Spoonwood

Hardscrabble Books—Fiction of New England

For a complete list of titles in the series,

please see WWW.UPNE.COM

Other Books by Ernest Hebert

The Dogs of March

A Little More Than Kin

Whisper My Name

The Passion of Estelle Jordan

Live Free or Die

Mad Boys

The Kinship

The Old American

Spoonwood
Ernest Hebert

Dartmouth College Press   **Hanover, New Hampshire**

Published by University Press of New England   Hanover and London

Dartmouth College Press
Published by University Press of New England,
One Court Street, Lebanon, NH 03766
www.upne.com
© 2005 by Ernest Hebert
Printed in the United States of America

5   4   3   2   1

Library of Congress Cataloging-in-Publication Data

Hebert, Ernest.
Spoonwood / Ernest Hebert.
p.   cm.—(Hardscrabble books)
ISBN-13: 978-1-58465-490-2 (alk. paper)
ISBN-10: 1-58465-490-2 (alk. paper)
1. Young men—Fiction.   2. New England—Fiction.   3. Fathers and sons—Fiction.
I. Title.   II. Series. PS3558.E277S66   2005
813'.54—dc22   2005011998

Contents

Contents

Part 2 The Calm

Acknowledgments and Dedication

I'd like to start by thanking my wife, Medora, for her companionship and wisdom. I am grateful to Sally Brady, Terry Pindell, and John Landrigan who read drafts of this work and offered helpful advice.

Many thanks to David Lawlor for teaching me the habits and psychology of white-tail deer; Robert M. Thorson for his absorbing book on stonewalls, *Stone by Stone;* Tom Wessels for writing *Reading the Forested Landscape,* and Brian D. Cohen for his etchings and illustrations in the same work.

I want to offer a special thanks to Rad Dike for his aesthetic sense in regard to land and art. I don't think *Spoonwood* would have been written quite the same way without Rad's extraordinary example of pursuing happiness through nature and the human need to make something meaningful and personal out of the experience.

The first inspiration for this book was Dan Dustin, who like myself is a New Hampshire guy. Dan makes beautiful, elegant, and useful spoons from native woods. I would like to dedicate this book to Dan and the people out there whose hearts, minds, and livelihoods intersect with the forest. Consulting foresters, loggers, truckers, sawyers, cross-country skiers and snowmobilers, environmental kooks and old-style conservationists, craftspeople and artisans—I love you all.

Spoonwood

PROLOGUE

APRIL 1985

When he reached the ledges, where the trees fell away, the sky opened and he could see quite clearly. Moonlight washed over the granite. It was getting cold. Winter was returning. He hiked over the rocks until he reached the Indian camp. Lilith was only a few feet away, curled on her side, under the cover of hemlock branches.

"Lilith?" He crawled into the lean-to. He felt the blood on his hands; he could feel it soaking into the soil. He'd seen blood like this before, from the burst arteries of deer shot with high-powered rifles.

"Frederick. Frederick? Is that you?" Her voice was soft as the hemlock boughs.

The baby was at her breast.

A ray of moonlight fell on the infant's face. "Beautiful," Frederick said.

"You came back. I didn't think you would. I thought—he's gone, gone forever." Her voice was soft as the sound of mist.

"I came back to take care of you." He knelt by her. He knew he was too late.

"Frederick, I'm happy. For the first time in my life, I'm happy." She put her hand on his beard, and then it slipped away. She shut her eyes.

He slid his hand between the baby and Lilith and put it over her heart. He could feel the child's strong, steady heartbeat and Lilith's weaker beat. He knew that even at the end dying creatures can hear clearly, so he whispered, "I love you."

She opened her eyes for a long moment, and then they closed of their own accord. Each heartbeat was weaker than the last, and then there was none. The child's heartbeat continued strong and sure, and his son drew in life from his mother's breast.

PART 1   The Storm

UP FROM DOWN

Dear Mother, now that I am about to die in this terrible blizzard, all my powers of telepathy have returned. I remember everything. I remember being born under the lean-to thirteen years ago. I remember the comfort of suckling on your breast. I remember I could not quite read your mind, because you were already between worlds. I know what you were feeling, though, because I am there now. I'm no longer cold, mother, just tired. I'm curled up in the snow waiting for you. I'm afraid when I get to your heaven I'll forget this world or I won't care, so before you come for me, while I can still remember, I want to tell you all that's happened since you died giving birth to me.

It's June of 1985, middle of the night. I'm two months old, not sure whether this new existence is worth the trouble. Sudden light wakes me. Dad leans into my crib. His breath is rich. He runs his fingers through his beard and stares down at me. He steps back, pauses, lurches this way, then that, reaches into his pocket and pulls a snapshot out of his wallet and holds it in front of my eyes. "Birch, this is your mother, Lilith," he says, the words slushy. "It was taken just before she was pregnant with you. She was nineteen." At this moment I cannot say what I'm looking at. I can't even tell up from down. Even so I memorize the shape and colors and sounds. Maybe someday I'll know what they all mean.

Grandma Elenore comes into the room.

"You woke him," she says.

"He's not fussing. He's got eyes like a little man from outer space." Dad laughs nervously.

"It's one o'clock in the morning, and you're drunk as a skunk," Grandma says.

"Don't worry, I won't spray." Dad totters back from the crib, and now the light is in my eyes again. I'm thinking that if only I knew up from down I'd recognize the "you" he was trying to show me.

"Are you all right?" Grandma Elenore says to Dad.

"I'll be fine, just fine, couldn't be better if my hair was on fire," Dad says.

I live in the "guest room" of my grandparents' mobile home. It has a creamy ceiling with warm, bright globes, a maple wood dresser, and a picture on the mauve wall of Jesus and his sacred heart. I have questions. Why do lights go on and off for no apparent reason? Do shapes exist in the dark, or do they come into being only with the light? Which way is up and which way is down?

I drift off to sleep to a young woman's voice. Though I have yet to learn language, I understand her in the dream. It's you, isn't it? Your first visit following your death. You say, "You, me, your father, we are one." If, as Grandma Elenore says, there are three persons in one God, can there be three persons in one me?

When morning comes I wake to the fragrance of a woman kissing me. I think for a second it's you, mother, but it's Grandma Elenore. I'm in the crook of her plump bicep. In smell and feel, not to mention sight, it's like riding in the bite of a pear—nice. We're moving toward the kitchen in slow steps, accompanied by Grandpa Howard, a mug of coffee in his hand. I scrunch up my face to exert mind control over Elenore in order to hurry her along, but the attempt fails.

"Isn't he cute?" she says, whistling through her buck teeth in that maple syrup manner of elders that even at my young age makes me want to puke.

"God creates them that way so you don't flush 'em," Howard says.

"Our Freddie is having a nervous breakdown," Elenore says.

"Seems more like a two-month drunk to me."

"Don't be *hash*, Howie."

"I'll admit he does a day's work, I'll admit that, but he goes out every night to the *bah*. He's going to get himself busted for DWI."

"He's had it hard. Lost his girlfriend, blames himself."

"You're too easy on him, Elenore."

"Why did that girl have to go up there in those rocks and bleed to death having her baby?"

"I can't imagine."

We arrive in the kitchen. Grandpa puts his cup down with a wham and a spill. Grandma places me on my back on a towel on the kitchen counter. I try to roll off but have no luck. Immobility is one of my many frustrations at this age. I smell cake; I smell the cutting board.

"I don't think it's grief. I think it's more like guilt," Elenore says. "I know because I feel it myself. She came here. I could have helped that girl."

"You could do no such thing. He ran off, that's why he feels bad," Grandpa Howard says.

"Any boy can make a mistake."

"Boy? He's pushing thirty. He left her because he thought somebody else got her pregnant."

"But he came back—Freddie came back!"

I hear the alarm in my grandmother's voice, and it troubles me. What does alarm mean? I expect the warm, bright ceiling globes to dull any second. But they don't.

"Too bad he was late in arriving at her side," Howard says.

"That's why he's drinking—because he was late in arriving."

"I think he just likes to knock down a few."

"Why did she go up there, why there?" Elenore raises her eyes in the general direction of the ledges. Good question, Mother.

7

Why did you go up there? It's the one question we all want answered. Maybe you'll tell me when you take me to heaven.

"Bad judgment—it could happen to any of us," Howard said. "Anyway how could she know that she would be a bleeder?"

"Or maybe she really did want to die. I have prayed, and I still don't know what to think."

I hear the sadness in my grandmother's voice. I have grasped the notion, but I lack the vocabulary to express myself. I try to invent my own words but only succeed in producing a series of gurgles.

"Isn't he precious," Elenore says, then the tone changes. "Freddie can't raise Birch without a woman around."

"Seems like he don't want to try."

"It's, I don't know, unnatural for a man to bring up a child alone," Elenore says. "How can a man be both womanly and manly at the same time, unlike a woman, who can be manly when she has to, but still be womanly?"

"Maybe he just doesn't take to fatherhood." Howard rubs one of his big, rough hands across my head. "Poor little guy. He's got his mother's complexion and blue eyes. He'll likely tan like her too, all gold."

"I bet he grows up to look like Squire Salmon, tall and handsome." Elenore pronounces your maiden name correctly, *Sahlmohn*, not *Saminn*, which is the way Howard says it.

"Good point," Grandpa Howard says. "We sure don't want him looking like me and Freddie. Two bulldozers is plenty for one family. Thank goodness he has my hair." Grandpa Howard runs his hand over his bald head and laughs.

"Cut it out, Howie. Let's get going with breakfast. The boys will be here in a few minutes."

By "boys" Grandma Elenore means Grandpa Howard's trash collection crew—Dad, 28, Pitchfork Parkinson, 37, and Cooty Patterson, senior citizen.

Grandma Elenore perks coffee, makes homefries, and scrambles a dozen extra-large eggs in half a stick of margarine in an iron fry pan. She serves bacon or whatever leftover meat is hanging around the fridge. Grandpa Howard's self-appointed job is to make toast and lay out the table with five plates, silverware, coffee mugs, and glasses for orange juice. The table always holds salt and pepper shakers, sugar, Coffee-mate, peanut butter, paper napkins, and Grandma's strawberry preserves in a mason jar.

Howard never uses the toaster. He rips open a loaf of Wonder Bread and spreads the slices on an oven rack under the broiler coil. He always makes perfect toast, and he always makes too much, requiring the Elmans to eat dry toast at noon and evening meals, because throwing out food is unthinkable.

Meanwhile, Dad hides out in his pickup truck camper parked in the driveway. It's where he sleeps and sucks his brew. He spends as little time in my company as possible. He'll wait for Pitchfork and Cooty to show up in Howard's older trash collection truck before coming into the house. Pitchfork lives with his mother and retarded sister in the town of Donaldson, so it's no trouble fetching Cooty at his cabin.

Pitchfork will stop at Ancharsky's Store and buy some Life-Savers, a grinder, a Pepsi (he's given up on Coke since they changed the formula), and a *Keene Sentinel* newspaper. On his way out Pitchfork will check the bulletin board at the town hall for bargains on used cars, tractors, firewood, notices of grange meetings, quilting bees, wild game suppers, births, deaths, EMT classes, and so forth.

Cooty remains in the cab of the truck. He loves the rumble of the idle, the smell of exhaust fumes mixed with the aroma of garbage. Cooty has no ambitions or desires. He is content to enjoy his own thoughts and what comes on the waves of his senses. Or anyway that's what everybody around here believes.

Breakfast at the Elmans' is served every weekday morning "at more or less six o'clock sharp," as Howard is fond of saying, and at more or less six o'clock Pitchfork pulls the Old Honeywagon into the yard and parks it in front of the New Honeywagon. Pitchfork, the big man in his prime, and Cooty, the frail little older man, take their seats at the Elman table and dig into the food without even a hello. Howard gives his men breakfast, calls it a business meeting, and deducts the costs of the food from his income tax. Lagging behind is Dad.

That particular morning he sits down at table and looks at nobody.

"Pick him up and love him," Elenore says.

Dad hesitates.

"Afraid he'll drop him," Howard says.

"He wasn't afraid last night. Go ahead," Grandma commands.

Dad plucks me off the counter, nuzzles me with his shaggy beard, quickly withdraws. I smell last night's drink on his breath. He hands me back to Grandma Elenore.

"He stinks," Dad says.

"Isn't it about time you learned to change a diaper?" Elenore says.

Howard laughs—a cutting laugh. "That'll be the day."

Dad tries to speak but can't get any words out.

Grandma Elenore dismisses Dad with a wave of her hand.

Elenore whips off my diaper, washes my behind, powders it, puts on a new diaper, and hands me to Dad, who hands me to Howard, who hands me to Pitchfork, who hands me to Cooty. I like breakfast time, being passed from arms to arms, the various breaths, the fast-moving shapes in the background, and voices shouting and laughing all around me. I remain in the cradle of Cooty's ancient arms.

Pitchfork digs right in, eating the way he drives. In two minutes he's done, ending with a self-inflicted thump in the chest to force a belch.

"Isn't that disgusting—so inelegant." The words come from the cat (more about him later).

"Hey, I made toast," Howard says for the umpteenth time.

"That's all right—I like the bread soft," Pitchfork says.

I feel Dad tense up, fatigued by the banter between Howard and Pitchfork.

Pitchfork sips coffee, scans the newspaper, and reports his findings.

"Oil Can Boyd won another one for our Bo Sox—Oil Can, that's my man," Pitchfork says, because he likes the way "can" sounds with "man."

"How did Rice do?" Howard asks.

"One for three, a double," Pitchfork says. "I can't stand that guy—nasty attitude."

"That's because he reminds you of Howie," teases Cooty.

"No, I like Howie. He gave me a job."

"Ignoramus," Howard says out of the corner of his mouth.

Pitchfork's feelings are hurt, and he folds the newspaper.

"Show a little sensitivity," Elenore says to Howard.

"I like Jim Rice," Howard says as if he has not heard Elenore. "He's an honest man. Pitchfork, I'm sorry I called you an ignoramus. Not that I take it back, mind you."

The cat comes over to me and Cooty, who squinches his ears. For years the Elmans had unneutered cats and for years they would wander off and disappear, getting hit by cars or ending as meals for coyotes. Elenore brought a kitten home after responding to a desperate note on the bulletin board of Ancharsky's Store—"FREE kittens! Call Soapy Rayno." Howard named him Spontaneous Combustion. Against Howard's wishes, Elenore had Spontaneous Combustion fixed as soon as it was medically permissible. From that day on, as far as Spontaneous Combustion was concerned, the Great Outdoors was a vast and potentially dangerous toilet. He does his business and hurries back into the mobile home. On occasion when he's trapped outside he'll yowl let me in, let me in, until one of his servants complies with his demands. You see, Spontaneous Combustion regards himself as king and us humans as his subjects.

He transfers his thoughts to my mind. "You look like something the human dragged in," he says.

"How come I can talk to you but not to them?" I say.

"Because you're a superior being, which is the only reason I choose to communicate with you. Enjoy your powers while you can. Your IQ will drop a few points each day of your life. Eventually you'll flatten out to normal human level, at which time you will no longer interest me."

"I don't plan to lose my telepathic powers," I say.

"We shall see. Meanwhile, what am I going to do with you? You are too big to eat and too helpless to wait on me. Human babies are the most totally useless creatures in the lamina kingdom."

"You're just jealous because I get all the attention."

That momentarily shuts him down. I watch him slink among feet, waiting for something eatable to come his way.

"Howie," says Pitchfork, "I won't have to take your truck home no more. I'm getting my own vehicle."

"Watch out, Trooper John." Howard raises his eyes heavenward.

"A Ford Falcon with seventy-seven original thousand miles."

"Who's selling it?"

"Chester the poacher."

"Oh-oh. You better let me have a look before you put any money down," Howard says.

"I already gave him a couple hundred."

Elenore prevents Howard from using the ignoramus word by kicking him under the table.

Howard makes a pistol out of his hand and points the barrel at Elenore. "What day is it?" he says.

"It's your birthday, Howie—the big six-oh—maybe."

Howard bows toward Pitchfork and Cooty.

"I thought you were older," Pitchfork says.

"I'm ancient."

"Actually, Howie's not sure how old he is," Elenore says. "We were both fosters, but we celebrate Howard's birthday in the marrying month of June."

"You ever going to retire, Howie?" Pitchfork asks, his voice shrewder than usual.

"Never," Howard says.

"You can't say never," Pitchfork says. "You'll kick the bucket one of these days."

"Not me. I'm neither going to die nor weaken."

"Leg hurts him, various other aches and pains," Elenore says.

"Not retiring today or on the morrow," Howard says, "and if I do it won't be because of any ache or pain."

"When you do retire—Freddie, he going to take over the business?" Pitchfork asks.

"There's times, Pitchfork, when I'd just as soon duct tape your mouth to your backside."

"I was just making conversation."

"It's a sensitive area with both of them," Elenore says.

"I should of guessed," Pitchfork says.

"Everything is guessing—don't you just love it," Cooty says. He nibbles at his food, leaving most of it. It pains Grandma Elenore that Cooty prefers his own cooking to hers, accomplished in his stew pot, which has been on his wood stove for a decade without ever being emptied and which has produced a crust on the rim an inch thick all the way around.

"How about we celebrate my birthday?" Howard looks at Elenore.

"Tomorrow, Howie."

"What's wrong with today?"

"I'm driving up to St. Johnsbury on genealogy business and likely will be late for supper. I'm going to see a lady up there who claims to have a line on us. You remember that farm we worked at where it was said the Indians used to come?"

"After all these years, what difference does it make now?"

"Roots, heritage—for our grandchildren. Don't you think they have have a right to know where they came from?" she says.

"I live in the here and now," says Howard.

Elenore turns to Pitchfork, says, "He's a liar," then looks Howard in the eye. "Tell me you don't miss your mother."

"I refuse to submit to the calling of bad dreams, and that's that." Howard turns away from Elenore to Cooty. "How old are you, old man?"

"It varies from day to day," Cooty says.

Dad says to Elenore, "If you're leaving town, where's Birch going to stay?"

"Why, I'll take him with me, that's a simple simon."

"Oh," Dad pulls at his beard and long, greasy hair. Dad is not what you would call a snappy dresser. He wears blue jeans, solid-colored tee shirts with no messages, and work boots. Only his belt is distinctive, wide, Western style with a brass buckle; Dad bought the belt at Wall Drug when he was traveling the roads of America because he liked the jackknife inscribed on the buckle. Dad has been whittling since he was a kid. In learning to keep his knife blade honed, Dad developed a knack for sharpening tools. He can sharpen anything, always at the correct angle, and he works fast. He sharpens all of grandfather's tools. Sharpening is a talent Dad has that even Howard acknowledges and appreciates. Since you died, Mother, Dad does two things in his spare time—he drinks and he whittles.

While Howard and Pitchfork argue and Cooty and Elenore play the audience, Dad removes one of his boot laces and drags it on the counter.

"Watch this," says Spontaneous Combustion, and he leaps off Cooty's lap. He stalks the string, then pounces on it as if it were a mouse.

I'm fascinated, trying to gauge the relative importance of the string, the cat, the man. And then it hits me: Spontaneous Combustion can be found on the furniture, on the floor, even climbing the walls, but he is never on the ceiling. The ceiling, which is the part of the building I view for most of my waking hours, is a separate realm. The ceiling is up, everything else is down. It's taken me quite a while to arrive at this starting point for reality, because I was tricked by my relative position, in my crib on my back looking up, into thinking up was straight ahead. Spontaneous Combustion has shown me the true way.

Spontaneous Combustion soon grows bored with Dad and assumes his sentry position on top of the fridge. Dad laces up his boot.

"Dad likes you," I say to Spontaneous Combustion.

"Your Dad doesn't like anybody," Spontaneous Combustion says. "He patronizes me out of envy, because I'm free and he's burdened with the likes of you, you pitiful hopeless fool."

Eventually, Howard rubs a hand over his bald head, pinches the crack in his chin, grimaces. "Production calls, my friends," he says, and lights a Camel cigarette. Which is the signal: breakfast meeting over, time to go to work.

In a few minutes Howard and Pitchfork drive off in the Old Honeywagon, Dad and Cooty in the New Honeywagon; Elenore does the dishes, then takes off with me in search of her identity.

Up From Down

I'm not good company. I don't remember the trip to St. Johns-bury very clearly, because I sleep through most of it. (Riding in a car does that to me.) In the town I do remember being lugged here, lugged there, fawned over by various strangers, and then the drive back, Grandma Elenore crying her eyes out.

FREDERICK ELMAN

There's no air conditioning in the cab of the Old Honeywagon, so Cooty Patterson and I drive with the windows rolled down and converse in the roar of engine and wind. It's like the sound of a blizzard. I devised our system for picking up trash. I do the work and Cooty does the psychotherapy. Cooty doesn't work even when he's riding with Howard or Pitchfork. Of course, he isn't paid either.

"You like your baby, Freddie?" Cooty shouts into the roar.

"I don't know," I say.

"I like him too. I like all babies," Cooty says.

"They don't do much," I say.

"You've got to admire them for that," Cooty says.

A minute goes by. We leave the hardtop on Upper Darby Road. The dirt lane narrows, and I slow down. I like driving slow, unlike Pitchfork.

We're on a downgrade and someone passes, but it's not a car. It's Garvin Prell on his bicycle. He wears a European racing suit and helmet. I gun the engine and roar on by. It doesn't bother him. It's well known around Darby that Garvin has no fear of motorists. He treats us as if we were not there. It's that arrogance more than anything else that infuriates me about Garvin and his kind. Not that my kind is any better. We're just arrogant in different ways.

It's quieter now. You'd think I could relax, but it's the other way around. In the quiet, pressure builds inside of me. Strange thoughts flash in and out of my mind. It occurs to me that I could relieve the pressure caused by my resentment of Garvin Prell by shoving Cooty through the window.

"You like being a father?" Cooty asks.

I shrug my shoulders.

"You're afraid of it, right?"

"I feel bad for the kid," I say. "Mother dead, and his only parent not fit to care for him."

"You still sad, Freddie. I thought you'd be cheering up by now."

"Don't you start in on me, Cooty."

"Gets on your nerves, living at home?"

"Cooty, I don't know who I am, what I am, I don't know anything. I got this kid who just creates resentment in me. I'm all bottled up. I hate to think what will happen when I blow."

"Make a move."

"What do you mean, a move?"

"Do something even if it's wrong."

"I'm thinking about a road trip. I hate to burden her, but Mom would take care of Birch while I thought things out."

"You have a destiny in mind?"

"Cooty, the word is destination, not destiny."

"Isn't that funny. You got—what?—a year of college and know destiny from destination and me, well, it all seems like one thing."

"Cooty, you ever get hemmed in by the damn trees? Ever have the urge to go someplace with wide open spaces?"

"No, I don't have any urges at all. But I do plan to retire to the wide open spaces."

"Retire from what? You haven't had a job since the mill closed down."

"Retire from the cold winter, to South Texas to live with my half-brother, Kenneth Riley."

"I didn't know you had a brother. Is he as crazy as you, old man?"

"I like to think so. He owns a nice trailer."

"Cooty, what do you believe in?"

"Wow! What a great question."

"It's not a great question, Cooty. It's an obvious question."

"Let me think." Cooty rolls up the window, rolls down the window, rolls up the window. "I believe in my stew pot. What about you, Freddie, what do you believe in?"

"Nothing right now."

We're in the heart of Upper Darby, traveling through the deep forest of the Salmon Forest Trust Conservancy, which Lilith's father established before he died. The landscape hurts me with its beauty—the great sugar bush of maples, stands of pine and hemlocks, but mainly a mixed forest of white birch, yellow birch, red maple, sugar maple, moose wood, white pine, cedar, red spruce, ash, red oak, white oak, shagbark hickory, and other species. Underneath the canopy, new ferns sway gently in the breeze. On each side of the road are stone walls. Lilith's spirit still resides in these woods. I try not to think selfish thoughts.

"All the more reason to go west," says a voice inside my head. "Even in death she's smothering your freedom."

"What was that?" says Cooty.

"Just talking to myself," I say.

The old man pats my shoulder. Cooty can tell when I'm in my grief.

"I'm going to pull over for a sec," I say. "I want to shut the engine and listen to the woods."

Cooty's puzzled. He doesn't know what I mean. That's all right. Cooty has lived a lifetime in uncertainty and confusion. He's grown to accept this condition as normal and even, in its own way, exciting. I wish I had a little bit of him inside of me.

I park the Honeywagon as close to the ditch as I dare. Even so, the big truck fills a third of the road. I shut down the engine.

"See that path?" I point.

Cooty nods. "Deer run?"

"Deer run, coyote run, hiker run, snowmobile run—all the critters run that path. Lilith and I often walked it."

"Where's it come out?"

"Lonesome Hill."

"The old hippie commune?"

"Right. Lilith always liked that hollow between the summits. We would go there and picnic."

I get out of the truck. Cooty remains inside. It's an effort for him to mount and dismount the high steps into the cab. I stand in the middle of the road, looking at the stone walls, the trees, listening, trying somehow to connect with Lilith's spirit. But I don't really believe in spirits. Did she cheat on me? Did she have her baby at the ledges to get rid of it? To get away from me? To spite me? To spite herself? These thoughts make no sense, but they're in my head, as if put there by some malevolent being. Lilith's spirit—if it was ever with me—must surely have departed in disgust. Now I'm visualizing a road out west someplace, long and disappearing into the horizon.

I'm still standing in the middle of the road when an old Chevy Impala, traveling very slowly, approaches from town and comes to a stop just as I make way. The car has Louisiana plates, which give me a stab of nostalgia for a state I'd lived in for a brief period some years back. Behind the wheel is a woman of about twenty-five with a serious face, skin light-brown, hair long and blue-black and straight, her face broad, nose wide and flat, eyes green, lips delicate and curved.

"Excuse me," she says. "I'm looking for the Salmon estate."

"You're almost there," I say.

"I thought so, I just wanted to check." She looks around, not nervous really, just wary.

"You one of the new people, right?" I say.

"Not exactly." The woman speaks softly and with confidence in an accent that is slightly British, slightly American southern, and slightly . . . I search in my mind for language and come up with the word "musical." I've never quite heard anything like this woman's lingo before.

19

I point. "The estate is about a half-mile on the left. Drive in between the stone pillars. You won't see the house from the road."

"Oh, yes. I remember the pillars now. Thank you."

I watch the woman drive off. I'm thinking about the Salmon mansion, the Italianate architecture in the middle of a New England setting, the greenhouse where Lilith grew flowers, the lane where she planted lilac bushes on the day she gave birth and died. Even my nostalgia goes sour. Now I'm thinking about Persephone Salmon, Lilith's mother, and how much I hate her and how much she hates me.

Cooty hollers down from the cab. "What—what was that?"

"I said, no doubt Persephone Salmon hates me for good reason," I say.

"Right—right," Cooty says, blinking, in awe at the incomprehensibility of everything.

At the end of the day I drop Cooty at his cabin in Donaldson and return to my parents' place in Darby. I park the Old Honeywagon near the barn and go right to my camper, break out a bottle of Old Crow, and get a cold beer from my propane fridge. I pour myself a double shot, glug it down, and follow it with suds. It's deathly hot in the camper, but I don't intend to leave it until I get a good buzz on. I could drive right to the bar, but I want to be alone to enjoy the first hit of the booze. When it starts to wear down, I'm headed for a bar in Bellows Falls. I'm not even going to bother to shower—let the bastards smell the garbage, in the seams of my clothes, in the pores of my skin, in the interstices of my soul. Let them know what I am, even if I do not.

Through the little aluminum frame window I can see my parents' place. It used to consist of forty or more acres, but Howard had to sell off most of his land when he lost his job and the house burned down. My people are reduced to less than an acre. Every square foot is used—mobile home, barn, garden, shrine to the Virgin, junked cars (for parts), and just junk that Howard keeps for reasons of his own. My father recovered from his down days, a fact that gives me hope for myself.

I note now that the Ford wagon, my mother's vehicle of choice, is not in the lot. She must still be in transit from St. Johnsbury. I do some quick calculating. I have one chore that must be done—dump my camper toilet in the mobile home system. If I do it now, I'll be able to avoid my mother and Birch. But first I must enjoy my fifteen minutes of euphoria.

I go in just as Howard has finished his supper, beans and hot dogs. When he comes home from work he wants to eat right away. He'll wait for no man and no wife. We exchange grunts for greetings. I've finished my business when my mother shows up with Birch. It's her third trip to St. Johnsbury, and something about the way she looks at me catches my attention. Usually I can read her face— fallen with a bout of sadness, glowing when she prays, furrowed brow when she's displeased, peaceful and open when she talks on the phone to my older sisters far away. But this evening I cannot tell what is on my mother's mind. She certainly doesn't look like a woman who has failed in her mission, because she's smiling as if she's about to tell a joke. At the same time she's twitchy, as if she'd seen some bad news on TV. I tell myself she's just tired, or maybe I'm projecting onto her a wedge of my own despair.

"Stick around, I have some news," she says to me. She puts Birch on his back in the easy chair behind the dining table. I look at him for a second and he looks at me. "Why did you have to happen to me?" I say in a low voice so Howard and Elenore don't hear.

Birch responds with some spit-up, as if he understood me.

"Sit down, have something to eat," my father says to my mother in a slack tone of gruffness that is as close as he can come to tenderness. "I'll make you a plate." He gets up from the table.

"Thanks, Howie. I'm pooped." She sits down. I sit down.

"You want something?" he says to me.

"No, I'm not hungry," I lie. I'm planning to grab a bite at the bar.

Howard warms the beans and two hot dogs in the microwave. "Tea?" my father says.

"Please," my mother says.

Howard turns up the kettle, removes the plate from the microwave, and with a theatrical gesture places the meal in front of his wife.

"Toast?" he says.

"Just one," she says.

Instead of placing the slice on her plate, he tosses it artfully and it falls on the side of her plate. He stands, waiting for orders.

"Sit down, Howie," Elenore says.

Howard sits down.

Spontaneous Combustion and Birch watch from the sidelines as if they know something is going to go pop. I just want my mother to finish her meal and dispense her news, so I can head out. I understand now what my father must have known from the start. My mother has something to say, but she's hungry and she won't deliver her message on an empty stomach.

My mother is a slow, finicky eater, and she soon uses up my father's meager store of patience.

"Well?" he yells.

"I'll finish my *suppah,* thank you." Two more bites to go.

"Want more tea?" my father says, in a tone suggesting Elenore is about to be indicted by a grand jury.

"Hold your water," my mother says. One bite to go.

"Sorry," my father says, and he clasps his hands in something like prayer and looks at the ceiling. It's one of his stock gestures and never fails to infuriate me.

Finished, my mother pushes her plate away. "I got some pretty good information today," she says. And she goes on, telling the whole story in her exasperating way, the drive up to St. Johnsbury, the weather, the road conditions, getting to her point in her own good time, finally speaking of her profound disappointment in the same chatty tone as the unimportant information. The records of her origins were lost decades ago.

"All's I could find out was that I was put up for adoption, but there were no takers. Imagine that—no takers."

My mother is left with her childhood memories—the orphanage, the Sisters of Mercy, a series of foster homes—but no knowledge of her roots.

"I'm sorry it turned out that way," Howard says. "I know it meant a lot to you."

Suddenly, my mother's face lights up with that funny look I noticed when she came into the house. She focuses the look on my father.

"I didn't find my people but I found yours."

"This does not bode well," my father says in a low growl.

"We're not Elmans in this house." My mother looks at me, and she looks at my father, and then she reaches into her handbag and gives my father a copy of a birth certificate. "This is you, Howie—you."

My father puts on his reading glasses and cautiously sniffs the document. He's only learned to read in the last few years, and he always makes a big production out of the act, his mouth drawn tight, face puckered. Without a word or even a warning shot over the bow, he hands the paper to me.

My father was born in Caribou, Maine, sixty-one years ago May 29. But it's the name that catches my attention. My father was christened Claude de Repentigny Latour.

I can't help a snicker. "A Frenchman—you always made jokes about Frenchmen."

"I've been putting my foot in my mouth all my life," he says. "The taste didn't bother me before, don't bother me now. Long as my driver's license says Howard Elman, I'll know who I am. Let's have dessert."

"Well I think it's promising," my mother says.

Birch makes a noise, not a cry, just a yelp, like he wants attention.

"Excuse me, I'm on my way," I say.

"Where are you going?" my mother asks. Her tone of concern fills me with self-loathing.

"Where does he always go?" my father says.

"Why do you have to talk about me as if I wasn't in the room?" I want to hit him.

"In a manner of speaking you aren't in this room," he says. "You're already in the *bah*."

"You're not going to be seeing Tubby again, are you?" my mother asks, voice pained.

"Tubby is with Giselle. He's a lot better since they've been going out," I say.

"Does it have to be every night—do you have to go out every single night?" my mother says. "And what about him?" she points at Birch.

"Well, what about him?"

"You haven't brought him to a priest to be christened."

"And I won't. I can't believe what you believe," I say.

"Oh, Lord, please forgive us," she says to the Almighty.

I tremble involuntarily.

My mother suddenly softens. "I'm sorry," she whispers, and her anguish angers me all the more. My father begins to pace, unable at the moment to deal with either son or wife. He makes hurrumph noises.

Suddenly, there's a loud, screeching sound, like a train braking at a crossing where a car is stuck on the tracks, or anyway that's how the sound feels to me.

"He's crying. Look what we've done," my mother goes to Birch, then stops abruptly.

I back away. "Now what?"

"Pick him up and love him," my mother repeats yet again. "He needs you."

I picture myself accidentally breaking his neck. "I don't know how," I say. "I don't know." And I storm out before I do something I'll regret.

"What do you mean, do something you'll regret? Think something original for a change," says the voice inside me.

I drive my pick-up ten miles to North Walpole, where I cross the bridge into Bellows Falls, Vermont. Growing up, my friend Tubby McCracken and I used to call Bellows Falls "Fellows Balls" or "Buffalo Balls." It's an exhausted railroad town with a perpetually downtrodden economy, but I like it. It has the Miss Bellows Falls Diner, Nick's Restaurant, a Newberry's for cheap shopping, and plenty of free parking. With my beard and long hair, I feel less combatively self-conscious in Bellows Falls than in Darby or Keene. Tubby and I meet at our usual hang-out, Nick's. Last night Tubby told me he had a "business proposition" to discuss.

On the way in, Rubric Fritz at the bar hollers "Hey Freddie," and I flash him the peace sign. You know you're on the skids when the barflies recognize you as one of their own.

I know what Tubby wants me to do, and I should be mulling it over, but I can't concentrate on anything for more than a few minutes before useless thoughts fill my head. Just when I think I know who I am and where I'm at and what's going on, I realize I'm looking back at an old me and Now has escaped me again. I'm like an artist trying to paint himself from a mirror image. He dips his brush and strokes the canvas. He looks up at the mirror, and a year has gone by. He paints another slash of color. Ten, twenty, thirty, forty, fifty, sixty years pass, and no matter how well he paints he can't capture the image in the mirror because it changes faster than he can work. He has to die in order to sit still, and perhaps then his ghost can paint his unchanging ghostly image, but where was the man?

Tubby, like me, is sturdily built, but not really fat. He has long blond hair that he's very vain about. He got his nickname in junior high school when he divulged his surefire seduction method. He would give girls baths. Until recently I hadn't seen Tubby since he and I were pulling guards on the Keene High School football team. We had little in common except that we were both Darby townies who spoke with stronger upcountry accents than the Keene kids. We were reunited six weeks ago when we bumped into one another at the Miss Bellows Falls Diner, where Giselle is a waitress. All my friends from high school have left the area, or they've married and settled down. Only Tubby is available to pal around with. Tubby occasionally works construction or drives truck, but he's unemployed most of the time; even so, he always has money.

Giselle is twenty-two, with pistonlike legs, a big wide perpetual smile, and freckles, a female Alfred E. Newman. (Actually, practically everybody I know resembles Alfred E. Newman.) She has two kids and a husband, current whereabouts unknown. She and Tubby plan to marry as soon as the ink is dry on the divorce papers.

Tubby is buying the rounds. He has a wad of bills in his money clip half an inch thick. I feel strange, the emotion gone out of me, outside of myself. I see an ugly young bearded man in the mirror staring into the void; I want to punch him in the face. I'm grateful for my rage; it masks my confusion.

Tubby is in no rush to get to his point. He's waiting to feel the booze before speaking, I know, because I myself am waiting. We down a couple shots of Canadian Club and two tall beers and hardly say a word to one another before Giselle ignites a conversation.

"How's the kid?" she asks.

"I can't bring myself to pick him up," I say. "He scares me in a weird kind of way. It's like he knows me all too well."

"Babies got wisdom, no doubt about that," Giselle says. "They lose it as soon as they begin to talk. Then they get like everybody else, and you can't handle them—they call it the terrible twos, but it's really . . . what was that long word you came up with the other night?"

"Existential angst—I didn't make it up. It was something I got out of my reading in college. You mean he'll get worse?" Something in my voice must be pitiable because Giselle bursts out laughing.

"What's so funny?" Tubby asks.

"Him"—she points at me—"Freddie is such a riot."

"Frederick—call me Frederick," I snap at her.

"Watch the way you talk to my woman, boy," Tubby says.

I ignore Tubby's superior tone for now. "Listen, Giselle, I admire you," I say. "You have kids, a job that must tire you out, but you never complain. You seem downright serene."

"You do what you have to do," Giselle says. "You just go day by day." She repeats the words, half in song. "Day by day, I go day by day."

"That's what I'm doing now," I say. "I want something else out of my life, but I don't know what it is. Tubby, what do you want out of life?"

"I want another beer."

"No, seriously."

"Seriously? Me and Giselle and her kids, and the kid we're going to have . . ."

"Really?" I look at Giselle.

"Really." She pats her tummy.

"We're going to Arizona and start a new life," Tubby says.

"You have to have money for that," I say.

"I got money."

A few minutes later Giselle's friend Joyce drops by the table. She's thirty, been around, lots of make-up, short skirt. Her buck teeth make me think of my mother. Suddenly, I'm full of rage at the people who raised my mother and never fixed her crooked teeth. I'm angry with my father for not insisting she get braces, angry with her for her self-sacrificing personality.

Giselle introduces me to Joyce, who holds out her hand. I refuse to take it and I avoid eye contact. I can't bear to look at a woman on the make. A minute later Joyce leaves and Giselle follows her.

Tubby laughs.

"Was that your idea?" I say.

"No way. I know better. You keep avoiding women and people are going to start thinking you're queer."

"If it'll keep them away from me, that's fine."

Giselle returns to the table alone.

"Freddie—Frederick, you can't carry a torch for a dead girl," Giselle says.

"It's like she sucked him dry, and he's got nothing left," Tubby says.

With Tubby's words my rage builds inside, but I hide it with a bashful smile.

"You can be so crude." Giselle's laugh says she likes Tubby crude. "Frederick, what do you want out of life?"

"I don't know. I got this idea that if I could get away for a year maybe, drive across the country, learn about the country, just myself, I could, like, you know."

"Pardon me, but it sounds pretty vague," Giselle says.

"I'll tell you what you need to straighten out your sex life and get your confidence back." Tubby reaches into his wallet, pulls out a hundred dollar bill, and slaps it down.

"Money is the root of all evil," Giselle says.

"Call me the Devil," says Tubby. He nudges the bill toward the beer glass with the tip of his index finger.

I'm thinking about the money. Money is freedom. Money is escape. I order another round of drinks. Tubby pays. I slurp half the shot, and almost immediately slurp the other half.

"I don't want my shot, just the beer. You want mine?" Tubby slides it over.

I knock it down and drink half my beer in one swallow.

"All those rumors about you are true, Tubby, is that right?" I say.

"If they are it would account for the money, wouldn't it?" Tubby grins.

"Excuse me, I really must powder my nose," Giselle says, in fake Upper Darby diction.

Tubby watches her walk away. Giselle has a very nice tush.

"She meant powder up her nose," Tubby says.

"What?" I say.

"Why do you think she's so confident? You know where I'm headed."

"I don't have any experience in that line of business," I say. "I'm not even a regular user."

"Last thing I want is a user. You have something else that's perfect for what we have in mind."

"We?"

"Nobody does anything alone, Frederick. You got to realize that. Listen, I'm just a small part of a very big operation."

"Who's in charge?"

"If I knew I wouldn't tell you. Nobody knows, but right here in southwestern New Hampshire is a Mister Big. That's all I know. What you have that we like is your truck, the camper body. You could go to a campground and nobody would suspect." Tubby breaks out a map of New Hampshire and puts his finger on some blue.

"It's Great Bay," I say.

"Right. Looks like a big lake, but really it's part of the Atlantic. Lobster boat goes out into the open ocean to do some business, lobster boat comes back in with its valuable cargo and docks right here." He points at the map. "Guy with a camper pick-up truck drives to the dock at a certain time and says howdy, I'm here for the lobsters. You and this other guy load the lobsters in the back of your pick-up. You call a number and you say I have the lobster order. You get directions, you drive there, you drop the lobsters. It's as simple as that."

"Except my cargo is not lobsters."

"It's lobsters, okay?"

"I have to think about this, Tubby."

"Of course you do. This is not a business to be taken lightly. I'll tell you this, Frederick: what you're doing is totally safe. I'm starting you with the easy stuff. The fact is—I mean, I love Giselle—but except for you I don't have any male friends."

"Me neither."

"This is a business where you can't trust nobody. It gets lonely. You and I have known each other a long time. You're not going to betray me." Tubby pauses for effect, then adds, "You're too stupid." Tubby laughs loud and sips his beer. "Seriously, Frederick, I know you. You never betrayed anybody in your life."

I'm thinking about Lilith now, how I had gotten angry with her, suspicious, and walked out on her when she needed me most.

"I'm at a time in my life where I need to get away," I say.

"Listen, Frederick, I know you're sick of Darby and your folks and your kid. Think about this. You can work the lobster trade all over the country. You make a call at every port. Everybody likes lobster, am I right or what?"

I pretend to think for a long moment, a long good moment actually. The moment I've been seeking all day. My mind goes blank. I'm past the buzz; the booze has negated my thinking apparatus. Which is what makes the moment good. I can pretend to relate to people more or less, function more or less, but I can't reason or scheme or create. The blankness is good. There's no pain in blankness. I wish I could crawl into the kernel of this moment and stop time.

"I'm not the right guy for this, Tubby. I'm too unstable right now." With the sound of my own voice, the good moment passes. Nothing good can happen for the remainder of this evening.

"Unstable—everybody I know is unstable. You think Giselle is squared away? Ask how much Kleenex she goes through in a month. Don't you want any of this?" He waves the hundred dollar bill under my nose.

"Tubby, I don't know where I'm going with my life, but it's not going to be on a track to run drugs."

"You are demeaning my livelihood." For the first time in the evening Tubby's words and the expression on his face match. I am suddenly sobering off, readying myself for an emergency. It's a good feeling, specific and uncomplicated.

"Fuck your livelihood," I say.

"Who do you think you are?" He tosses the hundred dollar bill in my face. I watch the bill fall on the table, slip off the side onto the floor. I turn my head toward the bar in full knowledge that Tubby will be insulted, and I wave at Rubric Fritz.

Rubric Fritz waves back.

"Look at me when I'm talking to you." Tubby slams the beer mug down on the table and beer jumps into my face. I grin at him.

"Just because you knocked up the Squire's daughter doesn't mean your shit don't smell."

My rage surfaces like a sea serpent. "No ambiguity is a great thing, Tubby boy," I say in a menacing whisper.

"You really are stupid," Tubby says. "Everybody in the state of New Hampshire knows Lilith was creeping on you."

I see Giselle out of the corner of my eye. I'm already thinking that she will be a court witness. I throw the first punch (as she will later testify in her deposition). It's a left jab that hits Tubby square in the nose and draws blood. Tubby leaps across the table just as I am standing up. The two of us grapple-waltz around the room in each other's arms, knocking over tables, drinks, and scattering patrons. Along the way Rubric Fritz catches an elbow or a fist on the right temple and falls to the floor unconscious. By the time the police arrive Tubby and I are on the floor laughing and bleeding, friends again. For the first time since Lilith died, I am completely relaxed and in touch with myself, a feeling that will last one hour and sixteen minutes.

The police find cocaine in Tubby's car. No one knows who hit Rubric; he spends two days in intensive care. In the end, Rubric recovers and declines to press charges. Tubby, who has violated his parole, is sentenced to the state prison in Concord for seven years, but the sentence is suspended when he testifies against a Maine lobster man turned drug lord. Tubby takes his considerable savings and heads for Arizona with Giselle. I, a first offender, plead nolo to battery and am sentenced to thirty days in the house of correction. I'm happy, relieved, grateful. For tension relief, my shame and disgrace are almost as good as whiskey.

HOUSE OF CORRECTION

The Superintendent of the County Farm and Jail, a.k.a. House of Correction, allows me to keep my beard and long hair, because I'm "only a thirty-dayer." The fellow is a dying breed who opposes capital punishment and favors the rehabilitation approach to prisoners. The county jail is not a real prison; its main purpose is to hold inmates for trial and to incarcerate persons convicted of minor crimes, persons such as myself. It includes three major structures—the old jail, a brick Victorian building that at a casual glance can pass as, say, a prep school library; a great big hip-roofed barn with white clapboards; and a brand new concrete-block lock-up. My quarters in the old jail include a toilet and two cots; graffiti on the walls call for relaxed drug laws. Not a bad space as jails go. For the first week I'm alone in the cell.

I'm in a mood, as my mother would say. It's as if I've been in a car crash—sick to my stomach, things happening in slow motion, outside of myself; my life is a bad movie and I'm in a hell doomed to watch it for all eternity. On the plus side my ability to experience emotional pain has greatly diminished, and for a while the discovery of same cheers me, until I realize I can't feel anything else either.

I lie in my narrow bed thinking about the fight with Tubby, the excitement, the strange hope that I would land one of those perfect punches that sends the bone in the nose up into the brain and kills the opponent, or that Tubby would land such a punch on me and put an end to my useless life.

When my mother and Birch visit she remarks that our screened cubicle where we meet reminds her of the confessional at St. Bernard's Church in Keene.

"Who's taken my place on the route?" I ask.

"Long Neck McDougal, some felon Howie rounded up from Critter Jordan's crowd."

"Did Cooty leave yet?"

"I don't know where he's at. You know Cooty, comes and goes as he pleases."

I nod. I'm thinking about Cooty Patterson's stew pot and the hand-sawn firewood neatly stacked between trees. I'm going to miss the old man.

"Tell Dad I'll work until he finds somebody to replace me permanent," I say.

"Oh, Freddie, you're not leaving us, are you?"

"I don't want to, Mom. I'm just a mess right now."

"I'll take care of Birch."

"He's not too much of a burden?"

"He's not a burden . . ." She stops herself before telling me that I'm the burden. "I love him," she says, "and I will care for him."

Week two I'm assigned a cellmate, one Hank Johnson, who is awaiting trial for passing bad checks. Can't raise enough money for bail. Every day Hank and I and the other inmates work on the county's farm. We herd Holstein cows, operate milking machines, and shovel the stuff that ends up in Congress. I like the work, because it keeps my mind occupied. I like the cows, because they have no secret cravings.

One day we're out in the field picking string beans in the hot sun when Hank tells me he has a "party lined up." Hank has bribed one of the guards, who will bring us a bottle of Wild Turkey bourbon. Sure enough, when we return to our cell we find an old GI water bag partly filled with whiskey cut with water about two to one.

Hank takes a long pull on the bag and hands it to me, and I do the same.

"It's great stuff, but I don't believe it's the Wild Turkey I ordered," Hank says.

"It's Old Crow, my favorite," I say.

"You like that cheap shit," he says.

"Doesn't have the bite of the pricey stuff, and the buzz is the same," I say, realizing as I speak that I'm actually repeating something my father told me years ago.

Hank and I talk about nothing in particular until the bag is well deflated. I'm drinking a lot more than he is, but he doesn't seem to mind. Even so he's getting on my nerves, his mere proximity. It strikes me as odd that he's a bad check artist. His body is artificially built up, as if he's been working out obsessively; his hair is closely cropped, sideburns cut high. His curiosity about me is touching and annoying. I want to hit him just to shut him up. With some effort to keep my voice civil (I mean, I'm still grateful to him), I say, "Hank, I want to be alone with my buzz for a while, okay?"

"Sure, Frederick, I respect that; we will talk later, okay? I mean I need to keep my tongue wagging or else I go crazy."

"Sure, Hank, we'll talk."

We lie on our bunks, his on top, me on the bottom. I convince myself I'm alone. I start to imagine myself driving on a two-lane road, no traffic, western mountains in the far distance. But I can't keep the fantasy going.

Did she cheat on me? I ask myself. Why do I care? What difference does it make now? Why can't I just remember what I loved about her? Or even continue blaming myself for her death—there's some honor in that. But this, this obsession with fidelity, why does it consume me? It's so low, so ugly, and yet I can't deny that it lingers inside me, a hungry worm.

Out of my brooding comes an intrusive thought that's different from ordinary thought: the thought speaks.

"Why do you think she went up there?" the voice says.

"Who are you?"

"I'm the spirit of your best friend."

"Old Crow."

"Yes, I'm Old Crow. You haven't had access to me until now. That's why my voice sounds strange to you."

"What do you want?" I ask.

"I want to guide you toward Reality."

I can see Old Crow's words in my mind now, the capital "R" in reality. Surely this is a part of myself I cannot trust.

"You're skeptical, Frederick. That's a-okay for now. Go ahead, test me with one of your profound questions."

"Why did she do it? Why did she go up there to die?"

"The answer is in what she left behind."

"Birch."

"You've hated him from the very beginning. Am I right?"

"Yes. Why? Why do I feel this way? It's so awful."

"Examine your hatred. That infant is the only being you have ever truly hated."

"I hate my father."

"No, you don't—you love him. What you feel is your suspicion that he doesn't love you. Which is only just. After all, you don't deserve anyone's love, let alone a father's."

I'm breathing hard, as if I were having sex, or dying. I try to control my breathing. I don't want Hank to know I'm breaking down.

"Howard is merely a source of anguish, not of hatred," Old Crow says. "Let's return to the issue—the infant. Does he look like you in any way?"

I understand now what Old Crow is trying to tell me. Lilith went up to the ledges to have her child because she knew it wasn't mine. She went up there to have it and kill it, so she could start over. Something like that.

"He is not yours, he is not yours, he is not yours, he is . . ."

Hank's head appears from the top bunk. "Hey, you okay?"

"I'm fine. What do you care?"

"Sounded like you were arguing with somebody," Hanks says.

"What did I say?"

"I don't know, pal. It's like you were praying, in a crazy way. Look, let's have a drink together," Hank says, hopping down from his top bunk.

I'm thinking that this man is an angel. He smuggled in booze, and he's maintained a warm attitude toward me even though I've behaved badly. "I'm sorry, Hank."

He hands me the bag and I take a drink. We sit on the side of my bunk and talk.

"Who do you hate?" Hank asks.

"You mean besides myself?" I attempt a laugh.

"No, for real. Me, I hate cops—who do you hate? You hate cops?"

"I hate everybody. Except for you, Hank. You supplied the fun."

"Look, Frederick, I'm in here for a petty crime born out of desperation. I had some business setbacks. I was trying to be an honest guy. I'm not perfect. I drink some wine, I smoke a little weed, I snort some powder—I like to recreate. I think I could do something for myself and my family and the world at large if I got into the business of giving people what they want, like Tubby McCracken." He hands me the bag. "You know Tubby, right?"

"Tubby's been a friend since high school. Actually since grade school."

"I heard you guys played football together. Then you and him have a fight. You go to jail. Why doesn't he go to jail?"

"I'm not sure exactly."

"Come on. We know he sold somebody down the river. You, you didn't sell anybody down the river. They interrogated you, right?"

"How would you know?"

"I wasn't born yesterday. Listen, I know you have connections." Hank pretends to snort cocaine. "My lawyer's going to get me off. Technical error regarding my arrest. I'm out of here in a week or so. But I lost my job. I need work. I'm reliable as a railroad man's watch. Give me a name or two. People who might help me out, like I just helped you."

Hank keeps at me. Dropping Tubby's name. Asking where he can buy drugs, sell drugs, move drugs. He brings up the rumor that Tubby mentioned, which is that a very important character in the drug trade lurks about in southwestern New Hampshire. I want to do what I can to help Hank out, but the fact is I don't know anything about the underground drug trade.

The next day Hank is removed from our cell and disappears from the jail altogether. It dawns on me in the middle of the night that Hank is a police officer planted to gain information from me.

I begin to brood. The world is an evil place. Relatives, loved ones, friends, government entities, institutions—all are untrustworthy; all have plans that do not include me and agents who wish to change or destroy me for their own purposes.

I used to have an academic interest in social class, a subject that Lilith and I were both passionate about. We had names for various groups—the criminal class, the out-of-work class, the Bohemian class (which we'd adopted as our own), the rural working class, the urban working class, the public school teacher class, the professor class, the clerk class and the cleric class, the techno class, the entrepreneurial class, the inventor class, the scientist class, the small business person class, the corporate managerial class, the boss class, the big boss class, the newly rich class, the old rich class, and on and on. Once you start you cannot stop. I'd been brought up in a rural working-class household, Lilith among the old upcountry rich class. As we saw it each class is a tiny island among many.

Nothing is the way Lilith and I envisioned. The working class is disappearing, not in reality but in consciousness. So is the Bohemian class. And all the others. Everybody today wants to call themselves middle class. Nobody owns up to the idea of class. But the Reality sits there like a Romulan starship with a cloaking device, ready to strike.

"Please," says Old Crow, "I find pop culture metaphors distasteful."

"All right," I say. "I was never comfortable in my parents' class, which is why I can never take over Howard's trash collection business."

"In your own way you're a snob. Problem is, Frederick, you had a taste of college, but the things you learned weighed on you instead of freeing you. You don't see yourself as a teacher, a doctor, a lawyer, or a businessman; you're not fit for any white-collar profession: the middle class, vast as it is today, is unavailable to you."

"When Lilith and I were in love I wrote poems. We were Bohemians."

"Frederick, you only wrote one good poem in your life. No Bohemian would ever accept you as one of his own."

"In the back of my mind I'm thinking maybe I could fall in love again."

"Even the idea of having sex disgusts you. You're pretty much permanently impaired. You, my friend, are an outsider, a loser of the worse stripe, a menace to loved ones, an enemy of society, too self-pitying even to take yourself seriously."

"I have my animosity, Old Crow—that's worth something."

"It's not even good hate—it's more like revulsion and fear. Too bad you can't find some religion, like your mom. It's done wonders for her," Old Crow says.

"I can't bring myself to believe in either God or the Devil. I'm like Howard, who believes only in clockwork."

"But Howard has something you lack—character. Only I and the lonely life of the road offer you any solace. Why should you bear the responsibility of caring for a child who is likely not your own?"

I lie on my prison cot through the hot, sultry nights and think terrible thoughts through Old Crow. He shows me news reels of Birch falling off the kitchen counter and cracking his head open, dying of spinal meningitis, getting run over by a rowdy teenager in a hot rod, drowning in his own bath water.

. . .

My parents can see that I'm not fit to care for Birch, and Elenore proposes that she and Howard adopt Birch. I tell her I'll think about it, pretending that I'm agonizing over the decision. Secretly, I'm gleeful. I agree to let my parents raise Birch until I am better able.

"You're doing the right thing," my mother says, a remark that cuts me.

Alone in my cell, I try to create a benign thought, as if through will I can trick Old Crow.

"At least my son will have a good home, which is more than I can provide," I say.

"Be truthful, Frederick," Old Crow says. "You don't think of him as 'my son,' or even someone else's son—he's hardly human, not even an animal but the physical embodiment of some malevolent force that aims to reduce you to ashes."

I'm not so far gone that I don't realize something inside of me is awry, but I have no mechanism for coping except to seek escape. The jail has a small library that includes a Rand McNally book map. Every chance I'm allowed I look the map over, planning trips or just mooning over various places. I'm attracted to areas where few people reside—the Maine woods, the swamps of south Florida, the Big Bend area in Texas, the Four-Corners section in the southwest, north into the Alaskan interior, south into the canyons of Mexico, into the empty places. I have my limits, however. The thought of leaving North America fills me with dread. It's as if part of me is not in my body but in the soil of this continent. To lose contact with the soil is to lose contact with the small core of self I can claim as my own.

By late July I'm three months old and bitterly disappointed with my progress so far. Spontaneous Combustion rubs it in.

"You should be half the size of a fully grown human by now," he says, "running around, talking, getting into trouble, giving detailed excuses for inexcusable behavior. But look at you, still on your back, sucking on bottles for pleasure, unable to speak, moving only your bowels, sleeping sixteen to eighteen hours a day."

"We babies sleep so much because we're depressed," I whimper. "It's hard to grow when you're depressed."

"You're stealing sorrow from your cubby of memory—a misdemeanor of stealth-pity, but I should not criticize since my own demeanor is often amiss."

When the cat isn't tormenting me, I torment myself. The whole infant thing is all about working through a major depression brought on by the trauma of birth and the realization that one has a small, useless body, an immature brain, and no sex life.

I compensate by drifting into nostalgia for the old days right after birth, when I'd been naive enough to think that my grownups were part of me.

"Your logic is sound," Spontaneous Combustion says. "Trouble is, you are departing from a clawed premise. You have needs, your elders responded to those needs; all creatures work to promote their own interests, but yours promoted your interests before their own. Therefore, you reason—what? Tell me what you reason."

"I am one with them. We must be all One. We are One."

"Your mother put that idea in your head through dreams. We—who is we? Well, if you are one with them, you can refer to yourself as me or us. Can move back and forth between first person angular and first person rural. I plus we cannot equal one, no? Yes. In the end, as you now know, having abandoned the ideas of your immature mind, linguistic trickery is a trap: pursuing the meaning of words makes a creature mute or cynical, or moot and cyclical, and what's lost is the feel of knowledge, as in: let's just say we are not one; we are One. (Note the breakdown in logic.) Or, even, we are won. More ridiculously, we are Juan. Was that what you meant, a confusion of Juan?"

"I don't know," I say.

By the end of the second month I was beginning to see that my grownups were not me, that everyone in the household was not me. My needs were not tied to their needs. Because I cried, because I was cold from a wet diaper, and because a grownup came to my rescue did not mean that the grownup was cold, that the grownup was myself. Not only was I helpless in the world, I was alone, outnumbered by the not me's. Not to mention confused and abused by the family cat.

Flash ahead to my third month. I ask Spontaneous Combustion the big question: "Why do my grandmother and grandfather take care of me?" His answer: "They are meeting their own neurotic needs to help somebody who is cute. Cute is all you have going. When you're living on your looks you can't help but be insecure, because you depend so much on other people for validation as well as sustenance."

I avoid these philosophical dilemmas posed by Spontaneous Combustion by sleeping as much as possible and when awake concentrating my efforts on physical pleasures—savoring nourishment, wallowing in the temporary euphoria of expelling bodily waste, and in my spare time sucking everything in sight (I am especially fond of my feet).

It's summer in New Hampshire, no air conditioning in the mobile home, so the windows are open all the time. Sounds of the outdoors distract me from my introspection—songbirds in the morning and at dusk; coyotes howling at night; owls asking the eternal question *who who who;* crows squacking off and on all day; wind blowing through trees and over the grass; cars going by on our road, producing a Doppler effect (which I like); various courtship rites of loudmouthed insects and frogs, *peep peep, seep seep;* the distant hush of the distant interstate. I don't know what to make of these languages, just too many for me to learn. I'm realizing what Spontaneous Combustion has been pointing out all along—my human stupidity. Disappointment leads me into a new and exciting strategy. If I cannot reason out noise into meaningful utterance, why not just internalize it for enjoyment? In other words, I have discovered music. My despair lifts.

The outdoor sounds make me realize what I should have known already, that the ordinary noises of the indoors are also music.

"It's about time you figured out that one can make music by attentive listening," says Spontaneous Combustion. "It's neither the quality nor the organization of noise that makes music, it is the quality of attention paid to the noise that makes music."

Four days before my release I'm in the fields pulling weeds. Behind me is corn, tall and almost ready for picking, peering critically over my shoulder. A house guard shows up, says something to the field guard, who tells me I have visitors. I and the house guard walk back to the jail.

"What would you do if I ran away?" I say to the house guard, whose name is Earl.

"I'd chuckle," Earl says. "No doubt you'd swim across the river, like they all do, figuring you'd have a better chance in Vermont. Sleep in the woods at night. Then what?"

"Good point, Earl," I say, but I'm thinking about this idea of sleeping in the woods. It doesn't seem so bad. "Who wants to see me? Is it the cops?"

"They don't tell me nothing," Earl says.

Since it's not visiting hours, I think maybe the police are going to interrogate me again. The first time they talked to me I was nervous and truthful. This time around I will be relaxed and deceitful. I will give them names of people in Upper Darby I despise. I will tell them that Upper Darby is the drug capital of northern New England. Drugs maintain their standard of living, their prestige, their influence at the State House in Concord, in the halls of Congress. I will perjure myself in court just to see the Upper Darby snobs squirm.

My fantasy suddenly vanishes. I loved Lilith Salmon. How could I slander her people? What's the matter with me? Why this unreasonable anger? By the time we walk into the building I'm frightened as a child at what I imagine will be this interrogation. All I will have to offer them will be the naked truth. I know nothing. In every sense of the words, I know nothing.

It's soon clear that it not the police who have come to talk to me. I'm not called to the visitors' lounge, nor to an interrogation room, but to the superintendent's reception parlor. I sit down in the biggest easy chair. Earl is relieved by another guard I don't know, who says, "On your feet."

My body stands, but my mind remains in the chair.

The prison superintendent enters with Persephone Salmon, Monet Salmon, and Garvin Prell, the very people I had in mind to incriminate in my crazy musings.

"Have a seat, young man," the superintendent says. He looks a little bit like President Dwight D. Eisenhower, but with a full head of graying, reddish hair. I'm thinking about *Mad Magazine* line art, how every president resembles Alfred E. Newman. The superintendent says a few words to Garvin Prell and leaves the room. After he's gone it occurs to me that he never looked my way. A prisoner is noticed only if he escapes. In other words, his identity is acknowledged by his absence.

Garvin is a couple years older than myself, and I remember seeing him around from time to time when I was growing up. But he went to private school and we had no more than a nodding acquaintance. He's a runner and bicyclist and looks the part—not big, but lean and hard and fit. It's obvious from his looks that he eats right and works out. He's wearing a suit and a red power tie. His sandy hair is artfully tousled. He's known around Darby as a swordsman. Birch looks more like him than like me. The bile collects at the bottom of my throat.

Monet Salmon is Reggie Salmon's younger brother. He's tall, squared away, wearing khaki pants, light hiking boots, and a blue button-down shirt, his face tanned gold the way all the Salmons tan. Monet is an impressive-looking man, a country gentleman in his early fifties, and never mind that he doesn't measure up to his older brother, who was taller, better looking, more forceful, and a visionary, the founder of the Salmon land trust. Local people will always think of Raphael "Reggie" Salmon as the Squire, Monet as the Pocket Squire. I'm surprised to see Monet here. He and Persephone never got along.

I've seen the snapshots, and I know how beautiful Persephone Salmon was when she was young, more beautiful than Lilith, as Lilith was aware. Lilith's features were like her father's—strong and handsome and cleaved, her body, as her father was fond of saying, like a racehorse. But Persephone's features are delicate, fine, proportioned, from her little turned-up nose to the double-upsidedown "V's" of her upper lip. As a young woman she was compared to Grace Kelley.

I haven't seen Persephone since the funeral. I barely recognize her. Age and wear and tear had begun to catch up with her anyway, but Lilith's death has speeded up the process, done something bad to her on the inside that shows on the outside. A flare-up of arthritis has rounded her shoulders, twisted her body, gnarled her hands. She has bags under her eyes, a thousand wrinkles, loose skin under her chin and cheeks; her lips are dry and thin. Her hair has stiffened and turned an ash color. Her alabaster skin is roughed and reddened by a rash. Chain-smoking has stained her fingers and teeth. What amazes me is why she's done nothing to make herself look better.

"This is quite the prison," Persephone says for openers.

"This is not a prison, Mrs. Salmon. It's a house of correction" I say, addressing Persephone but looking at Garvin.

"Well, we do stand corrected?" Garvin says, not sarcastic exactly, just trying to be clever.

"You knew Lilith quite well," I snap at him.

"Everybody in Upper Darby knows everybody else," Garvin says.

"Garvin is like a son to me," Persephone says.

"We're a tightly knit community," says Monet.

I want to ask Garvin if he had an affair with Lilith, his sister, since Persephone thinks of him as a son. But I'm too weary to play word games. Instead, I say to nobody in particular, "Why are you people being nice to me when deep down you're not nice?"

Persephone looks at me directly. I cannot hold eye contact with her. "What do you plan on doing when you get out of here?" she asks.

"What do you care, Mrs. Salmon?"

"I don't—not really." Her voice is thick with a cigarette rasp. She turns toward the guard, who stands by the door. "Is it all right if I smoke?"

"Yes, mam. We ask that you use the ashtrays." The guard points to a black plastic ashtray with holders scooped into the edges.

Persephone lights a cigarette. "Forgive me, I'm nervous. A year ago I had a husband and daughter. Today they're gone. All I have is my grandson."

"You never came to see him," I say.

"That first month was pretty difficult for all of us," Monet says. "Persephone was sedated for most of the time, weren't you?"

I fight off an involuntary surge of sympathy for this woman, who (correctly, it turned out) advised her daughter to stay away from me.

"Garvin, you'd better take over," Persephone says. "I'm a little too wrought up."

"It's okay, Persephone—it's okay," Monet says.

"Shut up, Monet," Persephone says.

Monet steps back, embarrassed. Garvin whispers a few words in Persephone's ear, calming her down. I admire Persephone's anger. It, if not her, is embraceable.

Garvin opens his briefcase and pulls out some papers. "We've drafted an agreement. We will leave it with the guard for you to study. Will you need a reader assistant?"

"I've been to college, Mister Prell," I say.

"Well, I guess I knew that," Garvin says in a soft voice. "Mrs. Salmon wishes to adopt her grandson."

Suddenly, I'm alert. "He would live with you?" I say to Persephone.

"With me and my niece, Katharine Ramchand," Persephone says.

"Think of what Mrs. Salmon can do for that boy that you cannot," Garvin says. "She can send him to the best schools, introduce him to influential people, give him a stable environment."

"What else? What's the catch?" I say.

"We ask that you surrender rights of visitation and that you leave Darby," Garvin says.

45

"You want me to give up my son," I say in a huff, but it's all acting. I'm thinking about the road, the freedom. I visualize myself sitting on a rock out west someplace, a beer in hand.

"It would confuse him and probably confuse you if you both lived in the same community," Persephone says.

Now I'm thinking about my mother, her search for roots. Not finding. Her disappointment. Her offer to raise Birch as one of her own.

"It's only right that he knows who his father is," I say.

"That's correct," Garvin says. "And Mrs. Salmon has thought of that. When the boy reaches the age of eighteen he will be told who his father is. He will then be able to decide whether he wishes to make contact with same."

"Eighteen years—it's like a prison sentence," I say.

"Think of it as eighteen years of free child care, unburdened by the responsibilities of parenthood," Monet says. This despicable man has seen through me; I guess it takes one to know one.

"Mrs. Salmon has included a generous financial settlement of fifty thousand dollars," Monet says.

"Fifty thousand?" I say.

"That's correct—direct payment upon signing of the papers and surrender of the child," Monet says.

"Sleep on it and get back to Garvin in the morning," Persephone says. "The superintendent will allow you to make a phone call."

That night I lie on my back on my prison cot, thinking. The smell of cow manure sashays in through the open, barred windows. My truck is in good shape, outfitted as a homemade camper with gas stove, a comfortable bed, a portable toilet. I'll see the country right into fall, go down to Mexico for the winter, head for Alaska come spring. Pick up odd jobs along the way. With fifty thou for back-up, I can live forever on the road. I visualize the money in various denominations, like green snow fluttering down from the heavens. I do not think about my family. My only inner conflict is whether I will have a drink before or after the signing. The following day I leave a phone message with Garvin's secretary that I agree to the terms. Signing is set at the Salmon mansion for two PM of the day I'm to be released from jail.

My last week in the house of correction, the superintendent resigns his position for coddling or cuddling prisoners, maybe both, or so the rumors go. The word goes out that the farm part of the jail will be phased out. Hard time ahead. I should be grateful that I'll be out before the new punishment regimen, but something in me thinks hard time could save me.

BABY IN A DUMPSTER

It's 9 AM on the day of my release from prison, the weather warm and sultry, and my mother shows up with the Ford to bring me back home. Home? My parents' place has never been home. She has the baby with her, which disappoints me. On the way I tell my mother about the agreement with Mrs. Salmon. I am too ashamed to mention the money.

"She can do a lot more for him than we can, that's for sure," my mother says, her voice breaking at the edges.

In the rear is Birch, strapped into a car seat. At the moment I am no longer thinking of him as "Birch," as "my son." He's an alien, put here to make me crazy and unhappy.

"You think I'm doing the right thing?" I ask. I don't really care what my mother says. I'm just trying to sound concerned.

"I don't know, Freddie, I just don't know. You think she'd let us come and visit? I mean, Birch is family."

"I imagine so," I lie.

"I'm going to miss him. I love him. Don't you love him?"

I won't say what I am thinking, which is that I don't love anybody. Instead, I say, "Of course I love him. I'm just trying to do what's best for him."

"Of course you are," she says.

I'm wondering whether now she's the one lying or whether she's just gullible. Either way, I wish she hadn't spoken, and I wish I didn't have a mother to make me feel so ugly inside.

"I want to be there this afternoon when you meet with Mrs. Salmon," my mother says. "I want to scope her out." She hurries her words now.

I have never really understood my mother, which seems like a task worth pursuing. "What do you mean, Mom?"

"I always wanted to snoop in that house," she says, unaccountably silly and malicious now.

"Everybody has a false face," Old Crow says. "Even Elenore. Don't you just hate her? Don't you just hate them all?"

"What was that?" my mother says.

"Nothing—nothing," I say.

Minutes later I'm home, but it doesn't seem real to me. I feel weightless; I'm hyperventilating.

"What's the matter?" Elenore says.

"Bit of an anxiety attack," I say.

"A what?"

"Never mind, Mom. I have to go somewhere and think." I hurry out of the house.

I drive my pickup to the liquor store in Keene with an idea to buy a bottle of the warm brown stuff I am so fond of, but I settle for a half gallon of Uncle Fred's vodka because it won't show on my breath. I don't even wait until I'm out of the parking lot before tipping the bottle and sucking out a corner of it. Another. I'm waiting for the feeling. And it comes. Food has let me down, people have let me down, weather has let me down—but never Old Crow, even in his potato incarnation as Uncle Fred. I wait.

I'm driving five miles under the speed limit. I take another long pull, stop the bottle (still in the brown paper bag), and shove it under the seat. In a few minutes I'm in that easy state between mellow and cross-eyed. I think about the money.

I show up at my parents' place a few minutes before Howard and Pitchfork arrive unexpectedly for lunch. Usually, they eat on the road.

"Pitchfork, you can get along without me this afternoon for a couple hours," Howard hollers up at the cab after he's stepped down. "Drive slow now."

My brief good humor vanishes. "Don't you think this is hard enough for me without the entire family on hand to witness it?" I say.

"Not nearly as hard as it should be," Howard says through a crook in his lips.

My father has lost all respect for me. Suddenly, my protective anger falls away and I am outside of myself, and I see Howard's slight limp where he favors his bad leg, then the bouquet of wild-flowers Elenore has picked and put in a vase, no doubt in honor of my return. I can't bear it, a little thing like this sending me plummeting to my depths. Because of my son I don't even have the luxury of committing suicide. The best thing I can do for him and my family is to disappear entirely, like my sister Sherry Ann. This sudden concern for others upsets me. It's as if without my anger I'm not me. I try to blink it away. I want desperately to watch TV, to finish my drunk, to go back to work in the fields at the House of Correction, anything to keep from seeing. I struggle inside to find my wonderful, armor-plated anger.

"Don't I get to eat?" Pitchfork hollers down from the high-horse of the cab, his voice like the bray of a blind goat trying to mate.

"Not from up there you can't," Howard says without rancor or humor.

Pitchfork hesitates, dismounts.

After lunch the Honeywagon roars off with Pitchfork behind the wheel, gears grinding, tires kicking up pebbles and dust. Pitchfork is about as emotionally solid a citizen as you can find in North America, but he's a wild man behind the wheel. Howard cracks a little smile and mutters, "Ignoramus."

I'm happy to go for a ride, not realizing of course that my fate is about to be decided. We leave in tandem, Grandpa Howard and

Grandma Elenore and me in the Ford wagon and Dad in his pickup.

"We're going to lose them both—I can feel it," Grandma says, voice flat. "The Salmon woman gets Birch, and Freddie will just bug out."

"Like Sherry Ann," Grandpa says.

"What is he looking for? What does he want?"

"Beats me. Maybe he's just sensitive."

"That don't tell me anything."

"Well, I don't know anything, okay? I don't understand any of our kids. Sherry Ann was the one that seemed so happy-go-lucky. Why'd she run off? Why do they all run off?"

"They're not running, Howie. They're moving away, for opportunity and to escape memory and cold weather. I love all our grandkids, but this one"—she pats me on the head—"he's such a treasure. Special circumstances baby. I expect Mrs. Salmon will do a better job raising him than us."

"You believe that?"

"No."

"Mistake I made with Freddie is, unlike the girls, I berated him."

"Someday he'll wake up and realize you're just a horse's ass, Howie, an easy fault to forgive. You know what bothers me the most?"

"Birch won't be raised Catholic."

"He's not even baptized. You know what that means?"

"Heaven's a long shot?"

"Yes, that's what it means."

Dad lags behind us two or three minutes. We wait in the car for him to show. Grandma Elenore is excited by the sight of that great big beautiful house. By contrast, the house has a dampening effect on Grandpa. He goes suddenly shy. Me, I'm taking mental snapshots for later retrieval. The gardens are all grown over, and the trees—once famous for topiary—are shaggy. The smell of cut grass is in the air. The house is stuccoed a tan color, with big windows and a red terracotta roof.

"This place is more run down than I remembered," says Grandpa Howard.

"It's beautiful," says Grandma Elenore. "Looks like a villa on the Mediterranean Sea."

Except for one New Hampshire touch, a row of lilac bushes that you planted, Mother, only hours before I was born and you died. Did you really want me? Why did you go up to the ledges? I refuse to think the worst of you. You had reasons, and I have faith.

Dad arrives and we all meet at the grand entry of red paving bricks underfoot. At each end of the big doors are huge pots sprouting geraniums.

Grandma Elenore says, "This may be the last time we're together as a family."

We're met at the door by a pretty dark-skinned woman, who smiles and leads us through the echoey hall to the drawing room, with its huge fireplace, chairs and couches with bowed legs, long mirrors with little gowns on the frames, and a couple of bookshelves for show.

The house changes my state of mind somewhat. For one thing the vodka I've been nipping away at is having its effect. I'll be pleasantly detached for a while. I just wonder what I'll do when phase two of my drunk sets in. Something else, a tug of nostalgia and familiarity. After Persephone left for Tasmania, I lived here with Lilith in this house—she regarded it as her house, not her mother's—and something about the place still feels like home. This relatively pleasant mood vanishes the instant the door opens. Standing in a poised, almost arrogant fashion, is the woman I met a month or so earlier on the roadway. I resent her for the simple reason that she's not Lilith.

"How do you do, I'm Katharine Ramchand, Mrs. Salmon's niece and personal assistant," she says politely in that accent I can't place. "Mrs. Salmon and Attorney Prell will be right with you. Please come in and have some tea?"

"Tea—wonderful!" Elenore says in a tone a little too friendly to suit me.

Howard bobs his head "yes yes yes" even though he doesn't drink tea. He's intimidated by this place. I want to shake him and tell him to be himself. At the same time I'm secretly gleeful that he's showing weakness.

"Do you remember me?" I say to Katharine as she walks us in.

"No, should I?" she says.

"You stopped and asked me directions a little more than a month ago."

"Oh, yes, the trash man," she says, only slightly flustered.

That's the way it is when you do the route. Everybody needs you, but they don't see you.

We arrive in the living room. I sit on a clawfoot chair outside of the target zone of the conversation area, two couches that face each across a coffee table of curly maple cut on the trust lands. My parents and Birch take seats on one of the couches. Lilith and I often built big fires in the fireplace, and then we would make love on a couch or even on the floor.

Persephone bursts into the room. She's wearing a solid-colored tan skirt and one of her signature high-collar white blouses. She's bent and frail, slightly round-shouldered. By contrast, Garvin, the picture of health, stands behind her with Monet, who is smoking a meerschaum pipe. Garvin is carrying a briefcase. Persephone turns to Garvin. "My word, but he's brought the whole tribe." She turns away from Garvin to me. "Look at him, just a perfect little creature. I'd weep if I had a tear duct left."

Persephone has a way of talking that puts a twist of mockery in everything she says. She could tell you it was a nice day and make you hate yourself.

Persephone holds her arms out and Elenore, as if hypnotized, hands Birch up to her.

Grandma Persephone smells like soggy, spoiled spinach and cigarettes. Her hands are like a hawk's claws that threaten to drop me for their awkwardness. She nuzzles me with her mouth. Prickles of mustache hairs scratch my neck, and little teeth probe my flesh like a vampire's searching the right place to sink the fangs. I love the embrace, so much more daring than Grandma Elenore.

Still holding Birch, Persephone sits on the couch beside my mother. I'm hot, not perspiring, the heat going directly to my core.

"Wouldn't you just die to have skin like that?" Persephone says.

"I don't know's I'd go that far," Elenore says.

Katharine returns with a tray of cookies. "Folks, you've met my niece, Katharine?" Persephone says. "Doctor Ramchand recently received her Ph.D. in geology. She has a grant to study New England rock walls and cellar holes. Is that correct?"

"Quite close," Katharine says.

"Katharine is a citizen of Trinidad," Monet says.

"Actually, I have dual citizenship. My mother was an American."

"Katharine is my late sister's child. Katharine, this is Elenore Elman, her husband, Howard, and their son, Frederick. And this squirmy handful must be . . . Raphael?"

"We don't call him that. We call him Birch," Elenore says.

"A birch boy in a family of elm men—this is too good," Persephone laughs, looking at Garvin as if he were the only one who could appreciate her sense of humor. And maybe that is the case.

Katharine slips out of the room.

"The name comes from Lilith's favorite tree," I say.

"Her favorite tree was the mountain laurel," Persephone snaps.

"I guess we could disagree about that," I say.

"I imagine she told everybody a different story," Howard pipes in, momentarily stopping all conversation.

Persephone, who is one given to sudden unnaccountable bursts of laughter, breaks the silence with a short ha-ha, then turns to Garvin. "Do you want to hold the baby?" She doesn't wait for his answer but hands him over.

Garvin pumps Birch above his head as if he were part of his weight-training program. Birch smiles big, which magnifies my envy and hatred.

"He looks more like Garvin than anyone else in the room," Persephone mutters to Monet, but I hear her because Persephone is not good at muttering. It's suffocatingly hot.

Garvin goes to hand Birch back to Persephone, but Elenore snatches him away.

"I'll take him—please," Persephone says, the "please" drawn out and pleadingly insistent in the way of the Upper Darby elite, a slightly superior smirk on her dry lips.

Howard suddenly comes alive. "We won't stand for this," he says. "Freddie, don't give this baby to this woman. She'll ruin him."

"He's not giving him to me. I'm adopting him and paying your son a considerable sum of money for the privilege."

Howard is taken aback, but only for a second. He looks at me. "Well, I guess we should hear the particulars."

"Fifty thousand dollars," I say.

"I don't like this, not one bit," Elenore says. "What are you going to do for his religious education?"

Persephone doesn't answer. She's too busy stifling a laugh, the result being that her facial muscles go into convulsions. Birch starts to cry.

"We'll give you fifty-five thousand dollars for him," Elenore says. "We have the money."

"I don't think we should get into a bidding war; it's unseemly," Persephone says. "But if I have to I will."

"You're not fit to raise a child," Elenore says.

"Really. I can give him the best education possible. I can give him a family legacy, financial advantages, a climate of civility and decency. What can you offer him?"

"A home."

"With trailer trash for playmates?"

The "trash" word draws the blood right out of Elenore.

"She was just kidding. We should all lighten up," Monet says.

"You buddinsky out of this," Persephone says savagely. "I meant just what I said."

"Well, Mrs. *Saminn*," says Howard, "trash is my business, and the likes of your kind produce a lot more of it than our kind."

"Too bad you had to dump it on the trust lands," Persephone snaps at him. She's referring to one of Howard's more shameful episodes, which cost him a big fine.

Garvin prevents any further discussion by making a show of removing the papers from his briefcase and handing them to me with a pen. "You should read this before you sign it," he says.

Monet withdraws, his face amused, as one watching the antics of children. He's enjoying the show. I reserve a special hatred for him.

I take the papers, look at them for two minutes, see nothing. It's as if I've had a stroke and lost my ability to read. I put the papers on the coffee table. The heat is so intense that I must do something to escape it.

"Mom—" I hold my arms out for the baby.

Something in my demeanor, or perhaps my voice, causes her to start shaking. "Please, Freddie. You're not going to hurt him, are you?"

"What is she talking about?" Persephone says. Apparently, I'm not sending any dangerous vibrations to her. It's only my mother who can read my true intent. I don't even know what it is myself.

"He's mine—mine!" I scream. Everyone in the room is stunned for a moment. I jerk Birch out of my mother's arms.

"Who gets the baby, her or us?" she asks.

"Don't you understand?" Persephone says. "He's going to keep him for himself."

Persephone had to say it for me to know what was inside me.

"Come on, let's get out of this den of snakes," I say. I hold Birch under one arm like a football and march out of the house.

The pickup barrels down Upper Darby Road, kicking up stones and dust, Birch lying on his back on the passenger seat, no safety carrier, which remains in my parents' car. For the first few minutes I have no thoughts at all, only my fine, blind rage. I reach under the seat, grab my Uncle Fred, and suck on him. The liquor calms me, the false calm inside the storm. My anger has cost me fifty thousand dollars. I want to be alone on the road, but I've sabotaged myself. How can I be free with a baby on board? I can't bear to go crawling back to the elders, and anyway I don't want either my parents or Persephone to raise this child.

"Read page one in tomorrow's *Keene Sentinel*," Old Crow says. A headline in bold type appears in my head:

Murder-Suicide in Darby

Father Kills Son, Self

How to do it?

I can drive to the ledges where Lilith died and throw myself and Birch off the cliff. For a moment everything is quiet, everything is peaceful in my head. It's as if the sunlight has been dimmed, the sounds of the road muffled; I am outside myself, already in the afterlife, watching my last hours from the future in a time rearview mirror. I see a storm, me fighting my way into its vortex, my last chance for salvation. And, puff, the vision vanishes.

Which leads me to a philosophical question. If there really is an afterlife it's only worthwhile if you can keep some semblance of your earthly identity and experiences and memories and feelings, because identity, experience, memory, and feeling are what makes you you. But what about the poor infant who has neither an identity nor worthwhile memories, nor even an inkling of gender? If the baby is killed off, can the baby ghost grow into a grown-up ghost? If a baby has no personhood, how can one consider him a candidate for the afterlife? All Birch has is his name, which I gave him. The name is only an idea: it's not him. He has formed no identity. Therefore he does not exist as a person. Birch the baby is merely a collection of pulsating cells, no more or less important in the scheme of things than a birch tree.

"Hold on," says Old Crow. "We may be miserable, but we do not want to die. We are a person. We have a personhood to protect. Scratch suicide from the murder-suicide option."

"That leaves murder," I say.

"How can you kill a being that has neither identity nor self-awareness? Infants do not distinguish between themselves and the people who care for them. And what difference does it make? Everybody you know is sick or stupid. Take your mother, for example."

"She's the only person I can think kindly of."

"She's pathetic, and you know it, Freddie boy," Old Crow says.

"Don't call me that name."

"All right, Frederick," Old Crow says. "Look at Howard—overbearing piggish. He'd kill to advance his trash collection business." After a pause when I hear the road under my feet, Old Crow says, "Who do you hate the most?"

"Persephone."

"No, partner," says Old Crow. "You don't hate her. You merely loathe her as she loathes you."

"It's Garvin."

"It's the baby you hate most. Here's what I propose. Lose the kid, change your name and identity; new, I, you, we will have no guilt for the crimes of the old Frederick Elman. You could mail Birch's body to Garvin's law office. That would get their attention."

"What do you mean 'their'?"

"Everything is about getting attention. Don't you understand anything? Attention, the quality of it, makes you you."

I hear Dad laugh out loud. I laugh, too. Or anyway try to. I'm working on my sense of humor. I'm not sure what's funny and what's tragic, but I do enjoy listening to laughter, which strikes me as an interesting thing to do with vowel sounds. I practice laughing every day, not that anybody notices. My grownups often confuse my laugh with calls for food or cries of discomfort, or even the untreatable disorder of infantile hysteria.

By the time Dad and I reach the interstate highway Dad is drunk and crazed by rage, which has gone from hot to cold. He turns off at the Putney, Vermont, exit, which winds around to a gas station. He stops at the end of the parking lot near the dumpster. He goes into the rear of his truck and comes back with a plastic trash bag. He puts me in the trash bag and lowers the bag into the dumpster.

"See you later," he says to nobody.

It's hard to breath in the plastic bag, but it's warm and the darkness is a comfort. I try to voice my ambivalence but am frustrated by sticky plastic on my lips; still, I'm not panicky. After living nine months in a submarine an infant does not fear suffocation. However, from the heat and the taste of my own breath I know something is wrong. I send my thoughts into the deep. The response is almost immediate. I hear Spontaneous Combustion in my head.

"Booze and anger have combined to make your father something other than your father," he says, no sympathy at all in his tone. "Such swift changes in identity brought on by the accidental collusion of events can happen to any human being. It can happen to you; perhaps it is happening in the storm years hence, where you are waiting for that moment when the chrysalis breaks apart and the new you flies off to bring your kind a major motion picture or, better yet, a snapshot of reality taken with a pinhole camera, an epic[urne] feast of literature or a few delicate[ssen] lines of poetry, something better than your telepathed thoughts to me or your mother, such thoughts being already weaker . . . weaker . . . weaker."

I'm about to drive onto the interstate when I see a bent figure by the side of the road, an old man with his thumb out for a ride. Hitched to the back of his knapsack is a never-washed cast iron stew pot.

I stomp on the brake, stick my head out the window, and holler, "Cooty, what are you doing here?"

"Bumming the entry ramps," says Cooty Patterson. "They won't let you hitchhike the interstate."

"Get in. Where you going, old man?"

"Brattleboro, to get on the Amtrak to Texas."

"Why didn't you call Howard or Pitchfork for a ride?"

"Good idea. I never have good ideas." He gets into the truck. "You look peculiar, Freddie, like you bumped your head. What's going on?"

Cooty has always had a sedative effect on me, and the old hermit works his magic now. I'm still drunk, but my anger breaks, replaced by the horror of what I have done. I'm suffocating, just as Birch must be suffocating.

"We have to turn around," I say.

I do a U-turn in the middle of the entrance ramp, almost run into a car coming in, and highball it back to the gas station. I leap up into the dumpster. My first thought is that he's gone. All the plastic bags look the same. I start ripping through them, but carefully. Third bag, I find him. His eyes are closed, his flesh warm to my touch, his body still. I flick his nose. His arms fly up and he cries out "Hey, watchit!" or words to that effect. It's the happiest moment of my life. In that dumpster I break down and weep, as much for myself as for Birch. For the first time since Lilith died I feel real.

We drive on to Brattleboro. I pour out my story to Cooty, who listens as he always does—in delighted confusion. For Cooty there is no such thing as usual. Cooty never learns from experiences outside his ingrained habits; even the most common event is new and exciting for him. Accordingly, he can never tell common from uncommon. For Cooty every day and every action is like a walk in a mine field. With an attitude like that a man must go crazy. Which Cooty did. But he came out the other side of crazy serene. Somewhere along the line he's taught himself to appreciate chaos. Because everything is perpetually new and strange for Cooty and because he's stopped being afraid he can enjoy every moment as novel and entertaining.

"You didn't like Howie and Elenore and Mrs. Salmon trying to take Birch for themselves, the fighting, I expect," Cooty says in his own mysterious, half-crazy, half-insightful way. "You were thinking Garvin might be Birch's real father, not you. You got mad, the mad was you. The mad took it out on Birch, like mad does, going for the little weakies, and you met me, a weakie not mad, and me not mad made you not mad any more, and now

here we are plowing down the highway, me holding this baby—
nice, nice, very nice."

"That about sums it up, Cooty, but I don't know what to do.
My anger scares me, especially when I'm drinking."

"You know what I think, I think Birch was sent."

"What do you mean, old man?"

"I never know what I mean. Words come out of me. I wish I
had Birch for myself."

"What would you do with a baby?"

"I would talk to him like I'm talking to you now."

"Talk to him," I say, then repeat, "talk to him." Possibilities
open up.

"You going back to your folks' place?" Cooty asks.

"I can't live there anymore—I just can't," I say. "I was thinking of a road trip, but now I'm not so sure. Cooty, if I go anywhere near a bar, temptation, I'll just revert. Get a few drinks in
me, and I commit rash acts. I left Lilith, I started a fight with a
friend, and look what I did to Birch!"

"You know what the biggest troublemaker is? It's electricity.
Camp out on some forgot land where there's no wires and you'll
heal yourself over time."

"Forgot land?"

"Land that nobody's using. Move in. All's they can do is
throw you out."

I'm picturing the abandoned hippie commune on Lonesome
Hill.

FORGOT FARM

After Dad delivers Cooty to the train station, he stops at Kmart and buys a baby car seat for the truck, some paper diapers, a set of bottles with baby formula, and a book on how to deal with people like me. The author is a Doctor Benjamin Spock. (No relation to the Star Trek guy as far as I know, but I do like to think that Dad had an idea to raise me on Vulcan principles.)

The last leg of the drive to the former hippie commune is a mile up a dirt road that is not maintained by the town of Darby. It is barely passable in the summer and closed in the winter by snow and ice and in the spring and fall by mud. It winds upward through a dense forest. Just about where the road ends and carries on as a hiking path and snowmobile trail, the land levels out more or less into a ten-acre saddle between the twin summits of Lonesome Hill.

"Here we are, Birch," Dad says. "A tribe of young people in the 1960s started a commune on this spot. They abandoned their land in the late 1970s, and it's been forgot land ever since."

Dad parks his truck just off the road, beside a stone wall and cellar hole where a farmhouse had set maybe a hundred years ago. The stones hold many colors in an aura of deep gray. Before anything else, the tall trees, even the wildflowers in the clearing, the stones draw the eye. They seem more like religious objects than parts of a falling-down, no longer useful wall. I want to touch them, and I reach out. Dad seems to know what's in my heart. He brings me over to the wall and puts my hand on a rock. It's hot from the sun and rough as his beard. He laughs out loud, me too, and the forest laughs back, or so it seems in my memory. It is our first joyous occasion.

Just beyond the wall, partially hidden by the trees, is an exempt yellow school bus painted in psychedelic colors and designs. A few tattered tie-dyed curtains hang in the windows. The door is gone and Dad walks in. The bus seats are gone, the inside gutted except for a clothes rack and an old dresser with the drawers open and empty, as if someone left in a hurry. On the clothes rack are half a dozen dresses on metal coat hangers brown with rust. Moths or something have eaten away parts of the dresses. On top of the rack is a bird's nest, empty.

"Amazing how nature makes beauty out of everything," Dad says. "It's a little mildewy, but the roof doesn't leak—not a bad space."

I memorize Dad's lyrics but do not understand them at the time and therefore do not answer.

We walk into the clearing, where the hippies had cut down trees but had not bothered to pull the stumps. Now a decade later suckers grow out of some stumps; others lay rotting. Dad walks me to a huge raspberry patch, maybe sixty feet long and twenty feet deep. Inside is an abandoned Volkswagen Bug, the blue paint faded so that it looks as if a piece of sky has fallen into the briars. Dad spends a good twenty minutes picking raspberries and popping them in his mouth. When I complain, he crushes one between thumb and forefinger and I suck the juice from his finger.

Scattered here and there in the woods in a circle around the clearing are rotting tent platforms, a collapsed yurt, and a rather dignified outhouse with a peace symbol drawn inside a half moon on the door. Dad finds a dug well covered with a large flat stone grown over with moss. He moves the stone and drops a rock into the dark. It makes a splash. We will have water. In the middle of the clearing is a ring of fire-blackened stones.

"When I was kid, Birch, Tubby and I used to sneak up here and watch from the woods, hoping to see hippie girls get naked, which they sometimes did. Everybody danced and sang to guitar music. They smoked their homegrown and held long discussions about the coming revolution. It was all going to be based on peace, love, and sharing."

Dad builds a campfire close to our truck, starting the fire with birch bark, building it up with dead pine branches, and adding hardwood once the fire is going well. Dad is well-equipped for camping. Inside the plywood shell in the bed of the truck is a small propane refrigerator, a cook stove, a sleeping platform, and cabinets for gear. With a bow saw he cuts maple poles and builds a tripod over the fire. He ties rope around a plastic bucket, lowers it into the well, and fills a big aluminum pot, which he centers on the fire.

He fills a couple of bottles with canned baby formula. He is very careful, reading the directions three times. He warms the bottles in the heated water. He changes my diaper, putting the used one aside; he washes me, dresses me, then takes me in one arm and feeds me with the other hand, as per instructions in the Doctor Spock book. Unlike lightning-quick Grandma Elenore, Dad does everything slowly and deliberately. I enjoy the change of pace. I don't remember the meal. I do remember that Dad follows Cooty's advice and talks to me. As I mentioned earlier, it isn't as if I know what he's saying (mercy, I don't even know what I'm saying), but I memorize every vowel and consonant as musical notes. Today when I remember Dad's speeches they sound like opera in my head.

After my meal Dad puts me down on a blanket on the ground and constructs a baloney sandwich.

I'm about to eat when I remember the bottle of vodka under the truck seat. In an instant Old Crow is back in spirit if not voice. I put the sandwich down and go around to the cab for the bottle.

I'm of two thought-meisters. One says pour the bottle into the ground, and the other—Old Crow—says pour the bottle into the throat. In the end I can do neither. I return the bottle to its place under the seat. I pace, and pace some more. I must drink something—anything. I rummage around in my foodstuffs and find a jar that my mother gave me years ago, when I took off on my first road trip—Ovaltine. I boil some water, pour it into a ceramic cup (made in pottery class back in college), dump in some Ovaltine, and, thinking about my mother, drink with, surprisingly, immense satisfaction.

I spend the next four or five hours sitting by the campfire. I read Doctor Spock by firelight, then whittle. Read, whittle, read, whittle, knock down the Ovaltine: something a man can do instead of boozing. When it's time to go to bed, I dump the remainder of my wash water to douse the fire. A flaming stick captures my attention. The god of fire is teasing me. I pull the stick out of the fire. It's part of a maple branch that has fallen from one of the ancient trees on the property. The stick is burnt halfway through. Something about the texture and shape of the stick, almost scooped at one end, intrigues me. In this object I see something I don't in myself—possibilities—but for what I cannot say; I'm just responding to a feeling. I put the stick in the crook of a tree.

That night Birch and I sleep under the stars. He wakes me twice for feedings.

The next morning I bathe Birch, dress him, and give him a bottle. I make a long list of things I need, things I might need, things I do not need but want. Like my father, I'm very handy with tools and imaginative in using them. I spend most of the morning cutting maple and birch saplings and shaping them with my jackknife into a crude crib lashed together with fish line. Later I put Birch in his car seat and we drive off.

"Better get used to me, buddy," I say. "We'll be spending a lot of time in each other's company."

We're headed for Ike's Auction Barn. On the drive I tell Birch about the Jordan clan, because they're part of his heritage. Ike Jordan was murdered a couple years back. His son Carleton, a.k.a. Critter, took over the business, and some people believe the murder was a family affair, that Critter did in his old man, or maybe it was Ike's brother, Donald, who runs the junkyard in Keene. The Jordans have been in this county since the last ice age, maybe longer, but nobody really knows who they are inside. They don't know themselves, or maybe the it's the other way around: they know themselves too well. Ollie Jordan, another brother, was Howard's best friend until he froze to death in the woods. Elenore hates the Jordans because, I suspect, she secretly fears she might be one. Anyone can see the resemblance around the mouth—bad teeth.

"Elmans or Jordans, we're both pretty close to being in the same place—at the bottom," I say. "You come from both the top on your mother's side and the bottom on my side. I think that's okay. What worries me is you don't have a middle in your background, and in America the middle rules. Let me look at you and see if you have perspective."

I take my eyes off the road and look at Birch. He grins at me.

"There's the auction barn," I say. "Used to be a real, hip-roofed cow barn, the Flagg place, until Ike bought it. It's still called Ike's Auction Barn, but there's not only no Ike, there are no auctions. Critter revamped the place into a mini–shopping center and flea market. In the rear there used to be a porn shop, but it closed up. Now it's headquarters for Critter's used car lot."

While Dad is speaking I feel buzzy on my bottom.

"Don't look so alarmed," Dad says. "We just hit the bumpy parking lot. Any time you deal with a Jordan think bumpy.

"I made a budget last night. We have enough money to last a year, provided we live real frugal, I mean the bare necessities. The woods are going to be hard on both of us, damn hard, but, Birch, I feel free and eager for the first time since you were born."

I leave the auction barn with a chain saw, a splitting maul, wedges, a sledgehammer, a couple of blades for my 21-inch bow saw, and a front pack designed to carry babies. On impulse I buy a dozen versions of an item I'd never seen before. It's called a bungy cord, an elastic rope fastener inspired by the latest craze, bungy jumping. I drive to Ancharsky's Store for groceries and look over the town bulletin board. There's usually a boat for sale and an unspoken story featuring an outraged wife and an irresponsible husband. But not today.

I spend another two days gathering provisions and shopping for a reasonably priced boat, which I want for recreation and, more important, as a platform to catch fish—free food. I like the idea of a boat because water separates me from other people. I finally find a ten-foot aluminum johnboat with life preservers and oars leaning against the side of a garage in Keene. A leader line and sinkers are tangled in a rivet. I buy the boat for fifty dollars from the widow of the former owner. The craft is unwieldy, but light—no problem to lift it on top of my pickup camper and tie it down.

My camper is crowded for one-man living. With a baby added it's downright jammed. I go to work on the school bus to make it habitable. I haunt the flea markets for worn rugs, candles, kerosene lamps, shelving. I buy a used Franklin stove and piping for a crude chimney, a rusty set of chisels and gouges that appear useless but only need sharpening. With my bow saw I cut saplings and tree branches to make stick furniture—an improved crib, a highchair, a table, a frame for a sofa bed. No clocks. Human beings started down the road to unhappiness with the invention of timepieces. Birch and I are going to live by sun, stars, and weather.

Abusive as he is, I miss the Elmans' cat, but other than that I'm content with Dad. Two weeks have gone by when Grandpa Howard and Grandma Elenore show up at mid-day. Must be Sunday. We're outside by Dad's cookfire.

Elenore pushes by Dad to reach me, comfortable in my new twig crib that Dad has lugged outside. She picks me up and inspects me.

"We heard you were up here, thought we'd pay a visit," Howard says, his voice full of cheer and sarcasm. "How you doing?"

"I'm gaining," Dad says.

"You have a job yet?"

"No, and I don't intend to get one."

"I knew you had bad habits, but I never thought being a deadbeat was one of them," Howard says.

"I never thought you were wrong about anything, Pop," Dad says.

"Me neither. It's dispiriting to learn different."

Grandma Elenore strips me, checks my orifices, my skin, my joints, dresses me, rubs her cheek against my face, and produces those idiotic kitchy-kitchy koo noises grownups make in their attempts to relate to babies. "His color's good," she says, "and he's put on a little weight—I guess you're taking care of him. What are all these red welts, mosquito bites?"

"That's right," Dad says.

Grandma Elenore furrows her brow. "You have a toilet out here?" she asks.

"I bought a second-hand medical potty."

"What do you do with the poop?" she sniffs. Points to the outhouse. "I don't smell anything."

"I don't use the outhouse. I burn it," Dad says.

"You burn it?"

"That's right—I burn it. I have plenty of firewood."

"Freddie, you can't bring up a child in the middle of the woods, no electricity, no proper toilet, no water . . ." Grandma Elenore says.

"We have water," Dad says. "We just don't have running water."

Elenore looks at our school bus home. "What's that?"

"Come and take a look." Dad walks toward the school bus, and the Elmans follow. They see an outdoor grill, stacks of fire wood, a clearing for a future garden. They do not see the fire pit where Dad burns paper diapers, sewage, and other refuse. They see Dad's new front door of rough-cut pine boards. At the top of the door he's carved into the pine the words "Forgot Farm."

Inside Dad stapled, nailed, and glued carpeting to the walls and ceiling as well as the floor. On the carpet walls he's started "sewing" sticks into the carpeting with fish lines. Eventually the whole place will be sticked or stuck or whatever you call an interior with twig walls.

"It's like being in a beaver lodge," Howard says. Hard to tell whether he speaks in admiration or admonition.

"That's the idea," Dad says.

"It upsets me, Freddie," Elenore says. "You should move back into a regular home."

"I'm going to raise Birch my way, Mom."

Howard doesn't like Dad's tone of voice to his mother. "You won't work, won't live like a normal person—how you going to make a dollar?" Howard is no longer droll. He is more obviously exasperated. "Moreover, you'll be marooned out here when the snows fly."

"I guess I will," Dad says. When Dad tells me this story years later, he'll say it was the first time he'd felt satisfaction in a verbal duel with his father.

"I fear for that child," Elenore says.

The Elmans visit for an hour or so every other Sunday after church. They bring canned goods, diapers, paper towels, household cleaners, and clothes for me. Dad is more or less cordial, but relations with his parents are obviously strained.

Elenore likes to tell Dad the town news, even though he insists he doesn't want to hear anything about the world outside Forgot Farm. This particular day in August we are sitting around a picnic table Dad has whacked together from lumber parts he pulled out of a construction dumpster.

"Lawyer Prell has moved in with Mrs. Salmon and her niece," Grandma Elenore says.

"They all deserve each other," Dad grumbles.

"Lord knows that mansion is big enough," Grandpa Howard says. "Freddie, maybe she'll rent you a room cheap?"

"Don't make jokes, Howie," Elenore says. "Prell is running for county attorney. He's quite the rising star, that fellow."

"Do I have to listen to this?" Dad says.

"All right," Grandma Elenore says, her voice suddenly full of false cheer. "Let me take Birch. I'm going to change his diaper."

"I just changed his diaper twenty minutes ago," Dad says, exasperated.

"She just wants an excuse to admire his body," Howard says.

"Howie, you can be so disgusting," Elenore grabs me out of Dad's arms the way he grabbed me back at the Salmon place weeks ago and walks away.

"I'll help you out," Dad stands.

"No," Elenore says in alarm now. "I want to do this. It's important."

"All right." Dad sits down.

Grandma Elenore brings me to the well, which is screened from the picnic table by some trees. Dad built a wood housing and roof around the well and installed a hand pump. Grandma pumps water into a bucket. She changes my diaper, washes me, and powders my behind. It's a great feeling, a giant and gentle hand grabs your ankles, hoists up your butt, and sprinkles talcum powder on your privates. Afterwards she dresses me in my finest boy blue.

Then she drops to her knees, puts her elbows on the well housing, and prays in a loud whisper. "Dear God, send me to hell for what I am about to do, but save this baby."

She sticks her hand in the bucket, puts her forefinger and middle finger on my forehead, raises her eyes to heaven, and says, "I baptize thee in the name of the Father, the Son, and the Holy Ghost."

The water trickles into my eyes and blurs my vision. I do not cry, but I wonder if I'll ever be the same again. How I long for the good old days before eternal life was bestowed upon me.

At that moment, I hear Dad's voice. "What's this? What's going on?" He picks me up.

Elenore backs away, her face full of guilt.

Dad notes the water on my forehead, and now he knows.

"You christened him!" he shouts.

"Take it easy," Howard says, arriving on the scene.

"I did it for his immortal soul," Elenore says.

"That's it—we're done," Dad says. "Don't come back here. Understand? I don't want anything to do with you people."

Dad with me in his arms walks away from his parents. They follow him, Elenore crying, Howard trying to calm both Dad and Elenore down. But Dad is angry, and when Dad is angry he isn't what you would call reasonable. He just keeps walking away into the woods, not following the path, bushwhacking until Grandma Elenore and Grandpa Howard have disappeared behind the foliage.

Finally, Dad stops. We hear Elenore calling out to us until she goes silent. When we return to Forgot Farm, the Elmans are gone. They will not come back.

EXPERIMENTS IN LIVING

What does it mean to love another human being? Probably the fact that I am asking the question suggests that I can never know the answer. But I must try to deal with the question. I feel something like love for my mother, or perhaps I am mistaking anguish at disappointing her for love. I cannot claim to love my father the person, but I do love those qualities of character in him that I lack. I feel a sense of duty toward my siblings, but since they are so far away I rarely think about them, and I cannot say I love them. I conclude that my feelings for family, while strong, are not really mine but mandates delivered by culture. My love for Lilith seemed real for a time, but it was accompanied by sexual desire and dreams of conquest, and in the end tainted by jealousy and tension brought on by our differences and insecurities. I'm beginning to understand that I've always been more interested in others loving me than in me loving them. Love was something I grabbed and ran away with to gnaw on like a dog with a bone. At its best love was never part of me but a beacon shining down from on high that illuminated me. I am not capable of loving family, friends, or a woman. My salvation lies in honest answers to certain questions, answers that must be tested through actions. In a word, care. Can I love this child by providing good care alone? Or is love apart from loving care, and if so what is its nature and value?

As a man, as a father, I see myself more as a protector from dangers than as a conveyor of affection. I lack any natural inclination to nurture him. In other words, Birch needs a mother. If I'm to raise Birch properly I must become his mother. I worry over this problem. I fear that eventually resentment and selfishness will take me over, as they did when I was living with my parents, as they did when I was living with Lilith. I cannot wait for love to shine down on me. I must act. I must create my illumination so that love departs from me and spreads across the globe. I must become the beacon. But how?

After only a week or two caring for Birch I realize that what I lack in my relations with loved ones is intimacy. I know this idea to be true because, quite magically, intimacy with Birch has come my way without me seeking it. I begin to understand that intimacy is an aura created by care. Since Birch is helpless, he can give me nothing. I must give to him. The more I care for this child the closer I am to him.

The rewards of a baby are partly tactile—softness, smell, baby thrashings and how they reverberate through the hands; I love the strange little sounds he makes. It's as if they contain meaning that even he is not aware of. God is speaking to us through our infants. (Not that I believe in God, nor do I disbelieve. I understand the need for a god, understand the possibility of same; it's just that God has chosen not to manifest Himself to me in a convincing form. He is like the thought of a shadow in a dark room: an idea without form and outside the empirical method. I'm a spiritual drifter, hoping for a hand-out from this stranger that is called God and that I cannot see or hear or touch, but whom I want to exist.) I sleep with Birch the first few nights, a delicious feeling, but I'm afraid of accidentally smothering or crushing him in my sleep, which is why I build him an improved crib of maple saplings, lashed together with waxed cord, the nails judiciously placed. I often lie with him not in sleep but for comfort. He pulls the hairs on my chest with his tiny hands and makes puckering gestures with his tiny mouth. At first I think this is a game, and then I realize he wants to nurse. What to do? I don't know.

It's odd but I actually talk more now than I did when I was living in the world and participating in unnecessary conversations. I talk out my practical thoughts to Birch. I want him to know what I am doing, why I am doing it, and what the likely consequences will be of my actions. Birch is learning everything I know, from driving a pickup truck to recognizing dry from green firewood on the stump. He's learning by my actions and speech. Unnecessary conversation disrupts meaning and encourages misinformation. Unnecessary conversation always deteriorates into a contest, with all of the accompanying tension of a competitive situation with a winner and a loser, but a voiced monologue with a specific purpose allows both listener and speaker time to analyze and verify its information.

It's late summer. I work very hard, gathering firewood and making a home out of a school bus, but I allow myself a part of the day for adventuring. We fish on Grace Pond, which is on the Salmon trust.

Dad and I drive regularly to Grace Pond. Forgot Farm is only about a mile and a half trail-walking to Grace Pond, but it's five miles by road. We have to drive down our nasty road, turn onto the paved town road, onto another dirt road, and finally onto a two-rut car path into the trust lands to the pond. Dad says, "The Salmon Forest Trust Conservancy is closed to motorized vehicles, with one exception. New Hampshire law requires public access to all water bodies because they are owned by the people. I know you don't understand me now, but my words are sinking in, and some day they'll rise to the surface." We drive down the narrow dirt road to the pond, nothing but forest on each side. The only sign that people ever stepped foot in those woods are stone walls.

When we arrive, Dad pulls the boat off the top of the pick-up and carries it to the sliver of beach that serves as a public boat landing. There are no cottages on the pond and no fishermen. The state does not stock the pond with trout, so the only fish are perch, hornpout, pickerel, and rumors of smallmouth bass. Some of the local guys come at night to fish for hornpout, but nobody but Dad fishes for perch, because perch are small and do not tug on the line, which is what gives fishermen the thrill they seek. The boat landing is only fifteen or twenty feet wide. Trees grow right down to the shoreline. The boat is very tiny, light enough for a strong man to carry.

With bungy cords Dad ties the car seat with me in it to the stern seat of the boat, while he rows from the middle seat. He rows me to a beaver lodge at the rocky end of the pond, where the trees came right down to the shore and lean in over the pond as if about to drink, not water but light. Dad picks up some beaver-chewed wood to bring back with us as an ornament for our house. "The beaver," he says, "ranks with the skunk as the most magnificent nuisance animal of the North Country." We catch a pail full of perch that day. Dad cooks them back at Forgot Farm, the tiny fillets dredged in flour and salt and fried in bacon fat in an iron fry pan on the outdoor grill. Other fishermen stalk the aristocratic trout, the union card bass, or the action-adventure-hero pike, but Dad goes after the down-home perch.

Another day on the pond we are treated to the sight of an osprey dropping from a great height to take a fish out of the water. "Imagine being able to see so well that you're a couple hundred feet above a windy lake and you can spot a six-inch fish below the surface," Dad says. "You can calculate where it will be after you begin your drop. You can see it rushing up to meet you, and you can make an in-flight course correction at darn near your terminal velocity. Fantastic!"

On one side of the narrow boat launch is the expanse of the pond; on the other side is a marsh, where a great blue heron has taken up residence in a huge nest at the top of a dead pine tree in the water. Watching the heron fish becomes a meditative activity for both Dad and me. Dad anchors the boat, waits quietly five or ten minutes for the heron to get over the upset of our presence. We watch the bird fish. She walks very deliberately, very stately until she finds a station. She stands still, as if posing. The tension builds in Dad and me. We hardly breathe. Suddenly the heron darts her beak into the water like a spear and comes up with a fish. Then the heron with fish crossways in her mouth begins a laborious takeoff, flapping her huge wings, tucking her legs behind her like a knife in a sheath, wings sometimes hitting water as she strains for altitude, finally rising on an air current, circling, and back into the nest at the high point of the dead pine. Dad lets out a whoop, and I throw up my hands and imitate Dad's whoop. I don't know if it qualifies as my first word, but close. His whoop is my whoop.

Another late summer day, the heron breaks off from fishing and flies away, but in the opposite direction of the nest, as if never coming back. Dad watches her fly across the pond. But I keep my eye on the marsh where the heron had been. I note that some fall color has appeared on the swamp maples. Something begins to emerge from the tall marsh grass. Only when Dad hears a splash does he turn around to see what I have seen, a moose in moose knee–deep water, munching some growing thing.

"Birch," Dad says, to me, "this is my favorite time of year."

Birch and I are taking one of our walks in the woods. It has misted all day and the sky is almost clearing, so that the sun shines strong but with diffuse light. The mist has collected on spiderwebs, making them visible. Glistening spiderwebs in the grass, in the trees, in spaces between rocks. I tip a moose wood leaf toward my son's mouth, and the collected droplets of water quench his thirst.

I break off the path and start bushwhacking. It would be easy for the average person to get lost out here, but I know these lands. I walked them as a kid-trespasser and I walked them with Lilith, and now I walk them with our son. I know the trust as well as the Squire did, but there's always something new to learn.

We've arrive at a patch of young white pine trees on the north side of a hill. I know this grove and have avoided it. Here young pines grow, their lower branches all entwined with one another.

The walking is hard and snarly and dark under the canopy, and underneath my feet is a desert. Young pines and their acidic needles kill everything in their shadow, including, sometimes, each other. I'm skirting the pines when my eye catches sight of a darker branch growing at a forty-five degree angle. The branches of pines grow ninety degrees from the trunk, so it's more the anomaly of the angle than the branch itself that I notice. I go in for a closer look, breaking dead pine branches with my hands. Birch does not like the sound, and his hands flutter with alarm, but he does not cry. The odd branch is not a pine at all; it's from an apparently dead apple tree. I explore some more and discover that I'm in an ancient apple orchard. Decades ago the orchard was abandoned and the pines took over and are in the process of strangling the light from the apple trees.

The branches of dying apple trees have grown tremendously long, reaching as high as they can for light. But the pines reach higher, and over the years the apple trees are losing this little war in the woods. In their struggle, I see my own and the inevitability of defeat. I decide that I might be doomed, but these apple trees are not, for while there is no one to save me, I can save them.

The tree I'd first seen and thought was dead holds a few small green apples that grow on a single branch that has found a shaft of light. They'll be ready in the early fall if the tree can get some more light. I return the next day with my chain saw and cut some of the pines, and the light pours through, and the apple trees thank me. I cut the pine wood into firewood lengths. Split, it will make good kindling next year.

At the ledges Dad shows me the secret place where you and he used to go to be alone. "You were made in this lean-to beside that little hemlock tree and born nine months later in the same place," he says. "I think maybe your mother's spirit is still here in some form."

Mother, dear Mother, that is why I have come here in the terrible storm.

One afternoon we walk to Old Darby Cemetery on the edge of the trust and marvel at the gravestones. Men died from accidents and infection, and women died in childbirth, and children died in droves from diseases, but from the looks of the gravestones it appears that if persons could reach forty-five or fifty, they'd make it into their eighties and often their nineties.

As the summer gives way to fall, I continue my great experiment in living, making rules as I go along. To raise Birch properly and keep myself from going crazy or committing a criminal act, I will have to enforce our isolation. I will avoid the temptations and corruption of the material world, what my Catholic mother calls the near occasions of sin—bars, liquor stores, televisions, radios, theaters, shopping centers, and schools.

My philosophy is based on the idea that the root cause of human confusion is unnecessary conversation. Which leads me to the practical matter of educating my son. If I refrain from conversation, how will Birch learn to speak? I decide that he must hear the best of human speech, but without trivialization or argumentation. He must be instructed in practical matters, for we are alone in the wilderness. I will never talk down to him. I will speak in complete grammatical sentences. I will refrain from all small talk. Together we will learn about the world through observation and through library books that offer instruction, wisdom, and beauty. I resolve never to criticize him, and to give him the tools that will allow him to do whatever he wishes.

We leave Forgot Farm once a week to shop for necessities. If a clerk speaks to me about the weather, I do not answer. I speak to no one on the street, and if anyone speaks to me I do not answer. We spend an hour at the Darby Free Library, which is the only place in the civilized world where I feel halfway comfortable. I return books and check out books. Later, at Forgot Farm, I entertain myself and teach my son language arts by reading out loud to him. We read the classics, history, literature, how-to manuals. We read about religion but stay away from the sacred texts such as the Bible, which are fraught with scientific errors, exaggerations, and mistakes in judgment, not to mention violence, ambiguity, pretentious language, and reports of unnecessary conversations with the Deity. Children should be protected from books like the Bible. However, I am most offended by so-called children's books, which range from stupid to trite, from insulting to patronizing, from left wing to right wing propaganda, cunningly or crudely disguised. I do admire some of the artwork in children's books, but the evil in the texts outweighs the good in the illustrations.

Over time my personality becomes integrated with my philosophy. In our woods I am cheerful and optimistic; in town I am guarded and sullen.

Part of my plan for Birch's education is to create an intellectual, moral, and emotional framework to give him the tools so that he can make himself intimate with this land that his mother and grandfather Salmon were so wrought up in. If I cannot introduce him to society at large, I must make do with the natural world, for a person must have a context to fit himself into or, conversely, to escape from. If he leaves the land, denies it, hates it even, he must know it to begin with so that he can place himself outside it. Without context he will drift on an endless sea. Through books and observation I will teach myself all I can, and I will pass on that knowledge to Birch. I am already well-equipped to teach him the practical arts of survival—sheltering, cooking, heating.

However, I lack in any but rudimental medical training. I cannot perform an appendectomy. I have no license to prescribe drugs. What will I do if Birch or myself sicken? Working in the woods is dangerous. I could gouge myself with the chain saw. A tree could fall on us. Medical care and the expense it entails is so overwhelming to me that I cannot face up to the problems. I simply refuse to think about them.

I am one who cannot exist in the material world without succumbing to drink and rage and confusion. However, as my father pointed out, eventually I must earn a living in that same world—but how? At the moment I do not have an answer. The best I can do is to refine my way of life here and now. The larger questions will have to wait for another day.

I've cut enough standing deadwood for the stove to get us through the winter. Once the snows fly my pickup will be stuck at Forgot Farm until spring, so I'm careful to stock up on bulk items such as paper diapers. Not that Birch and I will be marooned. It's only a couple miles into town on a hiking trail. The leaves have started to turn color, and I've decided to walk in with Birch and enjoy the views.

On the way I spot a figure in the woods off the trail—Katharine Ramchand. She's holding a rock in her hands, studying it intently. I stop and watch her. I'm waiting for her to notice me. I want to startle her. I want the Darby elite to know that Frederick Elman walks in their midst. I want them to fear me. I want to hurt them. I want to . . . I'm suddenly aware of my thoughts—how injurious they are. My chest tightens and my breath comes quicker. Birch in the baby carrier stirs from the euphoria of motion. He must sense the disturbance in me.

I want to apologize to Katharine Ramchand, to tell her that I do not mean to spy on her. "But that would be a lie." Old Crow's voice is barely a whisper. Katharine doesn't notice us, because she is so intent on the rock. What could be so interesting about it? I want to ask her, but I just don't have amenities in me. I decide to wait until she notices me and see what develops.

She replaces the rock in its niche in the wall and starts down the path. I could follow her, but I don't want to give in to the vague desire to stalk her. I'll let some time pass before I return to the trail. I walk over to the rock wall and inspect the rock she'd been holding. It looks like any other, pitted grey with flecks of mica schist and a streak of green (perhaps) fluorite. Suddenly, I'm grateful to Katharine Ramchand, for the rock is beautiful. I hold it above my head so I can see it with the fall leaves in the background. The rock deserves the attention she paid it. Katharine Ramchand did not toss the rock aside. She placed it in the exact location she'd found it, so I do the same. I decide to follow the wall into town instead of the path. It's maybe an extra half-mile of walking.

We're almost at the field where the wall breaks out of the woods. Not a farmer's field (mowed for good reason) but a homeowner's field (mowed for no good reason). Birch has fallen asleep, which he frequently does when the rhythm of my walking becomes steady. A movement in the woods catches my eye. I go over to investigate. Lying on her side is a sow bear in plain view, two cubs nursing on her. Unlike Katharine Ramchand she notices us, but she does not move. She just keeps her eyes on us. She's depending upon me to show good judgment. I back slowly away, impressed. A woman, a rock, a bear and her babies, fall leaves: entertainment in the woods. I feel blessed, lucky to be out today. Such are my simple pleasures. I want to express my thankfulness, so I wake Birch and tell him the whole story as we skirt the field and head into town.

Later that day back at Forgot Farm I'm still thinking about the bear, the look in her eye—wary, guarded, but without fear. The entire scene was odd. Odd that I should come upon it. Odd that a mother bear would nurse in plain sight. I don't doubt what I saw. I doubt its meaning. It's as if the bear mother was sent to me for some purpose. What could it be?

Usually, Birch's demands are easy to satisfy. He's hungry or he has a wet diaper. But there are times when he cries out of some need that I do not understand. During these moments I become nervous and upset. I attempt to feed him, and he knocks the bottle away; I rock him, I talk to him, and still he cries. On this day, I bring him to my bed, lie down, and put him on my chest. He somehow finds my nipple underneath my t-shirt. He sucks on the fabric until I can feel his wet mouth on my skin. His effort calms him down. Soon he falls asleep.

The following day: same situation. This time I remove my t-shirt and let him suckle on my nipple. The feeling gives me the creeps, but I persist. He wants this, not a bottle. I will give him this. After four days something strange and magical happens. Nursing changes me from the inside out. I begin to respond. The feeling is sensual, but not specifically sexual. I'm enjoying the kind of physical intimacy I could not have conceived of only a few weeks ago. I will not want to give it up. On day eight I produce a small amount of milk.

VISIONS IN FIRE

In October I build a shaving horse, which is a vise to hold wood for whittling, and at a flea market I buy a draw knife. It has a blade about a foot long with a handle at each end, so you can whittle with two hands. You put the stick in the vise and pull the shavings off. Making shavings satisfies my whittling urge, and the shavings do not go to waste. I use them for starting fires and to provide light. Open the stove door, throw in some shavings, and you are treated to a quick burst of light from the flames.

A few inches of snow fall on election day in November, but it soon melts. It doesn't count as the first snow. Never mind what the calendar says, in New Hampshire the first day of winter begins with the first major snowstorm. On an Indian summer day, I read the town bulletin board and learn that Garvin Prell has been elected county prosecutor. Envy and resentment ruin two hours of my life, but only two. I resolve never again to read the bulletin board. News is a form of unnecessary conversation.

One night I hear high-flying honkers, and I take Birch outside into the clearing so I can show him the "V's" of the geese silhouetted against the moonglow. The "V-birds" are flying south and making an awful racket. One feels privileged to witness such an event.

Late in the month a couple of deer hunters in blaze orange vests wander by while I'm stacking firewood. I recognize them as Chester Rayno, the poacher, and his son, Junior, who's about twelve; they're hunting legally right now since it's deer season. They look at me with amusement. The old rage, the old hatred of humanity comes roaring back. I try to ignore them by not looking at them, but they come over anyway.

"You're Freddie Elman, right?"

I answer with a bare nod.

"Seen any tracks hereabouts?" says Chester.

"I saw a blaze orange buck yesterday, but somebody shot him dead," I say.

"It's inadvisable to speak down to an armed man," Chester says.

I pick up my chain saw, start it, walk casually toward the men.

"I could shoot him down," the boy says.

I rev the saw.

The boy's debating whether to flick the safety off, when Chester grabs his gun. "Take it easy, Junior," Chester says.

They back away, while I continue to rev the chain saw.

By the end of the month the ground lies bare and brown, the ferns and grasses fallen, matted over with autumn leaves. Birch and I have settled into a routine that suits us both.

I sit up in my couch/bed and look outside at the trees, still and solemn under starlight and moonglow. I can't say exactly when I start my day, because I refuse to wear a watch or own a clock. Nor do I keep a calendar. My aim is to live in the present moment. Not easy with a brain that roams through time. I can say that our day starts hours before the dawn.

I light a candle, come over to Birch, and stick a finger in his diaper. It's a little moist. I'll wait until he wakes before I change it.

I open the door to the Franklin stove and throw some wood shavings in to give more light to the room. Watching dancing shadows in firelight entertains me the way a movie used to. A heightened awareness and appreciation of light is one of the un-expected pleasures of life without electricity. I add fat wood on the shavings to crank up the heat. Later, I'll put on some logs and close the fireplace door. The stove will run for hours without a reload.

I make my bed, sweep around the hearth, toss the dirt into the fire. The broom and carpet-sweeper are in use off and on all day. I keep our yard-sale imitation Persian rugs from collecting dirt. I'm discovering that, unlike Howard, I like everything to be just so. I pee in an extra-large empty Hellman's Real Mayonnaise jar. I screw the cover back on and place the jar behind the curtain, where the potty resides.

I pull the shaving horse close to the fire. I will move the horse back and forth throughout the day in relation to the fireplace to catch the right amount of light and heat. Against the wall is a pile of sticks. I place a stick on the shaving horse, push with my foot, and the "dumb head" comes down on the stick and holds it fast. I work with great concentration, pulling wood off with the draw knife, shavings flying. My goal is to make the stick smooth and shapely.

I've stapled and nailed carpets to the walls and ceiling of the school bus for insulation. I've sewed sticks to the walls for deco-ration. I try to bring out the beauty of each stick before using it. My goal is to finish the entire inside of the school bus with shaved sticks. I've made a kitchen chair for myself, a crib and high chair for Birch, shelves, and smaller stuff such as a mirror frame and candle holders, all with sticks. My latest project is a playpen for Birch. I expect that he'll be crawling soon. The playpen began with an ash tree I cut down. It's a tree the local Indians used to make snowshoes and dogsleds with, because the wood bends easily, especially when it's heated in a steam box. I rived the bolts with a froe and shaved the pieces into rounds with my draw knife. Presently, the shape of the stick is to my liking, and the sight of it makes me happy. I follow the natural bend of the wood, so no two pieces are the same, and none is exactly straight.

The stick is almost ready, and I can hear excitement in my breath. I sweep up the wood shavings and toss them into the space between the simmering front and back logs. I kneel on the floor, watch my shadow jig and jitter on the walls. I look around in satisfaction at the silhouettes of my modest homemade furnishings.

I hone my tools, inspect the floor to make sure every speck has been picked up; I move the shaving horse slightly so that its angle to the hearth is pleasing to my eye. Everything has to be neat and clean, as if company were coming. I go through my woodpile, choosing a piece as much by feel as sight. Every piece has to have some figure in it, some twist in the grain, some digression. Sometimes Old Crow speaks to me. "You don't want to do this, Frederick. You're tired, Frederick—tired. If you had a clock it would say 2 AM. It's dark, it's always dark—why is December so dark?" But my self-doubt is transitory, a function of my loneliness. I am soon back to my shaving horse, throwing ringlets of wood with the draw knife.

Birch wakes cranky and needy. I change his diaper and set the diaper outside by the door on top of the two other used diapers. I bring him to my bed and lay on my side so he can nurse and I can watch the fire. He suckles and I nap, that sweet hour of half-sleep, half-musing before the dawn. For me nursing is calming and meditative. Worries and animosity empty from my mind.

Years later I'll ask Dad was it was like to nurse me. He'll say it was a pleasant sensation that spread out across his body, like being in a hot tub, which won't be all that helpful since neither one of us will have any experience in a hot tub. I love Dad's warmth. It's during these times when we are almost glued together that I think of Dad as you, Mom.

I've listened to the *zz* of Dad's bow saw, the *whoosh-thuck* of his ax, the *sip sip sip* of his knives on the wood; in excursions outside I listen to the talk of birds, the talk of wind, the talk of distant coyotes, the talk of tree toads, the talk of Dad's footfalls. I've tested out all those languages with uncertain results thus far.

At the moment I'm trying to talk fire. It crackles, it sighs, it roars, it hisses, it spits, it squeals, and it farts, all in all quite a complicated series of syllables and sentences whose meaning eludes me. I practice speaking fire until suddenly I feel hunger, and then I turn to my own, more effective and precise, if limited, language—the FEED ME! holler. Dad's milk is soothing, but there isn't all that much of it. It's more an appetizer than a meal.

I cry and Dad ignores me for a minute. He's the most selfish when I wake him up. Finally, he puts me in my stick high chair and sets the stick table with silverware and cloth napkins. He insists that we dine with some decorum. We eat corn flake cereal in milk with fruit, no sugar. The propane refrigerator from the camper is Dad's only modern convenience.

After breakfast Dad puts me in my new playpen. He wipes the bowls and spoons. He shakes the table cloth, folds it, and places it on a shelf. He carefully arranges the chairs behind the table. He sweeps the floor and puts the broom away. He stands back and makes sure everything appears well-ordered.

Birch is in deep thought, or so it seems to me. I wonder if babies really think or whether thought arrives riding shotgun on tactile stimuli. I go outside, where I've set up my kitchen, the centerpiece being a stone fireplace hearth with a cooking grill vented by a metal chimney that rises up through a porch roof I built against the school bus. I call it the cook shed. With a roof and open sides I can cook year-round outdoors on wood fires.

I follow our trodden path to the well and pump a bucket of water. This goes on all day. You don't know how much water you use until you have to pump it and lug it by hand. The labor makes one appreciate water in the same way that one appreciates a hill by walking it as opposed to driving it. I dip the pot into the bucket and scoop out some water.

I put the pot on the grill in the cook shed. I have plenty of firewood but a limited amount of propane, so we rarely use the camper stove, allocating the propane to the fridge. Then I go around to the other side of our home and start another fire in a circle of stones. One of my future projects is building an ice box for the outdoors, useful during the winter months when we won't get out much to buy fresh food.

Once the water is hot, I bring the pot inside, strip off my clothes, and give myself a sponge bath. After diapering and dressing Birch and putting him in his playpen, I trim my beard and comb my long hair. I have a horror of lapsing into recluse-dishevelment. I want the trees and the rocks and the peeping-tom critters of the forest to note in their gossip that the father and the son in the wilderness are neat, clean, prim. By contrast, when I go to town I mess my hair and beard and wear dirty, wrinkled clothes. My purpose is to make people want to flee at the sight of me. I take a long look at myself in the mirror—hairy, thick all over. I'm proud of the body. It is built for utility rather than show.

I note the vanity in the eyes. But wait—what is this mote floating in inner space? Alarm? No, fear. Why be afraid? And then The Obvious speaks to me. I cannot afford overconfidence; any excess of self-satisfaction could lead to distraction and an accident. No accidents in the woods, please. I remind myself that if I die out here Birch dies too. I put the mirror away.

In well water I'd boiled the day before for drinking, I brush my teeth and clean out my juice bottle.

I clip my fingernails and put on fresh underwear and blue jeans, which I fold along a crease every night so they will appear pressed in the morning. I slip on tan moccasins (my cabin slippers). I pull a clean white t-shirt over my head and put on a blue oxford button-down shirt. Lilith bought a bunch of them for me. I have a row of them on hangers to keep wrinkles to a minimum.

I wash my dirty underwear and socks and hang them in front of the Franklin stove on a twig laundry rack. I dump the pan of dirty water outside the door in a homemade leaching field of small stones. I tuck Birch into my front carrier. He waves his hands and makes those *oo-ah* bird calls babies are famous for. He knows we're getting ready to go into the great big world of the forest, and he is happy and I am happy.

I place my slippers beside my couch/bed, put on my boots, grab the mayo jar of pee, and go out, pausing at the door with

Birch to listen. A pair of birds high in the trees sings to one another. I scan the trees, trying to locate the birds, but they are not to be seen, and I cannot tell from their song what they are. Bird identification is one of my weak areas.

I check my weather center, which I've hung in a hemlock tree because I enjoy hemlocks, their embraceable branches, their reddish bark. The thermometer says eighteen degrees, and the barometer has fallen overnight. The wind is blowing very gently from the west. I've considered a battery-powered radio to get weather forecasts, but in the end I've decided to depend on my gauges, observation, and intuition.

"We're at the tail end of a cold front," I say. "See the high clouds moving in. Maybe this is the day the first big snow falls. I hope so. Come on, let's do our chores."

Dad talks to me only about "necessary things," as he would say— what he is cooking, what he is making on the shaving horse, the practical matters of day-to-day living, various facts—or maybe should I say so-called facts—about the world. He likes to imagine that I, though I have not yet learned to speak, already understand him. Which is true, sort of. I have the score of his musical sounds filed in memory.

With his twenty-one-inch bow saw Dad cuts several lower dead branches off a nearby pine tree and tosses them in the fire pit. He adds some of the smaller branches from a brush pile he'd made from the tops of trees he'd cut down the day before. When the fire is going strong he tosses in the brown paper bags of his waste and my dirty paper diapers.

Dad dumps dribbles of pee from the mayo jar here and there. "It's called marking our territory," he says.

Dad removes the front pack (with me in it) and hangs it on the low branch of a maple. I look up into the trees at a couple of wise-guy crows. Crows of course imitate or perhaps even speak human languages. At the moment the crows are talking the language they learned from me, my desperate cries for attention or food. They're mocking me, though at the time I think they're admiring me.

"Listen, now, I'm going to teach you," Dad says, pointing. "That is a white birch, the state tree of New Hampshire. A lot of people think birch and pine and poplar are no good as firewood, but the truth is any wood will give you warmth as long as it's seasoned a year when you burn it. It's best to have lots of different kinds of wood handy, the lighter woods for quick hot fires and the denser woods for longer-lasting fires.

"White birch has medium density. It's kind of an all-purpose wood. The bark is oily but aromatic when it's burned, great for starting fires . . ." On and on he goes.

From my place hanging on the tree, I double my fists and swing them at Dad. I'm trying to create some entertaining chaos. Every time Dad talks, I work on speech recognition. I have learned to discriminate between vowels and consonants, but meaning continues to escape me.

"We do everything here with care and reverence and a touch of whimsy," Dad says. "We cut a tree down, and we apologize to the tree. Our care is our prayer.

"Now about God, I'm vague on the details, which is where, it is said, you'll find the Devil. I don't know if God is a Catholic like your grandmother Elenore, or whether he's just a whisper in my ear from the Universe. That's how your mom used to define her religious belief: the whisper in her ear. She'd say, 'God speaks to me in the sound of the wind, the sound of water.' Lilith the pagan was as close to God as your grandma Elenore, but in a different way. Or maybe a different god. I don't know. God, if He exists, likes to play with our minds. Even worse, with our hearts. Maybe He has a mean streak. You're going to have to work out the God business for yourself, because that's another one of your dad's weak areas."

Dad leaves me momentarily to fetch his woodcutter tools from twig shelves built on the porch—chain saw, gas can, chain oil, felling wedge, sledge hammer, and walking stick, which doubles as a rule, because Dad has notched it at various intervals. I must explain that Dad doesn't deal in inches and feet. He's invented his own measurement system, based on my appendages. He discovered that I'm about the length of a piece of firewood for our stove. He laid me out on the walking stick, and marked a Birch. From there he created other units—a leg, an arm, a fore-arm, a hand, and finally for the smallest unit of measurement a dink. For example, one of Grandpa Howard's cigarettes is a baby hand long, or about two baby dinks.

By late morning the temperature holds steady into the high teens. The sky is overcast, all the color gone out of it. The wind has risen. The barometer has fallen some more. No doubt it will snow. But how much? Only the radio can tell with any accuracy. I am grateful I do not have a radio. I have learned a little mental alchemy over the last few months, turning worrisome uncer-tainty into eager anticipation.

Back in the cabin, Dad sticks me in the new playpen. The first months at Forgot Farm I experienced bliss because I accepted my infantile state. But lately I sense changes within myself. I am big-ger, stronger, still an infant, that's true, but beginning to hope for better things. There's nothing like hope to make a person un-happy.

I lie on my back looking at my new environment, wooden bars all around me, smell of raw linseed oil. The experience makes me philosophical. I cannot be free unless I am mobile.

My first idea is to fly, for outside I have seen the birds, and their mobility is superior to Dad's. I flap my arms and legs, but I do not fly. I rest, contemplating the matter. Perhaps it is pure will that achieves great desires. I concentrate, seeing myself soaring, but I do not soar. Am I doomed to spend my entire life like this, unable to fly or to change the world to my liking through will power? The answer that comes to me is yes, that is the way things are. I weep with rage.

"What's the matter?" Dad says. "You don't like your playpen?"

The sound of Dad's voice calms me, and I have a moment of clarity. I cannot fly because I am not a bird. I am some kind of creature like Dad.

From what I gather watching Dad, leg propulsion isn't all that difficult, so perhaps I can walk. While still lying on my back I send orders to my brain: walk. Unfortunately, I only succeed in whirly-gurgling my feet. Walking seems as remote a possibility as flying.

However, whirly-gurgling does amuse Dad, because I hear him laugh. Encouraged by his mirth, I ponder the problem more deeply, finally figuring out that you can't walk while you are flat on your back. To walk you have to be on your feet. How to get there? I experiment, reaching upward with my legs, my theory being that if you move the legs the feet will take the hint and start walking. The feet do not take the hint. Another theory dashed to pieces by Reality. I sense Spontaneous Combustion eavesdropping on my thoughts. He's amused.

I'm not discouraged—well, maybe a little. I won't quit, though. If there is one thing I am not it's a quitter. However, I do need a break from mobility training. Accordingly, I embark on another project: handling the fire across the room for possible consumption. I reason that since fire is entertaining, it must also be edible.

"Now what are you doing?" Dad says.

I'm trying to make my hand longer by reaching. I extend my arm and my hand grows smaller in the distance. It's just a matter of extension now. I reach. The hand blocks my view of the fire, so I believe I've touched it. But I don't feel anything but air. Are air and fire one? Won? Are air and fire Juan? As I contemplate these questions I inadvertently grasp one of the bars on my playpen and—whoop!—pull myself vertical. I am standing up.

Dad cheers.

It occurs to me now that I'm on my feet that I should be able to walk. I take a step and fall backward on my bottom. I cry, not out of pain—it does not hurt to fall on your bottom—but for the usual reason of frustrated desires. I will abandon the entire walking venture—I am a failure; I will never walk. I will spend a lifetime brooding on my failures. Naturally, thinking about failure leads to more thinking about failure, such as my vain attempts at speech recognition. Without mobility or speech, all I can do between feeding and napping is to think, and thinking only leads to anguish.

"You want out. Well, okay." Dad lifts me from the playpen and puts me on the floor. "Let's see what kind of trouble you can get into."

I now have a clear view of the fire, and I am optimistic again; out here in the wide open spaces of the floor, away from the bars of my playpen, I believe I can be all that I can be. Be what? I hardly know what I am, let alone what I might become. But this is not the time for introspection. Without bars to hold me in I can expand outward toward the fire far far away. It is moving—the fire is always moving; it's the motion that calls to me. The motion says, Come and eat me. I will be a fire eater. How to get there? I must either lengthen my arms or close the distance between myself and it.

I reach with my right hand. The fire is no closer to the hand than it was in the playpen. The hand, connected to the arm, connected to the body, will never be long enough to reach the fire: a basic truth, as it comes to me now. Previous experience tells me that walking is out of the question. Can't fly, can't walk—what to do? I resolve to devise some unique mode of transportation.

I remember that long ago, long long ago I could swim. I'm not exactly sure what swimming is, because the memory is more a feeling than a picture or an understanding. But the feeling is so strong and so convincing that I know it has to be true—I can swim. I lay on my belly and extend my arms and legs and move them sinuously. I am swimming. It is a very nice feeling. Unfortunately, I am not making any headway.

I struggle over onto my back and swim. No perceivable movement. I fight off a tantrum. I go through the usual difficulties to sit up. Now I see the fire better. Hint: The better you see the fire, the better chance you have of getting to it.

What next? I sit stupefied for quite a while, perhaps six or seven seconds, and study my predicament. My hands have dropped to the floor. My bulk is on my bottom. Experience tells me that the bottom is the most powerful and important body part. Hands on floor, bottom on floor—think, now. Think! I push with my hands and scoot with my bottom. Forward march! Well, not quite. My feet are in the way. If only I didn't have feet. But I have feet. Therefore feet must be relevant.

I flap the feet. No effect. I hear Spontaneous Combustion in my head. "You've been defeated," he laughs. I take a break and suck on my toes. Very satisfying. Invigorated, I work some more with the feet, and by digging in my heels succeed in engaging them with the floor. This technique assists slightly in scooting. I am moving, but slowly and not very straight. Still, scooting is fun, and I practice this motion just for the enjoyment, which takes me away intellectually from my goal of reaching the fire. That ancient memory of swimming comes back to me, mesmerizing me, as I scoot along. Too much reminiscence distracts a person from more important matters. When I snap out of my reverie I realize that I am further away from the fire than ever before.

The problem, I conclude, is turns. I will have to practice turns. It is difficult to turn and scoot at the same time, but turn I do. Wrong direction. Now I cannot see the fire at all. If you cannot see where you want to go, how can you get there? I answer my own question: trial and error.

I scoot, lurching this way and that, and inevitably I overdo it and topple on my side, banging my head on our carpeted floor. Usually the surprise factor combined with frustration would make me cry. Not this time. This time I right myself, not exactly sure how, but I do and find myself on hands and knees. Quite magically, I am moving. Hands and knees seemed to have a mind apart from the command-center head and the industrial bottom.

I have discovered crawling. Partly in exuberance, partly in a mission to test out my new technology, I crawl from one end of the school bus to the other and take stock of my new powers. I turn wherever I want to with accuracy, stop and resume speed at will. Always under control. I have found a means of locomotion that is toppleproof. I can transfer inertia to the other major positions of sitting and reclining with a minimum of effort. I will never have need for flying or walking. I believe that this skill will set me apart, for no one I know crawls.

I am happy but not content. No doubt I have invented a unique method of locomotion, but something is missing in my triumph. Mere success is not enough. I have to know why I succeeded. What is the source of this new power? The answer creeps out from under the question. The bottom propels the hands and knees. Discovering the technique was difficult because the action is counter-intuitive. Logically, one should proceed backside first; in reality, one proceeds backside last. I am, I believe, a theorizing entity. Some day when I have mastered speech recognition I will share my theories with Dad and the rest of the pathetic human race.

Now that I am rested, now that I have basked in my success, now that I have delved into its meaning, now I must exercise the powers given to me, for power that lies dormant is not power at all. It is mere potential. Through this round of thinking, I return to my desire to divine the secrets of the fire. Now I will test the flames for touch and taste.

I go forward on hands and knees. The flames are very pretty to look at. I conclude that they are alive. I want to play with them, but as I get closer to them I feel terrible heat. Just when I decide that this, like most of my experiments, will fail and I'd better back away, I see a shape behind the flames. It's you, Mother. What are you doing there? A moment later you're gone. Then back again. It occurs to me now what the meaning of the fire is. It is the thing between me, here, and you, there. It is a barrier of pain.

"My word," I say, excited and proud as any father can be. This is one of the rare times since we moved to Forgot Farm that I wish other people were around, so I could shout hey, look, my son is crawling!

He stops about three feet in front of the flames. I swear he sees something in the fire he wants. A toy? I discourage toys on philosophical grounds. I have to teach him not to get too close. The heat should drive him back, but he edges closer.

At the last second I sweep him into my arms. He struggles. He does not wish to be touched.

"Hey, bub, you can't touch fire," I say, but he fights me. I put him back on the floor and again he crawls toward the flames. I stand behind him, ready to grab him. He's very close and the fire is very hot. My philosophy is to allow Birch to find his way, never to criticize him, to support his every whim, for I believe that ultimately our whims are ourselves. Should I let him be burned? Three more times he attempts to crawl into the fire before I pull him away at the last moment. Finally, he lies on his back and cries in exhaustion.

I put him in the playpen with a bottle, but he knocks it away. He lies on his back, fighting the air with his fists. This is not a tantrum. It's something deeper.

I pull my shirt up and lie with him while he nurses. In his crying I hear an emotion that I'm well-acquainted with, but I cannot understand how a son barely nine months on the planet can feel it—inconsolable grief.

8

THE OLD RULE

Eventually, Birch calms. I put him on his back in the playpen, and he's soon asleep.

Outside, I freshen the fire in my outdoor cooking grill. Back inside, I fetch the stew pot from the propane refrigerator and put it on the outside fire, along with a pot of well water for washing.

While the stew is warming, I set the table, run the carpet sweeper over the floor, and dust our stick walls. The down side of heating with wood is dust and wood grit. It is all I can do to keep this place picked up. Everything has to be just so, everything has to be clean, or I'll backslide into the person I was.

I check the weather gauges. Temperature twenty-two, barometer holding steady. The great thing about weather is that if you pay attention you can be part of it. It's a comfort, it's like you're not alone.

I wake from my nap, and it's as if it's years later. I feel older, stronger, more able. I expect I'll be able to talk and dance and sing and dress in jeans and wear shoes, and drive my own truck, but I'm a little ahead of myself. Turns out I'm still a damn infant.

Just wiser for the lesson of the fire. After Dad eats his stew we go outside again. We follow the stone wall downslope a short ways. For a fellow who's banned unnecessary conversation, Dad can ramble on. Years later he'll claim he was trying to teach me:

"This wall was built a couple and a half centuries ago as a property line, or maybe it was a fence to hem in the critters, or both. Just imagine this hillside a rocky, grassy pasture and you have an idea of what was here long ago.

"Your grandfather Howard and grandmother Elenore lived on many a farm when they were foster children. One of the places had a rule. Before going to school in the morning—when they were allowed to go to school—they were required to throw a rock from the field into a pile. Coming home same thing. There was no end of this work for the hill farmer of New England, because new rocks would appear in the spring, pushed up by frost, I imagine. Or maybe the Puritans were right, and the rocks were put there by the Devil. If so, thank you, Mister Devil. I like rocks and I like rocks of some size."

I love to be outside in the cold with Dad, love the sound of his voice ringing in the air, the moisture of his breath, the reassuring jostle of his walking, which reminds me of the bliss of swimming long long ago.

When I stop talking, I feel suddenly pensive and preoccupied, almost forgetting that Birch is attached to me. With his outburst earlier in the day, with my anticipation of the first snow, something subtle in me is changing. I'm not quite sure what it is. In my quest for self-knowledge I'm always a step or two behind my intuition.

Without the amusements of mass media and peer companionship, I have become attuned to the moods of the forest. The way another man anticipates watching an NFL playoff game on television in December, I plan to watch the first snow fall.

There's still work to do. I will build a sled to carry Birch and groceries on the snow, and of course his care is a neverending task. Presently, I'm cutting firewood to season for the following year and the year after. But I have all winter to do that chore. The fact is I've done the hard work, I and the chain saw. Now I will have some leisure time. I worry about filling the lonely hours in winter.

"I see you and me at Nick's," Old Crow says. "Picture a glass of beer, a shot of whiskey on the side. Picture the liquor store in Keene, you walking down an aisle, reaching for a quart of me. Picture the glass now, the warm brown whiskey, the swirls, infinity inside. Here's looking up at you from the vortex of time. It will be a Christmas present, from me to you."

"Why are you back—I'm not even drinking?"

"Cabin fever. Same difference. A drink will ease your mind. You can ration it out. One drink a day. Well, maybe two. Everybody does it around the holidays. Why should you be different? Why deny yourself?"

"Have two, I'll have three."

"Have three and the toll gate to heaven opens," says Old Crow.

"Or maybe it's the other place," I say.

"You still have time to get away. A phone call to Attorney Prell's office that you are giving up the baby to Persephone will set you free. Picture yourself: drinking and driving across the country, alone, free of all duty. Free—Free!"

A few snowflakes begin to fall, which snaps me out of my thoughts. I have been having an unnecessary conversation with myself.

Was it cabin fever? Or just the power of my desire for drink? With all my work, my achievement, as I like to think of what I've done with Forgot Farm, I am still far away from self-mastery. I exist in a perpetual danger zone.

We return to Forgot Farm.

Dad puts me in my high chair, feeds me peach-flavored yogurt, and talks to me. "We live primitive out here, Birch, but nothing like Cooty Patterson back in the old days. He'd pick up roadkill and put it in his stew pot, along with veggies he'd pull out of dumpsters. He never emptied the pot to clean it, just kept adding to it. Best damn tasting stew I ever ate. Took the pot with him to Texas."

Dad dips his little finger in the yogurt and licks it. I look at him crossly, trying to tell him to get his grubby paws out of my chow. Dad laughs, and then I laugh, and Dad laughs some more, and I laugh some more. I'm quite proud of my laugh. My first laughs were practice laughs, in order to determine what a laugh is for. I've discovered that the action of laughter often leads one into mirth. The conclusion is obvious: the purpose of laughter is to feel funny.

It is good to laugh with Dad, though in the beginning shared laughter confused me. Laughing as one means we are one. It troubles me that sometimes we laugh separately. I wonder if Dad understands the difference, for he continues to behave in a manner suggesting that he is unaware of our separation of being. Though not always. Such are the ongoing problems of establishing and maintaining a me.

Dad does not laugh very often out of sheer mirth but for purposes that still remain unknown to me, though I suspect they have something to do with food, because when I am eating, Dad often breaks out into laughter.

"Hey, look, Birch," he says, "it's starting to snow."

But I'm not interested. I've had a long day, and I want to go to bed.

After I feed Birch and put him in his crib, I make my own supper, popped corn flavored with grated cheddar cheese. I eat at the table, alternately watching the snow fall, or the fire, and reading snippets from this week's library book, *Living the Good Life* by Helen and Scott Nearing. I always read out loud for Birch's benefit, even if he's sleeping. It's a dreamy book that pleases one such as me, though I can't understand how the Nearings make a living boiling off maple sap.

I eat very slowly, one kernel at a time, so that each provides a distinct and separate experience in taste and texture. With my meal I drink Ovaltine.

After I finish, I start some hot water on the outdoor cook grill and clean house while the water is heating. Birch is deep asleep. I undress, give myself a sponge bath, and put on fresh underwear. I wash my soiled clothes and hang them up to dry on sticks in front of the Franklin stove.

It's dark out, but the freshly falling snow captures light and gives everything outside a blue cast, not night, not day, but a magical twilight. I go outside and run in the snow in my bare feet. About an inch has fallen. I dance in the snow until my feet burn with the cold, and then I start back inside. On the way I spot something. It's as if the snow has given me eyes for this object—a beautiful, curved salad spoon. The vision vanishes, and I'm looking at the charred stick I'd pulled out of the fire that first day of our arrival back in June. I'd forgotten about it. Now there it is in the crook of the tree where I had placed it months before. I shake the snow off it and bring it inside.

I put my slippers on and light two candles, placing them on the nightstand beside my couch/bed. I put the night logs on the fire and go over to Birch's crib, kneel, and speak in a whisper, praying for his health and good fortune, not because I believe in the efficacy of prayer but because I believe in the necessity of prayer.

I pick up the charred stick and open the door to the Franklin stove with an idea to toss the stick in, but the stick won't let me. I drop it on the floor and throw some shavings in the fire to give myself more light. I carefully inspect the charred stick, seeing the flow of the grain, the topography of growth rings, feeling my way into thought through the touch of the wood. What to do with this stick? I'm not sure at this moment. I grab my hewing hatchet, hold the wood against a brick and knock off an edge for a better look at the grain. The raw wood, freshly revealed, gives me an idea.

I place the stick perpendicular on the brick, the edge of my hewing hatchet on top of the stick. I tap the head of the hewing hatchet with a wooden mallet until the stick starts to split. I inspect the grain and swing the hewing hatchet—which now holds the wood securely—onto the brick to complete the split.

I straddle the shaving horse, which is called a "horse" because you fit it between your legs like a horse, and I put the stick on it, pressing down with my foot to bring the dumb head firm on the stick to hold it. With the draw knife I hog off wood until the shape I had seen in the shadow outside begins to emerge. I love the draw knife work. It goes fast, and it creates curled shavings lovely as flower petals. I am very careful not to remove wood from the charred end, which I've already decided to incorporate into the work.

After I've done as much as I can with the draw knife, I take the stick out of the shaving horse, use my left hand as a vice, and with my right make finishing cuts with my jackknife.

I open a wooden case of chisels and gouges nested in velvet, remove a spoon gouge, shut the case, and hollow out the bowl of a spoon, again holding the stick in one hand and carving with the other. A good spoon requires a shallow bowl, so I am very careful not to yield to the temptation to cut deeply into the wood. And now that the spoon had taken shape, I know I won't ruin the wood's natural curve, which had been there all along. My only duty as a craftsman is to honor that curve. I choke back a surge of feeling, gratitude and something else I cannot identify. I'm within some better part of myself, a garden where Old Crow has no entry.

After the bowl is gouged out, I look the spoon over. It needs smoothing. I break a bottle and use one of the shards as a scraper. I find a piece of 400-grit sandpaper in my junk pile. The sandpaper reaches places the scraper cannot. I don't like using sandpaper. I imagine that some divine craftsman is spying on me: Frederick—Frederick, you're cheating again.

I put the spoon down, leaning it against a stick-shelf I've built under one of the school bus windows, and I admire my work, a smooth, cream-pink wooden spoon with the top third of the handle charred black, something small and simple and not very important, but something of use, something that has beauty, something that was always there waiting for my touch.

I sweep the floor, hone my tools, and put them away. I close the door to the Franklin stove and retire to my sofa bed. The candle light flutters as if in speech: Read, the light says. I lie down, pick up the Nearing book, and plunge in. After five pages I am wondering why anyone would want to live in a stone house. One page later I determine that it isn't the stones in the house that put me off, it's the indifference to children in this couple's lifestyle.

It's maybe 8:00 PM, an hour and a half or so past my winter bedtime. I snuff the candles between thumb and forefinger and drop the book on the floor. I drift off imagining I can hear the whisper of the falling snow. "Better to sleep than to think, better to think while you sleep, better to wile than to slink, better to blather—slink wile you blather—blather to, blather too, blather two, blather tu. Tu? Latour, that's a French name." And so I fall asleep. Well, not quite. I soon pop fully awake. I've forgotten to oil the spoon.

I rise and light a candle. I pour a little raw linseed oil on my palm and rub it into the spoonwood. Life in the woods has made me a fussy man. Fussy. The realization strikes me with both ex-altation and some despair. Self-knowledge is coming to me, if slowly and incompletely. I lie down, content in watching the snow fall. I know what this fussy man will do during the long winter months. I will make spoons and live by the old rule of woodworkers: oil-finish the piece every day for a week, every week for a month, every month for a year, every year forever.

9

APPLE WOOD

The next morning I can tell by the sharp crunch of my footfalls that the temperature is well below zero. It is minus thirteen. Before doing my chores I listen to the quiet. It's like that moment when everyone's left the house and the TV is blaring and you shut it off and suddenly you and sweet silence are one.

"Birch, I think from here on in winter is going to be my favorite season," I say.

Winter in New Hampshire is the best time of year to be outside. No tormenting mosquitos, black flies, picnic ants, or noseeums. With the leaves off the trees, you can see way into the forest. I've planned to make snowshoes from ash wood, bending rived sticks in a steam box, but there is no need, because our road becomes a highway for the latest North Country craze—snowmobiling. I like the way the machines pack down the trail, which makes walking without snowshoes easy, especially when I'm pulling a sled full of firewood. But the idea of recreational snowmobiling strikes me as frivolous and in bad taste. I don't like the noise and speed, disruptive to the meditative spirit that resides in the forest; I don't like being hemmed in by humanity, an exaggeration, I suppose, when you consider that we might see half a dozen bands of snowmobilers on a weekend and few or none on weekdays. What really worries me, though, is that the word will spread to the owner of Forgot Farm that somebody is living on his property. I've become attached to this place.

I've read the trust charter and it bars all motorized vehicles. Either the trust board or perhaps Persephone herself has given the Darby Snowmobile Club permission to use the trust lands for recreation. The snowmobile trails spill over into neighboring trails and eventually go right by Forgot Farm. Part of me is amused thinking about the Squire in his special place in hell, the grinning Devil delivering the bad news: "Your conservancy appears to be serving a constituency you did not foresee."

During the cold wave I make spoons by the fire. Every cut, every flying shaving, gives me a little thrill. For the first time in my life I can say to a lie detector that I am content without watching the needle fly off the paper. Even so, I have much to learn before I master this craft. I have the tools, the eye-hand coordination, the aesthetic sense, the (accidental) practice in knife work from my whittling days, and the sharpening knack, but I lack experience in the particular problems posed by spoonmaking. I test each spoon and discover that most do not satisfy me. I cut the bowls too deep, or they do not fit the hand well, or the proportions are wrong. And then there is the matter of design. The wood makes its own demands. One piece wants to show the knife nicks, but even these subtle imperfections must harmonize with each other. Some want to be perfectly smooth, and one slip of the knife ruins them. Sometimes I misjudge the grain of the wood, and my hewing hatchet splits out a piece that wants to be part of the spoon.

I cannot bear to look at my rejects and I burn them. The spoon with the charred handle, my first spoon, a perfectly made thing, came my way not through my skill but from some mysterious agent in fire. The sight of it makes me humble and reverent. I will learn the craft of spoonmaking through work, study, trial, error, and prayer. I start writing down all the facts I can remember about the making of a spoon, from the nature of the wood to my own mood at the time. I call these little essays Spoonwood Documentations. They are my prayers.

Apple Wood

I test various woods. Oak, which splits easily and makes wonderful table furniture, is too open-grained for most kinds of spoons. Maple and birch make serviceable spoons, but the wood is often bland. I look for imperfections in color and grain to highlight. It is in imperfections that one sees beauty. Cherry is lovely, but not very hard, so it makes spoons that attract the eye but are fit for only moderate use, such as salad tossing. I wish to make spoons to last a lifetime.

When the cold snap ends I take Birch for a long walk—no wind to sting the cheeks and water the eyes, bright sunshine on the snow, like the beach. We go to the ledges. We've been here in the summer and fall, but not in winter. From the top of the cliff we can see across the Connecticut River to the Vermont hills and beyond the Green Mountains, where at this moment thousands of people from downcountry are skiing. They might as well be on another planet for what I have in common with them. They and their forest-stripped mountains intensify my loneliness. I am glad. I value my loneliness because it is so real.

The lean-to I built as our love nest and where Lilith died has partially collapsed. I cut maple saplings and rebuild it. I cover the saplings with hemlock branches and birch bark. I resolve to maintain the structure. I'm following a directive that comes from someplace within, inaccessible to the likes of Old Crow or even my conscious, functioning self.

While Dad talks to me at the ledges I look up in the sky at a great bird, circling. Maybe it's an eagle or an osprey or a hawk, or some bird of my imagination. I cannot say. All I know is that for a moment, Mother, you take my hand. For a moment I am the great bird. Below me I see a young thing, a possible meal, if only the parent would put it down and wander off to fulfill some desire, as a parent will.

I show Birch the tiny hemlock tree that Lilith loved so much, because it grew out of a crack in the ledge with no more than a cup full of soil for sustenance. I tell Birch that sad story all over again, how the world lost Lilith and gained him on this spot. I tell him Lilith's spirit resides in the little hemlock tree, and that she comes into the lean-to at night to stay warm and to remember him.

"'It's a tough little tree, a good tree—a good tree,' she would say," I tell Birch. "And look at this. Something new, scarred bark, where a buck deer scraped the velvet from his antlers.'"

We're about ready to start down when I notice the bushes that cover the ledges—mountain laurel. I remember that some of the oldtimers referred to mountain laurel as spoonwood. I cut a piece and bring it with us.

That night I make a spoon from mountain laurel, and with the first shaving—dark and firm—flying off my knife I know I have found what will be my favorite spoonwood.

Dad takes long walks with me to gather spoonwood and just to behold. He reads dramas in the snow and relates them to me.

"See those tracks of a bird in the snow, maybe a crow," Dad points. "It came down right here, walked a ways, flew six feet, and landed again. Then we have these other tracks, a ferret, I think. Note where they come together."

I see a blood spot in the snow, a few iridescent blue-black feathers, tracks of the ferret moving off. Dad is trying to teach me something about death, but I was born in death so I already know.

It's a nice winter day and I've set up the shaving horse outside. I should buy groceries but I'll wait another day or two. We walk to town less and less, only when in dire need of necessities and to return and take out library books. I always make a mental note to stop in at the town office to check the tax records to look up the owner of the property we are squatting on, but I never seem to find the time.

"The truth is you're afraid," says Old Crow.

"Just cautious. I don't like government entities."

"I think Dot McCurtin, our town clerk and premier gossip, intimidates you," says Old Crow.

"That's true."

"That was too quick an admission," says Old Crow. "The real reason you don't want to think about who owns Forgot Farm is because there's nothing you can do about it. You're living on meager savings; you have no job, no income, and no collateral to get a loan to make an offer on the land."

I'm so preoccupied talking to myself that I don't hear the snowmobiles until Birch screeches (his latest sound). My strategy is to ignore snowmobiles. If they stop I go on with my work and pretend they don't exist; by now the local people have gotten the hint and they zoom right on by. Not today. The snowmobilers pull into our yard.

They wear matching orange and blue insulated jumpsuits, the new velcro-buckled boots, shiny silver helmets, and faceplates that conceal their identities, though the curves in the suits tell me that one is a woman and one a man. I try to turn away but can't help watching long black hair cascade out onto shoulders with a shake of the head as the woman removes her helmet. It's Katharine Ramchand. She leaves the helmet behind on the seat of her machine, but her companion, Garvin Prell, carries his under one arm like a jet pilot.

I'm thinking that somehow Garvin has gained control of Forgot Farm and he's come to serve papers. I prepare myself for the worst; instead, his friendly demeanor knocks me off balance.

"I don't believe how much he's grown," Garvin says, looking at Birch.

"Care to come in for a cup of Ovaltine?" I say, in spite of myself.

"Great," Garvin says.

"Give me a hand," I say, grabbing the shaving horse. It's Katharine who takes an end. Garvin puts his helmet down and picks up Birch.

"You're already involved in an unnecessary conversation," Old Crow says.

"Why don't you shut up."

"I'm sorry, I didn't hear what you said," Katharine says.

"Nothing—nothing at all," I say.

I hadn't built our unique home to impress people but out of need and to please myself. The look of surprise and delight on Katharine's face is sweeter than sugar on snow.

"Beware—your guard is down, Frederick," says Old Crow.

Garvin hands Birch to me, and I put him in the indoor playpen; he resists, shaking the bars.

"He wants to be part of the action," I say.

"I'll play with him." Garvin pulls Birch out.

"Okay," I say, hypnotized by the man's good cheer.

Garvin crawls around on the floor with Birch and makes funny faces, and Birch pulls his hair.

Katharine sits on the stick chair at the stick table. I serve her Ovaltine and I sit on the shaving horse.

"We have come to inform you that I will be studying the stone wall on this property," she says.

"Why this wall?"

"For my doctoral thesis."

I repeat my question. "But why this wall?"

"Because stone walls are impacts of geology, artifacts of culture, and, of recent, aesthetic concerns regarding walls have been raised."

"Your diction," I say.

"Because I love this wall," she says.

"Okay, I believe that," I say. She breaks eye contact and rises. There's something she's not telling me.

Garvin returns Birch to the playpen.

"I heard Persephone left town," I say to Katharine.

"She's in Tasmania for the winter."

"You housesitting?"

"You could call it that." Katharine looks at Garvin.

"Maybe Persephone will like it down under so much she'll stay forever," I say.

"She will return," Katharine says. "She has a business deal to conduct."

"Please!" Garvin says sharply.

Suddenly, things are different. I'm alert, ready—no, eager—to fight.

"We mustn't spill our guts, such as they are, to the Hermit of Lonesome Hill—that is what they call me, isn't it?" I'm talking out of some gremlin in my head. I have no idea what the townsfolk call me. "Hermit of Lonesome Hill" just popped into my mind. It's the kind of unbalanced thinking that plagues me when I feel pressured.

Katharine ignores me and gives Garvin backtalk in the easy way of people intimate with one another. "There's no reason to be secretive about this, Garvin. The papers have been filed and are public information."

"Our host enjoys his peace and quiet around here. No intrigue. Isn't that right, Frederick?"

I pretend Garvin does not exist and I address Katharine. "What papers? What business deal?" I hate the sound of my voice, so strident.

Katharine looks at Garvin, turns back to me. "The matter will not affect you or your lifestyle," she says in her beautiful and formal accent. "I should not have spoken."

"Thank you," Garvin says to Katharine.

Birch is calm now, hypnotized, the way I was minutes ago.

"You have any business with me?" I say to Garvin.

"Persephone's offer still holds, if that's what you mean."

"I have no use for her money."

Garvin pauses, chooses his words carefully, delivers them in a friendly tone. "Frederick, you can't live on property you have no legal right to."

"Is that a threat?"

Garvin shakes his head as one might at the antics of a troublesome child. "If I wanted you out, you would be out. Okay?"

"We should leave," Katharine says. "Thank you for showing us your home." She's stoic, dignified, a mystery, as if a statue of an ancient goddess has come alive.

"Goodbye, little feller," Garvin says to Birch.

Off and on for the next couple weeks Katharine shows up alone at Forgot Farm to photograph the wall, scrape samples from the surfaces of rocks, take notes and measurements. Every afternoon I listen for the sound of her snow machine. I want to talk to her, and at the same time I don't want to talk to her. Not that it matters what I really feel, since she avoids me. Her presence is so disturbing to me that every time she arrives I leave and visit my orchard.

By now I've cut down scores of small pines so the apple trees can have some light. I haul the small pine logs to Forgot Farm by sled; split and seasoned, they will make good fat wood for the cooking fire. My goal is to bring back the orchard so the trees produce apples and there's grass underneath where one can lie down on a summer day and dream. I'm figuring on a five-year project.

Meanwhile, thoughts of Garvin playing with Birch and his sly reference to my status as a squatter eat away at me. I picture him with Lilith, and then I have to work to shake the picture out of my head. What was the real reason he came to my place? Is he working for Persephone? For himself? Finally, I overcome my fear of government and check the property tax records, where I discover that the owner of Forgot Farm is a Walter Sturtevant Jr. of Delray Beach, Florida.

I leave the town offices heady and dangerous. From the pay phone in Ancharsky's Store I call the Florida number I plucked from the tax report. The "hello" on the other end of the line sounds like an old woman.

"This is long distance calling. May I please speak to Walter Sturtevant?" I say.

"Who is this?" the woman says.

"My name's Latour," I say, the name slipping off my tongue so readily and without premeditation that I understand that it was in my mind all along, hiding. It doesn't sound like a lie, and now that it's out, I feel giddy. "I'm interested in Mister Sturtevant's Darby, New Hampshire, property on Lonesome Hill."

"I see."

"Is this a bad time?" I ask.

"Both my Walters have passed away."

"I'm sorry, Mrs. Sturtevant," I say. "Are you the current owner of the property?"

"I suppose I am. Mister, what was it, Mister . . . Laetrile?"

"Latour."

"Mister Latuna, I don't believe I'm ready to think about this right now. Call me back in the spring—maybe."

She hangs up, I hang up. I figure I have a year, perhaps more, before I'll have to do any serious worrying about being evicted from Forgot Farm.

I am frustrated by the complexity of my father's speech, though I'm expanding my musical knowledge of his voice, major chord when he works, minor chord when he mumbles to himself in thought. But the meaning—what is the meaning? And how to shape the sounds for my own lyrics? I cannot do it. At the very time when I need intelligence to formulate my own words, I feel my IQ decline by imperceptible measure day by day. My telepathic powers are so weakened that my old nemesis, Spontaneous Combustion, severs the connection between us. I wail in the night for the loss of brain power.

For solace, I turn my attention to other, more immediate speakers: the birds, the wind, the crunch of footfalls on snow, the howls of coyotes at night. In all of them I hear mainly vowel sounds. I pull myself up in my playpen and practice—*a, e, i, oh, you, wy, uh, ah, oo.* I also hum a little—*ummmmm*—a voiced vowel that pleasantly buzzes in my nose. I usually fall asleep to the sound of my father's knives on spoonwood—*sip, sip, sip.* It's a reassuring sound, a sound of love. I practice the sound—*sss, sss, pt, pt, pt*—and drift off.

Into the spring and summer and forever after, Dad makes spoons. He ties strings around them and hangs them from pushpins on our stick walls. He develops a formula for finishing a spoon that includes raw linseed oil, beeswax, and a couple of secret ingredients I am not at liberty to divulge, even to you, Mother. He loves to look at his spoons and contemplate them. He keeps detailed notes on each spoon—season, azimuth of sun, weather conditions, notes on the tree it comes from, soil, problems encountered in making the spoon, anecdotes relating to its creation.

. . .

We will not celebrate Birch's first birthday. I do not believe in birthdays or holidays, which are excuses for the unnecessary congregation of individuals. I do not believe in keeping track of time. Let the sun and stars measure the day. Let the moon measure the month. Let the seasons measure the year. Let us celebrate the good moments as they come to us. Hard winter gives way to something like a low-grade southern winter, our usual pattern. Just when I think the winter will never end, the days warm and the hardwoods, as if in secret collusion, all bloom the same week, producing a pastel version of fall foliage. It's spring, the best argument for the existence of God.

"Birch, this is my favorite time of year," I say. I'm in a good mood, happy even to give blood to the black flies. Our road dries out, and after I have lugged the truck battery to Ancharsky's Store for a charge (a tradition in the making?), it's now possible to drive to town instead of walking.

A week after the trees blossom the leaves appear, and as if by magic the forest is bright green. Another week of perfect weather and then it rains—a warm rain—and the humidity sets in and stays. Spring is gone; it's summer.

Dad visits his orchard in the trust almost every day, not usually to do work but just to be there. Sometimes we come only for a minute or two. Dad gazes at the trees and then we walk on. Other times he'll work for an hour, pruning the apple trees, knocking down some weeds, or moving rocks. I have to explain that Dad isn't satisfied where God put the rocks, so he keeps rearranging them to suit his own idea of design.

Around Forgot Farm Dad has taken up what he calls subtractive gardening. He cuts firewood trees at ground level. On these low stumps he stacks rocks, arranging them until they please his eye. He treats some plants as weeds, pulling them. Others he leaves be to grow—the early-season wonders of jacks in the pulpit, star flowers, violets, trillium, and various ferns. He makes walking paths paved with flat stones that wind between rock formations, flowers, greenery, and trees. Later in the summer wild daisies, lupin, and various grasses grow. Dad pulls out the plants that compete with the flowers. Soon there are flowers everywhere. Dad also weeds around the wild strawberries, raspberries, and blueberries. We and the birds are grateful and gorge ourselves in celebration. Dad calls moments like these Forgot Farm Holidays.

Dad does some additive gardening, too. We grow tomatoes, string beans, peas, carrots, parsnips, broccoli, cucumbers, and various squashes. Most of the veggies are eaten by deer. They never bother us in the daytime because in nice weather Dad brings his shaving horse outside to work. The deer come at night. With moonglow or starlight you can see them. They move cautiously, like the thieves they are. I learn to scan the woods to pick out the deer, two, three, or even more. They are brown with white on their tails. They move easily and gracefully. Dad prefers to watch them feed than to chase them out of the garden. I hear his breath catch, my breath catch, feel his heart beat faster, my heart beat faster. I think it's the way he used to respond to you. Maybe your spirit comes down from your ledges in the body of a deer to put some love in Dad's lonely heart.

One day I decide we should picnic at the orchard. We eat a lunch of yogurt and tomatoes. Afterwards, we lounge on the blanket and I watch Birch crawl and inspect bugs. He's quite busy these days learning about the ground, which is far more inhabited by living creatures than the air. He's inquisitive and meditative, broods over his discoveries rather than celebrates them.

I contemplate the winter to come. I have all my wood in and then some. I am prepared. I should be content. However, a financial crisis looms. I spend very little money, but I had very little to start with. I have no medical insurance for myself and Birch. I haven't been to a dentist in a year. Birch has never seen a doctor. I haven't paid the insurance on my truck. It needs tires and the engine is starting to burn oil. Even if I can manage to live without the truck, eventually I will have to generate some income for food and medical costs. I wonder about Birch, his future. His education. His health care. His social life. The condition of his future teeth.

"You should take a job, you lazy bum," says Old Crow.

"I'm not lazy."

"You're afraid of the world."

"Not the world, of the temptations: drink, anger, carnality, confusion, losing control, hurting someone. You, Old Crow; I'm afraid of you."

"How long do you think you can live on no income?" Old Crow says. "How long do you think it will be before Persephone and Garvin Prell find a way to spirit off our child?"

I pick up a ripe tomato and bite into it as if it were an apple.

I study ants and for the moment have nothing to say to my father. For one thing he is trying to wean me from nursing and I am resentful. For another I have nothing to say because I still cannot voice my thoughts. Vowels are not enough. Any day I will speak. I will not babble like a baby. I want to speak clearly and beautifully in complete sentences and in context. Dad has constructed a life based on simple living, clarity and beauty of expression. I know no other way. I await that moment of knowledge when I can converse on the terms he has set for me.

I identify with the ants, because they don't walk a straight line. They stagger the way I stagger. Perhaps I am an overgrown ant. When the time comes I will suddenly shrink, six-legged and armor-plated, all my tender parts on the inside. I will crawl down the ant hole, where, finally, I will speak in brilliant ant language, giving inspirational talks that will mesmerize my audience of thousands. They will bring me their young to eat, which will make me grow strong. The ants will be intoxicated by the eloquence of my marvelous speeches. At a final moment, I will pupate, crawl out of the ant hole, spread my wings, and fly away. See? I am not an ant after all. I am really a butterfly.

My musings are pretty intense and eventually I break down.

"It's okay, come to Daddy." Dad picks me up, brings me to the blanket. He pulls his t-shirt over his head and lies down on his side. I lay beside him. He puts his hand on my back and draws me toward him. I am instantly calm. All the difficulties of the world, all the worries go away for both of us.

On that particular day the Darby Development Committee is walking in the woods. The principles include Selectman Lawrence Dracut, town clerk Dorothy McCurtin, a consulting landscape architect, and three members of the Salmon Land Trust, Garvin Prell, Monet Salmon, and the chair, my grandmother Persephone Salmon. If Dad had kept up with Darby business affairs he would have known that the committee would be in the woods this day, making preparations for a land development that will change Grace Pond and the Salmon trust forever. Dad and I are in a state between wakefulness and sleep when the committee comes upon us.

We must be quite a sight: a large, bearded, half-naked man in the middle of the woods with a baby nursing at his chest. The man suddenly stands, glances at them with wild frightened eyes, and runs off into the woods with his charge.

Back at Forgot Farm, Dad tries to pretend nothing unusual has happened. He goes on with his spoonmaking and chores.

A week after Dad is caught inflagro delectable, or whatever that foreign phrase is, we are outside, Dad splitting firewood, me brooding on the nature of Reality (the universe, I've concluded, is shaped like a boomerang), when we hear a vehicle working its way up the last leg of Lonesome Hill Road.

I recognize the sound of an ancient glass-pack muffler, and I flirt with the idea of running off into the woods with Birch. In the end, I stay, bracing myself. Why is my domineering father paying me a visit?

As Howard steps out of the cab of his pickup truck, what surprises me is how much he and I resemble one another—widebodied, thick-necked men, both wearing white t-shirts in the late summer heatwave.

"Everything okay at home?" I ask. I know that my father would not come alone to visit unless he has good reason, such as a family disaster. I worry that something has happened to my mother.

"Just fine," Howard says. "The problem is . . . you. You."

"Me—it's always me, isn't it?" I flash with the old anger, the old resentment.

"Yah, you. I mean, you got caught with your pants down."

"My pants were never down," I say.

"Well, I didn't mean it that way," Howard says. "Look, Garvin is going to put a warrant out for you. Or so I heard."

"I didn't break any laws, except for living here, maybe, and nobody cares about that," I say.

"Yes, you did break a law. They're going to get you for cutting down trees on the trust land. And another thing."

"Another thing."

"Yah, another thing. I know for fact that Mrs. Salmon has filed a complaint that you're an unfit father."

I pause for a moment. "Well, I guess I should thank you."

"Well, I guess you should. You need any money?"

"No," I snap.

Howard turns his back on us, strides to the pickup, gets in like John Wayne mounting his horse.

"Don't say you weren't warned," he growls through the open window, and he rides off, the spinning tires kicking dirt in our faces.

10

GRACE POND

Our last day on Forgot Farm it's unseasonably hot and sultry, and I hear little creatures who live in the ground peeping and squealing, carrying on in business we humans cannot fathom. Dad takes a long walk around the farm, just looking at things for the last time—his favorite trees, the garden, the berry patch, the rotting frames of hippie housing, the fire pit, the outdoor cook shed. He loves it all, and goodbye. But he does not act that sad.

Though he'll never admit it, he knows it's time to start something new. The road trip he's always wanted to take is ahead of him for real now. Years later he'll admit this much to me: he was forming a plan for our getaway even before Howard warned us about the threats from Garvin and Persephone.

He puts the boat on top of the pickup truck and drives off, headed for Grace Pond. He's brought along his fly-fishing rod, day pack, camp stove, and toiletry kit.

With me in my car seat, tied down with bungy cords in the stern, Dad slides the boat half into the water. He steps carefully into the boat and sits in the middle seat. He makes no attempt to push the boat away from shore. We listen and look around.

After a few minutes, we hear birds in the forest. The pond itself is quiet, almost flat, with only a few riffles in the middle. Water lilies lie on their leafy pads, sleeping, it seems. I have a memory of smelling their fragrance, but probably it's only my imagination. I'm looking around, practicing focusing on objects at various distances. And still Dad does not row. This is how it is every time we come to the pond.

Our friend the great blue heron laboriously comes out of her nest in the tall dead pine in the marshy end of the pond. The bird makes an arc, as if to show off for us, flying low and with effort, her long feet folded underneath her belly. The heron lands ungracefully in some reeds, then stands patiently, waiting for a fish to come by. We watch her for what seems like a long time, and the heron does not move, and the time is not long at all. What is it for a bird just to wait without moving? What do you think about, bird? What do you feel?

Dad pulls an oar out of the oarlock and sticks it in the shallows and poles the boat free. The boat slides loudly off the gravelly beach into the pond. The heron jerks her head sideways toward the direction of the noise, up-flaps a single wing, then returns motionless to the sentinel position. Because of the aluminum, the boat rows loud, oarlocks clanking when wood ones would creak. As always, the metallic noise annoys Dad. He wants everything to be just so. I look ahead to distant waters, vast in my mind; Dad watches the widening wake of the boat and the receding shoreline.

I enjoy the rock-a-bye-baby experience of boat-on-water and think of you, Mother, that time that seems so long ago when you and I were one.

After a few minutes the heron pokes her bill into the marsh water and comes up with a perch about six inches long. The bird then flap her wings, splashing water as she transitions from settled to flight and carries the fish back to her nest. Even at that young age, I sense the concept of nest, but I cannot imagine what might go on inside it. The contemplation of such mysteries is what makes my life bearable.

. . .

I row out to a rock that juts out of the water, too small to call an island, only slightly larger than the boat itself. I step out of the boat onto the rock. For a second or two, I'm detached not only from the boat but from myself, and I let the pond carry the boat away and watch it, transfixed; for a split second I'm the man who stuffed his son into a dumpster. Meanwhile, the grin of freedom spreads across Birch's face. He enjoyed the sudden jolt as the boat jerked away from the rock. I pull off my shoes and socks, jeans and underwear. Naked, I step into waist-deep water.

The boat has drifted thirty or so feet from the island and into a finger of wind. Moving faster now, me panicky. I dive into the water and swim hard until I catch the bow line of the boat dangling in the water. I swim, towing the boat slowly. Only ten Birch lengths from the rocks my feet touch bottom and I pull the boat up on the ledge, metal scraping against rock and sounding like the lament of some prehistoric creature.

Dad takes me out of the boat, strips off my clothes and diaper. He walks into the water with me in his arms. He releases me to see if I'll float, which I do more or less. From the very first I can swim. I know to hold my breath when my face goes underwater. I know to flap my arms and legs toward the light at the surface. I know to breathe when I break through. I am back there with you, swimming. It is quite a heavenly feeling.

Back on the island Dad makes a little bed with a blanket from the day pack and puts me down. In the water I was able to move up, down, and sideways. Here the rough rock makes crawling hard on the knees. I nap in the sun while Dad fishes. He doesn't catch anything for half an hour, and then a school of perch comes by. In five minutes he has ten fish, two of them pretty chunky, as perch go. Dad has enough for our supper, so he stops fishing.

He sits naked on the rocks for a few minutes. Telepathy tells me that he is thinking that this will be our last good moment in this place. He reaches into his toiletry case and pulls out a mirror and looks at himself. I lose contact with his mind, so I have to make do with analysis. He's lost a few pounds, though he certainly isn't svelte. With his hairy body and hairy face and overly hairy head he appears more Sasquatch than human. Dad grew a beard when he turned eighteen to spite Grandpa Howard. Beardless he'd been "Freddie"; the beard had made him into "Frederick." In his fishing box he carries a filet knife, very thin, very sharp.

He comes over to me. I sit up and watch the knife in his hand. Little white sparks of light issue from the blade.

"I want you to see this, so you don't get too freaked out," he says.

He waves the knife blade in front of my eyes, then brings it to his face and slices off a hunk of beard. Dad works very carefully and meticulously, cutting hair from head and face. With the help of the mirror he gives himself a pretty fair haircut, and slices out most of the beard. Meanwhile, he heats some pond water on his camper stove. He works up some nice suds with bar soap and lathers his face. With a Bic, he shaves until his face is smooth. Then he shampoos what is left of the hair on his head and combs it straight back.

So this is the new Dad. The difference in the face hardly strikes me as important. It's his attitude that is threatening. He seems more interested in himself than in me.

I'm surprised by this face. Clean-shaven I look almost boyish. Though my body might be thick, my nose, lips, and ears are delicate. All the vulnerability and shaky self-esteem, hidden by the beard, is now on display for anyone to see. It isn't exactly like the face of a stranger, more like that of a long-lost brother, home after a decade of wandering. The face full-on in the mirror is wide, almost brutish in appearance. But from the side it's like a girl's. I look at Birch, look at my face. Is there a resemblance? Perhaps. I can't be sure.

My last act at Grace Pond is to capsize my boat just off the boat landing in about six feet of water and load it up with rocks until it sinks to the bottom. From shore I triangulate the location of the boat for future retrieval and use.

That night we eat the perch, the tiny fillets dredged in flower and cooked in bacon fat on my fry pan, our last meal together on Forgot Farm.

NEW YORK

Next morning I sell my boat and truck and just about everything in it for half what it's worth to Critter Jordan. All I have
now is a little bit of money, my son, a leaf bag full of spoons, and
a backpack with only the basics, plus spoonmaking tools (hatchet,
bow saw, mora knife, crooked knife). As I'm going through the
truck for the last time I dig out the bottle of Uncle Fred's Vodka,
a third full, under the driver's seat. I can't bring myself to dump
it. Hardly aware of what I'm doing, I put the bottle in the backpack. It's as if Old Crow himself does the deed.

   I'm going to miss fall foliage season on the trust lands, and
I'm sad as hell to leave Forgot Farm, but I'm excited too. Critter drives Birch and me the twenty or so miles to Brattleboro,
Vermont, and we board the train to New York City. Birch and
I are headed for a shop called Kitchen Elan that sells, among
other things, wooden spoons. I discovered it in *Functional Arts
Magazine* on the rack at the Darby Free Library. First Birch and
then I drift off to sleep on the train and wake sweaty but re-
freshed when it pulls into Penn Station six hours later. We
saunter east, then turn south on Madison Avenue; people, ap-

parently in a hurry, walk by us. No one makes eye contact and yet I have the impression that everyone is here to see and to be seen.

I stop at a window to look at spread rugs on the walls and rolled rugs on the floor. A man behind the counter reads a newspaper in Arabic. An expensive and beautiful rug in a stick house: the mental picture brings me pleasure.

The city is like the forest, full of tall spires for mischief makers to hide behind with the resulting wariness and suspicion among the occupants. It's a haven for raptors, which I see working the air currents between the skyscrapers. The kindly folk of the parks feed the pigeons, and the pigeons feed the hawks. Birch watches the raptors, ignores the pedestrians.

I have the address of Kitchen Elan and I know that New York is pretty easy to find your way in. It's a shoebox-shaped island, with numbered streets running sidewise and avenues lengthwise. My miscalculation has been judging just how big New York is. On the map it seemed like a short distance from the train station to the store. In fact it's a little over an hour's walk.

At Kitchen Elan I pull out one of my spoons in front of a startled clerk. Out of nervousness, I speak bluntly and stupidly. "You want to buy handmade spoons?"

She calls the store manager. The store manager declines to look at my spoons; she says the company is owned by a firm headquartered in Germany, and all decisions regarding stock are made by the U.S. Office Distribution Management Center, which is in midtown, back in the direction I've come from. The store manager says the company's wooden spoons are imported from Africa. By my standards the African spoons are big, clunky, and only marginally useful. It takes me a while, as I inspect various gadgets in the store, to figure out that the African spoons are not supposed to be useful. Nothing in the store is there because it is useful. The spoons are decorator items, emblematic perhaps of tribal life in Africa or anyway somebody's notion thereof, whose purpose is to give an American kitchen a touch of the exotic. I leave in a huff, feeling let down but superior.

After I've been to half a dozen stores and it is getting dark and we have no place to stay, I see a sign, The White Horse, one of the ignition centers of two of my favorite flamed-out writers, Dylan Thomas and Jack Kerouac.

"Go on in. It's on the historical register," says Old Crow. "Toss down a beer for the writers who died young."

"Or maybe twelve," I say.

"You deserve a beer, Frederick. It won't kill you to have one. One wonderful beer. One should not go gently into the good night."

Birch twists in my arms the way he does when I talk to myself. No doubt he can feel the tension in me.

I turn away from the White Horse and cross the street into a tiny park designed for kids, with a slippery slide, swings, and a huge sandbox. We have the place to ourselves. Amazing how in a world of concrete, steel, asphalt, and brick, a desperate person can find an outbreak of trees. It's cooler in the shade. Street litter mixes with dead leaves. Pigeons patrol for eats. I'm a little disconcerted because I can't tell what kind of trees I'm looking at. A sign on a tree says Linden. I put Birch down, throw off my backpack and sit on a park bench. Birch runs in ellipses, gradually extending the distance between us, and then he begins a return trip. He staggers, not like a drunk but like a bad actor imitating a drunk.

I've only been walking for a couple of months and I still do not have the hang of steering. I motor just fine, but I'm always smashing into things and falling down. After all the practice I still move like an ant. I am bitterly disappointed. I expected that mobility would give me freedom, control, and joy. However, as best as I can determine, walking is a small improvement over crawling. Just to stay upright is a big enough job. When I do manage to move I find it hard to stop or change directions, and Dad never lets me go very far. The old dream of flying comes back to me now. If only I could focus my mind, I'm sure I could make myself sprout wings and gain perspective from on high. I plop down on my bottom, because I have yet to devise an elegant way of transitioning from standing to sitting, and I flap my arms like the raptors I saw in the canyons of New York.

It's almost dark in the city of New York when I see a woman out of the corner of my eye. Her head is bobbing from side to side. It takes another moment for me to realize that the woman is miming Birch's antics.

She's in her twenties, snake-slender, with a sprawl of frizzy black hair. She's wearing black jeans and a black t-shirt with white lettering that says "Alice Neel Lives." She has small, pretty lips, troublemaking brown eyes, minimal make-up.

"Hey," I say sharply, "don't make fun of my kid."

"I was getting into him, you understand what I'm saying?" she says.

She comes around through the gate and sits down beside me on the park bench. I smell burnt marijuana in her hair. Her exaggerated demeanor of delight tells me she is meditatively stoned. Something I haven't felt in a long time comes over me involuntarily and full of demand. All of a sudden I find myself in a euphoric, rapid-fire flirtation, betraying my "unnecessary conversation" principle.

"What do you think he was doing?" I say.

"You know him better than I do, so why ask me?"

"Because sometimes it helps to have an outside opinion."

"Look, I wasn't mocking him. He was dancing, and I was dancing with him so I could internalize the motion."

"So you're a dancer?" I say.

"I'm not sure I want to tell you what I am," the young woman says.

"That's understandable. Your mother told you not to speak to strange men in the park."

"I never do what Mother says. What do you think he was doing?" She nods at Birch.

"I think he was working out an idea," I say.

"He's a little young for that. You were probably projecting your own thing."

"You think anybody ever really knows anybody?" I ask.

"Never," she says, and turns to Birch. "What's your name?"

I'm not sure what I'm supposed to do, so I do what I feel. I smile widely and screech. I learned the screech from birds, a whoop with attitude, very effective in attracting attention, if lacking in profundity. I made the bird-screech my own, so that it sounds like an elephant getting a hot foot.

"His name is Birch," Dad says.

"Birch—I like it."

At the sound of my name on the tongue of this new person, I reach for her to be picked up. It seems like the logical thing to do.

She holds out her arms and says to Dad, "May I?"

"Please do."

She sweeps me up. I like those arms, a different, riskier swing than Dad's; I like the softness of her face; the nook in her bosom. I'm not crazy about her breath, though.

"He smells nice," she says.

"I just changed him."

"Birch, you said. Like the tree?"

"Yes, like the tree. He's named after his mother's favorite tree."

"I never had a favorite tree. I take it his mother's not in the picture."

"Birch's mother died giving birth to him."

"I'm sorry. I've spent the better part of my life loathing babies, and now, Birch, I'm looking at you and thinking holy shit, here's looking at you, baby."

"You've got a way with words," Dad says.

"Now you're mocking me."

"I'm sorry. I'm a little antisocial. Well, a lot antisocial."

"Me, too—sort of. So what are you doing at People Central, because I know you're not from the city?"

"I'm here looking for a market . . ."

Dad reaches into the plastic bag on the ground beside the park bench. He takes out three wooden spoons and holds them up.

The woman takes one in her hand. She shut her eyes. "It's beautiful, and I like the texture against my fingertips."

"It's designed to fit the hand," Dad says.

I grab the spoon, surprising the woman—opening her eyes. After a brief tug of war she releases it to me. I wave the spoon like a wand. I'm trying to turn her into you, Mother. Dad laughs, a big roaring laugh I've never heard before; the woman laughs, somewhat less delighted, but amused nonetheless. I laugh theatrically—practice makes perfect.

Her name is Rachel, but she goes by her last name—Bloom. Her father is a Long Island businessman and her mother a real estate agent. Bloom is a couple years out of art school, trying to make a name for herself in the art world.

"You asked me if I was a dancer. Well, I'm more a choreographer of color, light, and shape in two dimensions."

"A painter."

She nods in the affirmative. "Am I going to call you Birch's dad or what?" she says.

"My name is . . ." Dad suddenly stops talking, changes the tack of his thought, and says, "I've always hated who I am."

"This is America; you can be who you want—if you work at it."

Dad thinks for a long time. Finally, he says, "The name's Latour."

"Latour—no first name?"

"It's Frederick, but call me Latour."

"Where are you staying, Latour?"

"This park bench is my home. Isn't it obvious?"

"I have a spare room. But I'd like something in return, permission to do some drawing studies of you and Birch. About a week or ten days' work. They'll be preparations for paintings."

"This is how you get your models?"

"Actually, yes. I've put up homeless men, bag ladies, drug addicts, aging drag queens, runaway high school boys and girls—you name it. Here's the deal. You pose whenever I want. You leave when you feel like it or I no longer find you interesting."

"How do you know I'm not dangerous?" Dad says.

"You probably are," Bloom says. "Look, life's not worth much without some risk, and hey, I'm not stupid. I think the odds of a baby-carrying man being a mad rapist or a murderer are pretty low."

Bloom's apartment is in the meatpacking district. Trucks are backed up to bays, where men and women in bloody white coats pull carcasses out of the trucks and bring them inside cool spaces. A couple of male prostitutes in drag are getting an early start for the evening by hustling the truckers.

"I like the neighborhood," I say.

"It keeps an artist stimulated," Bloom says.

"Stimulation for your paintings—is that why you live here?"

"Should there be another reason?"

The apartment building is the former The Packers Hotel, but most of the letters have fallen off, leaving only ghostly outlines. All that remains of the original relief lettering is the "The," the "h," the "o," and the "t."

"The Hot," I say.

"Right—that's what everybody calls it." She lets us in the front door with a key. The hallway leads to yet another door, requiring yet another key. We walk up three flights of stairs to a large space with tall vaulted tin ceilings, big windows, hardwood floors, a door leading to another room, a ladder climbing to a loft. The studio smells of turpentine. Lying against the wall are paintings of New York street scenes: a homeless woman pushing a shopping cart, a sad man looking in a store window and seeing himself as a woman in the reflection, a middle-aged woman packer in a white apron cutting into the flank of a side of beef. On an easel is a painting in progress of the front of the building, The Hot standing out more boldly than in reality.

"Moody paintings," I say.

"Thank you—I think. Would you like a drink or whatever?" Bloom asks.

I know that "whatever" is code for marijuana.

"Just water for me. Birch might like some juice."

Bloom brings me a tall glass of ice water and Birch a small glass of orange juice, which I hold up to his lips as he drinks.

"Excuse me, I have to make a couple of calls." Bloom climbs the ladder to her bed in the loft, lies supine, and talks in hushed tones. Is she calling the police? I can just see her crossed ankles sticking out of the bed.

I wander into the tiny kitchen alcove. The sink is full of dirty dishes, a jarring sight to one as fastidious as myself. I turn the faucet on. Water pours out. It's a treat just to watch it run, listen to it, feel it tumbling over my hands. For fun I turn the light switch on and off and giggle with the wonder of it all.

When Bloom comes down the ladder I've finished the dishes and I'm on the floor with Birch and a dozen of my spoons, laid out neatly.

"The workmanship is superb. And you want to sell them," she says.

"Sometimes I want to bury them in a time capsule. Sometimes I just want to hoard them—it's a miserly feeling. I definitely do not want to sell them."

"But you need to," she nods. "Thanks for doing the dishes and wiping down the counters."

"My pleasure, the pleasure of faucet water. Everything in New York is a delight." I pick up one of my spoons, return it to its modest carrier, and burst into nervous laughter. "I'm sorry, but I feel a little giddy, wondering why I'm enjoying this so much."

"You're easy to please, it appears."

"I've been in the woods a while."

"That's a metaphor, right?"

"No," I say.

I'm scanning the premises for something to play with when a buzzer sounds and this new person in our lives presses a button and speaks to the wall. The wall answers. I'm in baby awe. Even walls have language. Minutes later I hear a knock on the door. Bloom answers it and comes back with paper cartons.

"Chinese," Bloom says. "They're just down the block. I order from them all the time."

"That's what you were doing on the phone. You're very kind," Dad says.

"Look, I also made a call to one of my father's clients. He does import-export, specializes in accessories for interiors. He's an old New Englander. He'll look at your spoons tomorrow at 10:15 AM." She gives Dad a card: "Brewster Wiley, Arts & Trifles for Good Living."

"Thank you. I'll look him up first thing."

"Better arrive early or on time. Brewster is a very scheduled human being."

"I guess I'll have to start watching the clock," Dad says, his voice falling. This is the beginning of a new way of thinking for Dad, the rules he made for himself at Forgot Farm slipping and sliding on the ice of Reality.

While Dad feeds me Chinese food, Bloom stands off with a drawing pad. Her face is very serious, very intense. She looks like a woman defusing a time bomb.

She draws Dad and me while Dad gives me a bath, and I splash around in her tub, quite a dreamy experience.

She draws me while I play on the floor with ashtrays.

Without saying anything she makes it clear she does not want any distractions while she draws, so she and Dad are quiet all during the time she works, and I'm quiet too. Except for occasional outbursts, I'm pretty civil for somebody not yet two years old.

Through the window I see the halo effect of lights flashing, vague shapes moving in the windows in the next building. Even in the dark Bloom is drawing pictures. I'm thinking about the refrigerator. When I was cleaning up I saw an open bottle of white wine. Old Crow pictures the bottle in my mind—green, label of a vineyard.

The spare room is full of junk, so for the night Bloom has made a bed of folded blankets for Birch on the studio floor. I'll be sleeping on the couch. She covers Birch with a blanket, his head peeking out.

"Don't you ever sleep?" I say, sitting up on the couch.

"Of course. I'm a night person." She puts the pad down, picks up one of the ashtrays Birch was playing with, and puts it on the coffee table. She remains on the floor, yoga style, and rolls a joint.

"I hope you don't mind."

"Would it matter if I did?"

"No."

She lights the noxious stick, draws the smoke into her lungs, offers it to me.

"No thanks," I say. "I already reside in a mildly hallucinatory state. What are you going to do with the drawings?"

"Make paintings out of them, which I hope to sell for mucho dineries. My goal is to accumulate as much fame and wealth as possible."

"I bet that's somebody in your family speaking."

"No, it's me," Bloom says. "I want money and I want notoriety."

"I think everybody would be better off if we all made the minimum, lived minimum lives, and nobody was famous," I say.

"You're like an old lefty, Latour."

"I never thought about it in political terms. It's just the way I have to live."

"But, Latour, you said 'everybody,'" Bloom says. "You implied we all ought to live like you."

"You're right. The absurdity of me," I laugh.

After her marijuana interlude Bloom goes back to work drawing Birch as he drifts off, and I take a shower and return to the couch and lie down with my eyes closed, not exactly awake or asleep, alert enough to hear if Birch stirs, listening to the sound of charcoal on paper.

I'm thinking about my new name, Latour. The moment I'd spoken it aloud I knew it had been mine all along.

Next morning, when Birch and I depart, Bloom is asleep. I climb the ladder to her bed and leave a note on the phone pad.

In a few hours this tough-minded and driven young artist has dented if not demolished the belief system I built on Forgot Farm. My hostility toward people seems to have lifted, if temporarily. The idea of "no unnecessary conversation" seems silly. What do I feel for her? Lilith used to tease me that I only had one erogenous zone. But what I feel for Bloom is not directly wired to my genitals. It's as if she's throwing off rays that touch every part of my body. The feeling, I am sure, is tied to my experience nursing Birch and making spoons, the touch of wood.

Like everything else in New York, Arts and Trifles for Good Living is farther away than I've anticipated, east from The Hot and among jazz clubs, cafes, and art galleries. The storefront is plain, with shiny black vertical lines in the brick. I lose confidence and pace back and forth in front of the store. If I didn't owe Bloom for going through the trouble of making an appointment for me, I'd probably leave. Eventually, though, the inertia of my pacing pushes me toward the door.

Inside, I know in an instant that my gut feeling was wrong. Everything here speaks of the "Q" word—from quality candle holders to quality book ends, from quality brass door knockers to quality framed marquetry landscapes from Russia.

We meet with Brewster Wiley in his office, which is simple and spare. He sits behind an antique wood desk with inlaid side panels in an abstract design of wood "made from all fifty states," he says. On the wall, in a gilded frame, is a dollar bill and a caption, "What It's All About."

I sit in a leather easy chair, Birch on my lap. Unlike myself Birch has an instinct for the importance of decorum in crucial situations, so he does not squirm or make funny faces or noises. After a lengthy chit-chat Brewster spends the longest time inspecting my spoons laid out on his desk, and it is impossible to tell from his scholarly demeanor what he is thinking.

As I will learn later, Brewster Wiley is seventy years old, fit, alert—rueful, like Howard in that way, but without the sarcasm. He manages to dress conservatively but still distinguishes himself with expensive gray business suits and black cashmere turtleneck sweaters. In 1959 it was said that he was a dead ringer for the actor Craig Stevens. Today his various toupees are all based on the Peter Gunn haircut. He'll claim never to have touched alcohol, mind-altering drugs, or tobacco. He eats only lean cuts of meat and then only two days a week. He has never used vulgar language, nor is he known to raise his voice in anger. With men he is courteous, with women courtly. His amusements include a partiality to Western movies, which he watches on his Betamax VCR, and a collection of antique cars, which he keeps upstate in a garage. He attends Trinity Church every Sunday, because he likes walking down Broadway to Wall Street. He has never married, and he is often seen in the company of younger men.

Brewster is an upcountry New Englander by birth, but he considers himself a New Yorker. Indeed, his New England accent has almost disappeared. He says "woid" instead of "wuhd." He will tell me that even as a boy he collected objects that interested him. In adult life he'd discovered that a man can combine his passion with his livelihood. After a series of failed businesses he'd found a secret to success. "I buy and sell items I fall in love with," he will say. "My tragedy is that I'm doomed to part with the things I love."

On this first day we meet, he puts my spoon down, faces me, and says, "Can you make Welsh love spoons, with ball and chain and link carving, Celtic designs?"

"That's stuff's gimmicky, it's for show, or some tradition I don't belong to," I say, unable to conceal my contempt and envy. "It requires power tools, and the wood is usually bass wood. My spoons are made of good hardwood, and they're for use."

"They're pleasing, I'll say that, and well made, but they lack something, a consumer hook—like if they were from Africa, or the Andes."

"They're documented. I bet nobody else has that," I say.

"Documented, demented—what are you talking about?" Brewster says, putting on the New York accent, perhaps because he knows it will intimidate me.

I reach into my backpack and remove a manila folder. I fish around until I find a couple sheets of paper. I pick up a spoon.

"This tells the story of this particular spoon," I say.

"The handwriting is sensational, I'll say that," Wiley says. "It's almost like calligraphy. But combining writing with crafts, I don't know. It'll confuse people."

All day yesterday, when he pounded the streets trying to sell his spoons as Frederick Elman, Dad was nervous, hesitant, resentful of every cross look. Now as Latour he is calm, relaxed, confident. I, too, remain calm. I can read Dad's mood by the beats of his heart, the smell of his sweat, the assurance of his hands on me.

"Read it—it'll change your mind," Dad says.

Wiley looks the spoon over, puts it down, and reads Dad's document, first to himself, then hissing a few words, and finally out loud. Little streaks of white foam form on the corners of his mouth.

By the time Brewster Wiley finishes, his New Yorker accent has dissolved and he is speaking in the Vermont voice of his childhood. He hands the paper back to Dad.

"You have documentation for all the spoons in that bag?"

"Yes, sir."

"That's book length. You must spend as much time writing about these spoons as making them." Wiley is amused.

"Almost."

"I think you must be a little or a lot crazy."

"A lot," Dad says.

I glower at Mister Wiley, not out of anger, just practicing my raptor stare.

"Can't you get day care for the kid?" Wiley says.

"I am the day care."

"You can work with him tagging along?"

"Look at him, look at me, look at my spoons."

"Well, all right," says Brewster Wiley. "You have a company name?"

"No, and I don't want one."

"What about signing your spoons? Don't you want credit for your work?"

"No, just cash."

"How much?"

"Just enough. I believe in just enough. It's my philosophy."

Brewster Wiley gives Dad a little smile and a nod. Even I can tell they're in business.

Brewster opens a wall safe, takes out money, gives it to Dad. Dad will come to New York periodically to drop off spoons and collect money—just enough.

12

BLOOM

Dad's ready to head out for the wide open spaces of the West, but he owes Bloom a debt for referring him to Arts and Trifles. He agrees to model for Bloom for a week.

Besides posing for Bloom whenever she needs him, Dad does all the dishes and keeps the place picked up. Not because Bloom asks him too, but because he likes things orderly and neat. Dad cleans out Bloom's spare room and we move in. The previous occupant (Bloom refers to him as The Ex) was a sculptor, and he left behind some of his creations, metal things that resemble car wrecks. The room includes a single bed for dad and an ancient, smelly (from mildew) settee, which is my bed.

I often stand on the settee, hold onto the window sill, and look out at New York. Across the street higher up than us is a balcony with plants in pots and a woman with dark, flowing hair who leans over the railing and gazes outward as if she is thinking of taking flight. I can relate. Below her two stories are a couple of unwashed smoky windows where the blurred shapes of people come and go carrying stacks of something or other. At street level, concertina barbed wire tops a fence surrounding a small parking lot. On the street in front of a meat-packing building boy/girls stand on the running boards of trucks and talk to the windows, or so it appears to me. Sometimes a truck door opens and the boy/girl goes in. I'm not interested in any of these matters. I am studying three-point perspective. From here, way up high and looking almost straight down, people have odd shapes, and I am trying to determine why and what it all means.

Bloom watches Dad and me closely. When she sees us in a position she likes she'll holler "Hold it right there!" We freeze. She touches Dad, touches me, gently adjusting our poses to suit her eye. Then she takes Polaroid pictures of us. We wait in freeze-frame while the pictures develop. She watches the Polaroid take shape, her eyes intent and hungry. (That's what I'll remember most about Bloom, those hungry eyes.) Usually, she grabs the picture before it's fully developed and chucks it in the wastebasket. Then she fiddles around with our bodies some more. I like the touch of a woman, satisfying in a different way from Dad's touch. When she finally finds a picture she likes she exhales audibly and says something like, "This is it—beautiful!" She files the picture in a box.

I am acquiring a new understanding of the world and my place in it. Instead of me watching other creatures—bugs, birds, and beasts—another creature is watching me. I have that understanding to this day. You pose for other people, and they process pictures of you in their minds, which they use to judge you, reward you, or dispense with you. You, Mother—do you watch me with doe-deer eyes? I hope so.

When she's ready to start a study, Bloom re-poses us in the studio against white, ghostly sheets, placing us in the correct position using the Polaroid as a guide. She lights up her obnoxious and smelly marijuana and draws with charcoal on paper. The drawings will serve as templates for the paintings. During the drawing stage she smokes marijuana, because "it frees my hand." She says she never smokes her nasty weed when she paints, because it messes up her ability to judge colors. When Bloom is working, her disposition changes from easygoing and wisecracking to sullen and silent. She draws all night and sleeps all day. Since Dad and I are on-call models, it doesn't take long before we're on the same schedule as she is.

. . .

It's early morning, after Bloom and Birch have finally gone to bed. I'm still awake, in an odd state of mind. I'm happy with my work, with its potential for the future; I'm happy it's making me some money. Well, not really. I don't want to make money with my spoons; I merely have to. I want to give them away. Money taints them, taints my efforts, taints everything. I'm happy to be here in New York with Bloom and Birch. Well, not really. I really want to be back at Forgot Farm. I miss the woods, the pond, certain trees, certain smells, certain feelings when one lives in self-imposed privation. I'm dependent for survival on a greedy old businessman and a sexy but obsessed painter. Even so, I'm happy. Well, not really. I'm thinking of that old Peggy Lee song: "Is that all there is?"

"Look in the backpack," says Old Crow.

"What do you mean?" I don't know what he's talking about.

"You know exactly what I mean."

It's not until I actually unzip a compartment in the pack and find the vodka bottle that I remember putting it in there. Without any thought or hesitation, I twist off the cap and take a deep swallow. Another. I stand there waiting for the feeling. For about a minute, everything is quiet, everything is perfect. I bring the bottle to the sink and dump the remainder of the contents. I listen for Old Crow's lament, but all is silence in my mind.

I'm as ambulatory as a Thanksgiving Day turkey running from a hatchet, but I have no more chance to find freedom than that gobbler. I want to be outside testing my theory of perspective: that people routinely change in size and angularity, which is why self-knowledge is so hard to come by. I want to hunt for raptor nests, find myself a raptor mother to train me to stalk pigeons and eat them. Climb the barbed wire fence into the car lot and steal a shiny one. Follow a road to the nth. Ride the meat trucks to where the meat comes from. Wear the dresses of the boy/girls I see daily outside The Hot. I'm afraid, Mother.

Tension builds up in all of us. Dad promised Bloom a week of our time, but two weeks have gone by. One night Bloom breaks down from overwork and frustration, and Dad hugs her. Dad closes his eyes, and Bloom closes her fists until gradually they open and she completes her part of the hug. I do not—repeat—do not like to see them all wrapped up like that, and I cry hard to break them apart.

Dad isn't getting enough sleep. He's up at all hours sitting for Bloom or cleaning the studio or making spoons from New York wood, of which there is plenty in Central Park, about a hundred different species of trees. Dad can't sleep in daylight. He grabs naps during the twilight hours of dawn and dusk. Bloom might be up all night but during the day she sleeps like the dead; I, too, sleep like the dead. On occasion Bloom and I meet in our sleep in a church. In my dream I hide in the pews, because Bloom is trying to kill me, which is quite a trick since I am already in the land of the dead. She fools me by posing as a statue. I suck on her toes, and she snatches me up and envelops me in a crushing hug. Bloom and I share the same dreams, because she tells her dreams to Dad and he tells them to me, and they are the same as mine, Mother.

Dad has been trying to wean me since we arrived in New York, but he doesn't try very hard. He depends on me as much as I depend on him. Nursing is our magical time.

One week goes by, another, another; an hour or so after a session, when Dad goes to bed, I lie in my settee thinking. The air is pure and fragrant, and we are alone with flowers. Is this my dream? Dad's? Or maybe—and now I think I'm getting closer to the truth—it's your dream that you put in our heads. I get confused sometimes.

I wonder about that fragrance, and wondering lets me experience fragrance in my own hair (it's coming in sandy-colored, like yours). Flowers? But the fragrance changes. I smell the thick aroma of burnt marijuana and sweat, Bloom's all-night, art-work sweat. I open my eyes a slit. Bloom has come into the room, and she is standing in front of Dad's bed.

"Is he asleep?" Bloom whispers.

"I don't know. I'd better check," Dad says.

"He'll be all right."

"No, I have to see." Dad comes over to my settee. My eyes are closed but I see him. He touches my cheek. His hand is warm.

"He's okay," Dad says.

"You check on him often?" she says, her voice still low.

"Yah."

"What are you looking for?" she asks.

"I just want to know he's alive."

"You're with him too much. It's not healthy."

"That's probably true."

I open my eyes. Dad is in his jockies. Bloom is fully dressed. He takes her hand, and they go into the studio. I slither down from the settee onto the floor and very quietly crawl through the half-open door and hide in the shadows. Way back when I was a newborn, I learned from Spontaneous Combustion how to watch unobserved.

Dad and Bloom stand by the window and kiss. My first thought is to scream out my anguish at this sight, but something about the embrace is different from the hugs I'd seen earlier. Through Dad, I experience the touch of Bloom's lips, sweet and good. Stop right there, I want to say. Let's just preserve this in memory before it's stained by anything else that might go on between the two of us. No, it's three of us, or even four of us? I tell you this tale, Mother, as if three persons were involved, Dad and Bloom in an embrace and me watching and listening, but at the time it seems as if the three of us are all part of this gathering action, and now that I'm sending you thoughts it seems as if you were there, too.

"I like it by the window; I can see you better," Dad says, his voice soft and teasing in a way it never is with me.

"I like it by the window so others can see us," Bloom says.

"Our contribution to the city," he says.

"Yes, New York is a great big mirror," she says. "That's how I want to think of it."

They keep pawing at each other. It's annoying and unnecessary. I want to break them up, or do I want to jump in the middle and join? Join what? I have no answers.

"What are you, Latour? You're not gay, but you're not like any man I know. At one end of the scale you're almost ridicu-

lously masculine. At the other end"—she touches his chest—
"you're like a woman. What are you, Latour?"

"I guess I'm some kind of hybrid."

"Hybrid painter, hybrid models—hybrid love," she says in a
whisper, followed by kissing.

Bloom lays out a canvas on the floor. She squeezes tubes of
paint on the canvas. She tosses her clothes away and lies down
on the canvas. Dad kneels beside her and fondles her, and then
she fondles him and then they sort of fall over each other and roll
around on the canvas, spreading the colors. Because of the dark
it is hard to tell what they are doing. They writhe like snakes in
a stone wall. I hear rustling sounds of their bodies on the canvas.
I hear vowel sounds I never heard before. I don't understand
those sounds, but they excite me. I picture the raptors of New
York soaring through the night, enjoying experiences unknow-
able by lowly persons such as myself.

And suddenly whatever happened is over. Bloom laughs. "We
better get cleaned up. This stuff is definitely not healthy for
skin."

"I'll give you a turpentine rubdown," Dad says.

"Latour?"

"Yah."

"You know what this means, don't you?"

"I do. You don't need models anymore."

"I plan to start painting right away, and I need privacy when
I paint."

"Birch and I will be gone in the morning."

I manage to sneak back to our room just before Bloom snaps
on the light.

Six months later Birch and I return to New York with a load of
spoons for Brewster Wiley. I visit The Hot looking for Bloom,
not sure what I am going to say to her, and am startled to discover that the building is being pulled down. I check a phone
book—no Rachel Bloom. An old feeling of unreality hovers over
me. It's as if she were never there, as if our odd lovemaking never

happened. Brewster tells me that Bloom has decided to travel the world in search of subject matter for her art.

Brewster demands more spoons. He wants me to keep in touch via telephone and written communication; he wants "production"; he wants me to sign papers. I refuse on all counts. I'll take cash only, and he's not to know my whereabouts. I will never own a telephone. I will never purchase a post office box; I will never have an address. If the IRS or Persephone Salmon or anybody else wants me, let them find me on forgot land. Let the world swirl around me. I'm not part of it, nor do I wish to be. I enjoy being a fugitive. I tell Brewster how greedy he is, and he tells me how stubborn I am. Both charges are true. Our frailties are our bond.

13

SPOONWOOD DOCUMENTATION

Dad and I spend five years touring America. We avoid cities, national parks, festivals, shopping centers, concerts, anyplace where large numbers of people gather. We hitchhike the two-lane roads, hop freight trains, take the bus. Dad's routes bring us to the Forgot Places. Everywhere we go Dad makes spoons from the local woods. He trades some for food and lodging, gives some away, and turns the rest over to Brewster Wiley for greenbacks only. By the end of the second year Dad has enough money to support the cash purchase of a used Dodge van, which he converts into a home for us.

I finally learn speech recognition and to walk in a straight line. Sorry, ants, but I've left you behind. However, I must confess some disappointment. Foot mobility is nice but I was hoping for a more liberating experience. What really surprises me is how boring straight-line walking is. I prefer running because it's more exhilarating. Speech recognition, too, is disappointing. People rarely say what they feel or think. Words projectile-vomit out of their mouths. Like everybody else, I can't really think and talk at the same time, and my speech rarely meets the standards of my imagination. But I try. I'm careful what I say. Dad and I sometimes meet strangers in our travels, and they're always amazed that I don't speak like a child.

In year four Dad officially changes our names. Frederick Elman becomes F. Spoonwood Latour. I become Birch Spoonwood Latour.

We drink a lot of Ovaltine.

Dad makes spoons commemorating American trails—the Mormon Trail, the Cherokee Trail of Tears, the Appalachian Trail, the Underground Railroad, the Lewis and Clark Trail, the train trail taken by Sister Carrie in the book of the same title, the trail of John Steinbeck in *Travels with Charley* and later William Least Heat Moon in *Blue Highways*. Dad also makes spoons commemorating places where certain people treated him kindly. In no particular order (since Dad travels in no particular order), here are some of the spoon places: Grand Isle, Louisiana; Vernona, Wisconsin; Window Rock, Arizona; Tabernacle, New Jersey; Lincoln City, Oregon; Fort MaKavett, Texas. I fall asleep every night to the *sip, sip, sip* music of Dad's knives.

Other people tie down canoes or kayaks or bicycles or four-wheelers onto their vans. Dad ties down our shaving horses, his and mine. You see, Mother, by this time I am making spoons, some of them good enough for Dad to sell through Brewster Wiley. When Dad starts me off he doesn't do anything to correct me so I often cut myself. Eventually I learn and do not cut myself and make good spoons. It is pleasant work. Some things you learn by thinking, others by experiences, but spoonmaking is learned by touch. Dad sells my best spoons with his own. I don't think the average person can tell our spoons apart, but we can.

Every time Dad makes a spoon he writes up a "documentation," as he calls it. Some go on for pages and others just for a few lines. He spends many hours copying over the documentation. He wants the handwriting to be as well made as the spoon.

SPOONWOOD DOCUMENT: *Black Spoon*

The story of this spoon began beside a bayou in South Louisiana. For miles the main view was delta prairie grass, the most distinguishing feature a single dead tree way in the distance. Running parallel to the narrow two-lane road was a bayou not much wider than the road, but it must have been deeply dredged because shrimp boats chugged up and down its waters. It was quite a sight to look ahead at the optical illusion of blacktop melting into the horizon, only to see a real boat appear on waves of heat.

I pulled off and parked my van to get a closer look at the water. With me was my three-year-old son. We walked through the grass to a narrow spit of sand. My son remained on the shore, while I kicked off my shoes and stepped into the water. I tasted the water. It was slightly brackish.

The water over the sand was clear to greenish, but it quickly darkened to black as it fell off into the channel. I imagined myself diving in, following an outgoing tide into the Gulf of Mexico, past Florida, in the Atlantic, catch a ride on the Gulf Stream, ending perhaps in Ireland to start a new life in another country of stone walls surprisingly similar to those in my native New England.

Something streaked from near my feet into the deep. I imagined it was a fish, but it was probably reflected light. The unanswerable question—what did I see?—troubled me.

I began to brood, thinking that vanity was at the heart of my failures. My father used to say there were three ways to catch trout—offer live bait, give them an imitation of what they're eating off the water at a particular time, and, last, cast a lure that excites or provokes them to attack. "The smaht fisherman fishes all three ways," he would say. Just to be perverse I searched for a fourth way. I would entice a trout to take the fly I chose. Once I located the fish I wanted I would cast him my fly over and over again. I rarely caught trout, but when I did the satisfaction was great indeed.

I have made the mistake to live the way I fly-fish—do things my way without regard to the real world. The triumphs are rare, the strain palpable, but I persist.

My morbidity vanished in a second flash. Clothes and all I dove under. The water was murky, but I saw something on the bottom. Not a fish. An eel lying in wait perhaps? Or something more malevolent? I grabbed. Not an eel—a stick. I pulled it out of the suck of mud. It was about the length and thickness of my arm. With my x-ray vision I saw a spoon inside the wood. Like the stick, the spoon was black.

I removed my homemade shaving horse, which was tied to the top of my camper van, and I set it up on the grass. The stick was soaked through from being submerged and the wood shavings parted easily. Following the grain of the wood, I made a spoon about ten inches long, with a narrow handle flaring upward slightly at the end with the grain of the wood. I can't say what kind of wood the spoon was made of, because it had been in mud so long the properties of the wood had undergone a transformation. The mud and minerals of the water were inside the cell structure. I let the spoon dry, thinking that its color might lighten, but it never did. I finished the spoon with my special oil and wax mix and the blackness shone like the flash of a fish in dark waters.

SPOONWOOD DOCUMENT: Dam Spoon

My son and I visit a magical place by a river just below a flood-control dam. A dirt road led downslope a short ways to a spot bulldozed flat. Sticking out of the flattened fill were old beams torn out of houses and whole trees cut up, some buried, some exposed and graying to the weather. Apparently the area served as a dump for wood refuse. Grass and a few wildflowers grew on the fill dirt. Below, through the screen of bushes and small trees, the river tumbled out a chute from the dam, then eased off lazily.

Where the road ended, the ground dipped forty or fifty feet precipitously to the river plain. A crude staircase of stone slabs three to six feet across and a foot thick led to some coarse sand. Carrying my son, I walked down the stairs. With each step something changed. I could no longer hear traffic on the road. I smelled the river, felt the humidity. And finally when I arrived on the gently sloping flood plain of the river, I discovered a heaven for a wood-working man.

Lying before me for hundreds of yards was driftwood, from the size of toothpicks to logs sixty to seventy feet long, all of it stripped of bark and glowing in the sunlight.

My son and I walked among the driftwood in the sand. Here and there trees grew, and they provided another spectacular sight. Every spring some of the surface soil was washed away, revealing the roots of the trees, which now stood on conical tangles of roots two to five feet above ground level. Bark had grown over the roots. Every tree provided what to my eye looked like a home for an ogre, which was what I told my son.

"Ogres eat people, right?" my son said.

"That's correct," I said.

My son got down on his hands and knees, stuck his head between the roots, and said to the ogre, "Eat me."

We walked on.

It passed through my mind to camp out here below the dam for a month or so and make spoons out of the driftwood, but some higher power stopped me. Any action by myself could only contaminate this place, since it was heaven to start with. I decided that the spoons in these trees should remain where Nature put them.

While Birch continued to explore, I sat on a log, not thinking, not attempting to account for time passing: I just existed.

When we finally departed from this holy place, I took some spoonwood with me but not from the river. In the wood dump above the stone stairs was the unwanted wood—the diseased, the rotten, the discarded parts of demolished buildings, the troublemaking trees whose roots clogged up septic systems. The stuff suited me, and I made off with a maple branch from a rotted tree. I whittled a soup ladle, the handle of spalted maple.

SPOONWOOD DOCUMENT: Trash Tree

One afternoon my son and I were passing through a little town in that fringe between North and South, Midwest and East, when a thunderstorm rolled in. We pulled off, parking on the street in *a nice old-fashioned neighborhood with modest, single-family houses, big trees, and sidewalks. The storm lasted only half an hour, but it was accompanied by violent winds and machine-gun rain.*

We heard the thump of a large tree falling nearby, but we could see nothing in the rain. Minutes later the wind died to calm, and the sun came out. I put my son on my shoulders and we went out to look for the inevitable rainbow, and there it was at the end of a driveway far above the garage. Below stood a man with his knuckles on his hips. He was looking at the fallen tree. It had clipped part of the garage and wrecked his flower garden.

My son dismounted from my shoulders and stood gazing at the rainbow while I walked over and told the man about my interest in trees for spoonmaking.

"This one's no good for that," he said. "It's box elder, grows like a weed around here. It's just a trash tree."

I remembered reading about box elders, trees that produced a weak, bland-colored wood, barely useful even for the stove. In fact, every time I read something about box elders I always came across the phrase "trash tree." I wanted to tell this man that no tree is trash, just as no person is trash, but it was not the time to start an argument with one who has just suffered a misfortune.

I asked the man if I could keep a stick three or four inches thick. He agreed, giving me an amused look that suggested he believed I was unbalanced. He was right, of course: I am unbalanced. My goal at that moment was to redeem the value of the box elder as a species, start it on its way toward a more respectable reputation.

Normally, I would walk around the tree, worry over it, until I saw spoons inside the wood, but the homeowner had already become suspicious of us, and I cut the first branch in front of me. By then the rainbow had disappeared.

I hauled our prize to the van, tied it down to the top, and drove off. Later at a campground I cut into the raw wood and it gave off a funky odor I hadn't noticed before, something partaking of compost heap and the morning bedroom smell of sleepers. I traced the odor to a moist, almost scummy layer between the bark and the sap wood. I was excited by the unknown in the wood. It's always this way: the anticipation of surprises in even so humble a task as making a wooden spoon.

My x-ray vision usually allowed me to see a spoon or spoons in a tree, and I would make my splits based on that knowledge, but this particular branch must have had the equivalent of a lead shield because I could not see into the wood. I assumed that no spoon was inside. This project would fail. Failure was acceptable. I'd failed many times. I burned my failures in my campfire. My failures warmed me, cheered me, and cooked my food.

Since I had no x-rays to go by I decided to split the wood down the middle to see what there was to see. The branch was four and three-quarters inches thick. I started the split with a hatchet ax and finished it with a froe. I saw what I had expected, blond wood, not particularly interesting, though there was a suggestion of curve to the grain a third of the way through and just a faint pinkish tint in a crack. I split the piece again along the line. And was delightfully shocked.

The split revealed a deep, lurid red streak in the light-colored wood. I had seen wood with all kinds of colors, the purple of lilac, burnt umber of laurel, oranges of oaks, pinks of maples, bright yellow in the pitch of pines, somber red of cherry, but never a red this vibrant, like a child's little red wagon under the Christmas tree.

After close inspection I found where the grain cupped sufficiently to suggest the location for the bowl. For the next hour I worked in that blessed state outside normal consciousness.

Box elder was ridiculously easy to shape. I could have cut the wood with a fingernail, and yet it did not splinter. The finished spoon was eleven inches long, with a thick handle and a broad bowl. The red streak looked like a stream that started at the top of the handle and meandered into the bowl. The spoon was so light, it was like holding air. I doubted that the spoon would hold up under use. Even washing would dent it.

My research at a local library confirmed my suspicions. Box elder wood was indeed weak. Moreover, my reading showed that the vivid red color in the wood was caused by a disease and would *fade over time, degraded by exposure to light. The only plus was that the smell would go away as the wood dried. My spoon had limited use and transient beauty. Did that make it trash?*

In my craft I seek to create strong, useful objects out of wood, letting the beauty of the material speak for itself. Not in the case of box elder. I hid the spoon in dark green felt to keep the light from it. Unseen, untouched, the spoon will remain beautiful but not useful. On rare occasions one can remove the spoon for handling (for only the hand can appreciate weight and texture) and view it briefly, and then return it to its case.

I failed in my attempts to make a useful spoon from box elder. Nor did I do anything to improve the repute of this much maligned tree. Indeed, my labors reinforced the idea that box elder is a trash wood, that is, by the human definition of trash. Long after I am dead and gone and my labors forgotten, the box elder will still be known as a trash tree.

SPOONWOOD DOCUMENT: *Radioactive*

We came down off the El Capitan Mountains on Route 380 in New Mexico in a celebratory mood, down through the tiny town of Carrizozo onto flat desert land. For the next sixty-four miles we would pass through only the ghost town of Bingham, which consisted of a weather station and a rockhound shop. Current population seven. Sounded like my kind of place—forgot and forlorn. As we drove I imagined establishing a homestead in Bingham, finding an abandoned shack where my son and I could set up housekeeping. Maybe grow some hot chili peppers, keep goats, hunt rattlesnakes for food. Of course I didn't expect to find such a place, but the thought of it occupied my mind. We had been crisscrossing the country for half a decade and I was looking for a place to settle down. Every time I found a landscape that I liked I asked myself, Is this home? The answer was always: not quite.

A few miles outside of Carrizozo was the Valley of Fires National Recreation Area, a broken landscape of mainly black rocks and black wrinkles in the earth, the result of volcanic activity.

I pulled our van off the highway and drove a short ways to the campground. There were about twenty camping sites that included outdoor grills, a rest room, and the dreaded (by me) RV hookups. Normally I'd avoid a place like this, but no other people were recreating here but us. We left the van to look around. It was March, the air cool but the sun hot.

I scanned the horizon and saw grass, junipers, a few other shrubs. No trees. And yet it was all so beautiful.

"This is God's country," I said. "God doesn't need living creatures to make Him happy. He can make do with sunlight, rocks, texture, and color—these are His amusements."

"What about people?" my son asked.

"Some people say that God made us in His image and likeness and so we're special."

"Maybe He likes bugs better," my son said, "because He made so many more."

As a toddler my son did not talk for a long time. All the evidence suggested that something was wrong with him. But I could tell from the very beginning that he understood everything I said or did and that he would talk in his own good time. When he finally spoke it was in complete sentences, without baby diction or baby elocution.

"Good point," I said. "If He exists. I'm a doubter."

"I believe," my son said with fierce conviction.

I have never treated my son like a child. I've always insisted that he speak clearly and articulately. I've kept him away from other children. Childhood is cruel, full of erroneous thinking, and like other kinds of abuse best left unexperienced. The result is that my son does not know how to talk or behave like a child.

A self-guided trail wound from the campground for about a mile across the lava flow. There had been no volcanic explosion here. Lava just slowly spilled out of the earth in a river forty-five miles long and five miles wide, olivine basalt, same stuff you see in Hawaii. We found a nice prospect and I gazed out and just tried to absorb what this place had to offer. I heard no car sounds, no wind stirring. And yet it was not quiet. I heard a hush, a huge deep-throated hush.

I pointed. "That's west. Somewhere in that wide open space is the Trinity site, where they detonated the first atomic bomb back in 1945."

The look on my son's face told me that his thoughts were elsewhere.

"Do you ever really listen to me?" I said, as much to myself as to him.

"Yes, Father. I remember everything," he said.

"Everything?" He'd told me this before. We were together so much that we repeated ourselves, not to inform one another but to signal importance and meaning.

"Don't you forget after a while?" I said.

"No, I keep practicing it in my head so it doesn't go away."

"Why?" I asked, though I knew what the answer would be.

"To tell my mommy," he said.

"And you'll tell her that we love her."

"And always will."

My son knew his mother was dead, but he pretended she was out there waiting for him and that he would find her during one of our trips. He told me he learned language so he could talk to her. I neither questioned nor criticized him. I've developed my own theories of parenting. I wanted my son to watch me and listen to me and learn from my faults as well as my few virtues but mainly from my actions. I refused to tell him his thinking was wrong. How could I when I was not sure of my own thinking?

"Dad, when are we going home?"

"Where do you think home is?" I asked.

"I don't know," he said, "but it's not here."

"If you don't know, how can you know it's not here?"

"Because you told me this was God's country, so it can't be ours."

I looked at him. The corners of his mouth were turned up in whimsy.

We continued west on Route 380; my intention was to return to the Valley of Fires campground for the night. I anticipated staying in this forgot area for a month or more, maybe until the weather was too hot. We had water and food enough for a week. I could always go back to Carrizozo for supplies.

Bingham consisted of a few tumbled-down buildings that could not have been grand even when they were standing and the remnants of dusty streets that went nowhere. The only places showing habitation were a rockhound shop and next to it a mobile home. Nobody answered my knock on the door and no vehicle was parked in the driveway. Off the highway beside the shop was a dirt road and sign: Desert Rose Mine. The road headed into the desert toward a rugged, jagged hillside. I told my son all I knew about the minerals to be found here—fluorite crystals, galena, barite, brochantite. I also told him about trinitite, which was the glassy substance created by the heat of the first atomic explosion, only about ten miles away.

We arrived at the hillside, and I could see remnants of the former mine higher up. I didn't dare take the van up the road, which looked as if you'd need four-wheel drive. We parked and hoofed it to the mine.

My son wanted to scout for rocks.

"Go ahead," I said, "but look before you reach. These lands are infested with snakes."

My interest was in the weathered wood that would inevitably find its way to a mining operation—support beams, tool handles, the remnants of structures, wagon parts. I enjoyed looking at such wood. Weathered wood is condensed history.

"Dad," my son called my name, not loud, not urgent, but something in the voice sent me running to him.

He was on his hands and knees, peering between two rocks at a creature that was peering back.

"Dad, is that some kind of land crawfish?"

"You're still thinking South Louisiana," I said. "That's a scorpion. His sting can make you very sick. Remember what I said before. Be careful where you put your hands."

"Yes, Father."

There was plenty of wood up here, but none of it intrigued me. I was disappointed but my son was happy. He'd found a rock he wanted to keep. It was about the size of a golf ball. Inside was a perfect glass cube, pale blue in color.

"I do believe that's fluorite," I said. "I know because I've seen fluorite on the trust lands where your mother's people are from."

"Are we ever going to go back there?"

"I don't know." Suddenly, I was thinking of a car-sized boulder shot through with green slivers of fluorite, the boulder dropped by God when he was experimenting with glaciers as a rock-transportation device. Must have taken some thousands of years to move the rock from Canada to that special piece of land in the USA. When you're immortal you have the luxury of taking your time.

"Keep the stone for good luck," I said. "We'll stop at the rock shop on the way back and see how much we owe for it."

We walked down the hill to the van. I gazed south at the two-rut road that led in the direction of the Trinity site. That was when I had the crazy idea to join the Army of Unauthorized Personnel.

"Son," I said, "let's go look at the place where they exploded the first nuke."

We were able to drive six miles before the road vanished into some soft ground in a dried lake bed. I packed a tent, some food and water, binoculars, and a bow saw; I took a compass reading, discussed the situation with my son, and we set off on foot, each of us carrying our walking stick. I calculated we would reach the Trinity site in a couple hours. We would be back by dark. If not, we'd camp out for the night. I was very careful to take accurate compass readings, jot them down, and share them with my son in case something happened to me. I frequently took risks like this. I should not have done it—because of the boy. He could read a compass, but could he really find his way out if I were, say, bit by a rattlesnake? I didn't know the answer. I took risks without answers. A death wish? But for two? Was that criminal? I was a fugitive from justice, but was I a criminal?

It was easy walking, the land flat, the footing firm, though it was grassy in places. The grass worried me, because we might surprise a snake, which would do what snakes do in the grass. I prodded with my walking stick, hoping that Mister Snake fanged the stick and not me or my son. We didn't see any snakes, but we did see a pronghorn antelope doe with her fawn a couple hundred yards away. When they caught sight of us the mother stared in our direction. The fawn stood perfectly still, waiting for marching orders.

"Can we follow them?" my son whispered.

"Why?"

"I want to see where they live."

"They're like us. They live everywhere."

"I can read the little one's mind. I want to follow them." His voice was full of urgency.

"We'd only disturb their lives." I took his hand and pulled gently. But he resisted.

"Okay, we'll follow them," I said.

The mother moved off, her fawn right behind. We were able to keep up with them for only five minutes before they outdistanced us and disappeared into the horizon.

"I wonder where they went," I said.

"They went to heaven," my son said.

We moved on, the compass our guide.

In the middle of this nowhere we came upon a sign: "White Sands Missile Range, No Admittance." There was no fence, just brush, sand, and rocks. No sign of civilization but the sign itself. You would think the government would build a fence. Then again, who in his right mind would wander into a wasteland where missiles might drop at any moment? In either my right mind or my wrong mind—hard to tell the difference—I was not worried. No doubt if the range were in use our movements would long ago have been detected.

"You think we are in our right minds?" I said to my son.

"Yes, Father," he said.

The sign had been there for decades. The paint was faded, and part of it was falling down. I pulled at the frame and ripped off a dry-rotted two-by-four six feet long. Sun-baked, grayed douglas fir. Pleased by my criminal mischief, I stared at the board at my feet. Twenty minutes and a mile later, we did see a fence, which *enclosed a flat area that did not integrate with the landscape. I surmised that the atomic explosion left a crater, which was later filled to keep the radiation down. I whipped out the binoculars. After scanning the area, I handed the glasses to my son.*

"Take a look," I said.

"I don't see anything except that thing in the middle," he said.

"Yes, I don't know what it is. Let's go find out."

We walked down to the fence. The "thing" inside the fence was a small obelisk. We went around to the locked gate. A sign said, "Welcome to Trinity. The use of eating, drinking, chewing and smoking materials and the application of cosmetics is prohibited within this fenced area."

Looking through the binoculars, I read the plaque on the obelisk: "Trinity Site where the World's First Nuclear Device was exploded on July 16, 1945. Erected 1965."

And that was that. Our adventure appeared to be over. I was thinking about Tubby's dad, who died when Tubby was fourteen years old. His father had been a soldier during atomic bomb testing in the 1950s, and the radiation eventually gave him cancer and killed him. Or so the old soldier claimed. He told us that the army put them in trenches as close to the blast as they dared. "When the flash went off you could see the bones in your arm through your closed eyelids," he said.

We started back, going 180 degrees from our previous compass reading, and then my son said, "Hey, wow." He was pointing at the ground.

"Another scorpion?" I asked.

He shook his head no. I bent to look and saw what could have been a pea-sized glassie from my childhood, colored with swirls of blue. It was trinitite.

"I don't think I want you playing with this," I said. "It's probably mildly radioactive."

"That's okay. I like the fluorite better."

I removed my backpack, fished around until I found the medicine box, removed a Band-Aid, and wrapped it around the trinitite for safekeeping.

On the return trip I stopped at the missile range sign in the middle of the desert and picked up the board I'd taken down. With the bow saw I cut off a piece of the two-by-four and stuffed it in my backpack.

By the time we arrived at the van it was almost dark. The lights were still out at the rock shop so we drove on to the campground. We had the place to ourselves. I built a campfire from brush. I used to read to my son every night before retiring, but these days he read to me. The Swiss Family Robinson *was his favorite book. It wasn't the adventures that excited him, it was the family atmosphere he lacked—siblings, pets, two parents, ordinary values. All my son had was a father, and not a very normal one at that.*

Later, after I tucked him into his sleeping bag, his eyes wide open and staring up at the stars, I set to work by the fire making a flattish spoon in the Swedish style with a wide handle, on which I carved a mushroom-shaped cloud. At the top of the handle I scooped out a pea-sized hole, where I embedded the piece of trinitite my son had found.

SPOONWOOD DOCUMENT: *Education*

It was high summer. We'd had a lot of warm rain, and everything was greener than usual. My son had reached school age. We'd spent the summer living on forgot land in a state that shall remain nameless. It was a good time for me to see the local school principal about my legal obligations to educate my son, since the school should not be too busy at this time of year. I made an appointment. My purpose was to discover how to dodge around the law requiring school attendance, for I had no intention of enrolling him.

I hate progress and people, but I love general knowledge, and I wished to give my son the best education possible. Accordingly, I felt it best to keep him far away from school. The trouble with school is that there are too many children in a confined space. It might be necessary for adults to congregate in large groups for one reason or another but only for a few hours and only for some rote ceremony, such as religious services, concerts, sporting events, political gatherings, or other marginally useful activities. But Nature did not intend for the massing of children in one building with only a few adults to preside over them. Children teach each other cunning logic, which invariably departs from false premises, a habit that persists until death. Children produce nothing, nor are they exposed to people who do produce something.

One of the tragedies of the modern world is that children no longer see their parents at work, a situation that breeds disrespect and keeps the child locked into the child's world. Who would want to live in such a world—paranoid, dangerous, uncertain, illusory, and so dreary that children constantly complain of boredom? Certainly not a child. Every child wants to live as an adult. Our culture conspires to keep children childish, which accounts for the high crime rate among child-men, not to mention hysteria among child-women. I suppose I am blaming my own failures upon the culture, for I was a child in my heart until the death of my lover. I can still be childish—petulant, self-absorbed, rash, violent. I do not want my son to grow up to be like me.

A new concrete-block addition, appalling in its ugliness, had been added to a charming wood-frame schoolhouse with its cupola and rows of clerestory windows. In the parking lot was a dumpster, brimming at the top with the kind of wooden school desks I grew up with.

We went inside. The principal came out of his office, stormed past the secretary, grabbed my hand, and introduced himself. He was very young, on the job only a couple weeks, eager.

"Mister Latour? Hap Conroy here, come on in. I was tied up talking to a school board member." He smiled as if I should understand. As an afterthought, he said a few words of mishmash to my son, who looked at him with pity in his eyes.

"My son is eligible for school in the fall," I said.

"He seems to be a bright boy. Let me guess, you had him in Montessori?"

I shook my head no. "My son has never been to school, nor do I want him enrolled. I'm here to ask you how I can educate him myself and stay within the law."

"Home schooling."

"Is that what it's called?"

"It's the coming thing, especially among certain church groups. Are you part of a religion?"

"In a manner of speaking, I suppose I am."

As it turned out, Mister Conroy was very helpful, only too happy to explain the law and home schooling. My son would be one less headache for him.

On the way out I asked Mister Conroy about the discarded desks in the dumpster.

"We're getting new computer stations. Those desks will be useless in the twenty-first century."

Outside, I climbed into the dumpster and rummaged around the desks until I found one that suited my purposes, nicked with graffiti cut by a child's jackknife and filled with color by a ball-point pen—in other words, a desk very similar to my own when I was in elementary school.

I believe children should be exposed to knowledge without distractions or prejudices. Keep kids away from each other, away from TV, expose them to the livelihood of their parents or guardians, put them to work, and they will learn.

I'd been reading to my son since he was two months old: works of literature, history, geography, art, and philosophy. My son had already learned mathematics, because in our work as spoonmakers we were constantly measuring and calculating. He knew the names of trees, and how each species behaved. He knew birds, rodents, and insects. Instead of stuffed animals, he enjoyed the company of the deer, the woodchuck, the porcupine, the red squirrel, the mink, the otter, the raccoon, the coyote. We lived in the eddies of society. I saw no good reason to send my son to school.

Back at our campsite I inspected the school desk I'd pulled out of the dumpster. The legs and the cubby under the desk top were a drab brown, the result of darkening over time by exposure to light and faded varnish. The top, three-quarters of an inch thick and edge-glued, had been sanded down to bare wood and covered with clear urethane, dreadful stuff that, in effect, imprisoned the wood in an envelope of plastic. The wood might have been sugar maple or yellow birch—hard to tell the difference even when you sank a blade into it. Also it could have been some alien wood, for I wouldn't put it past the school government to purchase wood desks outside the local area. The top included a routed groove for pencils and an ink well, which was out of date even when I was a student.

The legs had been scratched by a child's jackknife. I know because the jackknife was my preferred tool for marking up desks.

The graffiti had faded over time. Someone had the initials L.W. The artist had carved triangles, various indecipherable marks, and the words "yellow submarine." Elementary school students received too much credit for being creative.

I knocked the desk apart with a sledge hammer and put the pieces in a galvanized tub. I poured water in the tub, dumped in some forest duff, and swirled it around until the desk pieces were in a wet slurry.

Every few days for three weeks I periodically added water to the slurry. Green wood responded best to my knives, but wetted was almost as good. During this period I made a plan for using the wood. It was always hard to start a spoon series (demanded by my dealer), and I kept putting off the job, making single spoons instead. I work better on the fly, but one cannot plan a series through serendipity alone, because the spoons must fit together in some way. In other words, I had to plot the wood, and that was difficult for me. Then on a chilly morning in late September, I saw a skim of ice on the galvanized tub. I broke it with my hand, enjoying the shatter on my fingertips. I rolled up my sleeve and mucked around for the wood pieces in the thick, icy soup, so cold it hurt.

The desk pieces were almost black, swollen with moisture, dirt embedded in the wood fibers. I set to work, following the plot that had been shuffling around in my mind all these weeks. From each of the four legs, I made two small teaspoons, almost identical. My secret finishing oil brought out some pink in the blond wood. I knew now that the wood was maple. From the desktop, the book nook, and the side supports I created twelve nearly flat stirring spoons. All sixteen spoons had individual designs on the handles, a notion I borrowed from my son. I asked myself what the appropriate design for these spoons should be and how best to incorporate it into all the spoons while allowing each spoon to attain its own identity. Further, how could the design represent the wood, specifically that intermediate zone between forest and the human hand, between formal education and the wild knowledge of experience?

With my jackknife I simulated child graffiti—initials, circles, triangles, stars, and shapes of undetermined meaning. I filled the scratches with various colors and put a natural oil and wax finish over the entire spoon.

It was my practice to burn leftover wood in our campfire. My son was picking up the waste wood for disposal when he came across a piece about ten inches long. The markings were no longer visible to my eye, but he could see them or perhaps could feel them with his fingers. He traced the marking, revealing a meaning. My son completed our set by making a spoon with the carved words "yellow submarine" flowing from the handle to the back of the spoon. It was the best piece of the set.

14

IN THE YELLOW SUBMARINE

Since my father died and my mother was institutionalized, you have been both mother and father to me. These have been good years, but I sense they are coming to an end, though to what end I cannot say. Please remember my gratitude. Love, Your sort of son.
    —Letter sent to Persephone Salmon in Tasmania from Garvin Prell

I have an idea to linger in rural Massachusetts until after the foliage season, but one night I wake with a premonition that something is terribly wrong. I immediately check on Birch. He's awake.

"What's the matter?" I ask.

"The antelope in New Mexico, they're following us," he says.

"You were dreaming," I say.

"Am I dreaming now, Dad?"

I feel danger but I don't know where it's coming from. I do what I always do when I'm afraid. I run. Birch and I leave in the middle of the night and head south.

We spend the winter in the Everglades, making spoons from cypress and various found woods in the wetlands. I like the big sky, the sweet smell of the sugar plantations burning off the cane, the alligators basking in the sun, the catfish who come to my illegal gang hooks.

By late March it's getting hot and I'm looking at maps, scoping out our next forgot place. The van is parked on a turnoff on Alligator Alley, and we're sitting at a picnic table. I point at the Rand McNally.

"Birch, what do you think about this for a road trip?" I say. "It's Route 1. It goes all the way from the bottom of Florida in the Keys to the tippity-top of Maine."

Birch puts his finger close to my finger. "Why do they call it Frenchville?"

"I'm not sure, but it's probably because some people from French Canada moved there."

"Dad, if we go up Route 1 we'll be close to Darby?" He points at the map.

"Who do you want to see?"

"Everybody."

"Even your grandmother Persephone?"

"Yes."

"For all I know she's moved permanently to Tasmania, or she might even be dead. She didn't look all that healthy the last time I laid eyes on her."

"She's not dead. She's waiting for me to come home."

"Now, Birch, how could you know that?"

"I dreamed it. In my dream Spontaneous Combustion told me to come back to Darby."

"You miss that cat?"

"No, I do not miss him. I don't even like him."

"Do you remember Persephone?"

"Yes I do."

"And you'd like to see her."

"Yes, in that great big house. I want to live there."

"And Grandma Elenore and Grandpa Howard, you want to see them?"

"Yes, and I want to live with them, too."

"Do you want to live with me?"

"Yes."

"You can't live with all of us at the same time."

"I could if we all moved into the great big house."

I laugh.

"Don't laugh, Dad. Don't laugh."

"Let me think about it."

That night we eat steaks over the grill. We watch the sun go down over the cane fields. It's clear that I have to give Birch what he wants. His desires are not frivolous. It's part of my philosophy of child-rearing that I must honor all serious requests. I mull over the problem of returning to Upper Darby. I'm guessing that after five years the charges against me—misdemeanors?—are no longer in effect. As for Persephone, perhaps she will not seek custody of Birch if I agree to let her visit. And then there is the matter of Forgot Farm. I miss my life in the woods. Maybe it's still forgot land. Maybe I could buy it. I've been hoarding the money that spoonmaking has brought me. I don't believe in banks, so it accumulates in my cash box.

"Okay, Birch, here's what we're going to do. We're going to make an offer to buy Forgot Farm. Then we'll go back to Darby."

"Thanks, Dad."

Dad drives us to Delray Beach, Florida; he is determined to buy Forgot Farm from Mrs. Walter Sturtevant. He has her address from his visit to the town clerk's office five years ago. Mrs. Sturtevant resides in a twenty-story senior citizen apartment building on a manmade channel leading into the Atlantic Ocean. A high wall surrounds the building and we are met at the main parking lot by a uniformed guard. He has a big mustache and he is reading a newspaper in Spanish, which he puts down as we pull in.

"Mrs. Walter Sturtevant," Dad says politely. His clothes are neat and with me sitting beside him he looks respectable.

"She's over by the dock," the guard gestures with a head nod. "She likes to look at the manatees."

Dad thanks the guard, parks the van, and we walk along a pebbled concrete walkway, which is landscaped on both sides by palm trees, flowers, and grass without weeds, a scary sight for Dad.

"What's a manatee, Dad?" I ask.

"Like a sea cow," Dad says. "Up close they look like intellectually challenged walruses, but from far away they're sometimes mistaken for mermaids. You can't trust what you see."

"Can you trust what you hear?"

"Sorry, the answer is again no," Dad says. "You can't trust anything or anybody."

"I trust you, Dad," I say.

I take his hand. I look around, trying to understand what Dad is telling me, but the world as I see it at this moment does not seem untrustworthy.

An old lady is standing at the edge of the dock, pointing what looks like a gun at the water. In fact it's a 35 mm camera with a telephoto lens. She's tiny, with knobby wrinkled knees and a face with more lines and folds than our road map.

In the water I see two huge shapes about ten feet long, no distinctive features, just shapes.

"Do they bite?" I ask as we approach.

"What?" she asks.

Dad shouts my question.

"No, they're vegetarians," she says to Dad, and then looks at me and says, "Young man, you're not a vegetable, are you?"

Dad winces and shuffles his feet in annoyance. "You don't have to condescend to him," he says.

The old woman fiddles with her hearing aid. "I can never get this thing to work right." She points to the water. "Look."

The manatees lie suspended just below the surface, brown thinking blobs. I try my old telepathy trick. It works. Manatees are easy reads because unlike Dad they are very trusting. They are telling me to enjoy the day. I switch to Dad's mind, but nothing is coming through. More and more, I'm losing touch with his thoughts. Spontaneous Combustion the cat was right. My mental powers decline day by day.

"See the big one with the scar on his back?" the old woman says. "That's the result of hitting a boat propeller. They come into the channel because the water is warmer. They're basking in the sun like us old retired folks."

"Mrs. Sturtevant?" Dad says. "Allow me to introduce myself. My name is Latour."

"Latuna, Latuna, I know that name," she says. "You called me some years ago after my Walters passed away about . . . You were an old Army buddy or something."

"I called you about your New Hampshire property," Dad shouts.

"Yes, I remember now. My young Walter bought that land to recover his verities after the Vietnam War, but it didn't do the job. In fact, he never stepped foot on it. The land thing was all in his head."

"For that very reason maybe it did do the job, Mrs. Sturtevant."

"That's a nice thing to say. You can call me Gertrude."

"Gertrude, I'd like to make an offer on the property," Dad says softly.

"Okay, I've got it tuned," Mrs. Sturtevant says, removing her hand from her ear. "You'd like to what?"

Dad repeats his words.

"You're late, Mister Latuna. I sold that property two springs ago."

Dad is disappointed, but he is not too upset—until he discovers who beat him to the sale.

"I was contacted by a Mister Garvin Prell, attorney for some kind of conservation district."

"The Salmon Forest Trust Conservancy," Dad says.

"That's it. They bought it."

We leave Mrs. Sturtevant to her manatees and drive north on I-95. Dad is very quiet for the remainder of the day.

After the disaster with Mrs. Sturtevant the old hatred of Upper Darby that I thought I'd left behind takes possession of me. No doubt Persephone bought Forgot Farm to prevent me from ever having it. No doubt Garvin Prell gave her the idea—"He's like a son to me," Persephone had said. I begin to think back, how Garvin fawned over Birch, how Garvin was seen with Lilith when she was supposed to be with me. He was county attorney when the warrant was sworn out against me for cutting trees on the trust land. With the old hatred comes the old paranoia. Who does Birch belong to—really? Garvin wanted me and his bastard son out of Darby. I played into his hands by leaving. In my heart Birch will always be my son, but what about biologically?

We never celebrated my birthday until I turned five, because of Dad's philosophy, but along the way I got wind of the idea of birthdays and started complaining, so now Dad compromises. I suppose I should feel guilty, but I don't. I guess I'm just a selfish boy.

"What do you want for your birthday, son?" he asks.

I've been gearing up for this moment for a year, and my answer is ready.

"I want to go to McDonald's for dinner," I say.

I've see the signs all over the country, have used the restaurant restrooms, but have never tasted the food. Though Dad loathes not just the food at McDonald's but the very idea of McDonald's, he honors my request the way he honors all my requests. We will feast at McDonald's for my birthday.

It's not hard to find a McDonald's. Dad's in a bad mood. We don't usually frequent service roads. Dad doesn't like the traffic, the architecture, the people. I eat a Big Mac, large fries, and a cola. The food is delicious. Dad does not eat. He sits there glowering, which I find kind of funny. When Dad gets in a bad mood he looks like he's trying to stare himself down in a mirror.

I like the uniforms worn by the McDonald's servers. I'm thinking how nice it would be to wear a uniform with thousands of other McDonald's servers. Who serves the world better? I daydream that someday when I'm of age I will be a McDonald's server in service to my species.

After McDonald's, Dad decides he needs some "therapy," as he puts it, so we visit Cooty Patterson. The old hermit lives in a small trailer in a small trailer park in the small town of Port Mansfield, Texas. In sight is a lagoon that calms the roaring ocean so it looks like a great big gentle lake. Sport fishermen come and go. Sea birds circle and make argumentative noises. The town is surrounded by ranch land, miles and miles of prickly pear cacti and mesquite bushes. The next town over is twenty-six miles away.

As we pull in, Cooty, dressed in cowboy duds, is waiting outside as if he expected us.

"Hey Freddie, what happen to the baby?" Cooty hollers as we get out of the van.

"He grew some," Dad says.

"He don't look gruesome," Cooty says.

The trailer is very crowded, because every last bit of space is taken up by aquariums. Cooty feeds us a delicious stew that includes dumpster vegetables, lizard, snake, and some kind of road-killed creature that Cooty cannot identify.

After the meal, Dad starts carving a spoon for Cooty made out of mesquite wood. As Dad works, Cooty sips agave tea and I watch the fish.

"This mesquite is beautiful wood, but hard to work," Dad says. "Cooty, what do you do all day around here?"

"Take care of the fish and watch them. It's exhausting. Night comes and I'm ready for a good sleep."

"You don't get bored?"

"Never. There's always plenty going on."

Dad laughs in a tender way that makes me a little jealous. Only Cooty can make Dad laugh like that. I pick up *Texas Highways* magazine and start fingering through it under Cooty's nose.

"Hey, look, he's reading the magazine upside down," Cooty says. "I wish I could do that."

"He can read right side up too, he's just showing off. Isn't that so, Birch?"

"Yes, Father," I say, "but I really can read upside down, and backwards too."

I put the magazine away and return to the fish. I like the feeling of my nose pressed against the glass.

"Freddie, I mean Latour," Cooty says, "Garvin Prell and a couple bounty hunter guys were here looking for you and Birch."

Out of the corner of my eye I see Dad suddenly stiffen.

"Really, when?" Dad asks, his voice very soft.

"Last week, last month, last year—I don't know; I don't keep track of time," Cooty says. "Garvin, he told me that if I see you I should tell you that Mrs. Salmon got custody of Birch."

"How come it's always the wrong people who die before their time?" Dad says.

"Couldn't you work something out with her and Garvin?"

"What do you mean?"

"Make peace."

Dad laughs again, but this time it's a bitter, mean laugh. Suddenly, I'm afraid.

"Cooty, there's only one thing I know for sure," Dad says, "and that's that the Elmans hate the Salmons and the Salmons hate the Elmans, and that they both hate me—for good reasons, I might add—and that there's no end to it."

Dad hands the completed spoon to Cooty. "Here you go, old man."

"A fish food scoop," Cooty says.

"Right," Dad says. "Make sure you follow the old rule when you oil it with the stuff I gave you."

"The what?"

"The old woodworker's rule: Once a day for a week, once a week for a month, once a month for a year, once a year forever."

Cooty begins to weep. "Oh, that's so beautiful," he says.

I don't catch the rest of the conversation, because while I'm looking at the fish, profound things happen in my head.

I decide that we should tour the Big Bend country. It's beautiful and practically empty of people. I'm thinking that maybe this is it, maybe this is going to be our home, because after the information from Cooty it's clear we can't go back to New Hampshire, let alone Forgot Farm.

"Dad, what is it like to watch TV?" Birch asks.

"It's like watching Cooty's aquarium."

"When I was watching the fish, I remembered . . . I remembered." Birch can't seem to get the words out.

"Yeah," I say, encouraging him with a pat on the head.

"I remembered watching the fire when we were living at Forgot Farm."

"What did you see?"

"I saw my mother."

"She was in the fire?"

"No, behind it. She was safe, I was safe, but . . ." I fight back tears.

"But I pulled you away."

"It's all right, Dad," Birch says. Just then I spot what looks like a rental car in my rearview mirror. It's coming up on me fast. Up ahead is nothing but road as far as the eye can see, but I do spot a ranch road that appears to wind up into the mountains. The car pulls up beside us. The driver is a big man, the front-seat passenger a bigger man. In the rear is Garvin Prell. He's motioning me to pull over, and hollering something. Since my windows are rolled up to keep the air-conditioning in, I don't hear him.

I cut sharp onto the dirt ranch road and step on it. The car rockets past and the driver has some trouble with the U-turn, getting his wheels caught in some soft sand. He's spinning round and round, kicking up dust while I drive fast. The road grows considerably more bumpy and narrow. Three miles later the road dead-ends in a box canyon.

Birch and I get out of the van, and I grab my knapsack.

"Let's go," I say, and we start up a foot trail. It too comes to an end. Hundreds of feet below I can see the car pulling up behind my van. I don't feel trapped or afraid or angry. My emotion is relief.

I sit down on a rock and Birch sits beside me. He senses my peculiar mood. I start making a speech. Even though I haven't thought about what I'm going to say, the words come out with inevitablity.

"This is probably the last time I'll be seeing you for quite a while," I say. "You'll have new teachers, I'm sure. Make the most of your opportunities. Walk down the trail with your hands over your head. Garvin won't hurt you. You're too valuable to him."

"What are you going to do, Dad?"

"Something I've been thinking about for a long time, since we left New York, actually."

Birch starts walking down the trail with his hands up. I watch him until he's out of sight, then I reach into the knapsack and pull out a bottle of Old Crow. I unscrew the cap and take a long pull, and it's as if the last five years of abstinence was prepartion for this moment, this wonderful, serene moment.

I manage to get through a third of the bottle before Garvin arrives. I screw the cap back on, put the bottle in my knapsack, and greet him with a handshake. It's a surreal scene, not only because of my state of mind but because of the landscape—desert, big western sky.

On the return trip, Birch rides with the two bounty hunters; I ride in my van, shackled to a waist restraint on the passenger side. Garvin drives. Between us is my knapsack. For hours we say nothing to each other. We come out of the mountains on the flats, and I see pump jacks working the desert for oil.

"Permian basin," I say.

"If you say so," Garvin says.

"Don't you think that pump jacks look like dinosaurs?"

"I suppose."

"Garvin," I say.

"Yes."

"I've been wondering for a long time."

"Wondering what?"

"When Lilith and I started to get involved and we had that fight, she went to you, didn't she?"

"Maybe."

"What do you mean, maybe?"

Garvin doesn't answer.

"Garvin, did you and Lilith—you know?"

"What difference does it make?"

"It makes a lot of difference and you know it. Birch—who does he belong to?"

"If you were in doubt all these years why did you spirit him off, why did you—how can I put this?—take pretty good care of him?"

"I'm not exactly sure. Strange, selfish needs maybe. Did you make love to her? Tell me the truth. You owe me that."

Garvin hits the brakes and the van skids to a halt half on the shoulder, half on the road. Garvin unlocks my shackles. He starts shouting, not in anger, more in hysteria.

"I wish I knew, okay?" he says. "Okay! Listen, this thing has bothered me as much as it's bothered you."

"I don't think so," I snap back. "What do you mean, you wish you knew?"

Garvin settles back in the seat, raises his head, then drops it, burying it in his hands.

"Something was bothering her, she wouldn't tell me what, but it was more than you, okay?" Garvin says. "Me, I was in a bad state because my father had just died in my arms. In my arms! Okay? Lilith and I were drinking heavily and I'd taken some pills too. We made out, I know that much. When I woke up, I was hung over and she was gone. There's a big blank spot in my memory. Okay? Look, Katharine Ramchand and I are engaged to be married. I don't need any of this. As far as I'm concerned, you can have the kid."

"Then why did you come after me?"

"For Persephone, to save her—understand? To save her." He thumped himself over the heart.

The horror is that I do understand. Persephone and I both need Birch to stay sane. In which case she's been insane all these years. Now it's my turn.

"Garvin, I want you to do me one small favor."

"Okay, what?"

"Let me have my bottle. It's in the knapsack."

At that point the bounty hunter car has doubled back. The men come out of the vehicle with drawn guns.

"It's all right," Garvin hollers. "We were just talking."

Garvin puts the shackles back on my wrists but doesn't tie them down to my waist-restraint. He removes Old Crow from the knapsack, unscrews the cap. "Here," he says. With two hands, like a baby at his bottle, I bring Old Crow to my lips. Birch, still in the car, chooses that moment to turn his head and look at me. I don't care. I just want to kiss Old Crow.

The charges against Dad include income tax evasion (Dad kept no records, but Brewster Wiley did), child endangerment, failure to register a minor for education, and illegal woodcutting on the Salmon Forest Trust Conservancy. The Statute of Lamentations never expires.

Dad pleads guilty to all charges. He's forced to pay his taxes and a fine, reducing his finances to zero. In addition, he's sentenced to nine months in a minimum security prison. "I must be pregnant again," he tells the judge. Or so I was told, because I was not allowed to attend the trial. Dad is barred from making contact with me until I am eighteen years old, and then it will be my decision if I want to see him.

I go to live with Grandma Purse and her niece, Katharine Ramchand, who is now Assistant Professor of Social Geology at Keene State College. Grandma Purse and her lawyers fought to gain custody of me over Grandma Elenore and Grandpa Howard. The judge allows me one day a week with the Elmans—Sundays. It's kind of interesting to be the center of attention, but I wouldn't want to go through that experience again. You see, unlike everybody else I love, I an not—repeat, NOT—mad at anybody.

Everything is different for me. Instead of living on the road in a black van with crazy F. Spoonwood Latour, I'm in a mansion with crazy Persephone Butterworth Salmon. This is the part where the poor little rich boy is supposed to get all sad, but it isn't like that at all. I love my mansion. I love Grandma Purse— she's good to me. And she's fun. She drives so fast that our gardener, Roland LaChance, wears his sleep mask so he doesn't have to see the road. Grandma Purse likes to speed whether behind the wheel of her vintage Bronco or of the snowmobile she owns with the souped-up carburetion.

When I saw Dad drinking again I lost contact with Dad's thoughts. During the nine months Dad is in prison it's as if he does not exist in the material world but is only a collection of my memories. My therapist believes my recent change in thinking represents progress. I guess I don't know what progress is. Mother, I'm lonely sometimes, empty in a strange way. I don't miss Dad. I miss myself. I'm not all there.

Upper Darby has changed in the years Dad and I were on the road. Many local people have left town to start new lives in new places. Nearly all the farms on River Road have been sold to make way for house lots. Darby Depot's shantytown has mutated into a trailer park. In Upper Darby the old family estates have been subdivided, the big houses remodeled or even torn down and new ones built by new people. For example, the Prell property is no more since Garvin was killed on his bicycle by a hit and run driver. Dad was in jail at the time—pretty good alibi; even so, Grandma Purse believes that somehow he did it, hired a hit man or something. Of course I know Dad didn't do it, because I know how he thinks. I wonder if you and Garvin see each other in heaven.

My granduncle, Monet Salmon, tore down his old estate and built what Grandma Purse scornfully refers to as a post-maudlin house. It looks like a giant New England farmhouse collided and merged architecturally with a Victorian house and a modernist house. It has fake Greek pillars, lots of skylights, and wild colors—pink, purple, yellow. Inside everything is painted white, except the hardwood floors. Granduncle Monet Salmon appears to be the only Upper Darby scion who is richer now than he was ten years ago. He says he's been lucky in the stock market. Grandma Purse thinks that his wife, who is from Brazil, is the real moneybags behind Monet's success. At any rate the source of Granduncle Monet's money is a question mark.

Granduncle Monet is second in command to Grandma Purse on the Salmon Forest Trust Conservancy Governing Board. She's the chair, he's the vice-chair, and everybody else on the board is a flunky. I don't know much about what goes on at the meetings, but I know that Grandma Purse has no use for Granduncle Monet and vice versa. She calls him "Fuckbump."

Grandma Purse and Granduncle Monet do have one thing in common. They both have spouses living south of the equator. Granduncle Monet is a frequent flyer to South America, where his wife operates an import-export business. Two or three times a year Grandma Purse hops a jet to Tasmania to be with her second husband, Professor Hadly Blue. I stay behind with Katharine.

Our house, the Salmon mansion, is still the biggest in Darby. It's hotel-sized, "restored to its former glories," in Grandma Purse's words. She and her lawyers found a loophole in the charter of the trust, and she sold off all of Grace Pond and its environs to an international conglomerate, which established an entirely new part of Upper Darby—Blue Heron Village. A hundred or so homes were built in the woods overlooking the pond. Lot owners pay to maintain the roads, get rid of the trash, etc. Only certain designs and color schemes are allowed, and trailers and junked cars are banned. Despite the rules and dues, people flock to buy up these lots and build their dream houses.

My mansion is gigantic, with separate entrances, so days go by when I don't see Katharine. Besides teaching she's writing a book about stone walls. She tutors me twice a week in math and science. My therapist says I am not ready to play with other children. Dad brought me up to be suspicious of the younger generation, and I have to admit that on this point I think Dad was right on. The behavior and thinking apparatus of young children appall me.

I love my mansion. Every room is an adventure, beginning with the library. I am determined to read every book. I like the pool room too, where in olden days the men would retire to smoke cigars and play with their balls. It has great big parlors with fireplaces wide enough to burn four-foot-long cordwood. In those "days of yore," as Grandma Purse puts it, the mansion was maintained by a staff of more than a dozen people. Grandma Purse has a staff of three. Soapy Rayno is our cook; her husband, Roland LaChance, is our gardener and handyman; and Katharine is Grandma Purse's personal assistant. Katharine has her own suite of rooms on our bedroom level, floor two, but Soapy and Roland live on the third floor in what used to be the servants' quarters—small, cramped rooms, but a lot of them. Once a month a custodial crew from Keene shows up and cleans the place. Even with a reduced staff, the house is expensive to keep up. Heat alone costs a small fortune. The property taxes are high, and there is always a carpenter or a roofer or a plumber or an electrician or a house painter on the premises to keep up appearances.

My room is on the second floor beside Grandma Purse's. It had been your dad's room. I like the huge desk, the surprisingly small bed, the bookshelves, and a closet big enough to park the Bronco or a bronco in. On the dresser is a picture of your dad. It's easy to see why local people called him the Squire. He was tall, handsome, square-jawed, and square-shouldered, wearing country casuals. Grandma Purse says I am the spitting image of him, but I don't see any resemblance. I discover a secret compartment in my room behind the bookshelves. Inside is a safe. I apply mind over matter to open the safe but have no luck.

I don't have a shaving horse in my room, but I do have a couple of knives and a spoon gouge that our gardener found for me, and I carve spoons when I can't sleep. The work is not the same without Dad to encourage me. It's just a habit. I don't finish the spoons, because Dad never told me his secret oil/wax formula. I keep the spoons in a dresser drawer. Maybe when I'm eighteen and can see Dad again I will give him my spoons to sell.

Grandma Purse says I can do whatever I want with my room, so I draw a submarine across one wall—about twelve feet long—and paint it yellow. Instead of drawing a blue ocean as a home for the submarine I draw some hardwoods, green in high summer—birch trees, maples, red oaks. There's a song about a yellow submarine, but I don't want to hear it because I'm afraid it would ruin my own idea that the yellow submarine is a reminder of the good old days at Forgot Farm, when Dad and I lived in harmony and happiness in a yellow school bus.

Grandma Persephone had your room across the hall gutted, remodeled, redecorated, and turned into "a guest room." (Like we need one more. And in fact we don't have guests.) One of the first things I did when I moved into the mansion was sneak into your room to experience your presence, but I didn't get a feeling or a telepathed message. Grandma Purse won't talk about why she cleaned out your things, but she does show me pictures of you as an infant, as a kid, and as a teenager—you died as a teenager. I cannot connect the you in those pictures with the you I have in my mind. Except for one. It shows you in your bathing suit when you were a lifeguard. Your long legs and muscular body thrill me in a way I cannot explain. I know that the real you is/was/will be the you in the water, swimming to save a life.

In Grandma Purse's grand bedroom is a door—locked—that leads to another room where her "personal effects" are stored, and I am not allowed inside. I promise never to go into that room, but I'm lying. You see, Mother, I am not a good person. In my heart I'm a spy. I want to spy into forbidden rooms, spy into twisted minds, spy into mysterious crevices where crawfish, scorpions, and other interesting creatures reside.

One of the first things Grandma Purse does is have me tested to see if I am, as she puts it, "of sound mind and body." I score one out of two. My body is sound. Grandma Purse and I meet with my therapist, a Dr. Lester Mendelson, to discuss my evaluation.

Doctor Mendelson, affectionately known as Mendy by his friends and Doc Mendy by his patients, has an office in Keene, but he only goes there once a week. He prefers to see his patients at his home, one of the new houses built on the slopes surrounding Grace Pond. The house has a flat roof, big windows, and several decks on three different levels. Inside, the walls and ceiling are painted off-white, the floors tiled like a black-and-white checker board. Abstract paintings that look like gasoline swirls on a street puddle hang on the walls. Other features include sculptures of curved metal and glass tables held up by stainless steel legs. We sit on plastic chairs with a minimum of padding. I ask about the house, and Doc Mendy says something I don't quite get. Sounds like "Foam follows function." Doc Mendy's wife, Madeline—"Maddy"—used to be an art director for a magazine in New York. These days she's a consultant and goes to People Central two days a week to consult. I don't see her much. They have two daughters both in prep school, so I don't see them either. The Mendelsons' goofy golden retriever, Rorschach, has his own quarters in the yard.

Doc Mendy sits with crossed ankles in a rocking chair while Grandma Purse and I sit knock-kneed at opposite ends of a couch. Doc Mendy has long hair like a hippie out of ancient times. I remember when Dad had long hair and a beard. He looked like a Sasquatch. Doc Mendy looks like a street mime wearing a lion's-mane wig.

"Birch has a very high IQ, and for someone with no formal education he's surprisingly well-read and well-informed," Doc Mendy says, looking at the report in his hands. "He is mildly dyslectic. In his writings he sometimes confuses one word for another, especially common expressions. For example, on our test instead of writing animal, he wrote lamina; intents and purposes came out intensive porpoises. He claims to have memories going back to birth, and he supports these claims by supplying intimate details and conversations from these early periods."

"Is it possible that he really does remember conversations between the Elmans before he could actually speak or understand language, or that, more extraordinarily, he remembers his actual birth?" Grandma Purse asks.

"It's more likely he gained most of the information from third-party sources."

"You mean his father told him stories, and he internalized them as his own," Grandma Purse says.

"Exactly," Doc Mendy says—"exactly" is Doc Mendy's favorite word—"but we mustn't discount all of his stories. I'm sure he does remember further back and in greater incident than 99.9 percent of the population. You must understand that total recall is a sign of hysteria. It's possible that his birth trauma marked him early. A baby's brain is a powerful computer. He might well have absorbed conversations as the equivalent of digital bits and bytes. Later, when he learned language, he was able to decipher his memory data to make meaning of them. From birth to age three, Birch took in a lifetime of information. From age three to the present his processing power has been more or less normal. Indeed, his more recent memories are murkier than most people's."

"What does the future hold?"

"Because of his negative attitude toward children he will probably have a difficult time relating. Also, because his diction and body language are so much like an adult's, children will have difficulty relating to him."

Grandmother Purse suddenly jumps to her feet. "Do you mind if I smoke?"

"I'm sorry, I cannot permit . . ."

Grandma Purse wheels around and jabs her bony finger in Doc Mendy's direction. "With all due respect, fuck you, Doctor. I paid big money for this evaluation, and I have to smoke." She lights a Kool and begins to pace. I love watching Grandma Purse when she is in full Persephone mode. She's like a dragon.

Doc Mendy is not scared of Grandma Persephone, not too much anyway. He's used to dealing with crazy people. "Okay, all right," he says with a smile.

"You're telling me that his father has so screwed him up that this boy has had no childhood?" Grandma Purse's face reddens, which is how she gets when the subject of Dad comes up.

"Exactly. In essence he's neither a child nor an adult, but a kind of hybridized juvenile. Bottom line: He'll likely have problems adjusting to school and social situations."

"The brats will eat him alive."

"Exactly. Plus the fact that he's so far advanced in reading and computation skills he's sure to be bored. Also, culturally, he's in a different world, never having been to a movie or watched television."

"I'll school him myself," Persephone says, very excited. In fact, she's excited in the same way that Dad was when he decided to educate me in his own way.

Cousin Katharine and I meet twice a week to study the "y" stuff—astronomy (my favorite), biology, botany, geology (her favorite), and chemistry (nobody's favorite); along the way she throws in some algebra and calculus. Katharine is all business. She gives me tests, grades my papers, and makes comments. I'm studying the same material as her college students. It's not all that difficult. It's just boring.

What's not boring is Katharine's life. I learn about it in bits and pieces from her and from Grandma Purse. Katharine's mother was Persephone's kid sister. They called her Flower. She was even prettier than Persephone, but impulsive and, by my estimation, kind of stupid. She gave away all the money from her trust fund to a guru who eventually left America with his fortune and returned to his home in India.

Flower had a number of lovers, but her favorite—and Katharine's dad—was Nigel Ramchand, a steel band musician from Trinidad. Katharine says that her father bragged that the blood of all the races of the earth ran through his veins—East Indian, African, European, Native Carib, and Asian. Her parents never married, but they were together for ten years on a commune. Turns out that Katharine and I both lived on Forgot Farm. She remembers her mother sitting on the stone wall in the sunlight and singing "we shall overcome" to her. It was that wall that started Katharine on to a career in social geology. Katharine also remembers her father telling her the news that her mother had died. She had taken drugs, danced half naked in a cold rain at an outdoor concert, and perished, maybe from the drugs, maybe from exposure. No one was sure.

After Katharine's mother died the commune fell apart. The guru took his American dollars to India, and Katharine went to live with her father in his native Trinidad. When Katharine was seventeen Nigel Ramchand went to Guyana to entertain gold miners. There was a raid by revolutionaries, and he disappeared. Katharine's not sure whether her dad was killed or joined the revolutionaries. Katharine left Trinidad and enrolled at Tulane University in New Orleans.

Meanwhile, Mrs. Sturtevant's son, Walter Jr., a Vietnam War vet with a plate in his head, bought the land to build his dream cabin on, but because of mental illness and finally death he never lived on his property. He did pay the taxes on it until he died. Dad used to say that the government taxes everything—even dreams.

I respect Katharine as a teacher, because she knows so much and tries to help, but she's not much fun.

By contrast, classes with Grandma Purse are an adventure. We meet every weekday morning for "school" in her bedroom. Grandma Purse stays in bed for most of the day. It's a huge four-poster bed, complete with canopy. Grandma Purse sits fully dressed at the head of the bed, propped up by pillows, a tray beside her. Soapy brings her black chicory coffee all morning and homemade doughnuts from a recipe Soapy got from Katharine, who got it from the cafe DuMonde in New Orleans. Grandma Purse drinks her black brew. I drink Ovaltine. We both eat doughnuts. They are delicious.

Grandma lets me read any book I want in the house library, but I'm required to write up book reports and discuss them with her. Most of the time this exercise is pretty easy, because Grandma Purse hasn't read the book. When I ask why anybody would buy books and not read them, she tells me that in her family books were considered decorator items. We cover the topics in the official home-schooling packet, and we are done by eleven o'clock, and I am allowed to do whatever I want for the rest of the day. Like Dad, Grandma Purse is permissive, though in a different way. With Dad I wasn't allowed to stray too far, but Grandma Persephone lets me roam the estate at will. Which I do and then some.

We have another educational session in the evening. Grandma Purse makes herself a giant martini with one olive, and she lectures me on what she calls "life." On nice days we sit outdoors in the garden. On cold days we sit around the fireplace. She likes the fire, because she can throw her cigarette butts into the flames. For the first couple years I whittle spoons while Grandma talks. Sometimes Katharine, who drinks white wine, joins us, but not usually. Katharine always has something to do. Grandma Purse says Katharine's way of getting over the death of her fiance, Garvin Prell, is to keep busy.

"Today we will talk about the dirty little secret of our society." Grandma says to me one day. She always says "we," but "we" don't say much. She pretty much talks on, and I pretty much listen, or pretend to.

"People are born into and/or slip and slide into five social class categories revolving around the most important thing in American affairs. Guess."

"Love?"

"No."

"Family?"

"No."

"God?"

"No."

"Cars?"

"Close."

"Books?"

Grandma Purse bursts into laughter.

"The most important thing in American affairs is the big M. People today are willing to go on national television and discuss their sex lives, their addictions, their relationships, even their weight problems, but there is one thing they do not talk about. The dirty little secret is money. People might speculate on how much money others make, but they'll never reveal their own finances, unless to brag or lie. Young people pretend not to care about money, but that's only because somebody else is paying their bills. Once they pay their own way, they become obsessed like everybody else. The older a person, the more obsessed over money.

"The social class categories I want you to memorize include: Old Money, New Money, Funny Money, Hunger Money, and No Money.

"Most people from Upper Darby come from Old Money. You, my boy, are half Old Money. Remember that until your dying day. I've already arranged a trust fund for you, which officially makes you Old Money. It was Old Money that helped me gain custody of you. Old Money works through the unlisted phone numbers of judges, bankers, legislators, and corporate boards. Some of us are dyed in the wool conservatives, and some of us are wooly-minded liberals, except when it comes to the issue of Money, capital M. The problem with Old Money is the same problem as Old Age: slippage.

"It happened to me. During that awful period when I lost my husband and your mother and was forced to go down under to regain my wits, I learned that your grandfather had squandered the family fortune in establishing his land trust. Through persistence and minor criminal activity I was able to find that loophole in his damn land trust and sell off the Grace Pond property to those crooks from Belgium and restore our financial stability. Old Money I was born into, Old Money I will die.

"The largest category is Hunger Money. These people vary from that Massachusetts bastard, Selectman Lawrence Dracut, to your—pardon my French—dumbfuck grandparents, the Elmans, and even, bless his bleeding heart, Doc Mendy. They have enough money, but they crave more. They work themselves sick to get money, and then they spend it on things they don't want and don't need so they can feel hungry again, because deep down it's that hunger for money that brings meaning to their lives. Witness perfectly secure senior citizens buying lottery tickets. The Hunger Money people are never satiated. They live off their craving.

"Once in a while Hunger Money persons acquire so much money they can't spend it without gross effort. The Hunger Money folk now become New Money. New Money are the richest of us all. They also have the worst tastes, the worst habits, and the worst philosophies. These people rule. Any questions?"

"What's Funny Money?" I ask.

"Glad you asked," Grandma Purse said. "Funny Money people gain their wealth through illegal and extra-legal means. They include the mafia, drug lords of various stripes, Wall Street bunko artists, but also smaller fry, from building contractors to income tax cheats. The Funny Money crowd makes up a huge percentage of all the other categories, but they won't admit it. If they ever formed a political party they'd win in a landslide. Without Funny Money success is darned near impossible in the USA. Some of your ancestors on the Salmon side made their fortunes as Funny Money entrepreneurs, but not on my side of the family. The Butterworths have been Old Money since the Middle Ages. We're pure.

"The anxiety of the Funny Money people is in their craving to move out of the Funny Money category into New Money or Old Money or even Hunger Money. They're driven by the fear of going to jail and more subtle psychological forces, such as envy, and the desire for respectability. They are an unhappy lot, but then again so are the other groups. Money is not the root of all evil, it is merely the root of all.

"Nobody wants to be No Money—right?" I say.

"That's correct. No Money people have no ambition, or they have bad habits, or they missed out on how to live, or they're just unlucky. But it doesn't matter how they achieve their No Money status; they are not even loathed, they are ignored. The only attention they get is when they riot in the streets. To be No Money is to be unpatriotic, because our economic system and culture-values revolve around earning and spending. This is a commercial empire and not to partake of commerce is to be suspect.

"Your grandparents, the Elmans, for all their defects, are at least mentally stable, because they're secure in their category. They're Hunger Money people and will remain so until death. The people with problems are the ones who try to change categories. Katharine and your father are prime examples.

"Katharine is a divided person by money category. Her father was a moderately successful musician. He was Hunger Money. Her mother, my dearly departed sister, was Old Money who fell through the hippie realm into No Money. That was how Katharine grew up, conflicted and broke. As a college professor and scientist Katharine is forever doomed to be Hunger Money. She might have married Garvin to connect herself to her Old Money roots, but Garvin rejected Old Money for New Money, which went against Katharine's nature. His Old Money/New Money conflict led him to rash behavior, which I am sure put him in harm's way when he was run over by your no good father."

"My granduncle Monet?"

"Right—Fuckbump. He's another case of Old Money/New Money confusion. You know what he wants, what he really wants?" (I already know the answer to this question, but I don't let on.) "He wants the Salmons' trust for himself and that kid of his."

"Granduncle Monet has a child?"

"Right, he and that conniving Brazilian wife of Monet's are raising the kid in South America to take over the trust someday. Or I'm just a paranoid old woman. Probably both. There will come a day when you will have to confront the Salmons over the matter of the trust or be squeezed out of Upper Darby like everybody else."

"What about my dad?"

"Your father is a category of one. According to the testimony in his trial, he had a pretty fair income, which would qualify him as Hunger Money, but he lived a No Money lifestyle. Not only stupid, but unpatriotic."

"He called it his philosophy," I say.

"His philosophy is the reason he lost you to me. Anybody with any philosophy outside survival of the fittest is putting themselves in danger."

"But, Grandma Purse, I have to believe."

"In what? Old Money?"

"No, in Dad, in you, in God, in the great big world, in everything, in everybody. That's my philosophy. I'm a believer."

"You poor boy," says Grandma Purse, and she hugs me.

15

CATACLYSM CLASS

Every Sunday morning at 9:15 AM Grandma Elenore and Grandpa Howard show up at the mansion. They never come to the door but wait for me in the car. Grandma Purse never greets them. She peers at them through drawn curtains and mumbles to herself. I go out alone, carrying a lunch that Grandma Purse orders Soapy to make, a lunch that will not leave the bag because the eats the Elmans provide are more than enough.

Grandpa drives us to Keene to St. Bernard's Catholic Church for ten o'clock high mass. After church we go to Lindy's Diner for a giant breakfast. I always order bacon and pancakes with maple syrup. Then it's on to the Elmans' mobile home.

I think at first it will be stressful to have to deal with Spontaneous Combustion again, but he turns out to be less of a problem than I imagined. Way back when I was an infant the Elmans' cat had seemed almost godlike. Now he is just a cat, difficult but not frightening. Sometimes he stalks me or leaps on my lap for no apparent reason, but usually he leaves me alone. I try to make contact with him telepathically, but he refuses to cooperate. It is only once in a while that he makes his powers known to me. For example, Grandma Elenore always spends a hour teaching me what she calls catechism class. I can never make that word "cat-echism" stick in my brain. It always turns into "cataclysm." The cat amuses himself by putting the mix-up in my brain.

Grandma Elenore tells me that since I am baptized I have a good chance of going to heaven, especially if I make my first holy communion. That is why she is teaching me what it means to be a Catholic. She gives me easy quizzes.

"Who made us?" she asks.

"God made us," I answer.

"Why did God make us?"

"God made us to know Him, to love Him, to serve Him in this world and to be with Him in the next."

Grandma Elenore helps me develop an idea that has been in my head for a long time, which is that there is another world after death where I might find you, look at your face, hear your voice, feel your arms around me.

Grandma Elenore teaches me to pray. She does not pray like Dad. When Dad prayed he was more likely than not to argue with God, and he never demonstrated faith, which is what you have to have to believe in God since there's no proof. Dad prayed to let off steam. Grandma Elenore believes, and in a humble way. She does not even use her own prayers; she uses prayers prepared by her church—the Our Father, the Hail Mary, the Glory Be to the Father, the Apostle's Creed. She repeats the same prayers over and over again. She never asks for anything from God for herself, nor does she criticize Him; she offers herself body and soul. She is holy and I love her, and I want to be like her, but I know that I can never reach the heights of love for God that she has. How can I be a good Christian if I love Grandma Purse, who makes fun of organized religions and brags that she is an atheist? I can't love God the way Grandma Elenore does. I love Him for my own selfish reason: to reach you, Mother. My plan is to trick God into letting me find you by pretending to be holy.

After cataclysm class and prayers, Grandma Elenore retires for her nap, and I go outside with Grandpa Howard. He teaches me how to work on *cahz*, lawn mowers, snowmobiles, but mainly we keep his trash collection trucks tuned up. Thanks to Blue

Heron Village, Grandpa expanded his business. He now has three Honeywagons with two-man crews for each. He runs the business and does all the mechanical work, but he only goes on a dump run when one of his felons (as Elenore calls his crew members) doesn't show up for work. Grandpa plans to retire in a couple years. He's agreed to sell his business to Pitchfork (a.k.a. the ignoramus) and a silent partner, Critter Jordan. I'm already handy with tools, so I'm a quick learner, which pleases Grandpa.

He also teaches me about guns. We target shoot with Grandpa's .22 "plinker" every Sunday afternoon. We don't have to go very far. Grandpa Howard sets up targets in the yard. I shoot at bottles, tin cans, aluminum cans, plastic jugs filled with water, and various other inanimate objects. "More fun to destroy something than put holes in a paper target," Grandpa says to me one summer day.

"You ever go hunting, Grandpa?" I ask.

"Useta. Useta love it. I still love it."

"But you don't do it."

"I swore off hunting back before you were born."

"Why, Grandpa?"

"I've become a softy in my old age." He has a faraway look in his eye, and I know he has more to say on this subject, but he won't and he doesn't and I never find out his secret.

Sunday at the Elmans means we skip lunch and eat a giant, late-afternoon supper. They take me back to my mansion at 8 PM. They do not come in, and Grandma Purse does not greet them.

This goes on for a year, until one day Grandma Elenore tells me it is time for me to decide whether I should make my first holy communion. My answer is a definite yes. I want to be as close to God as I can. I'm nervous, however. I must confess my sins. What will the priest say when I tell him how selfish I am, that I plan to trick God? Perhaps I should not confess at all, because if I do then maybe the priest will tell God what I'm up to.

I know what you're thinking, Mother, that God knows all and therefore knows that I am joining His church under false pretenses. I thought about that, and I have concluded that God does not pay attention to lowly beings such as myself. No doubt God could know what I am thinking, but He doesn't pay attention because He has better things to do. I'm sure He listens to you. If the subject of my deceitfulness comes up, tell Him I'm sorry. Mother, is love a form of selfishness? Am I just pursuing this idea of loving everybody—especially loving you—simply because love makes me feel good? What if love didn't make me feel good? Would I still seek love?

I'm in this worry zone, in the Elman kitchen, alone, when I spot Spontaneous Combustion at his spy station on top of the refrigerator. He eyes me from a crouch position, tail swishing.

"You grow stupider year by year," Spontaneous Combustion says.

"Then how come all of a sudden I can read your thoughts?" I say.

"Happiness makes a person stupid. Strife focuses the mind. There's more of a self in strife. You are closer to being you, which is bringing on your misery and temporarily raising your IQ. What do you think of that, dummy?"

"I don't know," I say weakly.

"'I don't know' is one of the marking phrases of your generation, as in, 'Like, I'm going to the movies, to see, like, I don't know—you understand what I'm saying?' 'You understand what I'm saying?' being another marking phrase. I pity you poor youths; you don't know what's happening, and you constantly beg for understanding from those who beg you for understanding."

"What am I going to do, cat? Confess my sins? Take communion?"

Spontaneous Combustion leaps off the refrigerator and runs off into the other room, breaking not only visual but telepathic contact. I'm alone again with only my thoughts for company.

Another day back in the mansion I hear Grandma Purse on the telephone arguing and shouting. She's talking to Grandma Elenore. She bangs down the phone, lights a cigarette, paces around the house, then announces that she's taking to her bed. I follow her up. I learn about one of the many boners of contention between the Elmans and the Salmons. Seems as if when Grandpa Howard was starting up his business he dumped

SPOONWOOD

some rubbish on the trust lands. He was caught and had to pay a fine.

That Sunday at the Elman place, Grandma Elenore and I have a long talk about Jesus and forgiveness and sin and confusion and faith. I feel less confident than before.

"Grandmother Persephone called me the other day," Grandma Elenore says.

"She yells and swears but she doesn't mean it," I jump to her defense.

"Well, I don't know about that. She told me that your therapist believes you're not ready to commit to a religion. Much as I hate that woman I suspect she may be right."

"You mean I won't be making my first holy communion?"

"I talked to the priest and he thinks we should wait until you're out of therapy. What do you think?"

"I don't know what I think."

"Do you think you are ready to commit wholly and unselfishly to Jesus Christ?"

I'm tongue-tied. I want to cry but I don't. I just shake my head no.

"That's all right, Birch," Grandma Elenore says. "I shouldn't have rushed you. As long as you're living with your Grandmother Persephone it's going to be difficult for you to open yourself up to Christ. So let's just time our bide."

MY MYSTERIOUS BROTHER

Like Dad, your mom had a nervous breakdown following your death, and like Dad she more or less recovered. (I'm a little vague about what a nervous breakdown is. If nerves break down, you would think that persons with broken nerves would be less nervy, but the truth is the reverse. Persons with broken nerves are extra nervy.)

Dad is released from prison and disappears for a year or so. Then rumors circulate that he's back in the area, laying low. In the years from ages eight to eleven, I don't think about him much. I begin my explorations of the trust lands. When Grandma Purse thinks I am only playing on the estate grounds, I am going deep into the woods. You might think that life in the woods would be lonely for a boy, but it isn't like that at all. I find playmates everywhere. I do it by stalking. The habit—and skill—began with Spontaneous Combustion when I was an infant, and I refined it when I was living with Dad and I eavesdropped onto the lives of insects.

Ants are like fraternity brothers living in a communal house and getting drunk in the basement: they can't walk a straight line. Caterpillars are homeless wanderers and charter members of

Overeaters Anonymous. They snack continuously until they're too fat to make their legs go, and then they check into the Betty Ford Clinic, where they're put on a strict diet of no calories and subjected to chemotherapy and reconstructive surgery and emerge with wings. They spend the remainder of their short lives flying around looking for sex. I like the spiders best of all. They are easiest to find shortly after dawn, when the dew on their webs beads up and shines in the morning sun. A spider is like a writer or an artist who builds an elegant studio for himself that is so satisfying he sits motionless in the center of it for hours to contemplate his achievement, until somebody drops in for dinner. Like any good host, he probes the innards of his guests and draws out their vitals to sustain him.

Dad's interest is Wood. Grandma Purse's interest is Money. Grandma Elenore's interest is God. Grandpa Howard's interest is Mechanics. Katharine's interest is Science. Soapy's interest is Food. Roland's interest is Soil. Spontaneous Combustion's interest is Himself. My interest is Everything Else. While other boys watch TV, I watch the world around me. I go from observing insects to creatures that leave tracks in the snow—deer, hares, red squirrels, coyotes, bobcats, ferrets, wild turkeys, and black bears. I see them from the lean-to at the ledges where I go to visit you, Mother. I keep thinking we'll bump into each other, but it never happens. Below me, overturning a dead log, is the bear. He's eating the slugs and bugs that inhabit the moist zone between earth and rotted wood.

Late one fall day I stumble upon a bear's hibernation den. Before I see him I smell him, like a nasty kitchen sponge. He'd dug out the den from the side of a hill and covered himself with branches. I creep closer, until I see his long dark bristly hairs. An ear twitches. I shout, "I am one with you!" But he does not move. I slink off, elated. I visit the spot all that winter. I see where he came out briefly, rummaged around sleepily, then went back to bed. One spring day he's gone, leaving a big pile of bear poop full of twigs nearby. I try to follow him but quickly lose the trail. I never see him again.

. . .

I also explore the world of water. Scores of new houses have been built in the woods behind Grace Pond, but the pond itself has been left as a preserve, the part of the trust charter Persephone and the buyers of the pond could not dodge around. No development is allowed on the shoreline.

In the summer, Grandma Purse buys me a mask, a snorkel, and fins. She drives me to the pond and sits by the shore and smokes while I stalk schools of perch and punkinseed, the lone pickerel, and the whiskered hornpout, which raises clouds of muck motes when he burrows in the bottom. I explore beaver lodges, and I will tell you that no gloomier place exists than the home of a beaver—dark, dank, still, claustrophobic. The beaver lives in a stick house; I lived in a stick house with Dad, but it wasn't gloomy because it had fire. Beavers don't have fire. God said to the beaver, "To you, I give fur, a flat tail, and a lifelong companion to share the despair of your dismal abode." God said to man, "To you, I give tools—a Bic lighter and a Bic pen—go put on your pants." Or words to that effect.

My explorations cost a beaver his life. I dive down deep, and come up from the bottom into a beaver lodge, shocking a pair of beavers in their love nest. They scatter, and I am amused. But the next day, I find bones and some gristle of a beaver near the shore, along with tracks in the mud. A couple of coyotes had killed and eaten one of the beavers I'd panicked. There's a reason beavers build lodges—they're as much forts as dwellings. Beavers also mate for life, and my intrusion widowed one of the pair. I remembered Dad telling me that without a mate a beaver is a lonely bachelor or spinster. The beaver does what he has to do because he has to do it. He gnaws on a tree, never knowing whether the tree will fall to the ground and provide him with nourishment and building materials for his home, or will fall into another tree and get hung up, making his labors fruitless, or will fall on his head and kill him. His philosophy of life is that you never know what will happen when you gnaw on a tree, but that you must continue to gnaw.

A remarkable event occurs late in the spring of my tenth year. By now I'm going where I please without Grandma. I find a deer trail in the woods, and I climb a tree in hopes the deer will walk by me. I know a lot about deer, because Grandpa Howard has told me and because I read books. (At the moment I've read one-third of all the books in the Salmon library. I should be done before I reach my teen years.) I know that if I climb real high in the tree, my scent will not be picked up by the deer. I feel protected inside a tree, and I can see down at the underlings of creation. I'm a spy, Mother.

It's June and the leaves are bright and clean. I'm sitting on the branch of a maple tree thinking about that bright green color of fresh leaves when a doe deer appears below. She's brown, with a white patch on her rump. She's walking slowly, her head rigid, as if she has a stiff neck. She stops for no apparent reason, goes on again, in a small circle now; round and round she goes, and then she lies down on her side. I think maybe she's going to sleep, but then I hear a low moan. And pop! Out he comes, a little fawn, about the prettiest thing I've ever seen in my life.

The fawn stands upon his legs for the first time—and collapses. But he gets up again, and this time takes his first steps. I remember the old days when I crawled at great speed. I want to jump down from the tree (I'd need a parachute, I'm so high up) and tell that little guy that everything is going to be just fine, even though I'd be lying.

In a few minutes mom and child are gone, she nudging him along with her nose. I scramble down my tree and inspect the scene—blood in the leaves, tracks departing. Mom's hooves are sharp, and she makes clearly defined hoofprints, but her fawn is so light he barely stirs the ground. Eventually, though, I find a good print in soft ground. My fawn has a slight askew curve to his left front hoof. It will make him easy to identify among other deer.

That Sunday I tell Grandpa Howard about the fawn. We are in the barn in a pit, and Grandpa is putting a muffler onto one of his Honeywagons. He'd dug out the pit and lined it with concrete blocks, which are starting to bow in slightly, so that I worry that the whole thing might collapse and we will be buried alive.

"You like watching that fawn being born?" he asks.

"Yes, Grandpa," I say.

"Would you like to see this fawn again?" Grandpa asks.

"I sure would."

"Deer live in families, in which the females are heads of the household, and like most families they're as conservative as Ronald Reagan's socks. If you can learn your fawn's habits, you can predict where he'll be."

"So I can see him again."

"Right. It'll be harder than you think, but you go ahead."

"How did the deer happen to get born?" I ask.

"What do you mean?"

"How did the fawn get to be in the deer's belly?"

"Oh, that—that's called the facts of life," Grandpa says, and I can tell by his tone that he wants no more said about the subject.

That night, after the Elmans take me home to my great big beautiful mansion, I ask Grandma Purse to tell me the facts of life. She does, and in great detail. Grandma Purse is not one to leave out the necessaries. I learn about Sex, Birth, Old Age, Death, and do it all over again. In a word, ProCreate. Not that I understand at that moment what ProCreate is really all about, but I have the basics to brood over. In the next few years she and Katharine will tell me more facts—how ants mate, and birds, and frogs, and snakes, and fireflies, and bears, and wolves. The facts of life are part of my home schooling. Grandma Purse raises me to believe that sex is natural and more or less wholesome, except of course sex between people. She doesn't come right out and say so, but I have the impression that she doesn't think that having sex is a good idea. I try to imagine myself having sex, but I don't like the picture that comes to mind. The thought that you and Dad had had sex is even more disturbing. In those formative years I go out of my way not to think about human sex.

For the first year I don't really have an idea of how to keep tabs on my fawn or his family. In the second year I go from knowing practically nothing to being an expert. That's how I learn—from Not Knowing to All of a Sudden Knowing. I don't even need tracks to predict where my deer family will be. The season, the weather, the time of day, their ingrained habits tell me what I need to know. Books, Grandpa, pawprints, deer pellets, antler scrapes on hemlock trees—they all teach me.

From the tracks I count twelve different animals in the clan my deer lives with. (Ideally, a boy has a dear family; I have a deer family.) Every once in a while I'll see two or three in the group, but never all at once and never my mysterious brother. I can see where they have been, but not my deer. I keep track of what the deer are eating, where they sleep, the shape and consistency of their pellets, the types of scrapes where the bucks rubbed the velvet off their antlers, the difference in gender behavior. The does stay with their fawns and close to the family clan. The bucks prefer the lonesome rider life, but they sometimes join the family, and sometimes congregate among themselves. Once I see five bucks all together, gesturing and mooing at one another with such enthusiasm I swear they're discussing the world series between the Braves and the Yankees (won by the Yankees in six games that year).

In the spring the deer gorge themselves on all the sprouting leaves. They especially like the tender shoots growing out of logging cuts. In the summer they move to fields, where they graze on grass and alfalfa. In the fall they eat apples, beech nuts, and acorns. For a month in the late fall the deer all go crazy in their own kind of Mardi Gras celebration. Their sole interest is having sex. They are less wary and I am able to observe them. They are part of my sex education.

The bucks, who only a month earlier were enjoying each other's male company, are now locking horns (not a metaphor). Their necks swell, and the does show off their rear ends, and the bucks mount them, sometimes missing, sometimes connecting; sometimes the does are not interested and run away. The spectacle is scary and funny and disturbing. Some does seem frightened and confused. Some bucks are seriously injured in their battles. Once I see two big bucks fighting for the privilege of mating, while four females, looking a little bored, stand around waiting for the fun part, and other lesser bucks watch the fight, which seems to make every animal all the hornier. Meanwhile, a little spike horn sneaks in and mounts one of the does. I wonder if it's my deer who does the deed that rubs the face of survival of the fittest in the snow. I hope not. I hope my deer will be like me, lonesome and pure. Afterward, I find my deer's prints in the ruckus, but it's impossible to tell which one in the melee he was.

In the winter, the family moves into a deer yard, a small area where they hunker down, moving very little to conserve energy, feeding on hemlock buds, not a very nutritious fare but good enough to keep them going until the spring growth on the hardwoods. The deer make highways in the snow. By March the snow banks along the sides of these paths might be four or five feet high. The deer yard comes to look a little bit like a town that includes restaurants, roads, and motel bedrooms under the hemlock trees.

At this point, I've had enough experience in observing deer signs and in thinking about my dear deer family that my knowledge surpasses Grandpa's, as he admits when I start drawing maps of my deer's family haunts—fields, orchards, acorn havens, winter deer yards, fall orgy arenas. Every time I see a footprint from my cleft-hoofed buck, I put a check mark on my map, along with the date. Eventually I'm able to plot out his day-to-day course.

My work pays off one late spring day in year three of my deer's life. I stake out a trail between the field where my deer sleeps and the grove of young red maples where he eats breakfast. I sneak out of the mansion before dawn and climb a tree and wait. Nothing that morning. I get back to the mansion in time for a quick bite to eat and my lessons in Grandma Persephone's boudoir. Next dawn, same story. The third dawn I am treated to the sight of a new fawn. It walks right under me. I wonder where the mom is. When I come down from my tree I follow the hoofprints of the fawn and discover where its mother waited and watched, only a few feet into the woods from my tree. The print of the mother has a cleft in it. My deer isn't a boy, he's a girl, and a mother at that.

THE WOLF PINE

I stay away from people, especially other kids, for a long time (Lord knows they are easy to avoid in the woods, because they make so much noise and they rarely take notice). I imagine myself a wild animal, and so I have an animal fear of people. Well, it isn't fear exactly. It's suspicion that in dealing with people I am dealing with Unpredictability, which is what bears and humans have in common. You never know what a bear or a person is going to do, because they're not sure themselves. Another reason, according to Doc Mendy, is Dad. He never actually warned me against the human race, but everything in his behavior told me to watch out. I am not particularly curious about people. They don't strike me as any more or less interesting than, say, the daily life of a chipmunk living in a firewood pile. What gets me tangled up in human beings is the challenge of sneaking up on them. The key is get above them and don't move if they happen to look in your direction. I watch the trails from trees.

People, like animals, can be categorized. Each group has different habits and habitat and has to be stalked accordingly. My categories include kids, loggers, hikers, snowmobilers, and poachers. I write about my observations, and Grandma Purse corrects

my papers for grammar and style and spelling but does not com-
ment on the rightness or wrongness of my activities and opinions.

The most clueless of forest creatures are human children.
They make too much noise, and they tend to get scared for no
reason; as they age, they become destructive and disrespectful.
From my hidden perches in the trees, I watch teenagers shoot at
trees with their guns; I watch them party down and leave their
empties behind in the woods; I watch their struggles to fornicate;
I watch them argue and weep and laugh at nothing at all. I vow
never to be a teenager.

Hikers, cross-country skiers, and snowmobilers have a few
things in common. They stick mainly to trails. They tend to look
straight ahead (and miss 90 percent of the scene). They are always on the move. They are rarely found alone. They are easy to
locate and spy on. I'll climb a tree just off a trail, sit on a branch,
and watch. Snowmobilers I understand—the fast ride, the cold
air blasting in their faces, the excuse to dress up in funny clothes.
I figure cross-country skiers are looking for the same thrills but
don't have the money to buy a snowmobile. Or maybe the noise
of the machines annoys them (it annoys me). What I can't understand is the hikers.

I walk the woods, but I always have a reason. Hikers walk for
the sake of walking. They have no purpose but the next step forward. If they stop to look around it's from the top of a cliff,
which doesn't make much sense to me. If a person's kick is a sce-
nic vista, why go in the woods, where the vistas are mainly obscured by the trees? I suppose some of the hikers walk the woods
for exercise, but I can't sympathize with the concept of exercise.
Why would anybody want to exert themselves just for the sake
of exerting themselves when there is always plenty of work to do
that is exertion enough? I conclude that because of those ugly
backpacks and their peculiar clothes—big, clunky boots, short
pants, funny hats—hikers are ashamed to be seen in public, and
that is why they go into the woods. Their walking is no more
than straight-line neurotic pacing.

Loggers on the trust lands are not allowed to do their work
with skidders and feller bunchers (don't you just love that name?).

On the Salmon Forest Trust Conservancy horses are used to drag the logs out. I enjoy spying on the woodcutters. They refer to each other as "pardner." "Hey pardner, you got a cigarette for a tired man?" Or, "This is my pardner, he's more feller than buncher." (Actually, nobody said that, but it gets the point across.) The pardners live in a handmade house of rough-cut pine boards on an upland farm, no neighbors, on a dirt road. Obadiah Handy, like Dad, is a townie. His family has lived in Darby since before the stone age. But the Handys all died out or left town. Obadiah was alone. One day he had a chimney fire from creosote buildup. The fire leaked through the crumbling bricks and burned the house down and the adjoining barn, destroying not only dairy cows and buildings but all the farm equipment. No insurance. Obadiah did save his late father's prize Percherons. The draft horses had been his father's hobby, entered in pulling competitions at fairs. Obadiah could have sold the farm to a developer, for surely he did not want to farm, but he liked his land. "It's all I know or can feel," I hear him say to his pardner. For almost six months, he lived in the only structure left on his property, a shed. And then he met his future pardner, and they built their strange abode. Obadiah leased out his acreage to a working farmer and went into the horse-logging business.

I obtain the following information from Katharine. Charley Snow had showed up at the commune in the 1970s. He lived in my school bus home. He had been a draft dodger and peace activist. When the commune closed Charley stayed on in Darby. He liked the land; he was into organic farming, alternative energy, and handmade housing. He and Obadiah met at a contra dance. Obadiah called him Chahley. In fact everybody in Darby called Charley Chahley until he began calling himself Chahley, even if he never lost his New York accent. Obadiah is big and slow-moving, a scratch-your-head kind of thinker. Chahley is quick and impulsive, with a high falsetto voice and an aggressive manner. He talks a mile a minute, as much with body motion as mouth. In fact, he sometimes breaks out in a modified dance when he speaks. Chahley designed their house, though Obadiah did most of the work on it.

In their business dealings Chahley does all the talking. Loggers have to be pretty agile in the thickets of business as well as the woods. They have to make deals with consulting foresters, wealthy landowners, independent-minded truckers, and saw mill superintendents. Chahley won't stand for criticism of the men's work. He gives long lectures on the efficacy (his word) of horse-logging. He likes to dicker. By contrast, Obadiah is so shy that he blushes when he is asked a question, and he can't seem to hold eye contact with anyone or speak to a stranger and make sense. But in the woods, when the loggers are alone and there is work to be done, Obadiah gives the orders and Chahley obeys.

The horses are both geldings. Francis is mainly sienna-colored, with a big, almost white rump, a quietly stubborn beast. Obadiah talks sweet to him. "Now Francis, I know you think this work is beneath you, but believe me you're doing the world a favor. Now pull." Reluctantly, Francis pulls. Fenwick is gray with black spots and has long silky hair just above his hooves. He is smaller than Francis, not as strong, but he always takes the lead, and he never complains; in fact, he likes the work for the very reason that it is work; in attitude he is an "equine existentialist," which is what Chahley calls him.

One day the men are in a part of the trust I've overlooked because it is high up but ordinary—just unbroken woods, trees and rocks not particularly noteworthy and off the logging road a couple hundred yards, no views. The ground is covered with short moosewood trees, whose big leaves hide me well but obscure my view. I don't really know where the loggers are, though I can smell their horses and hear the chain saws running. I move slowly through the moose wood and come out into a clearing, under the deep shade of a huge lone pine. Actually, it's several pines that have grown together and formed a giant, ten or twelve feet across and rising far above all the trees in the neighborhood. I wonder whether the pines have actually become one.

"One!" I shout to the tree, and my voice returns in echo. Suddenly, I am no longer interested in the woodcutters. I want to climb that tree.

It is easy going, because dead branches project out like ladder steps every which way for the first thirty feet. After that I have to fight my way through living branches heavy with pine needles. Even if I fall I will land in a tangle of other branches. After more climbing, I break out of the dense part of the tree, and I can smell the sun in the pine needles. Eventually I reach a natural platform, where branches cross over each other and the view opens up. I can see where the tree has grown around charred wood. Apparently lightning hit the tree decades ago, and the tree (or trees?) healed over in such a way as to create a platform of maybe two hundred square feet.

I sit and gaze out at the world. Heck, there is enough room up here for a ping pong table, a couch, and a TV; I am above the crowns of the maples, oaks, and birches below. I see Grace Pond in the distance, fields, Upper Darby Road, the ledges, and my mansion and estate grounds. I've stumbled upon the best place to view the entire trust lands. I hear a noise and look down. The loggers are walking toward my tree, chain saws in hand. Oh-oh.

I scramble down the tree but don't quite make it to the bottom. I'm in the dense greenery just above them, and I hear them talking.

"Quite the wolf pine," says Obadiah.

"It's a lot older than anything else around here," Chahley says.

"There was a field here once, and they must have left this tree, or probably it was four or five trees, for shade for the cows."

"It would scale good. Some hundreds of dollars in this tree."

"Nobody's cut it before because there's no way to notch it so it knows where to fall," Obadiah says, "and you can't tell by eyeballing it. It's a widow maker."

"I'll cut it," Chahley says. "You can move the horses to a safe distance and stay with them."

"My life wouldn't be worth living without you, Chahley." Obadiah takes Chahley's hand, and the two loggers stare up at the wolf pine, right at me, though they don't see me. They stare for a long time, and then they go off, still holding hands, and the wolf pine and me remain untouched for another day.

18

STRANGER IN THE BIRCH MILL

Obadiah and Chahley are cutting white pine, rock maple, a few red oaks, and one solitary white birch. The whiteness of its butt log makes it easy to pick out, and I keep looking at it and looking at it, wondering what happens to a tree after it is cut by loggers.

I come back a week later with that question still on my mind. The loggers are gone and so are the logs. I follow the horse tracks until I smell the horses. I've arrived at the log yard, where the logs are separated into three piles—pine and hemlock; maple, oak, and yellow birch; and white birch. Somewhere in that stack of white birch is my butt log. The woodcutters, having just finished sandwiches, sit around and smoke and watch a man operate a cherry picker, plucking white birch logs from the pile and placing them on a flatbed truck.

Obadiah smokes Old Gold and Chahley smokes a French cigarette from a holder.

Mister Cherry Picker grabs a birch log and gently places it on the truck.

The horses munch their lunch from grain buckets, at the same time dropping turds and conversing in horse language. I tune in.

Fenwick does most of the talking. Francis just kind of agrees, muttering the horse equivalent of uh-huh, because he knows that Fenwick insists on being agreed with. The ability to eat, drop turds, and at the same time converse, while keeping the whole performance graceful, is a feat I admire.

Mister Cherry Picker grabs another birch log. Another. When he is finished, Mister Cherry Picker gets off his machine and chains the logs on the big truck and drives away. The truck is white with birth (typo, I mean white with birch). Me, I leave my vantage point behind a rock and climb a tree. As the truck moves slowly over the rough logging road, I drop from the tree onto the logs stacked on the truck and lie down flat. From the trust lands, the truck pulls out onto Upper Darby road, picks up speed, and winds down the long hill into the town, air brakes making that tortured sound. From there the truck turns onto the main high-way. Now the truck is going sixty. Every once in a while the en-tire load of logs shifts slightly. I am afraid of rolling off onto the highway, so when I see a space between some logs I crawl down into the notch. The load shifts and I am stuck. I might be crushed at any minute.

I remember my Grandma Elenore's statue of The Blessed Vir-gin Mary, so I pray to The Blessed Virgin Mary. "Here I am, The Blessed Virgin Mary, stuck and ready to die because of the sin of curiosity and the character flaw of bad judgment. Make it quick, and if I should go to heaven, please introduce me to my mother." The Blessed Virgin Mary shifts that load, the logs part a bit, and I am able to scramble up out of my death notch. Two minutes later we go around a corner and the space where I had been closes up.

We travel about ten miles, turn off onto a country road, and stop at a big square wood-frame building alongside a river. I climb down the rear of the truck using log chains for handholds and, as the truck slows, drop to the ground, roll four or five times, and pick myself up out of the dust. I smell cut birch wood, can taste it in the mouthful of road grime I'd bit into when I fell. I hear the river argue with rocks; I hear shop machines chug and groan; I hear a screech that scares me because it sounds like me when I was a baby. I have the feeling then that I am time-raveling.

The yard is beautiful in its own way, dominated by stacks of white birch logs high as houses and running for hundreds of feet. Here and there are little mountains of scrap wood and sawdust. The building is old and run down but solid, a fire trap waiting for a match and a turn of fate. I don't see any sign of recent improvements. The year could be 1950.

The double doors to the building are wide open, and it is obvious why when I walk in. The heat. I wait for someone to ask me who I am and what I am doing here. I wonder what I will say. I don't want to lie and I don't want to tell the truth. What to do? No need to worry, because nobody even looks at me. I expect they think I'm somebody's kid, waiting for his mom or dad. At the time, though, I think maybe I have been squashed to death on the truck, and I am invisible, a ghost like you, Mom. Do ghosts go on trips or stay put? Do they meet other ghosts and join clubs, go to war, shop at the Celestial Mall, sing, tinker, watch TV, whittle, attend concerts, hold down jobs? What do ghosts do with all the spare time that eternity provides?

I see right away where the screech comes from. The building might be fashioned-old, but the great big band saw is art of the state. I can't get over the feeling that the screech in that saw is the screech that was me as a baby. I wait for twenty minutes or so when my birch butt log comes down a chute from the outside, is grabbed by a machine arm and placed on a conveyor belt, and runs through the saw—zip, screech, and out. Boards spill onto another conveyor belt. My butt log has just had its butt kicked.

A woman in overalls and an apron stands beside the conveyor belt with a hooked stick. She flips a board over with the hook and tosses it onto another belt going in another direction. I follow the first board. It empties into a bin, where it is picked up by a man wearing red suspenders over a hairy, naked upper body. He feeds the board into a hole. Little birch wood shovel handles spit out another hole.

The machines make the wood pieces you never think about but that show up on toys and tools and gadgets. One machine births salad spoons, another salad forks. They are not like Dad's, though. They are all the same, and they came pouring out as if by magic. I wonder what Dad would think of all this.

My favorite machine births Scrabble squares.

All of a sudden the machines shut down and it is quiet. The sudden silence stops up my throat and for a moment I cannot breathe. I think everyone is looking at me. Or maybe that is what I hope, because I don't like the persistent feeling of being—like you, Mother—a ghost. But it isn't me that stopped the machines. It is some force, mysterious to me. The shop men and shop women gather into a coven and twist their bodies into unusual positions, as if somebody dumped itching power into their pants. This half-dance, half-exercise goes on for about ten minutes, and then it is back to work. All this time nobody looks at me. I am begging them with my eyes: look at me, look at me. I have a great realization then, a realization that keeps coming back to me, and that, I am sure, will haunt me all the days of my life. Outside the trust lands I'm a stranger.

I hitchhike back to Darby, getting a ride from a frumpy woman in a beat-up Ford Pinto. "A young boy like you shouldn't be thumbing a ride—it's dangerous," she scolds. I love her, and I want to go home with her and be her son, but I just hang my head, bashful and inarticulate.

Grandma Purse welcomes me as if I'd been gone for twenty years. She suspects something has happened to change me, but she never says a word; she takes me in her arms and hugs me with her clawlike hands.

I tell her what happened, except the part about almost getting killed by the moving load on the truck.

"I'm glad that woman picked you up," she says.

"How come nobody else would give me a ride?"

"Nobody owes you a ride, Birch," Grandma says. "In this society, you live on your own initiative, or you die."

That Sunday I tell Grandpa Howard about my adventure.

"I've done a lot of hitchhiking in my life, and I'll say this: rich people don't pick you up. It's poor folks and perverts that supply hospitality."

"What's a pervert?"

"A pervert is the reason a young boy should not be hitchhiking," he says.

"Oh, yes," I say, as if I know what he is talking about.

I tell him about the stacks of logs at the birch mill, and the fantastic buzz saw, and the lady with the hooked stick.

"She was grading the boards," Grandpa Howard says.

I tell him about how the machines shut down and the people gathered and made strange movements with their bodies.

Grandpa Howard smiles. "They were taking a tai chi break. It's in the union contract. The machine operators do repetitive work that's dangerous and tedious. Tai chi helps relieve the stress."

That night I ask Grandma Purse what a pervert is. She tells me what perverts do. I am astounded. It doesn't sound perverted. It sounds interesting, until she gets to the part about being murdered.

Later in my bed, staring at the moonglow on my yellow submarine wall painting, I am thinking about those machines birthing Scrabble squares. They rain down from the sky like the detritus of comets, landing on a big board, the letters making words, clever phrases, and oh-so-elegant sentences. In the dreams I can never understand the words, and no opponent is on the other side of the board for me to challenge. I wonder if any Scrabble player but me thinks about birch trees and their contribution to words.

I pity the poor machine operators, all the fun they miss out on. Make a spoon by hand and you touch the tree, touch the raw wood, hear the wood split as you drop the maul onto the billet, and you touch the wood again, carrying it like something alive, and then you cradle it in your arms as you inspect it, and you work the wood with knives, touching it, always touching it. I find myself thinking about Dad.

19

MISSY

At age twelve I meet someone who will change my life for the better. Her name is Melissa "Missy" Mendelson, the youngest daughter of the Mendelsons. Missy is a year younger than I am, mature for her age in one way, immature in another. We meet down by Grace Pond. The first time I see her I resent her for playing in my domain. I'm so selfish, Mother. I just can't help it. She starts talking about saving the whales, and I tell her there are no whales in Grace Pond, and she says wouldn't it be great if there were, and the next thing you know we are speed-talking. I make my first friend.

Missy is taller than I am and very skinny. She wears thick glasses. Like me, she is bashful. She goes to private school, and she doesn't really like her summers at home because she doesn't have any friends here. She is the first girl I meet to talk to, and her presence excites me very much. It isn't a sex thing—I don't have sex on the mind at that age; it is, well, I don't know how to describe the feeling, it is just a feeling of wonder. When I am with her I am happy, and when I am not with her I make myself happy by thinking about her.

Missy

Most Darby kids swim at the lake where you were a lifeguard, but Missy and I swim and fish at Grace Pond, even though there's no beach and the shoreline is weedy or rocky or both and the bottom is mucky. We like the privacy. We like to muck around. I show her the place where Dad sunk his boat, but it's gone, which confirms my suspicions that Dad is out there someplace, watching over me or maybe just spying. Afterward we walk a couple miles down off the heights of the trust to Ancharsky's Store, drink Cokes, and hang around the Green.

I show her how to stalk people in the woods, but she isn't very good at it, and so we don't do that very much. We climb trees, or build "nests"—Missy's word—among the rocks. To relax from our forays in the wilds we sit around her room with the doors locked and play board games and listen to music. Or sit out on one of the many Mendelson decks in lounge chairs and drink pink lemonade. During these times, Doc Mendy doesn't act like my therapist but like any other dad—or what I believe real dads are supposed to be like—and I am grateful to him for that. Missy and I talk about our secret fears and desires.

I show her Forgot Farm. My school bus home, the Volkswagen in the briars, the falling-down yurt and outhouses, all the old hippie remnants have been removed. Even the well is filled in. The land has been allowed to return to "natcha," as Grandma Purse would say.

Missy is never hateful, but hate is her favorite word. She hates her nose, she hates her dark kinky hair, she hates her thick glasses, she hates allergies that won't allow her to wear contacts, and most of all she hates her body. Missy believes she has some kind of terrible disease that prevents her from being a real girl. Her friends at school are growing boobs and some even have periods. (No reports of commas.) Doc Mendy and Maddy tell her she's normal, just a person who will mature late, but Missy is convinced that her parents are lying to protect her from the awful truth: that she will never mature.

I tell her she's lucky, that permanently immature people are the children of God. I tell her about my telepathic powers, and I suggest to her the possibility of remaining a child forever through sheer willpower. For the first time I am behaving like a child, talking like a child, in the grip of the wonder of childhood. After much discussion, Missy and I conclude that childhood is The Delightful State. We could stunt our hormone growth through willpower and telepathy, I tell her. We practice by levitating objects, but no matter how intense our thoughts, we cannot lift a dime. We do have some luck dissolving clouds. We lie on our backs and stare up at the sky, thinking deep thoughts, and eventually the clouds part for us.

"Do you want to become a teenager?" she asks one day as we lie on one of the many Mendelson decks while mentally locking in on a cotton-candy cloud.

"Never," I say.

"I have secret thoughts that maybe I do, and, like, maybe I don't," Missy says.

"Look at the terrible things they do," I say. "They litter, they drink, they take drugs."

"And they, like, have sex," she says.

"Do you want to have sex?" I ask.

"I thought about having babies, but not sex—no, not sex. I couldn't have sex or babies anyway. I'm just a freak of nature."

"What I hate most about teenagers is their dirty talk, using the 'ef' word all the time, worse than even Grandma Purse. I hear them when I spy on them. Look, I just dissolved that cloud."

"I don't enjoy their sarcasm," Missy says. "I wonder if you wanted to enough you could create clouds instead of, like, just dissolving them, which seems sort of violent."

We make a pact that we will never have sex until marriage (not that I intend to marry), or if we do have sex we will never tell each other about it, because it will be so gross it will ruin our friendship, which is sacred. And so forth, just kid talk, but it is serious business for us.

We play Monopoly and Scrabble and I tell her that these little wooden blocks are made by working people who do tai chi. Missy is good at Scrabble, but I am better. We watch rented movies on the VCR, such as *Third Encounters of the Close Kind*.

I find movie-watching liftupping and religious, and I wonder why Dad kept me away from the experience all those years. After the movie we have a long discussion about the possibility of intelligent life on other planets.

It is raining outside and we are in Missy's room. She is lying on her bed and staring up at the ceiling. I am lying on the floor, head on a giant beanbag sofa, and I am staring up at the ceiling. We have super-glued a mirror up there, so we can lie on our backs and look at each other and converse.

"You think it's possible?" she asks.

"That people would voluntarily be kidnapped by aliens?"

"No, that some people are, like, destined to live in a place far far away from anything they know growing up, even another planet."

"What do you mean by destined? What other planet?" I say.

"I don't know exactly," she says. "I have, like, this feeling that I don't belong anywhere I've been. That I'm not even on the right planet. That there's some far place where I truly belong—home, a real home."

"Not me," I say. "I was on the road for eons, and now I've arrived and for me the trust is not just a place, it's the only place. It's people outside the trust that creep me out, the way they live, and they're all so ugly."

"I'm ugly," Missy says.

"You're not ugly. You're beautiful, you're perfect."

She takes her glasses off. "Here, put these on," she says. "You need them more than I do." We both laugh. Laughing with Missy is about the most heavenly experience I can imagine.

"Who do you take after in your family?" I ask.

"My old maid aunt Priscilla on my mother's side," she says. "All the sisters are pretty but her."

I watch Missy in the mirror, a long lanky being, not a girl, not a woman, not a boy or a man, but some special kind of gender that I like a lot. "They used to say Priscilla was a look-alike for Eleanor Roosevelt. Who wants to look like her? Who do you take after? Your dead mother?"

"I guess I look like my dead grandfather Salmon."

"The Squire? Daddy says he was a great man."

"I guess. I think your father is a great man."

"I wouldn't know. He never tells me anything great. Your father is, like, unusual," Missy says.

"My father is the greatest of all men," I say. "I wish I didn't hate him and want to see him dead."

Missy can see my face in the mirror, and she says, "Birch, are you going to cry? Don't do it. It would upset me."

I master my emotions and do not cry.

"Do you ever see him?" Missy asks.

"I'm not allowed to, and Grandma Purse gets angry every time I mention his name, and the Elmans act real sad. Dad makes everybody sad. I just hate his guts."

"They say he's . . . well . . ."

"I know what they say, that he's the town drunk. And maybe he is but I still love him."

"I thought you said you hated him."

"That's what I just said, that I hate him."

"No. You said you love him. What do you think about when you think about him?"

"I'm a baby again, lying in my stick crib that he built, and he's working at his shaving horse making spoons, and I'm listening to the sound of his knives—*sip sip sip;* it's my lullaby."

"What do you mean, spoons?"

"Dad carves spoons out of wood, or at least he used to, and he taught me how and it's such a stupid way to pass the time. It all seems kind of useless and I don't carve them anymore, because, well, it makes me sad."

"You want to grow up to be like your dad?"

"I could never do it. I'm not good—I'm selfish. I don't care about anybody but me. I am basically evil. That's why I hate him. Because he's good."

"You're bad, Birch, but I'm worse. I'm spiteful to my mother and sister. I hate their beauty, that they've got it and not me. 'You're just a stick—honestly. Eat something,' my mom will say, like she's ashamed of me. And I'll just hate her when she talks to me like that, I'll just want to moosh her face into a meat grinder and throw my sister in for good measure. So you see I'm more evil than you are."

"I guess you are. I admire the hell out of you for it too."

"Thank you, but I don't admire myself."

"That's too bad, because self-admiration is the key to happiness."

"Are you happy, Birch?"

"I'm happy when I'm with you, Missy. Your friendship makes me happy."

"I'll be happy when I get boobs and I'm beautiful like my mother and she's old and ugly, and I can rub it in." Missy's words are mean but her voice is sad and full of love. "You don't know what it's like having a mother. You're better off because you don't have one."

I try to feel better off, but it doesn't work. I would take Maddy Mendelson as a mother even if she is a nag.

Missy and I don't hang around with the other kids, because we're Upper Darby snobs. We believe other kids are gross and stupid and violent.

20

POACHERS ON THE TRUST

After Missy leaves for private school, I go back to stalking wild animals and hikers, and home schooling. It's rewarding to read a book and write an essay about it and to listen to my grandma Purse discuss it; it's rewarding to learn new things about the world of science from Katharine. But there is a great big hole in my heart. I try to hide my feelings, but I can't fool Grandma Purse.

I climb into her bed and she puts her arm around my shoulders and hugs me and blows smoke rings for me to watch. "I made a mistake bringing you out here into this big and lonely house where you can't find friends," she says, her raspy voice full of regret. "I should have sent you to prep school, but I wanted you for myself. It's too late now. I don't know how to change myself, let alone change you. You want to go to Tasmania with me this year?"

"My mania is here, Grandma Purse," I say.

"I knew that. I'll be gone for a month. You'll be okay with Katharine and Soapy and Roland?"

"Yes, Grandmother, I will be okay."

I feel her strength flow into me. Unfortunately, it doesn't root and goes right through.

Missy comes home for the holidays, but I don't see her much because she and her family go south to vacation. Which I don't understand. There's nothing like the New Hampshire woods in the winter. Why go to a muggy, buggy place? I am more destitute than ever.

On the night of the first official day or winter four or five inches of fresh snow fall. It's over by morning, and there is no wind and the snow decorates the trees. The air is crisp, cold, and still. After morning home-schooling lesions I tell Grandma Purse I am going to go sledding. In fact, I am out into the chill looking for my deer.

It is her fourth year, middle-aged for a deer. Their bodies are still youthful at age five or six, but their teeth are getting on, which makes it harder for them to eat. By the time they're six or seven their front teeth are so worn they can't bite the hard twigs they have to munch on to strip buds for nourishment in the winter. Old deer usually weaken from lack of nutrition, especially after the snows begin to fall. Coyotes, or domestic dogs off the leash, chase them into exhaustion. If they escape the predators they'll lie down one fine day after a storm and just drift off to deer heaven. Death by jaws, death by starvation: why do you do this to your creatures, God?

I find the tracks of my deer family, though not of my doe. The deer are transitioning from fall to winter habits, though they have yet to move into their winter yards. Deer are like people. Some are smart, and some are stupid, and even the smart ones are stupid about something. The stupid ones use logging roads as trails for walking. They get shot in deer season. The smart ones stay off the roads, and the really smart ones, like my doe, devise hiding places and escape routes. But all deer are stupid about house and home. A deer family will stake out a territory and hole up for the winter until spring. The family will return to that same deer yard year after year. Sometimes they'll eat all the browse in the yard and starve to death even while food is in supply over the next hill.

I start back toward the main trail when I see tracks where a deer has come to a stop and stood still for a while. My doe. She's been watching me. I think about my doe and her wariness and the doom of winter; I think about you, Mother; I think about Missy. I stand alone in the woods, trembling with emotions I do not understand.

A big winter storm hits a week before Christmas, and then comes the hard cold that invariably sets in after the holidays. I stay away from the deer yard, because I know my scent could scatter the family. They'd return to the yard, of course, but they'd be weakened by the unnecessary exercise.

Grandfather Howard helps get me out of my funk. We are having a big bowl of popped corn, sitting around the wood stove.

"Look what I found in the snow yesterday," Grandpa Howard says. He puts a thirty-odd-six rifle shell-casing on the table. "Somebody's poaching deer on the trust lands, Birch. I saw blood on the snow and tracks beside this shell."

"Why do they poach?" I ask.

"Some do it to supplement the family food store," he says. "Back when we were short on cash, I was known to jack a deer out of season myself. That don't amount to much. Then there's ones who like the thrill. Kids mainly, not very good at the hunting part. It's professionals you got to watch out for. They kill deer and wild turkey, even ferrets and coyotes and porcupine. They sell the game to fancy restaurants in ski areas or as far away as New York. They sell to furriers, religious nuts, and quacks of various stripes." Grandpa Howard must be reading my mind, because he adds, "You stay out of the woods for a while. Understand? It could be dangerous."

"Yes, Grandpa," I say, but it's a lie. I am going to catch that poacher and turn him in. I think maybe if I can be a hero I'll have masses of adoring people surrounding me and I'll be less lonely. Suddenly, I'm thinking about Dad.

"Do you ever see Dad?" I ask.

"Only by accident," Grandpa Howard says, his voice flat, and he won't look me in the eye.

"I don't even know where he lives," I say.

"That's because he doesn't live anywhere. He moves from place to place."

"You think I'll ever see him?"

"When you're eighteen. If you want. That's what the law says."

End of conversation. Nobody I know wants to talk about Dad. I work hard at forgetting he exists. Dad, the man who lives in forgot places, is on the way to becoming a forgot person.

At the moment I'm interested in finding the poachers. I don't know exactly what I have in mind. I'm curious, I'm bored, but mainly I'm sad. I want something wild and strange to happened to me. I used to imagine that I was being watched by alien beings who were judging my behavior. If I'm a hero the regular people of the world, the Hunger Money people, will reward me with some kind of spectacle beyond my imaginings. I know it doesn't make much sense, but that is what I am thinking.

By now a fresh snow has covered any tracks that poachers might have made, but I am still able to discover where they have been. I check the deer yards in the area. Two of them show the routine of winter deer life, the paths in the snow, the chewed shoots of hemlock trees. Another deer yard has been harassed by coyotes. In a fourth deer yard I find what I am looking for— disturbed paths where the deer fled an intruder. The deer returned when it was safe. I bet that my poacher knows what I know, and that he will be back too.

This particular deer yard is the logical one to raid, because it is the closest to a town-maintained road. Even so, if a deer has been shot here the poachers would have to drag the animal more than half a mile, though most of the going is downhill. I inspect the area. I see broken branches and soft indentations where snow has covered clumps of tracks. From the disturbance I judge that two or three people have hauled a deer out.

The trail leads to a town road and a wide place where the snowplows turn around. No doubt the poachers parked their vehicle in this spot.

I try to think like the mastermind poacher. I plan this act very carefully. I am a hunter, and I know this particular deer yard. I know about the turn-around, so I'm probably a local guy. I am not a kid. A kid might take a pot shot at a deer, but he wouldn't know about the deer yard and he wouldn't have the wherewithal to get the deer out. A rifle shot at night would arouse suspicion, but it's not unusual to hear rifle fire during the daytime in the woods, especially on a weekend, when shooters do target practice, so I'll shoot the deer on a Saturday or a Sunday in broad daylight. I have a partner, maybe a brother or a best friend. One of us owns a pick-up truck or an SUV big enough to stuff a deer into the rear. Ideally, I'll watch the weather reports and commit my crime the day before a storm to cover my tracks.

Over the next couple weeks I learn some more about my poachers. He and his partner(s) are working on weekdays as well as weekends. They shot a half dozen wild turkeys and at least two more deer at another deer yard, the one that has already been disrupted by coyotes. I see from their tracks where one poacher has deliberately scattered the animals to panic them and another shot them as they ran down their paths. I have to stop them before they stumble onto my dear deer family.

I catch up to the poachers in an unexpected way, when I am not even looking for them. I am walking the snowmobile trail only a half a mile or so from Upper Darby Road when I hear the crack of rifle fire close by. Without thinking I start for the noise, clomping through knee-deep snow until I come to some rocks. I see movement not a hundred feet ahead. I freeze. I hear voices, but there is no alarm in the sounds so I know they haven't seen me. I creep closer, until I come to a big rock and hide behind it and peek over the top.

A big man in a red hunting cap and a full brown beard stands over the carcass of a bear. Beside him is a guy who could be his younger clone, maybe eighteen or nineteen, holding a rifle. His long brown hair is in a pony tail, which he constantly smoothes with his free hand. Beside him is a boy about my age. He is shorter than I, but very wide all the way around—head, shoulders, hips, chest. Not fat, just wide.

"Give me the bag," the man says.

The boy about my age fishes around in his pocket until he comes up with a plastic bag.

Meanwhile, the man appears to be feeling up the dead bear with the point of a knife. It is embarrassing to look at.

"I hear something," says the older boy.

I hunker down while they strain to listen.

"There's nothing out there," says the man. "Don't get trigger happy with that thing."

The older boy chuckles. Years ago when I was an infant I heard that laugh.

The man takes the bag from the younger boy.

"We're not going to shoot anybody, are we, Uncle Chester?" says the wide-bodied, younger boy.

"I'm tempted to shoot the Chinaman on general principals, but no, never mind. You're like your mother, Bez—you worry too much."

The older boy points the rifle at the younger boy and says, "You doublecross us, and I'll shoot you, okay?"

The man named Uncle Chester chuckles just like the older boy. "Don't scare him, Junior. Nellie won't like it."

"I wouldn't want that to happen. You're not a good daddy when you're shut off."

"Watch your mouth, Junior."

Uncle Chester stands holding the bag. I see a flash of red before he tucks the bag into young Bez's backpack. He wipes the knife on the hide of the bear and slips it into a sheath on his belt.

"Come on, let's hike," says Uncle Chester.

"What about the bear?" asks the boy named Bez.

"The coyotes and the crows will strip him clean."

The three poachers start walking away. I stand out from the cover of the rock. I have an idea to call out to them. Getting shot at or even shot seems grand. I have a good look at their backsides now and at the bear lying still in the snow. How could I be so stupid as to expose myself like this? I am about to duck behind the rock again when suddenly the young boy, Bez, turns around. He sees me, and the two of us stare at each other for what seems like an hour, though it's more like five seconds.

"Come on, Bez," Uncle Chester says.

Bez turns and walks off with Uncle Chester and Junior. I wait for them to wheel around and shoot me, but it doesn't happen. They just walk on, disappearing into the trees.

After the poachers are out of sight, I go in for a closer look. The bear is shaggy, not that big, about the size of a big dog, smaller and lighter-colored than the bear I found in a den a year ago. It has been shot behind the ear. I look around and can see now that the poachers found the bear's hibernating den, just some dirt dug out of the hillside, and shot it dead before it ever woke. They dragged it out onto the flat to do their dirty business. They didn't take the head or the hide or the teeth or the claws. Just what did they want with this poor creature, who was just trying to get a winter rest? The question is more disturbing to me than the carcass.

I don't tell Grandma Purse or the Elmans about the poachers. They became part of my secret life. A week later I am in Ancharsky's Store just hanging around. Joe Ancharsky was raised in Hazelton, Pennsylvania, but he had a dream to own a New England country store, and when he finally got one he made the most of it. The store is old-fashioned in looks but it keeps up with the times. It has a pot-bellied stove, necessities, a deli, and a movie rental section. Joe is the perfect storekeeper. He talks to everybody, he knows everything that is going on, but he never takes a position on local issues, so he has no enemies. Grandma Purse is checking the bulletin board, which she does every week or so, when I hear the ting-a-ling of the front door. A woman enters. She's pretty, but she has a wide body. With her is Bez, the boy poacher. We spot each other at the same moment. Bez's mom goes one way, and Bez goes the other—toward me.

"You didn't squeal on us," Bez says.

"You didn't squeal on me," I say.

"I was afraid Junior would of killed you," Bez says.

"How'd you find that bear den?"

"Dumb luck. We stumbled across it during legal deer season."

"You and those criminals coming back to the trust?"

"No, Uncle Chester and Junior don't work a place long enough for their truck to look too familiar."

I'm relieved. My deer family is safe for now.

"I won't tell on you then," I say.

"You're the Salmon kid, right?"

"My name's Birch Latour, but I do live in the Salmon house with my grandmother," I say.

"I always wanted to live in a mansion," Bez says.

That's the beginning of our friendship. Bez's real name is Bezaleel Woodward. He and his mom, Comfort "Nellie" Woodward, live with Bez's sister, Trudy, his uncle Chester Rayno (distant cousin of our cook, Soapy), and Uncle Chester's son, Junior. Chester is not really an uncle. He is Nellie's boyfriend. They live in the trailer park in Darby Depot. Bez and I sit around and dream up ways to assassinate Uncle Chester and Junior and get away with it, though neither one of us has it in ourselves to do the deed.

We make a pact, signed in our blood, promising that we will never squeal on each other. Uncle Chester used to work for a ski area in Vermont on the snowmaking crew. It's hard work—how would you like to be in a manmade blizzard every cold night?— and so he quit, but not before he made a deal with a restaurant owner in the ski town. Uncle Chester provides the restaurant with fresh venison and wild turkey.

The bear was a "specialty item," which is what Uncle Chester calls it. A rich skier from someplace in Asia wanted a bear gall bladder. Seems as if he could make a potion out of it that would perk up his sex life.

Bez knows almost as much about the woods as I do. Bez owns a .22, and he and I go shooting. We hunt coyotes, which is legal game during any season in New Hampshire. We track them, we harass them, but they are too smart for us, and it's only by accident that we get a shot off.

I happen to be holding the rifle at the time. I aim it and squeeze the trigger the way Grandpa Howard taught me, and the bullet strikes right where I aim in the shoulder of the coyote. But the coyote doesn't die. He runs off, leaving blood in the snow. It takes us two days to find the body. He had gone more than a mile before he bled to death. Bez is excited, but I am sick about what I have done. I am too squeamish to be a hunter. It's a dispiriting piece of self-knowledge.

HOUSE IN THE TREES

Summer rolls around and Missy comes home, taller, skinnier, and homely as ever. The three of us quickly form a gang. I am elected president, Missy vice-president, and Bez is, well, nothing. After a week of hanging around the store, swimming in Grace Pond, and target practice, the three of us are in bliss.

Things change all of a sudden. Bez shows up with a smashed-in face. Junior beat him up when Bez found his stash of dirty magazines. I don't mean *Playboy* or *Hustler,* I mean really dirty. Meanwhile, Missy has a big argument with her mother, who thinks she is becoming too much of a tomboy.

We hold a meeting in our "club house," which is the pool room at the mansion. I tell them about the Forbidden Room that Grandma Purse won't let me see, and we try to pick the lock, but it's too much for us. We are bored again.

"Something has to change," Missy says.

"Amen," says Bez.

I don't say anything. I don't want anything to change. I am happy just to have friends on the trust lands, on the estate, in my mansion—my domain. I am a very selfish person.

"Bez, Junior is going to kill you," Missy says.

"I'm not afraid to die," says Bez.

"I think we all ought to leave town for the summer," Missy says.

"Let's work on our tans at the pond," I say, though I have no interest in getting scalded by the sun.

"I have a better idea," Missy says. "Let's go to the ocean. I have, like, a friend from school whose family has a place on York Beach."

"I'm the president of this club, and we're not going to any damn ocean," I say.

"Birch, you spend far too much time in this big stupid house and in the woods moping," Missy says. "You need to see the world."

"There's nothing in the world I want. And I love this house."

"That is most stupid, Birch Latour."

"Stop fighting. I get enough of that at home," Bez says.

It is our first major argument, and we are all upset. We sit there silent with our own thoughts for a minute. Finally, Bez speaks. "No ef way our parents going let the three of us go to any York Beach without supervision," he says.

"You're right," Missy says.

"And you don't really want to be looked at on a beach by a bunch of creeps. You just want to get away from your mother," I say.

"She, like, nags nags nags—she's driving me nuts. And I don't like this pool room either. It's too, I don't know, old man."

"If you could have what you really wanted what would it be?" I ask.

"Freedom," Bez says.

"Like a great bird," I say.

"A home in the clouds, way up there, nice and cozy, where we would be, like, a family, just the three of us." Missy raises her eyes to the heaven none of us believe in (except, secretly, me). We are quiet, we are still; we are in some kind of rapture; we are one in our powerlessness and hope and dreams.

We finally agree that all of the grownups we know have one thing in common—Stupidity, with a capital "S." And then the strangest, most beautiful thing happens. We all have THE big idea at THE same time. In a few minutes we have set our course for the summer: We will build a tree house.

I know exactly the tree for our enterprise—the wolf pine that the loggers passed up a couple years ago. We head for the woods, and we climb the tree and I show my friends the flat spot where the tree house platform will go. The tree has changed some in the last couple years. Small branches have grown in, blocking the views. We decide that that is all for the good, because now our tree house won't be seen. We can spy across the entire trust by parting a few branches and peeking between the pine needles.

We climb down from the tree, build an (illegal) campfire, and hold a meeting.

"We'll need lumber, tools, all kinds of stuff," I say, and suddenly the project seems in doubt for our lack of experience, expertise, and confidence.

"We'll need money," Missy says.

"I don't have no money," Bez says.

"I've got money, but I'm not allowed to spend it," Missy says.

"That makes no sense," Bez says.

"It's supposed to be for my college education."

Bez blinks with incomprehension. Nobody in Bez's family has gone to college, and the idea that you have money and won't spend it immediately is alien to him. Me, I was brought up by Dad not to think about money, and now I have tons of money. Despite Grandma Purse's lecture on how money makes people who they are, I'm as confused as ever about money.

"I've got money, but it's in a trust fund that I can't touch until I'm twenty-one," I say.

We sit in silence for a while and look at the fire. We are never uncomfortable, even when nobody is talking. I am not thinking about the tree house. I am thinking about the wall between desire and possibility. Finally, Missy speaks.

"We don't even know what we're going to build. Let's start with a plan."

"I don't have a plan," I say.

"Me neither," Bez says.

"I have a plan," Missy says, with such importance in her voice that Bez and I gasp with admiration. She clears a space in the leaves, but she can't draw on the forest duff, so she picks up sticks and uses the sticks to show us the shape of what is in her head.

"We will build the cabin to follow the natural floor plan, which is irregular. It will be about eight feet long by seven feet wide, but it will have this alcove . . ."

"What's an alcove?" asks Bez.

"It's like a wing. Ours will be maybe six feet by four feet, with a curtain, so a person can go there for privacy, like if you want to go to the bathroom when boys are around."

Bez and I break out into embarrassed giggles.

Missy designs a two-room tree house with a deck about four feet in depth running the eight-foot length of the structure. The door is in the middle of the deck.

I look at the plan, defined by broken sticks, and it gives me an idea.

"We can build most of this cabin for free and without having to go far for our building materials. They're all right in front of us."

"A log cabin—no way," says Bez.

"Not logs, saplings. A house of sticks," I say.

"Be hard to nail," Bez says. "I can barely drive a nail through a board without smashing my thumb."

"We won't use nails," Missy says, excited now. "We'll use fish line and maybe wire. It'll be like sewing. We'll sew the sticks together."

"Lashed together," Bez says. We all like the sound of those two words, so pervy.

"Sewed, lashed, crocheted, knitted—whatever. It'll be, like, a stick-quilt in a tree," I say.

That day I build a shaving horse out of lumber laying around in the mansion's barn, and Bez and I lug it out to the big tree. It's almost a mile walk. Bez cuts saplings with a bow saw. I trim them to length, shave off the bark with a jackknife. I'm planning to get Roland to hunt up a two-handed draw knife. We rig a pulley so

Missy can haul up the sticks to our building site and start sewing the floor.

Grandma Purse may hide out in her bedroom for most of the day, but she keeps in touch. She soon wrings out most of the truth from me. I am surprised that she approves.

"It's about time you had friends," she says. She gives me the summer off from lessons.

Missy, Bez, and I learn a lot about ourselves that summer. We are up at 6 AM. We bring sandwiches into the woods. We sometimes stay until dark. We do overnights, sleeping out in tents and later on the tree house platform. I learn that I like being in charge. I like the responsibility. I work darn hard at figuring out how to get the most from Missy and Bez, how to avoid hurting their feelings, how to make decisions and look ahead for the good of the project. Missy acquires confidence for the first time in her life. She's our master builder. She has touch—that's the only way I can describe her work. She can visualize anything, and her hands know how to make the sticks fit together and look good. In that way she's a lot like Dad—hands that know. She uses wire, cord, and fish line to fasten the sticks together, and in the end everything is strong and beautiful.

Bez is our contractor. He can scrounge anything. He knows every dumpster in Darby and what you might find there. He keeps an eye out for carpenter pick-up trucks. "If you hang around building sites, or where somebody's renovating, they'll give you stuff they normally throw away," Bez says. "My mom and me built a shed like that once. Course it didn't hurt that she was going out with one of the carpenters." Bez will wander off by himself for a couple of days and come back with shingles, or a screen door, or a couple of windows, or a carpet, or caulking, and so forth. Without ever talking about it, we realize how much we depend on each other. Building that tree house with my friends is the single most rewarding experience of my thirteen years of life.

Everything is going fine. The floor, walls, and roof of the main room in our tree house are up, though the place lacks a frame for the windows Bez scrounged and a railing for the deck. Also the ladder's a little rickety. Missy has started laying the stick floor for the "privacy" room she insists upon.

And then in the dog days of August—the first disaster. Bez's mom is marrying Uncle Chester, and the family is moving to Killington, Vermont, nearer the ski areas, where they figure they can get jobs. Disaster number two: I read in the newspaper (newspaper reading being one of my new habits since moving in with Grandma Purse) that Dad has been arrested for drunk driving. Loses his license for sixty days.

I do something real private that day. I collect all the spoons I made at the mansion and put them in a leaf bag, just the way Dad used to before going off to see his dealer. I throw the bag over my shoulder and go into the woods. I start a fire with a match, birch bark, and dead pine branches. When the fire is going well I throw the spoons in and watch them burn. I'm trying to feel something, maybe regret or anger—something. But my thoughts are purely practical: make sure you put the fire out before you leave.

If it wasn't for our grand project, I would mope and turn back to my old tricks of tracking animals. (Funny how "moped" and "moh-ped" are spelled the same but said different.) But that summer I have Missy and Bez, and we have our project, and I am happy. Well, I am not happy, not exactly. Something demonic is happening to me. Missy and Bez and I sit around and talk about how dismal our various parents and guardians are.

Missy, Bez, and I continue our work, but it's not the same. Bez is going to be leaving us, and I'm worried about Dad, and then another disaster. Missy takes a couple days off, claims she's sick. When she comes back, she's quiet and gazes out at the dropoff from the tree house as if she's contemplating jumping. Finally, I can't stand it anymore. "What is wrong with you?" I yell.

"Never mind," she says.

"Don't fight," Bez says. "I hate fighting."

"We are not fighting," I say. "We are seeking the truth, and the truth is that Missy has a secret that she won't tell except with her lying eyes."

"All right," Missy says. "I'll tell if you both promise never to mention it again—never. Understand?"

Bez and I swear.

"I had my period," Missy says.

Bez and I are in awe at this news, mute with the wonder and catastrophe of it.

A few days later Bez gives us each a copy of a paper he's printed on Uncle Chester's computer. It's his last will and testament, leaving all his earthly possessions to Missy and me.

"You're not going to kill yourself, are you, Bez?" Missy says.

"No way, but I'm afraid Junior's going to murder me."

We complete the tree house a week before Labor Day. The moment isn't nearly as exciting as I'd hoped it would be. For one thing, I realize that the idea to build the house of sticks was not my own. It came from Dad. I'd been brought up in a house of sticks. I was just repeating my personal history. I begin to suspect that I lack creativity. Spontaneos Combustion was right. Every year I grow stupider. Eventually I'll be as dimwitted as Dad, Grandma Purse, Grandma Elenore, and Grandpa Howard.

We have an overnight, sleeping on beanbags; we barbecue hot dogs and marshmallows over the grill on the deck; we sing camp songs that Missy learned years earlier; we swear allegiance to our friendship. Even so, life isn't the same after the work is complete. The work made us one. Without the work, we are just good friends who soon will go separate ways. And so it happens. Bez moves to Killington, Vermont, where likely he will die at the hands of his evil stepbrother. Missy goes back to private school, with the three of us understanding that when we see her again she will have hips, boobs, an ass, and no doubt a revised attitude sure to destroy our friendship. Me, I am alone again.

THE FORBIDDEN

It's "glorious October," as Dad used to say, and I've just returned from the dentist, who has referred me to an orthodontist. Seems as if I'm going to have to have my teeth wired from wisdoms to incisors. I'll have so much metal in my mouth I'll probably be electrocuted by the first thunderbolt that comes over from the Vermont hills. Braces—how I dread them!

After I finish my home-schooling lessons I take long walks in the woods in search of creatures to bring me comfort. It's on one such jaunt that I find Dad's latest hideout. He's camping on the trust grounds. I see his stovepipe protruding from a house of poles, plastic, and what have you. The van is parked a couple hundred feet away, hidden in some trees. I think about leaving him a message, but we're not supposed to see each other. Grandma Purse has made it clear that if she finds out I'm with Dad for any reason she will have him arrested again. She has her spies. I back off. I do find it kind of funny that Dad is living on the trust lands. I wonder why. I wonder why he doesn't just head west like he said he would. I concentrate, trying to read his mind the way I used to, but no message comes through.

A couple weeks later, after some personally disturbing news (I learn that the birch mill has closed, and the logs are being sent to Canada), I accidentally sort of bump into Dad, but I don't think he sees me. Periodically, I hike up to the ledges and huddle in the lean-to, just to feel your spirit. I don't do anything. I just sit cross-legged under the cliff overhang and concentrate my mind on the tiny hemlock tree and send you my thoughts.

One afternoon after finishing my visit I hear a noise below me on the trail. I duck behind a rock. It's Dad. He's headed for the ledges. I start to follow him. I even have an idea to call out to him. After all, Grandma Purse couldn't possibly catch us out here. Then I notice that Dad is not walking like Dad; Dad is walking like an ant. At first I don't understand. Has Dad actually become one with the land in that he is now part ant? Well, no. Dad is drunk.

This is the end, I think. Not only will I never see Dad again. I don't believe I will ever want to.

I've been plowing through the hundreds of volumes in the Salmon library since I moved into the mansion when I was eight years old. I thought I'd have them read in two or three years, but it's taken longer. Part of the problem is that I don't like to speed read. I don't "see" words on a page; I "hear" Dad's voice in my ears. It's as if I'm back at Forgot Farm lying in his arms and he's reading to me. And of course there's that ongoing problem of continually declining IQ. However, despite all, I just finished the last book in the Salmon library, a quirky thing called *Mad Dogs* or *Mad Buns,* something like that. Can't remember the author either. I can never remember the names of the people who write books. They're probably best forgotten anyway. Upon completion I thought I'd be proud and thrilled. Instead, I'm empty inside. Will have to acquire more books. Doc Mendy tells me I have an addictive personality. Which brings up another issue—cigarettes.

I would never steal from Grandma Purse, but taking from ashtrays is not stealing. She rarely finishes a cigarette and leaves her butts all over the place. I "pick up" after her. I do my smoking outside, and the head rush is very good. Smoking calms me down, gives me a feeling of independence. A smoke is like having a friend. I'm not worried about lung cancer. I figure I'll be long dead before the ciggies can do me in.

Roland caught me the other day. "I didn't see that," he said, and he walked away. I got the point. He isn't going to tell on me, but he doesn't want me to smoke in front of him. That's all right. I like being sneaky. It's being sneaky that leads to my next misadventure. It's a Saturday, one of the rare times when Grandma leaves the house. She's gone shopping with Roland and Soapy.

The only person around is Katharine. She's supposed to be minding me, but she knows I often disappear for hours at a time and anyway she's holed up in her suite poring over her research papers. I'm outside having a smoke and since nobody's around I'm walking in plain sight around my magnificent mansion. It will be mine someday. Not sure what to do with it. Maybe convert it into an orphanage.

My eye follows a drainpipe that goes all the way up beside a window in the room that Grandma won't let me in. I'll open the window from the outside. The burglar alarm only goes on automatically after dark, or Grandma turns it on when no one is going to be in the house, or more likely she forgets to turn it on. I flick the cigarette away and shimmy up the drainpipe.

I'm not sure what I'm going to find in Grandma Purse's special suite. Maybe some Tasmanian stuff. Things come and go from the house, delivered in boxes by UPS or the US Mail. Often I'm told to leave when she's prying open the crates. Obviously she doesn't want me to know what's in them. What does she have to hide? I don't really care, I tell myself. I'm just curious. As I climb the drainpipe I consider the possibilities of I-don't-care. Seems like a foolproof philosophy. Dad's problem was that he believed certain things, and that he cared about them, or maybe tried to pretend he cared. What do I care that everyone I love hates everyone else I love? What's the point? "What's the fucking point?" I shouldn't shout. I tell myself to calm down. Katharine might hear.

The Forbidden

What I see makes me slip, but I catch myself. I see a picture of you, Mother. As it turns out the windows are locked. I shimmy down the drainpipe and go into the house to my grandma Purse's room. I open the drawer beside the bed, reminding myself to wipe the fingerprints off. This is my first major burglary. Inside I find a set of keys. One of the keys fits the door to the Forbidden Rooms. In I go.

The curtains are open, and the dyeing (not a misspelling) light of late afternoon sun pukes fall foliage colors into the room and hurts my eyes. Now I understand. Grandma Elenore created a shrine to honor The Blessed Virgin Mary, and Grandma Purse created a shrine to honor The Blessed Not-Virgin Lilith. She moved your things to the room beside hers. She wanted her little girl to be close to her. Your bed is big—even as a child you wanted a big bed, or so I've been told; the room is all too neat, as if nobody lives here, and of course nobody does. Unless you visit for ghostly kicks. The wallpaper is of laurel blossoms in the spring. A life-sized Big Bird doll reclines on the bed. No wonder I like herons and eagles and other large feathered critters. On the dresser is a line of Barbie dolls, no Kens.

I thought I'd read all the books in my mansion. Not so. In your room is a shelf of children's books with pictures of animals misbehaving more or less like children. The books puzzle me. Dad never let me read children's books, and the covers and big writing seem foolish and obvious or foolish and stupid, and I am disappointed in you for reading those books and disappointed in Grandma Purse for keeping them. A lot of the stuff in the room is for girls, and it hardly registers in my mind—funny-shaped bottles, numerous belts, a clothes rack of dresses, a doll house, dresses for the Barbies, but also some sporting goods, such as a tennis racket, a lacrosse stick, and a softball on which someone has written 1–0.

But the main show is a glass case containing more than a dozen trophies for swimming; on the wall are pictures of you in your lifeguard bathing suit with the Red Cross emblem on the hip. One photo shows you standing in the beach sand at the lake alone looking out, your long hair tucked into a cap tight around your head to make you sleek for the water; one acting dumb with a boy (my word, it's Garvin Prell as a teenager); one acting dumb with some other girls (why does a camera make people act so stupid?); one bashful with Persephone when she was beautiful, you bigger and looming over her; one stiffly posing with your dad, who looks strange at the beach, fully clothed in corduroy trousers and a wool shirt. I'm surprised by how big and muscular your body was, made for swimming (maybe you're a fish today; maybe I already pan-fried and ate you); your faces in the photographs sadden me, especially the ones in the pictures with your parents. The pictures seem full of questions.

I browse around your writing desk and look for something you said, but I don't find any secret diary or even notes. I do find some drawings in pencil, skinny girls like out of fashion magazines. On top of the dresser bureau in front of the mirror is a framed picture of you and your grandparents, I think, taken outside my mansion. Everyone is dressed to the nines, maybe even to the twelves. In the background I see a big car, a Royals Royce, maybe. I don't recognize the wood that the dresser is made out of. Probably it's mahogany. This is the kind of thing that would make Dad crazy with rage: the idea that the wood on the local lands is not good enough for the local occupiers. I open one of the drawers, but at that moment I see something in the mirror that attracts my attention—a flash of color from another room.

I go over to investigate. What I see is quite shocking. The adjoining room is a shrine to me! I find all the papers I've written for our home schooling, carefully filed by date and subject matter. I wrote about ants, spiders, herons, coyotes, beavers, and native fish such as perch. I never realized until now that most of my writing is about the trust lands. Framed in a glass case is a wooden spoon I made when I was with Dad. Grandma Purse must have bought it from Arts and Trifles. I open the case and pick up the spoon. It has the words "yellow submarine" carved on the handle. I remember being in a trance when I made that spoon.

But it's not the spoon or the papers that grab my attention when I first enter the room, it's the flashes of color: paintings on the wall—Bloom's paintings.

Dad coming down from the ledges carrying me as an infant, a ghostly outline of you in the background rising up in the sky, your face obscured, apparently because Bloom didn't know what you looked like.

Me as a baby staring into the fire in the Franklin stove, fear and awe on my face.

Dad standing on the rock island of Grace Pond shaving off his beard, me lying on my back on the rocks looking up at him.

Dad and I in the apple orchard lying on the ground, me nursing from him.

An abstract work that I recognize as the smears of colors and shapes that Dad and Bloom created while they thrashed around on the canvas.

But the painting that moves me the most is so simple and true that I shake uncontrollably. It's Dad's big hand holding my small hand holding one of Dad's spoons.

When I stop shaking I go back into your room and sit on the bed with Big Bird, not thinking, not feeling. Through concentration I try to go back in time. And then a whiff of something faint but perfumey strokes me. I stand, pacing for a minute, then return to the drawer I opened earlier. I find underwear and bras and lingerie. I am in forbidden territory, and I enjoy the feeling in a way that is new for me. I take out each private article of clothing, smell it, rub it against my skin, and carefully return it to its place. And then I stumble across the one-piece, tight-fitting bathing suit I saw in the pictures. The moment my hand touches the fabric I feel demoniacal in my pants. Seconds later I swoon deliciously.

23

FIGURES IN THE WHITEOUT

Right into November and December I make forays to the Darby Public Library, the magazine counter at Ancharsky's Store; I root around department circulars in junk mail and magazines in my new orthodontist's office. I search everywhere for pictures that show girls in one-piece bathing suits. I rip the pages out, bring them into the woods with me and do the Demon Swoon.

One day I see the imprint of my deer's cleft hoof and I'm back stalking my doe and her family. It helps—it really helps me get over my loneliness. She doesn't let me see her, but I can always find where she has been.

In the woods I happen upon a deer sex orgy, the does huddled around, watching the action, waiting for winners or deceivers to breed them, the bucks fighting for the right to breed. The ritual disturbs me. I hate the bucks for being so stupid and violent. I hate the does for their passivity. I hate that they are all naive about the fact that the event is a trick by God to carry on their species. I hate God for his tricks. I hate me as a child of God. In other words, I am thinking like Dad, and I am afraid . . . afraid there is no me.

My feelings about God trouble me in another way. I'm afraid to tell the truth because it will hurt my Grandma Elenore. I find it harder and harder to go to church, to pretend I am not angry at God. Then one Sunday Grandma Elenore brings up the subject of first communion again.

I am unable to say anything. I look at my grandma Elenore's soulful eyes, her quivering lips, her furrowed brow, her skin loose around her neck, her buck teeth, her plump little body—she reminds me of a koala on a bad day. I think about my own teeth, like hers screaming to get out of the mouth, but wired in. Can God love a boy who does to himself what I do in the woods? Something of my despair must cross my face, because Grandma says, "You want a piece of pie?" And I say yes, but there is no pie. There is cake, so I eat cake, not tasting it. The damage has been done. It's clear I've let down someone I love.

Back when I was an infant I theorized that the problem with the world, or at least my world, was Misunderstanding. Nothing has changed. Grandma Purse, Grandma Elenore, Grandpa Howard, Missy, Bez, and even Dad—the bastard!—all have good things to say to me, good ideas about something, strong and admirable feelings, but they cannot get their points across to one another. If I could only bring them all into one room I could make them see that their hatred is only the result of Misunderstanding. But I just don't have the whiz-bang to pull off that kind of caper. I was so much smarter when I was younger.

With no experience in human sexual affairs, and with a limited, academic understanding of human sex, I can't help but focus on deer as my role models. I can never be a buck or a doe. I am no longer a boy, not yet a man, nor am I a deer in fact but only in mime; I am nobody, I am nothing, abandoned by God, doomed never to breed or even to belong to a group. And yet I have some comfort. I have you, Mother. I have become like you, another ghost of the Salmon trust.

The only difference between us is that I have living tissue in my brain to create emotions to torment me. That is what it is like at thirteen when your friends leave: everything is exaggerated, which is what Doc Mendy tells me. We had been meeting once a month when he thought I was getting over my traumas, but now he wants to meet every week. I'm tired of lying to him. My lies sap my strength. I'm not even sure when I'm lying and when I'm telling the truth.

The tracks tell me that there are actually three separate deer families of does and their young ones, along with a number of bucks that come and go from family to family. In the mating season the families and bucks gather, but only briefly. They will eventually split apart and then come together again in the deer yard.

There is something special about my doe besides her cleft hoof. She is smart, real smart. Despite all I've learned I can never glimpse her. Now, as fall is coming to an end, she develops new habits, rare for a deer. Periodically, she breaks away from the does and fawns that make up her own greater family and goes off by herself. It is as if she's come to know that I am stalking her. Even so, I am able to map her movements, because it has been a wet fall and hoofprints are hard to hide in ground softened by rain.

One morning I'm up before dawn. It's dark, the air still and cold. I dress and slip out. My doe won't expect me this early, and she will be less wary. This might be the day I lay eyes on her. She'll be bedded under some hemlocks and upon rising will walk a short ways to what had once been Dad's orchard to feed on apples. Then she will move downslope to find acorns and beech nuts. I will climb a tree and catch her along her familiar route to the orchard. I'll be back at the mansion in time for my lessons.

Even in the dark I can find my way on the trust lands. It is late November, past the time of the rut, past hunting season. No one will be in the woods except me, or so I believe. Exuberant, full of hope and, dare I say it—love?—I reach the climbing-tree at the spark of dawn. I go up. Wait. She doesn't show. When I come down from the climbing-tree, I hear a noise. I walk toward the noise. See her tracks. She's been stalking me. But the noise? She doesn't have to make a noise. Was she taunting me? Was she that smart? I like to think so.

After that, day after day, I sense her presence all around me. I'll stop and listen—no sound. Just that feeling. I'll be walking and the feeling will come over me and I'll whirl around—no deer in sight. I'll climb to the tree house and the feeling will climb up with me. I'll even sense a presence above me, as if my doe can take flight. I am at peace.

Well, not really. I am the storm before the calm. I don't sleep well. I'm jumpy. Grandma Purse asks me a couple times if I'm all right, and I say, "I'm all right. Are you all right?" She answers, "I'm all right." This goes on for a week, so that we refine our responses. Grandma Purse looks at me, the question in her eyes, and I say, "All right." And she nods, "All right." I ask her if it's okay to stop seeing Doc Mendy. Answer: Not all right.

It's the middle of December. Missy's coming home for the X-mess holidays. I don't want to see her. Now that she's had her period I expect she's changed into a new being. The girl I loved as a friend will be no more. Meanwhile, I've become grotesque. My voice is changing. The demon in my pants is going crazy. My feet are growing but I'm still short and baby-faced, except for a two-hair beard on my chin, which I pluck out every three days. Missy will look at me and I will look at her and we will see each other as gross teenagers. She will hate me and I will hate her. I can't bear the thought of this encounter. At the same time I realize how stupid my thinking is, and I refuse to discuss us with Doc Mendy or Grandma Purse because they'll lose respect for me. I'm thinking all these things in Doc Mendy's office reception room in his home while I'm waiting for the Doc and Grandma Purse to conclude their conference. I imagine they're determining my fate. Finally, Doc Mendy pokes his head out the door and asks me to come in.

I enter just in time to see Doc Mendy settle down into his rocking chair. I imagine him in an old granny dress, looking like Norman Bates's mom. I hear the Psycho knife-music playing in my ears. My mind is polluted with images from movies and TV. If Dad in his far-off realm can read my mind he must be awful disappointed. Well, I'm disappointed in you too, Dad. Grandma Purse paces and smokes.

"We have to make this quick," she says. "We have to throw down some lunch and go to Keene before this damn storm hits."

"Exactly, let's get to work," Doc Mendy says. "Birch, your grandmother and I are worried about you. You've been very private lately."

"Private" is Doc Mendy's word for "lying sack of shit." I hang my head and shrug my shoulders in what must appear to be a pathetic gesture.

"There's something we want to talk to you about," Grandma Purse says, her voice unusually soft, which fills me with dread because it's so unlike her.

"We feel you've been spending too much time in the woods," Doc Mendy says.

I'm thinking that they've somehow figured out that I'm a chronic, disgusting, habitual Norman masturBAT(ES)or. They'll probably make me wear some kind of rig so that every time I reach for my demon I'll get an electric shock.

"Let's just lay it on the line, Doc," Grandma Purse says, normal raspy voice now. "Birch, you're too unstable right now to leave alone. You're coming with me to Tasmania until March first. You'll meet my husband, Hadly Blue. He has plenty of books, and we have nice neighbors in a lovely section of Devonport. It's a town about the size of Keene."

"Oh, wow," I say, but it's pure acting. I want to shout, Keene! That's huge! I don't want to live in some crowded metropolis of twenty-five thousand people. So many names to memorize, so much intrusive telepathy to confuse my own thoughts.

"See, he's very good at seeing reason," Grandma Purse says.

"I'm not so sure," Doc Mendy says.

"Birch, I feel that you've created a kind of fetish out of the trust lands. You'll benefit from an environment actually somewhat similar in climate to New England."

"Except it will be summer down under instead of winter," Grandma Purse says.

"Exactly," says Doc Mendy. "Birch, you sure you're okay with this?"

"I think it's a good idea," I lie.

An hour later we're back at the mansion, just finishing lunch. Something rises up deep inside of me. Not a voice exactly, but like a voice, a deep moaning call that I must answer.

We take off in the Bronco, Grandma Purse behind the wheel, Roland in the passenger seat, sleep mask over his eyes, me in the back. Just as we're going out the gate, I tell Grandma Purse I don't want to go to town. I want to study for my botany test. Grandma Purse leans on the brake and Roland slams forward, only the seat belt preventing him from smashing his head in the windshield.

"I thought you wanted to rent a movie?" Grandma Purse says.

"No, I just want to read," I lie. I'm amazed at how good I've become at lying. When I was with Dad it wouldn't have occurred to me to lie, and once in a while when an untruth accidentally came out of my mouth, I'd feel awful for days. I don't feel awful now. I feel in charge.

Grandma lets me out of the two-decades-old, refurbished, pristine, other-era Bronco. Her last words are "Make sure to stay in the house. This storm is supposed to be a nasty one."

My last words are "Bye Grandma, I love you," which is true. I know it's true, because I experience the hurt when I speak the words.

I'm wearing a winter coat, mittens and a hat in my pockets, but only track shoes on my feet. I should go inside and put on some boots, but I'm afraid Soapy won't let me go out again. I take my chances in street shoes.

The clouds came during the morning gradually and without wind. Now, by early afternoon, I can't see clouds, just a continuous envelope of gray. I know it's going to snow. I want it to snow. I am following my doe on a trail with her family when suddenly her tracks vanish. I backtrack and discover she's left the family and gone off on her own again. I don't think too much of this change at first. She's been straying from her normal haunts, but she always circles back to some familiar place.

She goes down by the pond, where the ice is brand new and thin. I see smoke curling from the metal chimneys of the new houses behind the trees. I see skid marks where my doe's hoofs bit into the new ice. Beneath I see new leaves on the bottom of the pond. I see perch. I see leaves and muck. I want to reach through the ice and scoop up the bottom. I see the reflection of the sky. I walk until the bottom disappears under my feet into blackness. The ice creaks and groans: I'm going to fall through and die that terrible death of cold water that is like burning. I am not afraid, Mother. I am at peace. I will follow my doe to the end, even if that end is the bottom of Grace Pond.

The tracks lead off the ice and for the moment I am safe, though the feeling of danger and doom remain with me. I am not afraid. It is as if I am hypnotized, not thinking on my own but controlled by an outside force.

A few flakes of snow begin to fall. The tracks lead back into the woods. I find a place where my doe stopped to spy on me. I am beginning to understand now: my doe is searching for heaven and she needs my help and I need hers. I must find her before the snow starts to come down hard, when all the tracks will be obscured.

I reach out with my mind or maybe she reaches out with hers. I'm not sure anymore. It doesn't matter because our minds have merged.

I lead her or she leads me toward the ledges. I can't feel any wind but it must be blowing along the tops of the trees, because I hear the aching sound of branches rubbing against one another. With all the leaves of the hardwoods fallen, I see deep into the woods, the tree trunks varying shades of olive and charcoal and silver and by contrast the forest floor bright hazel in color and crispy from freshly fallen leaves. Once the snow comes the leaves will pack down, the color will grow drab. I am witnessing that last vision of fall.

It begins to snow harder now and the wind picks up. In minutes I lose her trail. I should turn back but I go on; I am not afraid, Mother. During the entire ordeal to come, I will not be afraid.

I'm cold now and I can only see a few feet in front of me. We're not just in a snowstorm but a blizzard. I don't know where I am. My doe walked in so many circles and spirals and polygons and rhombuses that the blizzard and the math combine to leave me disoriented. Isn't it amazing that I who know this land better than anyone (except maybe Dad) do not know this land.

Time goes by. Minutes, hours, days, decades—can't tell the difference. What is that sound? It's not the blizzard anymore. It's what? Oh, it's that calling; it's the sound of mist that Dad told me about. Have I come home?

PART 2 The Calm

After math there is algebra.
—Birch Latour, in an email to Missy Mendelson

IN THE WIGWAM

The storm hit earlier and harder than predicted, so that Persephone had to put the Bronco into four-wheel drive to make it up the long hill from Center Darby to Upper Darby. She was thinking how much she loved a blizzard, which was rare on the trust lands because the hills and trees broke up the wind. But once in a while a storm would come straight from the northeast down the Connecticut River valley and the wind would howl and the snow would lash the trees. The road would suddenly disappear into the whiteout. A normal, prudent person would be frightened and slow down almost to a stop. Persephone grew more excited and speeded up, driving by guesswork, poor Roland Lachance rigid and stoic by her side.

It was only after her loved ones died that Persephone had become herself. That was the irony that kept coming back at her at odd moments in the middle of the night. After her husband died and then her daughter, she'd aged overnight. In grief the worries of losing one's looks, the failures of self-realization as a consort to a powerful and charismatic husband, had become irrelevant. It was no longer necessary to be pretty. She could just be. Despite the pain, she liked herself in grief. She was more honest, more real.

Garvin's death, coming without warning, had rocked her again. She'd adopted him as a son in her heart; his death had left her bereft both of hope and self. She'd thought of suicide after Garvin's sudden violent end. All that kept her going was the thought of her grandson. Since Birch had come into her life five years ago, she'd looked outward at the world without fear and with a sense of humor. During the rare moments she searched inward she saw an old dug well gone dry after a drought, nothing to see inside, nothing to fear but echoes. She'd narrowed her life to a single purpose: prepare Birch for the difficulties of the world.

The boy had made remarkable gains, but these days she worried about him. Doc Mendy was worried too. Birch had finally made friends, had plunged into childhood as if diving off a cliff into a boiling sea. He'd been happy, or so it seemed, but when he found himself alone again he was at a sudden loss. Doc Mendy had explained it this way: "Birch has had a brief but intense childhood. He's missed out on the normal defense mechanisms one builds as a child. Meanwhile, the defenses of his previous life with his father have been badly damaged by this selfsame childhood. The normal upheaval brought on by puberty is exacerbated by his peculiar past. We must keep an eye on him as he makes the transition into adolescence."

His father! Persephone felt a surge of anger at the thought of Latour. Every time Birch made progress, the specter of Latour loomed over the boy and herself, too. Latour had frustrated her in ways even he could not have imagined. For one thing she'd discovered that though she had gained custody of Birch, she could not change his name to Raphael Butterworth Salmon. Latour, who normally ran roughshod over the law, had gone through all the legal channels in changing his own and his son's name. Now only Birch could change his name but only when he came of age. Even now Latour was squatting on the trust just to spite her. Doc Mendy had advised her not to prosecute Latour as long as Birch remained in a teen state of confusion.

The Bronco slipped and swerved on their half-mile-long driveway. "When we pull in, get the jeep and plow this damn road," she said.

"If you don't kill us first," Roland said.

"Someday I'm going to fire you for insubordination," Persephone said.

"I wish you would. Only thing worse than riding with you, Persephone, is working with you."

And they both laughed.

She left the Bronco in park, the engine running, leaving the vehicle for Roland to put away, while she went to the house, stimulated by the storm, almost content.

Soapy was waiting for her at the door. "Katharine called," Soapy said. "She's going to stay the night in her office in Keene."

"Katharine is a wuss."

"Isn't Birch coming in with you?" Soapy said, looking past the open door into the storm.

"Birch is not with me. Isn't he in the house?"

"No, I thought he was with you."

"Oh, my God," said Persephone.

Persephone telephoned 911; she sent Roland to Ancharsky's Store in the jeep to recruit some help from local men who'd know the woods. Out of courtesy she informed the hated Elmans of the situation, and finally Mrs. McCurtin, knowing she would spread the word: Birch Latour was lost in the blizzard.

Persephone slid into her snowmobile jumpsuit, put on her helmet, and went back into the storm. She kept her snowmobile well tuned up and it started right away. She'd had it in the back of her mind to bomb along the trails after the storm, enjoy the first burst of hard winter before leaving for Tasmania. Even now, in the middle of an emergency, a possible tragedy, danger to herself, she couldn't deny the thrill of speed and cold, the exhilaration of pushing the machine and herself to the limits. About six inches of snow had fallen, but since there was no base every once in a while the machine would scrape against bare ground. She'd sail over a bump airborne and free, and she would scream like some crazed nymphomaniac.

In minutes on the trail she thought that she herself would perish, for the wind was blowing the snow every which way, creating great moving white clouds that obscured everything. She asked herself if she really cared whether she died. Damn right she cared. As long as she might help this boy she had to stay alive. She had a little bit of luck. The wind died when she turned a corner of the hill, and she could see. Below was Latour's shanty.

A moment later the wind smacked her again, and for a few seconds she lost sight of the shanty. She shut off the engine and stood in the whiteout, trying to get her bearings. She took a few steps downslope, fell, rolled to a stop against a tree, struggled to her feet. She wondered if it were possible to light a cigarette in this wind. "Hello!" she shouted to the wind.

The wind answered by slapping her face.

She continued down, almost walking past the shanty into sure oblivion, but the storm died down for just a moment so that she saw a vague shape, more the embodiment of the idea of shelter than anything else.

Latour had scrounged a second-hand door and fitted it into a wall of sticks, plywood, and plastic. She pounded on the door. No answer. She pounded again. She screamed. "Let me in, Latour— let me in!" No answer. She shoved her shoulder against the door and pushed. The door did not budge. The place was better built that she'd imagined. Then she did the obvious. She turned the doorknob, and the door opened.

In one sweep of the eye she took in the entire structure. No one home. But the wood stove was running, and the place was warm.

She experienced a moment of stupor, her worry dulled by exhaustion and shock. And then she remembered her cigarettes. She might forget her grocery list, the time of day, someone's name, but never the cigarettes. She lit one off a burning candle. With the first drag, the pleasant sear in her lungs, her mind cleared.

It was likely that Latour too was caught in the storm. She would have to face the storm and look for Birch. She had no idea where to go next—the pond, perhaps. She took another drag, put the cigarette between her lips, and opened the door. The wind blew the cigarette out of her mouth, and it flew away like a bird. She could not see her snowmobile. Could not see even a tree. She believed now that she, too, was destined to perish in the storm. Well, all right. She started up in the general direction of her machine.

And there it was—she sensed it before she saw it—a vision of her death, a moving obelisk coming to take her away. She stood still, waiting, watching the shape, formless and in soft focus, moving slightly from side to side, but slowly coming forward. The whole meaning-thing was right there for her to see: the infant son lost before she knew how to love him, the daughter she could not love, the husband who could not love her, the ghosts of Upper Darby proclaiming her obligations and damn any ambitions she might harbor, the meaning of her life a shapeless, shifting blob in a freezing, windblown fog.

In a twinkling the shape vanished, and now she could see only one form—Latour carrying Birch in his arms.

"Is he alive?" she shouted into the wind.

"I don't know," Latour said.

They went inside. Birch's face was pale, eyes closed, arms dangling limply from shoulder sockets.

"I'll take him to the hospital on the snow machine," she said.

Latour shook his head no. "He couldn't take any more cold, and anyway it's hard or impossible to see out there."

"Where are those damn rescue people?" she said, just for something to say.

"We'll have to do what we can for him here. Take your clothes off, Mrs. Salmon."

"What did you say?"

"Strip to your underwear." Latour put Birch on the bed and pulled off the boy's shoes.

Persephone took her boots off, wiggled out of her jump suit, stripped off her slacks and sweater, paused at the high-collar white blouse, then finished.

Latour looked her over, looked at the clothes at her feet. "You're messy," he said. He undressed himself and Birch, then he zipped two sleeping bags together. The boy was white as the snow. For a moment Persephone and Latour in their underwear stared at one another: the older woman with a body still okay but her skin raw, red, scaly, joints swollen with arthritis; the man in his prime, thick all over, looking like a wrestler in his jockeys.

She was aware that her black panties and white bra did not go well together.

They put Birch's cold, almost stiff body into the sleeping bags, then they crawled in with him, one on each side. They enveloped him with their arms and legs. Birch's body was so cold it made Persephone shiver. By contrast, Latour's leg, draped over her own, was warm and heavy. They lay in silence until the twilight came.

"In case you need to get up, there's a flashlight on the table," Latour said.

"Thank you," Persephone said.

And they were quiet again until it was dark in the hut. Birch's body was warmer now.

"I can feel him breathing," Latour said in a whisper.

"He'll live." Persephone, too, whispered.

"How the hell would you know?" Latour said, still whispering but louder, angrier, his tone giving her just a hint of the thrill of a fright.

"Because I insist upon it," Persephone said.

"You insist upon it. That's arrogant as hell."

She could barely hear him. They were like agitated lovers quarreling in a chapel, struggling to keep their voices down.

Where did you find him?" she asked.

"At the ledges."

"You knew he would go there?"

"It was just a guess," Latour said. "Well, maybe more than that. It's a mystery like everything else. Persephone, have you been to the ledges? The lean-to?"

"No, I couldn't bear to see where Lilith died."

"I'm sorry. I should have known how hard it was for you."

"It's all right. Grief made me selfish, too. I'm amazed you could find your way up there and back in this storm."

"I didn't find anything. The whiteout was so bad I couldn't tell up from down, and then something happened." Latour stopped talking, as if he was afraid of betraying a confidence. Then he went on. "I lost my way going up, and then I heard a noise in the wind. I followed the sound to the ledges, and Birch was lying down all curled up. Coming back with him, I was lost again, and then I heard that sound. The last time I spoke to Lilith, when she was dying, her voice was weak from loss of blood. I thought at the time it was like the sound of mist. That's what I heard in the howl of the blizzard, her voice, real soft but coming."

"It was your imagination."

"I suppose."

"Latour, what were you doing out there in the storm to begin with?"

"Birch. I've been following him for weeks, worried about him."

"We all have."

In the long pause that followed Persephone listened to Latour's breath, labored with anguish. Finally, he said, "How did you find me?"

Persephone couldn't stifle a sardonic laugh.

"You knew about this place?" he said.

"Of course, you idiot. Everybody knew about the homeless man who'd parked himself on the trust lands. No derelict would park himself so deeply into the woods. Nobody but you."

"You never thought about evicting me?"

"It would have given me great pleasure to kick you out, jail you, vaporize you, but Birch's therapist advised me to take it easy."

Now it was Latour who laughed. "Unbelievable," he said, paused, and went off on another track. "Birch didn't get himself lost accidentally. He went up to the ledges on purpose. What would the shrink make of that?"

"Birch was upset when his friends left the area, but there was something else bothering him. His therapist didn't know what it was."

"I guess we won't know until he wakes up. And maybe not even then. He always had secrets, even as an infant."

"He got that from Lilith. You love him, don't you?"

"I thought—I still think—he belonged to Garvin, not me. In other words, I didn't deserve to love him like a father. It was in the back of my mind: Maybe I didn't love him. I didn't know what I felt until now. I do love him. He'll always be my son."

"I used to imagine that he would grow up to be tall and handsome like Reggie or compact and athletic like Garvin, and maybe with a little bit of the classic lines of my own people, the Butterworths," Persephone said.

Latour interrupted her with a bitter laugh. "But not like an Elman. He would never look like Howard or me. And you were right about that; he didn't grow that way."

Something in Latour's voice made her think about Mendy and Maddy, Roland and Soapy, the great body politic of Darby, New Hampshire, the desperation of the Hunger Money people for acknowledgment or achievement, some damn thing.

"You haven't seen him in a few years," Persephone said.

"Only at a distance."

"Take a look, Latour."

She reached for the flashlight and shined it on Birch's face. "Look closely."

Latour parted Birch's lips with his fingers so that he could see the braces. "Elenore, my mother," he said.

"That's right, Latour—he's yours," Persephone said. She could feel Latour's body heave and shudder in the sleeping bag, his chest rising and falling, rising and falling, mournful hiccups barely audible.

"Lilith—how could I have doubted her all these years?" Latour said.

"It's okay that you're an idiot, Latour. Admit it to yourself, and you may be fit to join the human race."

They lay quiet for a while. Persephone knew she had won that round, but she hated herself for it. Whatever Latour's faults he had saved Birch's life. She didn't exactly want to apologize as to explain herself, her overreaching aggression a defense that meant no offense.

"Latour?" she said.

But he was asleep, and suddenly, she felt her own exhaustion.

Persephone dreamed that she had lived an entirely different life—childless, poor, happy, coming of age as an international grand prix race car driver.

When she woke it was warm in the sleeping bag but cold in the shanty. Latour slept with his arm around Birch. The object of Latour's and her mutual concern had reached normal body temperature, his breathing regular but faint. Morning light came in through a window. She crept out of the sleeping bag and lit a cigarette and looked around.

For a hovel of about a hundred and fifty square feet the place was surprisingly homey, a stick home, complete with a door, a window, shelves, a bed frame, one chair. No clutter, as if Latour had been expecting company. In a corner was a curtain and a potty, clean, no smell. She wondered where he dumped the stuff.

A backpack and some other clothes hung from pegs on a wall. A snapshot of Birch in blue jeans, taken a couple years back, was attached to a pole by pushpins. Persephone had taken the picture herself. Somehow Latour had gotten hold of it. Beside it was an eight-by-ten of Lilith laughing, obviously looking amused at the photographer as he snapped the picture. Persephone had never seen her daughter look so happy, so in love.

She stoked the fire, putting in a couple pieces of split red oak. The stove was some kind of homemade thing, small and simple, a crude but efficient heat delivery system for this space.

The walls were made of lashed-together saplings, very much like the tree house the kids built, except earthbound. On the walls hanging from push pins were scores of wooden spoons, strings tied around the handles. They resembled Japanese wood chimes. Carpeting covered the dirt floor. A single recycled window allowed some light in. On a shelf beside the chair was a bottle of Old Crow whiskey half full, a shot glass, and a notebook. She picked up the pages and read an account of the creation of a spoon made of apple wood stolen from the Salmon Trust. On the margin was a note: "Don't sell this one. Deposit in time capsule." Persephone didn't exactly admire Latour or his craft, didn't exactly envy him, or understand him, but the thought of this strange man absorbed by his labors touched her in its simplicity and humanity.

She'd had the same feeling when she'd stumbled across the ex-

pensive handmade wooden spoons in the Arts and Trifles cata-
log. When she saw "yellow submarine" carved on the handle of
a spoon she'd known intuitively that it had been made by Birch
when he was living with his father.

PAYING DEBTS

Obadiah Handy and Chahley Snow pulled Latour's van out of the drifts with their horses. They charged him fifty dollars—he gave them a hundred. They were surprised that the Hermit of Lonesome Hill had money. No one in town but Persephone knew of his trade as a maker of high-priced wooden spoons. Latour's original plan had been to let the van sit in the snow until spring, because he liked the solitude and the desperate living conditions imposed by winter. Everything had changed. He needed wheels to visit Birch in the hospital in Boston.

The boy lay still, but he did not appear to be in a coma. It seemed to Latour that he was living and thinking and feeling in some other realm where he might reach Lilith. Latour knelt by the bed and tried again to transfer a message of apology to Lilith through Birch. A blank space in time ensued. Latour knew he was failing. Birch had the power to deliver such a message, but why should he? Surely he sensed that his father lacked sincerity at his core.

On the drive back from the hospital in Boston, Latour bought a bottle of Old Crow. A third of the contents had gone down his throat when he impulsively threw the bottle out the window. He immediately regretted his actions and when he reached Keene a little more than an hour later he bought another bottle. He had a faint glimmer then of what he must do: seek the counsel of others. It was a disturbing idea for one such as he, and he shut himself off from it. He did recognize that in his anger and hurt he'd been blinded to other people. To make peace with himself, he must make peace with his world.

On Sunday Latour knew when Howard and Elenore would be back from church, and he timed his arrival accordingly. He'd been so long absent from his parents' mobile home that he knocked at the door. He had planned a long speech, asking for their forgiveness, but when his mother opened the door to let him in, his father standing behind her, he understood that they knew why he had come. His mother burst into tears, and then Latour burst into tears, and Howard said, "My word, but wonders never cease."

Latour ate Sunday dinner with his family for the first time in years. His mother made meat loaf with mashed potatoes, peas, and gravy from the can. Latour told them truthfully that it was the best meal he'd had in his life.

They talked about Birch, the boy's injuries, the eight toes that had to be amputated, the tissue damage, the possibility that when he woke, if he did wake, he might have brain damage.

Latour spoke only kind words about Persephone, who had risked her own life for Birch, who was paying all of his medical bills, who had demonstrated that she loved him.

Elenore talked for a good hour about their family, bringing Latour up to date on the recent adventures of his sisters and their children. It pained Elenore that they had all moved so far away. The annual Elman Christmas dinner was no longer a family reunion. The Elmans were scattered across the country.

Howard gave Latour that half-injured, half-angry look that told Latour that his father was disappointed in him for not taking over the business. In the past Latour (as Freddie Elman) would have left the table and sulked. Now he understood Howard's hurt and realized that there was nothing to do but accept the differences between them. Howard didn't say as much as usual, and in the end, almost in a whisper, he announced that he planned to retire "one of these days."

After a dessert of apple pie and ice cream, Howard went out alone to the barn to work on one of his Honeywagons. Latour stayed behind to visit with his mother.

"Is something wrong with Dad, or am I just remembering him wrong?" Latour said.

Elenore broke eye contact with Latour for a moment and then turned to him. "I hope this doesn't make you mad, but . . . it won't make you mad, will it?"

"I doubt it, Mom. I'm seeing the world in a different way since Birch's accident."

"It's your name. It bothers your father in a funny kind of way."

"Latour—it's his name, too." Defensive now.

"No, I don't mean the name itself. He doesn't care whether he's a Latour or a Howie Elman or an Elmo Dingleberry. It's just you grabbing the name on his birth certificate has got him to thinking about his mother and father, the past . . . you know, you understand what I mean?"

"I do, yes. But what about you, Mom? The last time I saw you, you were real upset about not finding your own roots."

"That I was, but I got over it because, you see, I faced it. It'll all true up after I die and, hopefully, go to heaven. But your father, he hasn't thought about the smoldering hurt inside of himself. Boom! It went off when you changed your name to Latour."

"I'm sorry. Should I tell him that?"

"He'd only get embarrassed, and he'd still have the ache. When a hurt steals upon you, it's harder to set it right."

"What do you think he wants?"

"Why, he wants his mommy and daddy. That great big man. It's really kind of sad."

SPOONWOOD

. . .

THE NEXT DAY

Latour liked Frenchville, Maine, at first glance. It reminded him of a set out of a 1950s movie on rural America, wood-frame houses and storefronts, limited neon, no food or restaurant chains, pickup trucks parked outside Rosette's Diner, the town built along U.S. Route 1, just a two-lane road this far north, roughly parallel to the railroad tracks, which were roughly parallel to the St. John's River. Rising up from the valley were low hills, some wooded, some open, potato fields in the broad river valley, a landscape both rugged and pastoral at the same time. More snow here than back in New Hampshire. It was soon obvious from the street and business signs that the town's name fit its people—Ouellette, Raymond, Gagnon, Cyr, Michaud, Pelletier, Guimond, Boucher, Dionne, Hébert.

He had come to Frenchville for a reason, but it would wait until he had a meal and a night's sleep. Latour had developed an instinct over the years for a forgot place to camp out, and he knew he'd find one nearby and did, a recent logging cut on a side road ten miles out and up. He had to shovel snow for an hour to clear the snowbank thrown up by the plow. After that he was able to drive in far enough not to be seen from the road. He smelled the sawed fir trees and branch detritus, which gave the area a messy, disreputable look that dirtied the snow. From this prospect he barely made out a church steeple across the St. John's River into Canada.

He started a fire and fried hamburger and onions, which he ate with good French bread, the last thing he'd bought at Ancharsky's Store when he left Darby in the morning ten hours ago. He tried to imagine Birch the way he was when he was whole, but he couldn't create a clear picture in his mind.

It was dark and he'd had his fill, but he kept the fire going. It was no longer a cooking fire but a meditation fire. He twisted open the bottle of Old Crow and poured himself a shot, downed it, another, and another.

"Do you see me in the fire?" Old Crow said.

"As much of yourself as you allow."

"Yes, I admit I am cagey that way. For a while there you seemed relieved of the burden of parenthood and happy with my company."

"Yes, I was relieved. Almost glad. I didn't think I would feel that way. When they took him from me I thought I'd have some sense of loss, regret—something other than what I did feel."

"Relief."

"That's correct, Old Crow. You know me too well."

"You were not truly a father."

"I loved him."

"It wasn't a father's love," Old Crow said. "It was a perverted version of mother love. You found a diluted version of the feeling in a father's weak milk. So I'll grant you some paltry imitation of mother love. But, Latour, you were, are, not yet a father. A father's love grows out of his own maturity since, unlike a mother's love, it is not innate. You have yet to mature, and that is why you cannot love him like a father. Why not just accept yourself as you are, a drunk producing silly spoons?"

Latour heard laughter come out of the fire, or maybe it was the wind in the fir trees.

"All I ever asked for was freedom," Latour said to the fire.

"You have no freedom, Latour. You're in bondage to this fire, to me, to memory."

Latour didn't bother with the shot glass. He took a long pull from Old Crow. His eyes watered, his throat burned, and the spell of the fire broke. Old Crow was not his friend or his lover or his confidante; Old Crow was some kind of twisted version of his mother and father that lodged in his thinking apparatus. He could not deal with Old Crow alone. That, at heart, was his problem—trying to go it alone.

The next morning at 9:00 AM Latour's van was back in Frenchville, parked in front of a renovated shed that might have been a chicken coop at one time. Now it was painted mauve, with flat blue trim. The sign on a picture window said Claire's Unisex

Salon. Latour had been waiting until 8:30 AM, when the place was supposed to open up. His mood had darkened; his old distrust of human beings ate into him like an acid. He wanted to flee, to hide, to contract. If only he could dispense with people and memory and the anguish they brought on. Finally, a stocky woman in her fifties arrived in an aging four-wheel-drive Subaru. The body might be thick but the face had small, pretty features. She was wearing make-up, but it was subtle. She vaguely resembled his older sister Pegeen.

"You waiting for me?" she said.

"If you're Claire, yes. I'm here for a haircut."

"Well, come on in," she said. "Usually people make appointments. You an ice fisherman, skier, or what?"

"If you mean tourist, no, not exactly," Latour said.

Minutes later he was in the chair, white sheet thrown over him, the stocky Claire in a white frock cutting his hair.

"You're getting a little thin on top," she said.

"The truth hurts," he said.

"I can't do anything about truth but I can about the consequences," Claire said.

"I thought your job was to make people look good, which is neither truth nor consequence."

"My word, a philosopher in my midst. I guess Rogaine would never be enough for you."

"Philosopher overrates me." He took a deep breath. "I didn't come only for a haircut, I came to see you, Claire."

"I'm flattered, but I'm a married woman." She never stopped snipping, so he knew he hadn't frightened her. One of his big fears was accidentally scaring people and provoking a crisis. His voice, his body language intimidated people. In that way, he was like his father.

"It's not that," Latour said. "I was in Caribou yesterday in the town clerk's office. I'm doing some genealogy, looking for my father's parents. According to his birth certificate they were residents of Frenchville. They told me that Claire knows everything that goes on in this town.

"Not everything, but close. What's your interest?"

"I'm looking for some history or background, any information, about a man named Claude Latour, married to a woman named Mary DeRepentigny. They were my father's parents. He was born seventy-three years ago. I checked the phone book, no Claude Latour in the area." Claire was cutting his hair very slowly now, snip, pause, snip, pause. "I suppose they've died after all these years, but I was wondering if you know the name, the family, anything."

"Anybody born in this town knows that Claude Latour was killed in 1925 on the river—he was a logger—but Mary, well, Mary is quite alive."

"You sure?" Latour was startled.

"I ought to know. Mary DeRepentigny is my mother. She gave birth to your father when she was only thirteen years old. She had to give him up when Claude died. Later, when she married again and raised a family, there'd be times when she'd cry for the child she gave away. Hello, nephew."

Claire and Latour talked for a long time, and then she took him to meet his grandmother—not Mary (a mistake in the Caribou register), but Marie.

The next day Latour returned to Darby and presented his evidence to his father. The look on Howard's face made Latour proud. Later, at Ancharsky's Store, he looked over the bulletin board advertising the time and place of the next county AA meeting.

3

CHRISTMAS AT THE ELMANS'

ONE YEAR LATER

Persephone had depended on Katharine Ramchand's good sense and calm demeanor to keep her own spirits up, but Katharine was flying to Tunapuna, Trinidad, to be with her half-sisters and their families for the holidays. Persephone had given Soapy and Roland a week off, and they had left for parts unknown. Persephone and Birch would have the mansion all to themselves. How to give the boy a proper Christmas when she herself could care less and had no talent for faking anything, let alone joy? It was not Christmasy-looking in Upper Darby that year. The early part of the month had seen a surprise storm and below zero temperatures for a week. And then everything changed. It rained, the snow melted, and now it was sunny, the temperature befitting October. The thaw was supposed to last two or three more days.

She had brought Birch home only three weeks ago from the rehab center. The doctors believed he had no permanent brain damage. Even so, his mind had been distorted. He remembered some events in minute detail, some not at all, and it appeared as if his imagination had filled file cabinets usually reserved for memories. His speech was oddly formal, as if he remembered how to speak from the books he had read. He'd pause in places where most people would motormouth. His diction gave him the power to command one's attention. Doc Mendy believed that the latest trauma had exacerbated the effects of earlier traumas.

The paralysis in Birch's face had diminished but it left a tic around the eyes, so that he often appeared to be squinting, as if poring over some very fine print. Persephone had no doubt he would grow to be tall, handsome, and strong like Reggie, but for now he was still weak, his muscles slack from months of inactivity. His smile, revealing a mouth full of metal, was rather hideous. In rehab they'd taught him to walk all over again without toes.

It was the day before Christmas, and they were decorating the tree in the Butterworth family tradition—real pine cones painted in wild colors for ornaments, family pictures from various periods starting with the 1870s, hair ribbons belonging to the Butterworth women, jewelry, family memorabilia (emphasis on the funky and bizarre, such as discarded sunglasses, pocket watch chains, tied trout flies), and popped corn, lots of stringed popped corn. If there was one thing that heartened Persephone, it was Birch's delight in popped corn, a Salmon and Butterworth family tradition. The tree reached to within inches of the twelve-foot-high ceiling.

Every Christmas season, even the years when Persephone was not in Upper Darby, Obadiah Handy and Chahley Snow would deliver a tree they cut from the trust lands. The trees were always perfectly symmetrical, and Persephone puzzled over this matter; she'd been in the woods, and she knew that young evergreens never had enough room or light in the deep forest to grow evenly. She marveled that her loggers could find a perfect tree. What Persephone Salmon did not know was that Obadiah and Chahley looked for a tree at least sixty feet tall, one that stuck out above the others. The top, exposed to the sun without competition from its neighbors below, would be perfectly formed. They'd drop the tree, lop the top, and leave the rest to be gobbled by the Nature-machine.

The tree was magnificent enough, but it did not dominate the room. The fireplace and its giant maw would always reign here.

Persephone told Birch how on the twelfth day before Christmas his grandfather Reggie Salmon would build a huge fire, and how it would take three or four days before the bricks were warm and then the fireplace would become a giant radiator and that would heat the huge room with logs alone for the holiday.

"Why did, he, do, that, when, the, furnace could do it better?" Birch asked, each word a question, an observation, a marker for the world to take note.

"He did it for fun."

"I would, like to, try it."

"You're too young now. We'll have to make do with smaller, occasional fires. Do you remember your father's wood stove?"

"I remember, the fire. My mother, my mother, was in, the fire." He spoke as matter of factly as you'd talk about the weather.

"Oh, goodness."

"It's okay. The fire, the fire, the fire, did not, her . . . hurt her. She"—Birch made a diving motion with his hand—"flew down, from the"—Birch raised his hand to heavens—"stars, to, to, to acquire, my attention."

"Acquire?" Persephone laughed at the word choice. "What went on between you and your mother, or rather her ghost?"

Birch shook his head, and when he spoke it jarred her because his voice was almost perfectly normal, "I don't, know. It's all mixed up in my head. I don't really know until I start talking and then I, I remember."

She gave him an encouraging nod. His memories from inside the coma were especially vivid, and she liked listening to them. "You talk, I'll listen," she said. "Tell me something you remember about your mother."

"Right now—nothing. I remember, remember, Dad. He held, my hand, and he, talked to me. I wanted, to tell him that, I, I, understood, but I couldadint. Is that, a word?"

"Couldn't, contraction for could not. Couldadint sounds like patent medicine."

"I knew, that, I already, knew that. I remember my mom now, in heaven, with my mom. She said, that Dad, was his own worst, worst, worst. Emmy?"

"Enemy."

"Right. Dad was his own liverwurst enemy?"

Persephone laughed. "Are you making a joke?"

"Yes, you, got it, good. Mom said, love Dad, anyway. Dad told, me, me, he told me . . ."

"When?"

"During my, coma. He talked, 'I did, one, good thing in my, life. I, found, your grandfather Howard's, mother. She's, she is, she's eighty-six and lives in Maine.' He, Dad, told, me, me that Grandpa Howard, drove up to see her. They had a re-onion."

"A re-onion?"

"Right. After Dad told me, about Grandpa, seeing, his mom, Dad, Dad, he sat in a chair, and he, he, was quiet, but I know what he was, was, doing. I knew, the sound. I, can't, think of the, idea, in verbal. But, the sound." He squinted, looking for words and diction, it appeared.

"Make the sound," Persephone said.

"*Sip, sip, sip, sip.*"

"He was drinking a glass of water?"

"No," Birch was adamant.

"You say you were with Lilith in heaven."

"Yes."

"Did she speak to you?"

"I, think, so."

"What did she look like?"

"Like the pictures."

"Apparently, one does not age in heaven." Persephone laughed, her bitter scraping laugh that could peel paint.

"Grandma, Purse?"

"Yes?"

"Can I, go and see, Dad, once, in a while?"

Persephone thought long on this question. "Let me think about it. Birch, is there something special for Christmas I can do for you?"

"More, presents?"

"If you want. What would you like? Your own TV maybe?"

"Okay, a TV."

"Really?"

His squint became more pronounced. "Not really. If I, could, have, it would be, to see, Missy Mendelson, and to eat Christmas, dinner, at Grandma Elenore and Grandpa Howard's mobile home, with Dad."

"They pack them in that trailer, and you'd rather be there than here?" She was talking to herself now, a bad habit, for the quality of the company was not up to her standards.

"Did, I, I hurt, your feelings, Grandma Purse? I love you."

"I know you do," she said. She wanted to hug him, but he was at an age where hugs embarrassed him.

They watched *A Wonderful Life* on the VCR, a recent addition in the Salmon house, because Birch had become addicted to television and movies in the hospital and in rehab.

Afterward, Persephone went into her office, closed the door, and telephoned the Elman residence. Elenore Elman answered the phone.

Persephone found herself unaccountably shy. She had to light a cigarette just to keep her voice steady.

"Mrs. Elman, Persephone Salmon here. Listen, I know this is the last minute, but Birch has expressed a desire to eat Christmas dinner with you folks. I was wondering if I could drop him off. I've made arrangements for Missy Mendelson's mother to pick him up and bring him to the Mendelsons'. They just returned from a vacation."

"Well, this is really something," Elenore said, and Persephone could not tell from her tone, surprised and a little suspicious, what her meaning was. Persephone's old animus gnawed her gut. She wanted to tell Elenore Elman to speak her mind, but she reined herself in.

"Birch says you eat punctually at noon," Persephone said. "I could drop him at a little before then, and Missy's mother will pick him up at 3:30."

Again there was a long pause. Finally, Elenore Elman spoke. "It used to be that all our children and their families would come to our place for Christmas *dinnah,* but they moved away, thousands of miles. Mrs. Salmon, maybe you'd like to help fill out our table."

"You're, inviting me—me?"

"Yah, you."

Suddenly, both women choked up with emotion. The very idea—the Elmans and the Salmons at the same table. Why had they waited so long? They lingered in some kind of telekinetic embrace conducted through the phone lines, then hung up at the same time without good-byes.

The Elman yard was appalling—junked cars, various discarded appliances with bullet holes in them, a bathtub Mary in a vegetable garden, garbage trucks in a dirt parking lot, things just lying here and there. The scene made Persephone fearful. She wasn't afraid of the inhabitants of this place; she was afraid of her own insulting, unmanageable tongue. For Birch's sake she resolved to put a clothespin on it.

On impulse she'd brought the Elmans special gifts, but now in the driveway she questioned her own judgment. How could these people appreciate works of art? She must have had a temporary lapse into insanity to agree to come here.

Inside, the mobile home was neat to a fault. Apparently the Elmans divided their domain into duchyes: he got the barn and the outdoors, she got the domicile. Persephone couldn't tell from the road, but another room with a shed roof had been added, making the kitchen and the adjoining "family room," as they called it, fairly good-sized and comfortable. But that wall-to-wall carpeting!

An Aubuchon hardware store calendar decorated a kitchen cabinet door. Magnets held notes to the refrigerator. In the family room was a framed print of a rosy-cheeked Jesus, with Joseph and Mary, and another print of cows grazing in a field. Persephone saw only one well-made piece of furniture, a gun cabinet, beside which was a plastic creche and an artificial Christmas tree. Framed portraits of children and grandchildren popped up everywhere. A couple of shelves spilled over with *Reader's Digest* condensed books. A magazine rack contained *Time, People,* and the *Catholic Messenger.* No ashtrays in sight. The poverty of art depressed Persephone. It wasn't that the Elman house was in poor taste; it was that it lacked any standard or even idea of taste. Still, it was neat and clean.

Birch embraced his grandparents in a cautious, reserved way. Latour and Birch did not embrace, but something passed between them—a smile, brief but penetrating eye contact, an intimacy that gave Persephone a pang of envy. She remembered that Latour as Frederick Elman had been an insecure, high-strung young man with a chip on his shoulder. Now, on the brink of middle age, he was a different person. Rueful—was that what she was seeing behind the calm exterior?

Persephone was introduced to the other guests: Pitchfork Parkinson and his sister, Delilah, obviously a sweet-dispositioned Down's-syndrome person; Long Neck McDougal and his girlfriend Janice (no last name given, bad teeth). Pitchfork and Long Neck were part of Howard's trash collection team. Persephone was impressed by the physiques of these men. They didn't have the pumped-up, poster-boy look, nor did they resemble athletes; they were a breed apart, slouchingly muscular from manual labor, eight hours a day Monday through Friday plus Saturday mornings, ugly, dependable, expendable bodies, like the machines they loved so much.

Birch tore into presents from his grandparents, a video game and a sweater from Elenore and a .22 rifle from Howard.

The grimace on Latour's face told Persephone he didn't approve of guns, but he didn't say anything.

"I'll take it back if you don't want him to have it," Howard said to Latour.

"Pop, you're going to do what you're going to do," Latour said with mild amusement.

Howard turned to Persephone. "I've been holding onto this little pea-shooter for a week, didn't even know whether I'd have the opportunity to give it to him. I probably should have checked with you first."

"As long as he takes a gun safety course, it's all right with me," Persephone said. "I've been shooting since I was eleven years old—skeet."

"I stand corrected," Howard said. He had a droll way of talking that suggested he never stood corrected.

Latour's gift to Birch was about the size of a box of chocolates and wrapped in birch bark. Birch closed his eyes and held the box for a moment.

"I bet you know what it is," Latour said.

"I do," Birch said. "Can I open now?"

Latour didn't say anything. He just smiled, and Birch opened the box. Inside was a Swiss Army knife and a sharpening stone.

"You remember how to use the stone?" Latour asked.

"I remember everything Dad."

"I knew you would."

Persephone experienced a complex emotion. It was joy and anguish and envy. She knew that Birch and Latour had reestablished the connection that had bound them in the years they were together.

Elenore and Janice served turkey, store stuffing, mashed potatoes, peas, Thanksgiving all over again. Dry toast in place of rolls—what was that all about? Persephone declined dessert, and despite her efforts to remain cordial and calm she began to fidget. Only Howard noticed. He made a motion with his fingers and pointed toward the door.

Elenore, who was standing by the sink with her back to the table, understood the silent communication between the smokers. "The filthy habit," she said, loud enough to be heard by all, her tone supplying the verb.

Persephone Salmon and Howard Elman stood outside on the deck, a butt can by their side. "Used to be I could smoke in the house," Howard said. "Every day you lose a little more hair, a little more freedom."

"Uh-huh." Persephone was reevaluating her recent impression of the Elman place. From this vantage point the barn and the junked cars looked like sculpture, a diorama of country life in the twilight of the century.

Howard lit a Camel with an old, brushed-metal, fluid-style lighter, and then he lit Persephone's Kool.

"I always liked the noise those lighters make," she said.

"Nothing like a Zippo—made in America—needs only a bit of love and a kind hand to throw the flame," Howard said, paused, and went on. "I've cut down, but I can't seem to quit."

"Me, I don't even try. I do change brands. Funny, but I only smoke when I'm in Darby. In Tasmania, I don't smoke at all," Persephone said.

"Really? You feel stressed here?"

"Not stress, loathing. I never did like Upper Darby. It was Reggie's realm, and I was just the Squire's wife. If it wasn't for Birch, I would have been gone long ago."

"Whoopsie-daisy. I never figured . . ."

"That anybody in Upper Darby had a problem?"

"I guess everybody's got some damn thing that nags at them."

"What's your problem, Howie—you don't mind if I call you Howie?"

"Just don't call me late for eats."

She could see he wasn't about to answer her question.

They smoked in silence for a few minutes, and Persephone could feel herself grow both calmer and more alert.

They talked about Birch for a while and then Latour.

"Freddie, he's doing okay by himself," Howard said. "He goes to AA meetings. Sounds like he's delivering the gospel sometimes. Talk like that can drive a man to drink."

"Is that so? Latour, growing up after all these years."

"I think he's going to be all right."

"I hope so, for Birch's sake. He needs a father."

"Mrs. Salmon . . ." Howard extinguished the cigarette in the sand of the butt can.

"Please call me Persephone."

"Persephone, some years back I poisoned the waters between the Elmans and the Salmons when I dumped refuse on your land." He didn't look at her when he spoke. He looked far away, as if he were talking to someone high on the hill that shadowed this property.

"Literally, you poisoned the waters," she said.

"Persephone," he practically shouted, "you ever need anything up there on the hill, I mean to fix—I can fix anything you got busted. I want to do it."

"Apology accepted."

He looked at her now, right in the eye. "I didn't apologize."

Persephone broke into laughter. "Howard Elman, you are such an idiot." She punched his thick upper arm.

"No, no," he said, droll and in command. "Pitchfork Parkinson is an idiot, Long Neck McDougal is an idiot, Freddie is an idiot—me, I'm only the biggest horse's ass in Darby."

"You can depend on me to kick your ass when necessary," she said.

"Deal." He offered his hand and she took it.

And that was that.

The guests cleared out fast after coffee. Persephone helped Elenore with dishes and clean-up. Latour, Birch, and Howard went outside. Persephone could hear the *pip pip* of .22-caliber gunfire.

She watched Birch through the window. He didn't walk with a limp exactly, more an awkward shuffle. His grandfather crouched beside him. Latour stood by, arms folded.

As the women washed dishes Elenore underwent a change in demeanor. She stopped chattering, broke off eye contact, concentrated on the chore at hand.

"Elenore, you look to me like somebody with something on her mind."

Elenore never stopped working, washing a dish, wiping it, putting it away, and she never looked at Persephone, who could see shame on her face. "When Lilith died, I was here and I did nothing," Elenore said.

"I always thought if I'd been here instead of Tasmania, I could have saved her—that's the guilt I carry," Persephone said, her voice suddenly clear of the rasp.

"But you had no chance; I did." Elenore's eyes brimmed with tears. "You see, Mrs. Salmon—Persephone—she came here, pregnant, upset, and I sent her away out of spite. It was only hours before she went up to those ledges to have her child and die. I've prayed for forgiveness, but I don't deserve it, and I'm not looking for it from you. I just want you to know. Because . . . it's necessary."

"I can see how hard this is for you, Elenore. You haven't asked, but I do forgive you, just as I forgave myself. We're just human beings."

The women embraced spontaneously and just as spontaneously they parted and returned to the kitchen work.

A few minutes later Maddy Mendelson showed up with Missy in a brand-new foreign-made four-wheel-drive. Persephone experienced a knot of resentment in her stomach. There had been a time when Reggie's Bronco was the only vehicle fit both for road and woods. Now four-wheel-drives were all over the place, operated by people who had no use for such vehicles. Persephone thought that if she could just get over these inconsequential biases she wouldn't need to smoke. If she could somehow purify herself before she died, she might leave this earth with some dignity and a sense of accomplishment.

She watched Birch hand the rifle to his grandfather, hobble over to the car; the rear door opened, and he entered. The car backed, turned, and drove by her window. Persephone waved but she couldn't be seen for the reflection. In the back seat of the car, the two young people were face to face. Persephone only had a glimpse but there was something fateful about the way they looked at each other.

In the barn Latour watched while his father changed the oil in one of the trucks. Latour wanted to make himself useful, but despite the fact that he and Howard had made peace with one another he couldn't feel comfortable around his father in the barn messing with cars and trucks. At any minute Latour expected to be ordered around, or criticized in Howard's oblique, sarcastic way. Part of F. Spoonwood Latour would always remain that small berated boy, Freddie Elman.

Howard went down into the pit and Latour followed. Latour had forgotten how much he hated the pit—the darkness, the smells of earth and machines all mixed up. Howard clicked on his light. It was on the end of a cord, the bulb encased by a rubber-covered metal cage. He shined the light on the undersides of the truck. Latour looked away, fighting off an unaccountable wave of revulsion.

"I couldn't survive in an environment like this," Latour said.

"Too unwholesome for you?" Howard said as he worked. He could never quite take his son's sensitivity seriously.

"Too ugly," Latour said.

Howard laughed. "Me, I come down here to relax. These vehicles, they might not run right but they never complain." He put a pan for the dirty oil at his feet.

"Freddie—oops, I keep forgetting you go by Latour these days."

"That's okay, Pop."

Howard cursed at something under the truck. "Would you hand me that wrench?"

"Which wrench?"

"The three-eighths."

Frederick handed Howard the wrench.

Howard put the wrench on a bolt, pulled, grunted, pulled again. It loosened. With his fingers he twisted the bolt until it fell off in his hand. Dirty oil dropped from the bowel of the truck in the pan below. Howard grabbed a rag and wiped his hands.

"Freddie—Latour!" he shouted.

"Yah, Pop." He knew Howard was working his way up to something.

"Oh, I don't know."

"You started to tell me something, and now you're backing off," Latour said.

"I never backed off from anything in my life."

Latour was puzzled and a little amused. He'd never known Howard to refrain from voicing an opinion, especially to his son.

"Go ahead, Pop. Don't be bashful."

"All right, goddamn it. I hope I don't jinx it, but I have to say it. About finding my mother—geez!" He stopped, unable to go on. "Oh, never mind. Listen, one thing I really missed when you were off by yourself was having to sharpen my tools. You got the knack, admirable, my boy—admirable."

Latour smiled to himself. His old man couldn't bring himself to thank him for finding his mother. Mother and son had had a great reunion. No embraces or tears or speeches; they'd immediately started kidding one another. No doubt they were two of a kind. Latour wanted to tell his father that he loved him, but such language in or out of the pit was unthinkable.

Howard aimed his light at a new location and in so doing the glow revealed his face for a moment—quizzical, optimistic. "You, me, the boy, Elenore, Mrs. Salmon—I think we're gaining," he said.

Outside, on the way back into the house, Latour noticed a junked car beside the barn, a Ford Falcon with a smashed-in grill.

"Isn't that Pitchfork's old car?" Latour said.

"Yep."

"What did he hit, a tree?"

Howard said nothing.

Latour went over to the car. He picked a twisted bicycle spoke out of the grill. "Pop, this is what is known as evidence. Tell me what happened."

"I don't know exactly—I wasn't there. But from what I gather the ignoramous was doing his usual . . ."

"Driving too fast."

"Right. Same time you-know-who came out of nowhere, also no doubt not heedful."

"Okay, Pop, I get it," Latour said. Pitchfork Parkinson, barrelling down the road in his Ford Falcon, had run over and killed Garvin Prell.

When the men came in the women were sitting in the family room in front of the TV, which was tuned to a soap opera.

"Hey, I wanted to watch that," Howard said with mock seriousness.

"Oh, shut up, Howie," Elenore said.

"You know, Persephone, I always wondered," Howard said, "why you go down under for months at a time."

"My second husband teaches and lives in Tasmania. It's my true home. I come to Darby purely for business and family reasons."

"You sacrificed your own desires for Birch," Elenore said.

Persephone winced. She didn't want these people to know how vulnerable she was.

Latour unwittingly came to her rescue with an accusation in his tone.

"I bet there's more to it than that," he said.

"You knew Lilith, but something's missing, isn't there?" Persephone snapped.

Latour's voice dropped almost to a whisper. "I want to know why she went to the ledges. Something was bothering her that I can't figure."

"It was love," Elenore said.

"It was spite," Howard said.

"It was money," Persephone said.

"Money, what do you mean? There was plenty of money," Latour said.

Persephone shook her head no. "Reggie frittered away the family fortune, or what was left of it, on buying properties for his damn land trust."

"It makes sense. I think she tried to tell me, but I wasn't listening. I couldn't imagine that the Salmon money had run out."

"You see," Persephone said, "that was her problem. She grew up as the rich girl in town. Nothing else would do."

"So it was shame that drove her up there to have her baby," Elenore said.

"That was part of it, no doubt," Persephone said. "We'll never know for sure. This much I do know. Lilith was branded with the Salmon hubris."

"What's hubris?" Elenore asked.

"Overweening pride," Latour said, but that didn't satisfy Howard.

"Wait a minute, I'll go look it up," he said, and stormed into the next room. When he returned he was holding the dictionary and wearing his reading glasses.

"Overweening pride, right?" said Latour.

"Hubris is pigheadedness, says so right here." Howard tapped the dictionary with his thick forefinger, slammed it shut, put it down, and then quickly changed the subject. "Persephone, you finagled the trust charter and sold off the Grace Pond property to get dough."

"I made a simple hard-headed business decision." Persephone turned a droll eye on Howard. "You understand the hard-headed part."

"Indeed I do."

Elenore addressed Latour. "Well, I guess they have that in common."

"They have us out-gunned, Mom," Latour said, then turned to Persephone. "If Reggie left the house to Lilith, then Birch should have inherited it."

Persephone smiled mischievously. "Well, of course. You understand the implications?"

"I'm beginning to," Latour said. "Back when I had custody of Birch I could have moved into the Salmon estate with him and kicked you out."

"This gets funnier by the minute," Howard said.

Persephone couldn't help feeling smug. She looked at Latour and said, "Since I now have custody, I have the house."

Latour smiled, an embarrassed smile.

"It's okay, Freddie," said Howard. "The Upper Darby people aren't any better or smarter than we are, they just learn tricks from the cradle that we don't."

"That's true, Howard," said Persephone. "That's why I wanted to raise Birch."

"So he could have your advantages," Elenore said.

"He'll need every advantage," Persephone said to Elenore, then to Howard, "and trick. When he comes of age he'll take my place as chair of the trust board."

"Where there are competing forces," Latour said.

"Monet—the Pocket Squire," said Howard.

"Yes, Reggie's brother," Persephone said. "He wants the trust."

"Where does Monet get *his* money from?" Howard asked.

"I don't know but I have my suspicions. Monet's wife is very connected in Colombia."

"Back when I was hanging out with Tubby McCracken, I heard rumours about a big-time local drug lord," Latour said.

"This is all loose talk," Elenore said. "There's no proof, right?"

"No proof," Persephone said.

There was a long moment of unease in which time appeared to stop and no one could think of anything to say. Finally, Howard shook the room with a large rueful laugh, and the clock of Darby began to tick again.

"Well, I guess we all confessed our sins today," Howard roared. "Better run and get those rosary beads, Elenore."

"Put a sock in it, Howie," Elenore said.

Persephone was pleasantly confused now. She didn't understand these exasperating people and they didn't understand her, but somehow because of Birch they would get along.

"I almost forgot," Persephone said. "I have a couple presents for you." She went out to the car and returned with two hastily wrapped oil paintings.

She gave one to Elenore and Howard, Rachel Bloom's painting of Birch staring into the fire, the other to Latour, the one of his hand holding Birch's hand holding a spoon. Elenore hung the painting in the living room beside the Jesus print.

"How did you come by these?" Latour asked, his voice soft and full of regrets.

"In Perth. I hadn't see my husband in ten months. We were on holiday. I had the paintings shipped to the states."

"Did you meet the artist?" Latour asked. "I owe her."

"I did, a remarkable woman. She remembered you and Birch with . . . well, I don't know if it was fondness, but it was with clarity. Last I heard she was cohabitating with an Aussie sculptor."

Missy Mendelson had known about Birch Latour's injuries and she had emoted greatly at the news, but inside she couldn't quite bring herself to believe that something was really wrong with Birch. Part of her thought that having toes removed and "brain dysfunction," as her father put it, were theatrical effects when it came to Birch Latour, not really real—those were the words in her mind, "not really real." When Birch, who had always been athletic as a monkey, staggered awkwardly toward the car, she'd thought he was making a joke. But after he started to speak in his halting way it began to dawn on her how damaged he was. Her realization made her feel fiercely defensive on his behalf. She would protect him against the world.

Later that day they left the house and went outside, where they discovered that each, unbeknownst to the other, had taken up smoking. They smoked.

"When you were, like, in the snowbank, what happened?" Missy asked.

Birch took a moment to gather his thoughts, and when he spoke his voice was normal.

"At first it was awful. The cold hurt, but then I wasn't cold anymore and suddenly I could see my mother, I could reach her, I almost touched her."

"Was she all there? I mean could you, like, talk to her?"

"Not exactly. I could read her thoughts and she could read mine. I telepathed her the big question."

"Why she went up to the ledges to have you."

"Right. Say my mother's name."

"Lilith."

"You like saying it?"

"No."

"Me neither. Lilith twists my tongue. Her father named her that because he liked the ledges and he read someplace that Lilith means woman among the rocks. She was a daddy's girl. In her mind, she was always 'woman among the rocks' because her daddy told her so."

"Your mom died because she had a lousy name."

"You like your name, Missy?"

"I do. You like yours?"

"I do. A person has to have the right name."

A SURPRISE FOR LATOUR

NEW YEAR'S EVE 1998

It was late in the afternoon, already getting on toward dark. The bank thermometer said fourteen degrees. Katharine Ramchand, back two days from her annual holiday trip to Trinidad, had just completed her shopping, and she drove to a renovated mill building. Outside, a couple of men in parkas and a woman in a cloth coat and a bright red and green scarf stood around and smoked cigarettes.

The woman recognized Katharine and said, "He's inside. I'll get him." She flicked the cigarette into the street. One of the men opened the door for her.

A minute later Latour came out. He always dressed up for AA meetings. Today his outfit consisted of pressed khaki pants, a dark green and black Pendleton shirt with a bright yellow tie, and a Tweed jacket. He managed to look both stylish and ridiculous at the same time. Persephone had encouraged him to help himself to the Squire's wardrobe. He'd resisted at first, but only for show. Despite his peculiar lifestyle, Latour was vain about his appearance.

She moved to the passenger side and he took the wheel; he kissed her lightly on the lips, put the car in gear, and drove off.

"Man, am I glad to get out of Keene. I hate New Year's Eve," he said.

"Is it the reminder of drink and revelers?"

"It's that, the biggest amateur night of the year, but mainly I hate to see so many people at once."

"A man who can't stand a crowd, how did I manage to find you?"

"Anything more than you and me and I get jumpy."

She smiled. He was romantic in his own way. They indulged themselves in the easy chatter of intimates. She regaled him with office gossip at Keene State College, where she was Associate Professor of Social Geology, and she talked about visiting her sisters in Trinidad. One made costumes for Carnival and the other managed a taxi business with her husband. They ate roti and dove through the surf at Maracas Beach. Katharine would miss her sisters, but not the heat. She was glad to be back in the cold. Latour talked about how pleased he was at the reconciliation between Persephone and his own family. Birch was going to spend a month with the Elmans while Persephone visited with her husband down under.

It was a forty-minute hike to Latour's shanty. They walked by starlight on a few inches of new snow that came in after the thaw departed.

Latour built up his fire, and the shanty was soon warm. They made love, then had something to eat. Latour laid out the stick table with cloth napkins, cooked hot sausages on the outdoor grill, serving them with good, crusty bread and a salad. She drank chardonnay, which she'd brought with them, and he Ovaltine.

"You shouldn't drink that stuff," she said. "It's loaded with sugar."

"So's your white wine."

And they made love again.

Afterward, Latour said, "Admit it, you like it out here?"

"I like it for sex and relaxation—it feels cozy and private; but I couldn't, that is definitely would not, live like you do. What would it take to move you into the mansion with me?" she asked.

"I love you, Katharine, but I'm in these woods until the next ice age," Latour said. "This is the only way I know how to live. It's not a matter of choice." He picked up one of his wooden spoons.

"I guess I knew that," she paused, and started again, "Latour?"

"What is it, Katharine, what is it you want from me?"

"I want to have your baby."

5

THE TRUST

DECEMBER 2005

Katharine Ramchand—full professor, author of *Society and History in Stone Walls*—began her lecture by lifting a rock the size of a grapefruit over her head and displaying it for her students. She said nothing for a minute and then she put the rock down beside her notes on the podium and began to talk.

"Your assignment over the holiday break is to find a stone from your hometown and bring it back to class for analysis," she said. "My hope is that you will become very intimate with that stone and in the end will know more about its origins, its eventual fate, and its implications and influence upon the kind of person you are in the world you live in."

Professor Ramchand commanded the attention of her class not only with the content of her course but with her voice, where one could hear the nuances of her complex heritage—England, France, South Louisiana, New England, the Caribbean, India, Africa, China. It was said that when Professor Ramchand talked about rocks she could make poetry out of them with the sound of her voice: quartz, barite, molybdenite, chalcopyrite, galena, fluorite.

"This particular rock beside me on the podium comes from a wall on the Salmon Forest Trust Conservancy in Upper Darby, New Hampshire," she said. "I will return the rock to the place where I found it. Why? Because the wall has become a cultural icon as well as a land form . . ."

For an hour she talked about the rock, its origins in ancient volcanic times, its transformations by natural forces through the eons, its similarities to rocks found on the British Isles, and finally how the rock played a role in the settling of North America by Europeans and today how the rock had found its way into the psyche of the people who inhabited its environs.

She dispelled some myths—for example, that the first New England colonists struggled with stony soil. Not true: the soil was deep and fertile. The stones lay well beneath good workable soil and rose into the loam through natural processes created by the clearing of the forests. "Indeed," she said, "Puritan farmers worried that they had offended the Almighty when they saw stones suddenly appearing in their fields after half a century working their lands.

"Another myth was that farmers built walls as fences to keep stock in or to use as boundary lines. In fact, most walls were built simply to clear the fields. The result: 240,000 miles of stone walls in New England. Perhaps if we realign the walls carefully we can walk beside them to the moon.

"The appearance of stones changed the character of New England. The walls became land forms, affecting agriculture and even climate; by now they have achieved the status of monuments. They are part of the identity of the region and the people. Nowhere else in the world does one find miles and miles of stone walls meandering through second-growth forests."

At the end of her day, Katharine carried the rock with her to her new Ford Explorer and put it in the rear. She would return the rock to its place on the wall that went through what had once been the commune where she'd spent part of her childhood. She had mixed feelings about the place. She remembered the joy, the music, the natural world, the feeling of being one with so many other people. But she also remembered rash acts, her mother's life cut short by her excesses. Katharine would not recommend commune living to her own children.

Her daughter, Persephone, was born a year before the woman she was named after died of lung cancer. "Sephy" would start school in the fall of next year. Katharine's son, Nigel, named after Katharine's Trinidadian father, was three, a handful. Katharine picked up her children at day care and drove on. She worried about the future, how to explain to her children the peculiar living arrangements of their family, she and they in the Salmon mansion with their half-brother, Birch, while Latour, their father, lived in primitive conditions in various places according to his whims.

Birch Spoonwood Latour and Melissa "Missy" Mendelson hiked to the tree house, not an easy walk for Birch with his bad feet. Every summer he and Missy and Bez made improvements to the structure. The ladder was now a staircase that wound around the tree and was protected by a railing. The deck had been widened and each of the two rooms expanded, with standard windows installed. The tree house was now fully furnished with comfortable chairs, a propane refrigerator and cookstove, and a wood-fired Franklin fireplace for heat and meditation.

Birch was home from Dartmouth College, where he was majoring in environmental studies. Missy was a physics major at Wesleyan University in Connecticut. They saw each other almost every weekend. The elders in both their families puzzled over the nature of their relationship. They seemed to be siblings; they seemed to be lovers; they seemed to be best friends; they seemed to be business associates; they seemed to be comrades in arms in ideological struggles known only to themselves. The young people did nothing to advance or retard the theories about them. They preferred to keep their elders guessing. Birch would be turning twenty-one in the spring, when he would take his place as chair on the trust governing board. Or would he? The current chair, his granduncle Monet, had his own ideas about how the trust should be administered.

Missy poured glasses of wine, and while Birch built a fire in the Franklin stove she scanned the trust through the window with binoculars. "I swear I can see somebody at the apple orchard," she said.

"It's Dad."

"How do you know?"

"I don't know how I know what I know. Even in school I get these funny feelings about Dad."

"Memories."

"No, it's like I'm in his thoughts and he's in mine."

"Weird."

Once the fire was going Birch and Missy sat on the stick couch in front of the stove, close to one another but not touching, and they smoked cigarettes and looked at the fire.

Birch was good-looking in a delicate way, but he never came close to measuring up in stature to his famous grandfather, the Squire. He took after his grandmother Elenore, and he still wore braces. They would not come off for another year. Because of frostbite injuries to his feet, his natural walking gait was awkward, as if he were dragging a ball and chain. He compensated by walking very slowly with his head bent down and his hands behind his back, like one in deep thought. If he had to walk fast, he would straighten his back and square his shoulders, not to help him move but to appear dignified, if not natural. He had learned to walk in this special way from his stepmother, Katharine Ramchand, who of course learned it in Trinidad. Despite his modest physical attributes, Birch Latour exuded confidence. He was never drunk, never out of control. He might be a worrywart, but he was without fear. His friends looked to him for leadership, which he was happy to provide.

At six feet in height Missy was two inches taller than Birch. The awkwardness of her early teens had vanished. She'd found contact lenses she wasn't allergic to, and she wore very subtle make-up. Wherever she went she turned heads; she walked with a natural grace, an effortlessly beautiful woman.

For a minute or two they said nothing, content to sip the wine and gaze into the fire. Then Birch stood and went over to the window.

"I can see the ledges from here," he said.

"Do you really remember being born there?" Missy asked.

"I do. I remember everything."

"That's so weird."

"It's even weirder than you think," Birch said. "For the first six years of my life I not only remember what I was doing and thinking, I remember what Dad was doing and thinking. You know that old saying about being of two minds? Well, I was of two minds. Unfortunately, I was going for a third, but I never did reach her."

"Your mother."

Birch nodded, came back from the window, and sat beside Missy, closer now, so at times they brushed up against one another.

"Maybe you did reach her but she made sure you forgot," Missy said. "You know, like, because it was necessary for you to be here and not with her."

"I like that idea, Missy. I like it a lot. I'm not a loner like Dad. I'm Catholic in more ways than one. I enjoy the company of people. I need people and they need me. I believe in the Communion of Saints and in my own memories as far as they go. We're all part of God—you, me, every little ant; this pine where we've built our refuge, that's my mother. The deer we jumped on the way here, that's her, too."

"You're part Catholic and part pagan, Birch. It's kind of mysterious and a little bit funny to me." She paused. "You think Monet's branch of the family is going to try to take over the trust?"

"They already have, Missy. Monet wants to sell off the rest of the trust to the Heron Village people."

"That's illegal."

"It's a murky area. Persephone was able to sell the Grace Pond watershed. Monet and his son will use the precedent. You follow? And it's all going to blow in three years."

"The twenty-fifth anniversary of the Salmon trust."

"Yes, the charter comes up for a self-review and renewal."

"It's going to be a war. You have three years to prepare yourself."

Birch held up his arm, like a police officer halting traffic. "No," he said. "I will not go to war with anyone. I will find a way without war, even metaphorical war."

"You're a dreamer, Birch."

"That's what Grandma Purse used to say." Birch took a long drink of wine.

"You miss her, don't you?" Missy said.

"She taught me so many things. I wish she were here to help me work out my philosophy. I don't really know what I believe. I don't even know if I want to keep my name. Inside"—He thumped his chest—"I'm half Elman, half Latour, and half Salmon."

"You have a math problem."

"Yes, aftermath. I was going through some of the family papers, and you know what I found out? The original pronunciation of Salmon is not *Sahlmohn*, it's *Saminn*, the way Grandpa Howard says it in mockery."

"And then there's—Birch. Your dad named you after your mother's favorite tree, right?"

"Right. Except he was wrong. My mother's favorite tree was the lilac. She planted a bunch of them the day she died."

They were quiet for a while, then Birch continued talking about what he was going to do when he took over as chair of the trust.

"People have been poaching deer, firewood, even saw logs. Damn dirt bikes tear up the trails, and there's litter everywhere. I'm going to hire a trust cop, the baddest SOB I know."

"Our old pal Bez."

"Right. He knows the trust and all the dirty poacher tricks."

They finished the wine and started back for the mansion, listening to their own footfalls, the creak of a tree in the wind, the squack of a crow. Finally, Missy spoke. "Birch, you don't have any big ideas, but I do." She paused and delivered her last words in that tone that told Birch she was serious. "I have a plan," she said.

"Really."

"Your house—it's, like, gigantic. Even with Roland and Soapy and your family, you still have, what, fifteen or twenty rooms you never use."

"Twenty-two," Birch said. He was thinking of his mother's room, which he had left preserved just as his grandmother Persephone had left it. He was thinking now of his grandma Purse, picturing himself in her bed beside her as she taught him his lessons. He shut his eyes. Missy knew that when Birch shut his eyes he was going back in time and she should leave him alone until he returned to the present moment.

Persephone wants to die in Tasmania, but the cancer has other ideas and she can't be moved from the medical center in Keene. Birch sits beside her bed, moistening his grandmother's dry lips with a sponge on a stick. She opens her eyes briefly and looks at him in the old ironic way of the atheist. Her hand quivers, and he understands that she wants him to take the hand.

He envelops the tiny, bony hand in both of his own. The hand is ice cold. Her body shudders and shakes, and then she is still and he knows she is dead. At that moment energy surges through the hand right into Birch. It spreads into and across his body, a warmth. She is leaving him her strength.

Birch opened his eyes, and Missy went on with the conversation as if no break in time had occurred.

"You, me, our friends, we don't have anything in common with our parents or anybody," Missy said. "We don't know what we're going to do when we get out of college. How about we start a commune right here? Everybody lives in your house or on the grounds someplace. The trust lands, they'll be our experiment."

"Experiment in what?"

"I don't know right now, environmental something or other. Government, God—so many things in the world are all fucked up. We have more than a year to figure it out."

"Right," Birch said. "I get it—yes, I get it. Right. A commune. We'll start with you and me and Bez—and Spontaneous Combustion."

"That cat must be ancient."

"Thousands of years old."

They were both excited now. They would talk some more about how young people can make a better world. All they needed was a philosophy, a religion, cultural institutions, an economic system, a government that worked for everybody, and of course a cat.

TIME

When Katharine Ramchand arrived at the mansion she found Missy Mendelson watching TV in the family room. The children ran to her. Through the French doors Katharine could see Latour and Birch splitting firewood. In the winter they closed off most of the house to save on heat, congregating in two rooms— a large eat-in kitchen and the library, converted into a family room with stereo system, television, and a "play" section for the little ones. Latour had installed a Vermont Castings wood stove insert in the fireplace. Though he'd never spent a night in the Salmon house with her, he was good with the children, taking them for long walks in the woods, talking to them, teaching them. His ability to mesmerize them sometimes frightened her. He held entirely different views of childraising than her, but he never criticized her more traditional methods. He simply subverted them with his charm and persistence. She hoped that eventually the children would sort the best from both their worlds.

Katharine paused for a moment before taking her coat off, and when she did her mind recorded a short mental video of the proceedings. The images were so vivid that she knew they would remain in her memory for retrieval at any time. Her children had joined Missy, and the three of them were all tangled up in each other as they watched a women's basketball game on television. Outside, Birch chucked round wood from a pile to his father, who caught it and ran it through the power splitter. A father and son dance. Suddenly, the rhythm of their labors broke. Latour held up a hand just as Birch was going to toss him a log. Birch put the log down. Latour bent and picked up a piece of wood recently created by the splitter, a crude but recognizable spoon shape. Latour handed the piece to Birch, who studied it for a moment. Father and son then engaged in conversation, serious and intimate from the look on their faces. Finally, Latour took the spoon shape from Birch and set it aside and they went back to work. The image that remained embedded in Katharine's mind was of Latour's hand, Birch's hand, the wood, for a moment all touching, a unity, like that painting that Latour kept in his work wigwam in the woods. The spoon, the hands, the bodies, the feet on the ground, the ground itself, the earth's shifting crust—she melted it and fused it in the heat-flux of her mind.

THE FUTURE

Who can say whether Birch Latour and his cohorts save the World, or even the Salmon Forest Trust Conservancy? Who can say whether Latour will be a good father to his children with Katharine Ramchand? Who can say where these people and this land fit into a world order or even whether there will be a world order? The forest might be cut down, houses built, and shopping centers established along with streets and streetlights. Or the trust charter might hold, and the mixed hardwood forest might continue to reign with the beaver, the bear, the deer, and the mysterious coyote. Or the climate might change and the trees vanish. The ice age might return and completely transform the landscape, even the rocks. Upon the retreat of the ice outcasts from other nations might settle here, call it their own. One can only imagine:

A surveyor, perhaps, is planting a stake, or a backhoe opera-
tor is dislodging a boulder, or, better yet, lovers on a picnic are
looking for a place to lay their blanket, when an object attracts
their attention. A time capsule has pushed its way up into the soil.
They open it to find a beautifully carved wooden spoon, along
with a few pages of explanation—unsigned.

SPOONWOOD DOCUMENT: Apple Tree History

Let me start with a little history, derived from archives available
at the local public library, mixed in with some guesswork and—
dare I admit it?—wishing.

In 1780 a New England farmer planted some apple trees. He
chose the north slope, which would remain cool in the spring,
thus retarding the blossoms from blooming. He believed that
late blossoms, besides being less susceptible to a late frost, would
produce juicier apples. He planted the twenty-five trees in rows
of five, thirty feet apart. The farmer started an orchard at the in-
sistence of his wife, who, like himself, was worried about their
eldest son, who had gone off to fight in the war for independence. For some reason she thought the orchard would please the
Almighty who would respond by protecting their son.

Fifty years later the son of the original homesteader was widowed in the fall of the year. He walked out into his orchard, a
noggin of cider in his hand. He stared out at the trees and field
and wondered what his life was all about. The next year he ap-
proached his son. "You can have the farm," he said. In return he
asked that he be allowed to live out his years in his sacred home.
The son turned him down. The old farmer offered the place to
his three daughters, one after the other, according to their ages.
They respectfully declined. His oldest daughter insisted he move
in with her at her home in Boston. He declined. The next year he
sold the farm, moved in with another daughter in Keene, and
died the following spring.

The new owner of the farm was very ambitious. He added to
the house, built a new barn, cleared more fields for sheep. He

pruned the apple trees for productivity. The farm thrived, but the farm couple's eldest son was reported missing in the Civil War. They were never sure whether he deserted or was killed.

By the standards of his place and time, the farmer died rich, and his heirs squabbled over ownership of his property, because he wrote several wills over a period of thirty years. In the end, the farm was divided up among six children, two of whom sold their lots to a party not in the family but who married into the family. The family expanded into a clan. They lived in less than grand circumstances. Most of the landowners worked in town and half-farmed their property. Some of the fields start growing in with woods. The orchard remained tended, more or less. The apples were wormy, but that didn't bother the cidermakers. Some of the trees died, but they were replaced by cuttings from live trees, so perhaps the trees didn't die after all. People are born and die one time each, but trees sometimes go on and on, new life sprouting from the dead. Two gods or perhaps two manifestations of one God inhabit each tree, one in the dark of the earth in search of water and nutrients, the other in the air in search of light and energy. The God-Manifests communicate through the exchange of bodily fluids.

Around 1910 members of the clan, like a chain of firecrackers going off, sold their small lots to a wealthy family from Massachusetts. The clan shacks were torn down. The dirt roads were transformed into bridle paths, for the new owners liked to ride their horses across hill and dale. Meanwhile, the forest grew relentlessly. What a hundred years before had been cultivated fields was now woods. An exception was the pasture where the orchard rested. The estate owner kept it mowed, though the trees were untended. The apples were deemed bitter and wormy, and the trees had gotten too big and the branches were too high to allow apples to be picked easily.

In 1930 the estate owner suffered financial setbacks. He died, it was said, from a broken heart. His heirs loved their New England property, but they no longer had the money to keep up the land and pay the taxes. By 1970, the orchard had been completely abandoned. The current owner, apparently pumped up

with new money (on this point the records are fuzzy), had a different idea for his property, a land trust based on conservancy
principles.

When I arrived on the scene I found the orchard overgrown,
mainly by young pine trees. Most of the apple trees were dead or
dying. I was terribly upset by the sight of these apple trees being
slowly strangled to death. I spent the next year reviving the orchard at the expense of the pines. The activity was my passion,
the place my church. I was too zealous with some of the trees,
and their sudden exposure to sunlight killed them. Some were already too far gone to renew. Others had died long ago, and only
their skeletons stood. But a few responded to my care. On the
day I write these words, a half dozen apple trees thrive.

I have plans for my son and me: make cider, make pies, eat the
apples raw. Do it now, I tell myself, for I expect to leave this
land. One is always leaving the places one loves. We make do
with memory. From my pruning cuts I've made spoons. In each
spoon is a little bit of the history of this land.

You can't find spoons with scrutiny. The spoon finds you
when you are least suspicious. Creativity is difficult for me because I am a suspicious person. One morning around 5 AM in a
lurid dawn I took my infant son outside to see the sunrise. I'd
completely forgotten about some apple tree branches I'd brought
in from my orchard. I noticed one now, wet at my feet, and in
that glance I saw into the wood with x-ray vision. Inside was a
spoon.

I yanked the branch up. I lost heart for a moment because at
the new angle the branch showed no promise. I persisted, cutting
it with my bow saw, placing the piece in my shaving horse vise,
and stripping the bark with my draw knife. Once the bare wood
was revealed the spoon that I saw appeared again in my vision
in template.

I cut the spoonwood from the branch, leaving the piece a little
longer than the intended spoon. With a hewing hatchet I roughed
out the shape of the spoon. (I love my hewing hatchet. I keep it
sharp enough to hone the points on my pencils, with which I
write these notes.) I continued refining the shape with the draw

knife, following the natural grain of the wood. I worked in great confidence and certainty. I don't say this in vanity but in humility, but for it was not from me that the vision for this object came but from a higher power.

I hollowed the bowl with a homemade crooked knife. Sometimes I use a spoon gouge to make the bowls, but the crooked knife is faster and better for shallow spoons (and most spoons should be shallow), and I enjoy the motion of my wrist in using it. Also, the crooked knife is an invention of the Native Americans in my region of the North Country, and in using it I can reach back in time to some ancient spoonmaker and hear the tiny slices of his knife.

I put on a coat of my special finishing oil, which will harden over time. Next day I smoothed out some rough spots brought out by the oil. I used glass for smoothing, some of it curved for the bowls. I have never cut myself with a knife, but I have with the glass, and so it happened that day. A trickle of blood stained the handle. I decided to leave it on because I liked the shape of the stain.

The next day I oiled the spoon again, and again the following day, and so forth for six more days until I had a suitable apple wood serving spoon. Every time I touched the spoon I thought about the desperate apple tree it came from. It had a little more freedom to grow, to live. Today I leave my offering, this spoon and these words.

Reading Group Guide

Questions for Discussion

1. *Spoonwood* opens with Birch addressing his mother's spirit while he is caught in a life-threatening blizzard. Why might the author choose to frame the first part of the novel in this way? How does it shape your reading of the material that follows?

2. Birch claims to remember experiences and conversations from the earliest months of his life. How do you respond to these claims? How do you view the claims by the end of the novel? How do you respond to a narrative apparently told from an infant's point of view?

3. Freddie Elman initially resists his responsibilities as a father. How does his response to his child shape your feelings about Freddie? At the end of the book, he still considers himself a poor father. How would you rate Freddie's success as a father?

4. Early in the novel, Freddie attempts to abandon Birch in a dumpster. How do you respond to this incident? How does it affect your feelings about Freddie? The episode itself is narrated by Birch; does the point of view affect the way you experience the incident?

5. Freddie objectifies his struggle with alcoholism by personifying his urge to drink and calling it "Old Crow." How do you respond to this "Old Crow" voice? What information or perspective does it offer that Freddie's own narrative perhaps cannot? How does his interaction with "Old Crow" shape your understanding of Freddie and his behavior?

6. How do you respond to Freddie's reinvention of himself as "Latour"? What sort of change in the character does it signal? To what extent do you think he succeeds in his reinvention?

7. Midway through the first part, Birch is taken from Latour and goes to live with his grandmother Persephone. What are the differences and continuities between his experiences with these two very different guardians?

8. How do you respond to the tension the novel presents between the solace to be found in the solitude of nature and the stress and confusion of living in society? How do Latour and Birch respond to this tension in ways both similar and dissimilar?

9. *Spoonwood* is largely set in New England. What expectations about contemporary rural New England do you bring to your reading of the book? In what ways does the book confirm or challenge your expectations?

10. Though it stands on its own, *Spoonwood* follows from a series of earlier novels that share the same setting and feature some of the same characters. What expectations do you bring to a novel that you know is part is series? If you are familiar with the earlier books, how do they shape your expectations and understanding of this novel?

Author's Statement

For me fiction writing is like telling a long lie to a psychiatrist. I'm the patient, and the reader is the therapist. I don't set out to tell my own story; quite the opposite. I'm telling a tall tale in order to divert attention from my flaws, frailties, and vulnerabilities. But in the end I reveal myself, and never more than in my latest novel, *Spoonwood*.

Most of my writing starts at a secret hideout in the woods of New Hampshire. Nearby is a gutted school bus, windows decorated with homemade tie-dyed curtains. Somebody lived in that school bus, trying to make a home in a place a mile from a plowed road. Once I was walking through red oaks, black birch, and maple trees when I spotted a flash of pale blue. I went to investigate and found an ancient Volkswagen Bug, small trees growing up through the smashed windshield. The school bus and Volkswagen and an imagined history found their way into *Spoonwood*.

Bordering my secret hideout on the north side of a hill is an intersection where two tumbling down stone walls meet. Here I build a campfire; I sit with a notepad, gaze out at the trees and rocks, and wait until ideas creep in from the gloom and accost me. God lives in these woods and so do the Devil, the ghosts of the hippies who dwelled in that school bus, the ghosts of English settlers who made this nation, the ghosts of dispossessed Indians, and the ghost of the glacier who departed ten thousand or so years ago. It's a spooky place, and I love it. It's my church.

I grew up very near a pine and hardwood forest on Beech Hill behind Robin Hood Park in Keene, New Hampshire. I used to daydream about living in the forest alone in the simplest manner—in rock caves or in trees, eating roots and acorns, with only the critters for company and the weather for entertainment. Such a dream is not possible in my real world of family, teaching, job, writing, career, friends, obligations, and commitments, but the dream has always been in my head. In writing *Spoonwood,* I went back into the woods of my childhood dramas, both as a boy and a man, through my father/son co-protagonists.

I tried to convey all my love of the forest in this book.

An Interview with Ernest Hebert

This is your first Darby novel in fifteen years. Why return to Darby now? How was the experience of writing this book different from (or similar to) writing the earlier Darby books? What were the challenges of returning to this landscape and these characters after a time away?

In the late 1980s my feeling was that *Live Free or Die* would be the concluding book in the novel series centering around the town of Darby. I figured that five books about one imaginary New Hampshire town was enough. However, no sooner had I finished *Live Free or Die* than I began wondering what happens afterward, that is, what happens after Lilith Salmon dies at the ledges giving birth. No doubt the future of the trust lands would center around the child that Lilith had given birth to. Since the Darby books are written more or less in real time, I had to let some years go by before telling the story. In fact, I was daunted by the idea of waiting almost twenty years, and I tried to forget the whole scenario, move on to other projects. But around 2001, after I'd finished *The Old American,* I found myself thinking about Darby and Lilith's baby and poor Frederick Elman. Soon I knew I just had to write the book to discover what happens to the characters, to the Salmon Trust, to the town of Darby, because in the same way that a reader learns about a story by reading it, I learn by writing it.

The main technical problem I had in writing *Spoonwood* was compressing the action over decades. What to put in? What to leave out? The second problem was creating a smooth narrative that cuts back and forth between different time periods.

One of the joys of writing this book was in reintroducing myself to characters that had appeared in previous Darby books, especially the Elmans

(Frederick, Howard, and Elenore), Cooty Patterson, and Persephone Salmon. It was kind of like meeting old friends after many years. You just pick up where you left off as if no time has passed. Howard, Elenore, and Cooty remained pretty much how they'd always been. They jumped out of my brain onto the computer and wrote their own lines. However, grief transformed Frederick and Persephone—part of them died when Lilith perished on the ledges. I had to reinvent them, just as a person at times has to reinvent him- or herself with all the accompanying anguish and difficulty. Frederick and Persephone are not the same people they were in the previous books.

One of the problems and pleasures was in creating Birch, Lilith and Frederick's son. I asked myself, What if Birch had total recall of his childhood or believed he did anyway? The resulting character and plot line is the answer to that question.

When I started *Spoonwood*, I decided early on not to reread any of the previous Darby books. I wanted to treat my knowledge of Darby as one treats one's knowledge of one's life, as memory with all the frailties of human cognition. Accordingly, I'm sure there are some inconsistencies between *Spoonwood* and the previous Darby novels, for unlike Birch I do not possess total recall.

Your most recent novel was the critically acclaimed *The Old American*, which was set in the eighteenth century. What are the differences between writing historical and contemporary fiction? Did the experience of writing that historical novel inform your work on *Spoonwood* in any way?

In one sense writing *The Old American* was easy, because the story of Nathan Blake and his captivity was already laid out in the historical record. I needed only to follow the dots, as it were. In addition, the research I did on the book, though time-consuming, laid out for me a set of values and historical details that enriched the novel. For example, if I say in a contemporary novel that a character wears a blue, buttoned-down shirt and tweed jacket, that says something about him, but it's hardly exciting information for the reader. But if I say that a Native American in eighteenth century Vermont is wearing a birch-bark hat, that is exciting to the reader because it's probably brand-new information. The difficulty in crafting historical fiction is in finding a persuasive voice for the book and the protagonist. How did people speak in 1748? I don't know—nobody knows for sure. You have to make it up without sounding trite or forced.

In writing *Spoonwood,* the technical problems were the reverse of those in *The Old American.* I had to invent a story and a complex plot from start to finish, but the voice came rather easily.

Writing *The Old American* neither helped nor hindered the crafting of *Spoonwood.* However, *The Old American* did affect the content of *Spoonwood.* The theme of identity flows through all my work. In addition, all my works are related in some way. (I don't actually see my books as individual entities; in my mind they're part of a long, single work that I am writing and that will only end when I die or go dotty.) In *The Old American,* Black Dirt, who is a Native American with a dollop of black blood, eventually marries a French-Canadian named de Repentigny (which, by the way, was the maiden name of Grace Metalious, the Manchester, New Hampshire, author who wrote *Peyton Place*). In *Spoonwood,* Howard Elman eventually learns that his real name is Claude de Repentigny Latour. I like to think that Howard and Frederick are descended from Black Dirt and that they have a distant cousin in Grace Metalious. In this way and in many other small ways I can connect the characters of all my books together into one fictional world. It's not something I do for the reader so much as for myself.

Much of *Spoonwood* is narrated by Birch as an infant and a child. What were the challenges (and pleasures) of writing from this point of view? What were the advantages of telling the story in this way?

I've always been interested in point of view. How does one show a scene or an idea? Often the most illustrative point of view is one that is outside normal perspective or thinking. I especially like to look into the minds of characters because I want to show my readers events and drama they can't see in the movies, hear on the radio, or even experience in real life. I read somewhere or somebody told me that, according to Freud, total recall is a symptom of hysteria. I took that idea into *Spoonwood.* Young Birch, my co-protagonist in *Spoonwood,* is doubly traumatized, first by his birth, after which his mother dies, and second by his experience in the storm. The data in his memory bank, accurate or not, includes imagery and conversations from when he was an infant. Indeed, he can actually remember not only his own thoughts and actions but those of his father. Birch believes he has telepathic powers; he even recalls conversations with the Elmans' cat, Spontaneous Combustion (which, by the way, refers back to *The Dogs of March,* the first book in the Darby series). In writing from the perspective of an infant and child, a damaged one at that, I hoped to gain deeper insight into my characters and their world. The technique also allowed me to see in a way that is different from my own thinking. I find I write better outside my own point of view.

How do you see this book in the context of the other Darby novels? It would seem to offer a more hopeful view of class and social conflict in New England than the previous books; would you agree with that? How have you come to this point of view?

I'm a born-again optimist, so I am sure that my state of mind influenced the work in the direction of the heavens as opposed to the other. But there's another reason that *Spoonwood* ends on an up beat. In order to create an interesting narrative arc—as opposed to a boring straight line—*Spoonwood* had to rise in tone and mood, because in the first part of the story the main characters are at a low point. They can only move in one direction—up. I designed *Live Free or Die* as a tragedy whose base was class conflict. It's the story of a fall. *Spoonwood* is a story of ascension.

Something else in my experience has also given me reason for optimism about the small New England towns that Darby attempts to represent. Back when I started writing the first Darby novel, *The Dogs of March,* in the middle 1970s, I held a pretty dark view for the future of North Country towns. I figured the new people would overwhelm the towns and destroy their identities. It didn't happen. Thirty years have passed since I started writing the Darby series, and most of the towns in my region have retained their identities. In the end the new people didn't change the town so much as the towns changed them.

Like several of your books, *Spoonwood* contains many passages about living in the woods and the natural world. Why is this an important topic for you? What is your own experience of the woods?

I'm a lapsed Catholic. I've always wanted to believe in a God, but the God of my upbringing and the gods of organized religion don't make a whole lot of sense to me. I would like to believe, but I cannot. Faith in God just is not in me. I've filled this vacuum in my life, this need for God, through my love of the northern forest. I spend a lot of time in the woods. I cut my own firewood. I hike. Sometimes I just sit on a rock wall and wait for something to happen. The woods are my church, where I go to pray. I must be some kind of pagan.

How did you settle on spoon-making as a livelihood for Freddie? What has been your own experience with woodworking or with spoon-making in particular?

As part of my religious love of the northern forest, I look for any reason not only to go into the woods but to touch and smell and even taste the woods, so I've always found excuses to work wood. I love to get slivers and pull them out of my fingers so they bleed a little. I cut my own firewood, and I've made furniture and "stick" sculptures. I always use hand tools; I'm not interested in production or even in quality but in the religious experience of handling the wood.

Some years back I was at the Sunapee Crafts Fair where I came across some elegant handmade wooden spoons by Dan Dustin. I have made some wooden spoons myself, but none are anywhere near as beautiful as anything Dan makes. Dan Dustin inspired me to write about a maker of wooden spoons, and that is why *Spoonwood* is dedicated to Dan and all the other people who work wood.

In *Spoonwood,* Howard Elman learns that he is Franco-American. What was the significance of giving him this heritage?

I mentioned earlier my attempts to connect Howard Elman with Black Dirt and her French-Canadian husband, as a literary mechanism for connecting the Darby series with *The Old American.* However, there's also a personal reason. I'd grown up believing that my ancestry was 100 percent French-Canadian. When I was twenty-one I learned that my mother's grandfather was an Italian who had migrated to French Canada. Some years ago a distant cousin of mine did a genealogical survey of the Heberts. I discovered that the line goes all the way back into the 1600s in Acadia (present-day Nova Scotia). I also discovered a Scottish ancestor in the gene pool, one Cormac McDonald. On her deathbed my mother alluded to a Native American ancestor. So I've learned over the years that I wasn't what I thought I was. I've learned that I am an American with New England Yankee ways and mixed bloodlines.

In previous Darby books, Howard Elman has no idea where he comes from because he was a foundling. I wanted the Elmans to discover something of their past, just as I had. Howard, secure in his identity, has no real interest in changing his name, though he yearns for some kind of link with his birth parents. Unlike Howard, Freddie is in search of identity right from the get-go; he seizes upon Howard's real last name, Latour, as his own. Latour is the most famous name of old Acadia. The story of the Latours is marvelous and strange, but it's too complex to go into here.

Freddie Elman nurtures many theories about life, child rearing, self-sufficiency, the virtue of handmade objects, the dangers of civilization, etc. Do any of his notions resonate with your own thinking or views?

Freddie's notions are only partly my own. Like Freddie, I'm an obsessively permissive parent. Unlike Freddie, I've never made an effort to keep kids away from TV or modern media. My feeling is they must be exposed to the world as it is, not as I wish it to be. I'm much more of a people person than Freddie, though there are times when I enjoy getting away from other human beings and, as Freddie would put it, unnecessary conversation.

What's the hardest thing about a writer's life?

I never anticipated that for me the hardest thing about the writer's life would be the feeling when a book goes out of print. It's even worse than when a book is rejected. Imagine that you are married to someone you love very deeply but, for whatever reason, you have to keep the marriage a secret. Imagine that this secret marriage partner dies. You must carry your grief around with you in silence. That's what it's like for a writer when his book goes out of print. In fact, the deep, emotional source of the grief that Frederick and Birch and Persephone feel at the death of Lilith comes from my emotion when my novel *Whisper My Name* was ignored by readers and critics alike and soon went out of print. That book died in the late 1980s, and I grieve for it even to this day.